The Skeptic's Playbook

The Skeptic's Playbook

BOOK ONE

HALCIE DAWN

Published by Halcie Dawn
Edited by Elaine York/Allusion Publishing, www.allusionpublishing.com
Cover Design by Stacey Blake, Champagne Book Design www.champagnebookdesign.com
Formatting by Elaine York/Allusion Publishing, www.allusionpublishing.com

Halcie Dawn
CARE ANNOUNCEMENT

Halcie Dawn's novels contain serious and complex content.

For a full list of Trigger Warnings and/or Content Warnings, please visit
https://www.halciedawn.com/my-books

For everyone who loves Crutch and Ella
I pray you love Holt and Merit too…
because this is just the beginning.

And

For everyone who loves Danny Kaye, Gene Kelly,
Clark Gable, James Dean, John Wayne,
Dean Martin, Cary Grant, and Elvis
This one's for you.

Author's Note

The Skeptic's Playbook is Book One in *The Skeptic's Duet*.
This is <u>not</u> a standalone novel and
should immediately be followed by...
The Believer's Game: The Skeptic's Duet Book Two

The Hill Family Universe

The Skeptic's Duet is a standalone duet in a larger, interconnected parent series of duets and novels—*The Hill Family Universe*. While *The Skeptic's Duet* can be enjoyed by itself, the reader will experience a more immersive and pleasurable reading journey if *The Reality Duet* (*Escaping Our Reality* & *Finding Our Reality*) is read first. *The Skeptic's Duet* <u>will</u> contain spoilers about your favorite Hill Family characters and events from *The Reality Duet*.

Halcie Dawn Novels

The Hill Family Universe

The Hill Family Universe is a large, interconnected parent series of duets and novels. While each duet—or singular novel, when applicable—can be enjoyed by itself, the reader will experience a more immersive and pleasurable reading journey if the suggested reading order is followed. Reading the duets out of order <u>will</u> result in spoilers about your favorite Hill Family characters and their defining life events.

Suggested Reading Order
The Reality Duet

Escaping Our Reality: The Reality Duet Book One
Finding Our Reality: The Reality Duet Book Two

The Skeptic's Duet

The Skeptic's Playbook: The Skeptic's Duet Book One
The Believer's Game: The Skeptic's Duet Book Two

Merit's Movie Playlist

White Christmas
(1954) Bing Crosby, Danny Kaye, Rosemary Clooney, Vera-Ellen

Singin' in the Rain
(1952) Gene Kelly, Donald O'Connor, Debbie Reynolds

The Wizard of Oz
(1939) Judy Garland, Jack Haley, Ray Bolger, Bert Lahr, Margaret
Hamilton, Frank Morgan

Anchors Aweigh
(1945) Gene Kelly, Frank Sinatra, Kathryn Grayson

An Affair to Remember
(1957) Cary Grant, Deborah Kerr

Blue Hawaii
(1961) Elvis Presley, Joan Blackman, Nancy Walters, Jenny Maxwell

The Court Jester
(1955) Danny Kaye, Glynis Johns, Basil Rathbone, Angela Lansbury

An American in Paris
(1951) Gene Kelly, Leslie Caron, Oscar Levant, Georges Guétary

The Ghost and Mr. Chicken
(1966) Don Knotts, Joan Staley

Mary Poppins
(1964) Julie Andrews, Dick Van Dyke, David Tomlinson, Glynis Johns

The Apple Dumpling Gang
(1975) Don Knotts, Tim Conway, Bill Bixby, Susan Clark

Rear Window
(1954) James Stewart, Grace Kelly

Teacher's Pet
(1958) Clark Gable, Doris Day

Some Like It Hot
(1959) Marilyn Monroe, Tony Curtis, Jack Lemmon

Yours, Mine, and Ours
(1968) Lucille Ball, Henry Fonda

It's a Wonderful Life
(1946) James Stewart, Frank Capra, Donna Reed

Giant
(1956) Elizabeth Taylor, Rock Hudson, James Dean

Spencer's Mountain
(1963) Henry Fonda, Maureen O'Hara

The Parent Trap
(1961) Hayley Mills, Maureen O'Hara, Brian Keith

Pillow Talk
(1959) Rock Hudson, Doris Day

McLintock!
(1963) John Wayne, Maureen O'Hara, Patrick Wayne, Stefanie Powers

Honky Tonk
(1941) Clark Gable, Lana Turner

Double Indemnity
(1944) Fred MacMurray, Barbara Stanwyck, Edward G Robinson

Butch Cassidy and the Sundance Kid
(1969) Paul Newman, Robert Redford, Katharine Ross

Rio Bravo
(1959) John Wayne, Dean Martin, Ricky Nelson

The Man Who Shot Liberty Valance
(1962) James Stewart, John Wayne

Prologue

Merit

I sneeze so hard my forehead ricochets off the steering wheel. Ouch.

I look down in resignation at my navy shirt, now covered in remnants of snot. There's nothing worse than having a cold in the middle of summer. And this cold is completely kicking my ass.

My throat is raw, my brain feels thick and sticky with the side effects of a fever, and somehow my nose is completely congested, yet still running like someone turned on a faucet. On top of all that, I've never gone home sick in the middle of the day before. That's just not something I do. The store is my happy place, a place I built from the ground up. It's more than stressful, but always more than rewarding.

Sighing in tired defeat—because all I want is my bed—I watch as the garage door slowly slides open. I'm shocked to see Edward's car. The afternoon sun reflects off the bright red paint of the sports car, making my eyes water more than they already are.

What is he doing home?

Concern seeps into my heart. Maybe he's sick too? If I got him sick, he won't be happy—he has a trial coming up. And, of course, it would never occur to him that maybe *he* got *me* sick. It's always me, I'm the one who's around kids every day, so by default, I'm Patient Zero...always.

It takes all my energy to climb from the car. If it wouldn't be completely pathetic, I would lie down right in the middle of the garage and nap, using one of his expensive golf towels as a blanket. Or maybe his car cover. I mean, it *is* made of supple leather and sheepskin. Could be comfy, you never know. And I'm just that desperate to get in the horizontal position.

But I don't think he would appreciate that much—Edward doesn't really like it when I touch his stuff—so I force myself to go inside. I actually have to give myself a pep talk with each step I take, mentally forcing one foot in front of the other.

One hundred more steps, and you can rest.

Ninety-five more steps, and you can sleep.

Ninety more steps, and you can pass out.

Classical music wafts through the house, worming its way downstairs like a slithering snake. If he is sick, he's obviously not as sick as me, because the soothing music does nothing but split my head wide open. Tossing my bags on the kitchen island, I trudge up the back staircase. The music grows louder, piping through the surround sound of our master bedroom.

Edward's obsession with classical music has completely soured me to the genre. But I still listen to it. For him. That's what marriage is. Give and take. Compromise. Right? So what if one of us happens to *give* more than the other. It can't always be even. Right?

My marriage is just different than what I thought it would be is all. Based on my parents' marriage, based on my grandparents' marriage.

A coughing fit pulls me into its nasty grasp. Hacking up a huge spitball, I pull a tissue from the pocket of my shorts and spit into it. I quickly tuck it back in place before opening the bedroom door. Edward hates all things gross, anything to do with bodily functions. And that includes a used Kleenex. You should've seen him three years ago when I caught a stomach virus—he actually rented a penthouse suite at the nicest hotel in town. He claimed he needed to stay healthy for work, but I know he ordered non-stop room service and had an in-room massage and facial. Turning the doorknob, I shelve those thoughts as my mind immediately knows that blessed relief is literally only two seconds away. I'm gonna flop on that bed and beach myself like a walrus.

Huh.

I must be sicker than I thought.

I'm seeing things.

I'm seeing really bad things.

The music is so loud, they don't hear me come in. But in all honesty, I don't know if they would stop, even if they had heard me. My husband's bare ass is flapping like a sheet in the wind. I can't see the face of the naked woman bending on all fours across my bed, but I do see enough to recognize that it's Edward's executive assistant. Her massive, fake breasts are swaying back and forth, fighting a war against the vigor of my husband's thrusts. Edward's gripping her waist so tightly his knuckles are white, his cheeks red from exertion.

The golden afternoon sun shines through the window. The navy draperies softly billow underneath the register of the air conditioner. The brown ceiling fan blades swirl around and around and around. My vision clouds with black spots.

Why am I seeing so many colors?

Gold, navy, brown, black.

Gold, navy, brown, black.

Despite the ridiculous volume of the music, the sound of their skin echoes in my ears, shattering any hope I might've had that this is all a dream, a delirious vision conjured up by my feverish subconscious. Pump, slap. Pump, slap. The noise churns my stomach, and I fight against the urge to vomit. When the fingers of his right hand disappear between her ass cheeks, bile rises into my mouth.

My husband is having sex with another woman.

He's cheating on me.

He never makes love to me like that.

He's doing things with her that he never does with me.

Things that he's insinuated are gross...you know, those bodily functions and all.

I wish I could say that I have enough common sense and grace to retreat, holding my head high. I wish I could say that I have enough gumption and dignity to demand they stop, get out of my bedroom, get out of my house. I wish I could say that I have enough fire and anger to beat them to a pulp, leaving them in a bloody mess on my three-hundred-dollar sheets.

But I don't.

The cold medicine I took earlier has left me dizzy and lightheaded.

So, instead... I faint.

I pass out cold in the middle of my husband's affair, and in my addled brain, I wonder if they'll even notice long enough to stop having sex.

Two Years Later

Chapter 1

Merit

"You have the prettiest toes I've ever seen."

The little girl loves my compliment and wiggles her blue-painted toenails right under my nose.

Her mom sighs, shifting her toddler son higher on her hip. "Macy, don't put your feet so close to Merit's face."

"I was just letting her see my toes, Mommy."

I secure the buckle on the white sandal and gently tickle Macy's leg. "All right, time to run and jump and twirl."

Jumping from the seat, she immediately starts racing around the store, skipping and dancing. Carla, Macy's mom, laughs. "This is her favorite part. She loves it when you say that."

I smile, watching her play. "It was always my favorite part too." In fact, I loved it so much, that's why I named my store *Run and Jump and Twirl.*

I call Macy back over and take a look at the fit, making sure the shoe is snug—but not too snug—with enough room to grow. Carla and Macy both agree with me; this white sandal is the winning pair. Boxing the losing shoes back up, I stack them out of the way and put Macy's old sandals in the shoebox because she quickly informs me and Carla that she will be wearing her new shoes home. Grunting, I pop up from the floor.

Kyra has just finished checking someone out when I make it to the register. "You check them out, and I'll fill out the card," she offers. Pulling Macy's index card from our handwritten database, she writes the name brand and size of the sandal, documenting today's purchase. "Macy, what's your favorite thing about your new shoes?" she asks.

Macy puckers her lips, giving it serious thought. "The insides are squishy. And I love the flower on the buckle."

Kyra leans over the counter, checking out the flower. She enunciates the syllables slowly, repeating the words back to Macy as she writes, "squishy and flower. Got it."

After I run Carla's credit card, I slide a couple of stickers and temporary tattoos in the bag before handing it over. Right then, the curious little boy in her arm reaches across and slaps a small container of paperclips with his chubby hand. My own hands aren't quick enough to catch it, and it falls to the floor on my side of the register, sending paperclips everywhere.

"Oh no, Merit. I'm so sorry!"

I shrug. "Don't worry about it, Carla. It's no big deal, it's just paperclips. I'll pick them up."

Her brow furrows. "Are you sure? I can help."

Macy then tugs on Carla's shirt. "C'mon, Mommy. Let's go show Daddy my new shoes."

I laugh and wave her on. "It's fine. Y'all have a great night. I'll see you next time."

The door chimes as they walk out. Kyra starts picking up the few paperclips that are scattered across the counter, and I squat down, trying to rake all the paperclips on the ground into a pile. "Macy's getting big."

Kyra nods. "Yeah, her card shows her last shoes were bought just four months ago, and she's already gone up half a size." When the door chimes with another customer coming in, she whispers under her breath. "Oh, shit."

Her tone catches me off guard, scaring me. I quickly grab her shin, pinching her skin harder than reasonable. "What's wrong?"

What if it's a robber? Oh please, don't let us be getting robbed.

What if it's a disgruntled customer? With a shiv?

What if it's an IRS agent? Did I pay all my taxes?

She looks down at me, lifting her eyebrows. "I think this guy is the best-looking guy I've ever seen." Then, she grunts, "And, ouch, by the way." She kicks my hand away.

Sighing in relief, I roll my eyes. "He's gonna hear you."

She shakes her head. "They stopped to look at the sales rack next to the door."

One by one, I poke the clips back into their container. I giggle, making myself snort.

She nudges me in the butt with her foot. "What?"

"I was just thinking that we really need to discuss what classifies as an *'oh shit'* moment. Dropping your keys in a porta potty? That's an 'oh shit' moment. Literally. Catching your panties in the zipper of your shorts? That's an 'oh shit' moment. Dropping your chewing gum in the open casket of your neighbor's dead mother? That's an 'oh shit' moment. Seeing a sexy man?" I jump up from the carpeted floor, and my hair tangles around me, shrouding my face. Spitting a strand from my mouth, I fling it out of my eyes and spin around, finishing my thought. "That's not an 'oh shit' moment."

My heart drops into my stomach.

Standing in front of me, with a drop-dead sexy smirk etched across his face, just as Kyra said, is the best-looking guy I've ever seen.

Kyra covers her mouth with her hand, trying to stifle her laugh. Slamming the now-full paperclip container into her hand, I scowl at her, telling her through best friend telekinesis that I'm not amused.

"And I assume all those things happened to you?"

His voice coats my eardrums in honey, the low timbre sending a chill down my spine. It's something I haven't felt in a long time. A very long time. And in all honesty, I don't even know if it's a welcome feeling. I shake my head, clearing my thoughts. "Pardon?"

He lifts an eyebrow. "Keys in the porta potty? Gum in the casket?" His tongue darts out, licking his lips, "Panties in the zipper?"

Oh, shit. The way he just said the word panties...

A bright red blush creeps across my face. I can feel it. Burning me, scalding my skin. I glance down, pretending to wipe something from the counter. "I must apologize for my language, sir. That was very unprofessional of me." Squaring my shoulders, I glance up, forcing myself to look into his eyes. "May I help you with something? Are you looking for something in particular?"

He cocks his head to the side, studying me. I guess he doesn't know what to make of my apology.

He really is gorgeous. Achingly gorgeous.

Tall. Built. Firm and muscular. His light blond hair is styled short, but still long enough to see the thick waves just begging to be touched. His eyes are the brightest, most intense shade of blue—they almost look fake.

Azure.

I think they call the color azure.

And the hue is even more offset by his tanned skin and the spattering of freckles across the bridge of his nose.

My fingers itch to count those freckles, itch to trace the lines of his face, and playfully tug on the two-shades darker facial hair decorating his square jaw.

And where would I tug that face once I had ahold of it? Just which lonely lady body part of mine would I push that face into?

Oh, holy mother of all shits...

For a second, his upper lip twitches, like he's trying to fight back a grin. Forfeiting the battle—or perhaps winning it—he gifts me with a brilliant smile.

A knowing smile, a smile that says... *That's right. Do it. I dare you to touch me.*

I think he can read my mind.

After a moment, he drags his hand across his face, rubbing his fingertips against his lips and chin. The thick cord of muscle in his forearm jumps, twisting with the motion.

Somewhere behind him, someone makes a sound. A whiny moan. He shifts to the side, and for the first time, I see who he's with.

A fake blonde with fake boobs, fake eyelashes, and a fake tan. And she's wearing a short, tight dress that would definitely look more at home in a Vegas nightclub than a children's shoe and clothing store. I look down at my own tank top, linen shorts, and tennis shoes, before glancing back to her. I think her ass may be fake too. Butt implants?

So, he's one of *those*.

Like Edward.

Reaching out, she wraps her hand around his and lays her head against his shoulder. Well, against his elbow, really. She's super short compared to him. Her voice grates against my brain. "Are you finished?"

What a stupid question.

Does he look finished?

He hasn't even started yet.

"Give me just a few minutes, Bonnie." He nods to the row of chairs in front of the back wall of shoes and big-screen TV. "Why don't you have a seat?"

I watch her sashay across the floor and seductively sit down. Why is she flirting with her ass? I don't know who she's trying to seduce. There's just me, him, and Kyra. Kyra and I are straight. And he's already with her, so I'm pretty sure that means he's a sure thing.

I tug my tank top away from my sweaty body. When did it get so hot in here? I clear my throat, asking him the same question as before. "Are you looking for something in particular?"

His eyes scan my body, making me nervous and self-conscious. After what feels like a century, he reaches into his pocket, pulls out a folded piece of paper, and hands it to me. "I'm here for this."

I'm very careful to avoid touching him.

Looking at the paper, I read the name of the shoe, style, and size. Biting my lip, I frown. "I'm very sorry, sir, but I only have one left in that size, and it's being saved for someone."

He smiles again. It makes my body feel restless. "I know. For me." He shrugs, "Well, I mean for Anna."

My mouth falls open in shock. "You're Will? Anna's dad?" Immediately my eyes dart to the fake woman named Bonnie. I can't believe he would step out on Raylee, aka his *wife*. She's so nice. How dare he? My face immediately absorbs my disgust.

Fucking cheater.

His laugh churns anger in the pit of my stomach.

"Will's my brother-in-law. I'm Raylee's brother, Holt." He tosses a look over his shoulder to his girlfriend. "But I'm glad to know that you're so protective of my sister."

How does he know what I was thinking? *Can* he read my mind? "Pardon?" I feign innocence.

"It's pretty clear what you were thinking. You wear your emotions all over your face."

Well, that's the first time anyone has said that in a very long time. A stranger, I mean. Kyra sees the real me, of course, but she's my best friend. Edward always preferred that I keep things civil. Calm. Monotone. He wanted me to be more mild-mannered. Growing up, I was pretty high-strung, so it took a lot of training for me to become someone who shelved my feelings, who only existed in public with a polite and stoic face.

Coming to my rescue, Kyra reaches across the counter, introducing herself with a handshake.

He politely nods. "Holt Hill."

Holt Hill. That name sounds familiar.

I guess Raylee or Anna have mentioned him before.

I walk away from the counter, using that as my excuse to avoid shaking his hand. "I'll just grab those shoes from the back."

"I'll be happy to get them, Merit," Kyra offers.

I shake my head. "No. I put them on the top shelf. I'll get them." The safety-angle rolling ladder broke last week. A new one won't be arriving until sometime next week. In the meantime, we're having to use an old wooden ladder that I borrowed from the maintenance guy at my condo complex. There's no way I'm having an employee climb on it. The last thing I need is a workman's comp claim.

Kyra rolls her eyes. "Yeah, and that's what we really need. *You* climbing up rungs on a ladder."

I glare at her, pinning her in place with my death stare. Well, I assume it's my death stare. It doesn't seem to faze her, though.

Holt is now behind me. I don't have to turn around to know it. I can feel him. It's like his body gives off an electricity, a current. It slices through the air and penetrates my nerve-endings. It's been so long since I've been around someone attractive. My body is having a visceral reaction without my consent.

If I got out more, this probably wouldn't be happening.

But what's the point?

I don't wanna go out. I'm happy with my life.

His voice stops me in my tracks. "Is that *Singin' in the Rain*?"

I turn around, watching him point to the movie playing across the big-screen TV. It's one of the best scenes—the *Make 'Em Laugh* sequence with Donald O'Conner. "Yes, it is."

"I've never seen it all the way through. My cousin, Ella, loves it, though."

My heart stops beating. Sacrilege. Utter sacrilege that he's never watched it in its entirety. Trying to wipe the shock from my face, I fold my hands in front of me and politely nod. "You should really take the time to watch it. It's a classic." Despite my best efforts to keep my emotions locked away, I make the mistake of glancing back up at the screen. Unable to contain myself, I laugh.

And snort.

Holy crap. I can't believe I just snorted.

Cocking his hands on his hips, Holt chuckles, watching me.

Bonnie smacks her lips, interrupting whatever moment we're having. "Old movies make no sense. They're outdated. I like *The Fast and the Furious* movies."

It takes all my strength not to throw her out of my store. "Let me get Anna's shoes," I say, retreating around the corner to the back.

I make a quick detour to the bathroom. Flipping on the switch, I study my image in the mirror. Same as every day. Store shirt, comfortable shorts, and comfy shoes—even though, half the time, I'm walking around barefoot before noon. Nearly every drawer in my dresser at home is filled with tops emblazoned with the *Run and Jump and Twirl* logo—tank tops, T-shirts, and sweatshirts. So, I'm never lacking in the work 'uniform' department. My normal makeup routine consists of tinted moisturizer, mascara, and lip gloss. Apparently, the makeup companies toss around the word 'tinted' very loosely because it's doing nothing to conceal the flushed embarrassment etched across my cheeks. But what do people expect? I'm not gonna dress up. I spend my days crawling around on the floor, inspecting little kids' feet. And pretending to bite babies' toes to elicit a smile instead of a cry. And jumping up and down like a kangaroo because most toddlers won't willingly try on a sweatshirt with a kangaroo pouch unless you turn it into a game.

Berating myself for getting swept away by this guy's good looks and charm, I make a silent pact to get him out of my store as quickly as possible.

Positioning the ladder, I climb up the rungs, carefully balancing myself at the top. Somehow, the box has gotten pushed back, and I'm struggling to reach it with my fingertips. I'll be so glad when the safety-angle gets here.

Right as my hand wraps around the box and I pull it toward me, a voice startles me, making me jump. The hard, cardboard edge of the shoebox hits me in the tender skin underneath my right eye and then clatters to the floor. The unexpected impact makes my foot slip off the ladder. My vision blurs with a nano-second injection of adrenaline, and I brace myself for a painful impact on the floor, praying I don't break anything.

But I don't fall. Onto the floor, that is.

Instead, I fall straight into the arms of the handsome Holt Hill.

It takes several seconds for us both to realize exactly what happened.

"Oh, shit! I'm sorry, I was just coming to see if you needed help. She said your ladder was broken." He scans my face. I'm not sure if he's reading my emotions again or searching for injuries. "Are you okay? It looks like you hit your eye."

See, that was an appropriate 'oh shit' moment.

I can't breathe. His body is literally pressed right against mine, and I can't breathe—I've forgotten how to inhale. It's been two years since I've been this close to a man, and it's confusing my brain.

Confusing my soul.

Confusing every single cell in my body.

I glance down at our tangle of arms and legs. Both of my hands are resting on top of his shoulders. He has one arm snaked around my back, and the other is underneath my left knee, propping my leg up against his waist.

Like we're dirty dancing. Or like I'm about to jump on him and wrap both of my legs around him.

That thought makes my mouth dry.

My feet dangle in the air. My heart pounds in my chest.

"Are you okay?" he asks me again.

Looking up, I stare into his deep blue eyes, struggling to find the right words. Eventually, I settle on the first thing that comes to mind. "You can put me down."

The movement of his hand against the bare skin of my leg stirs a heat low in my belly. He sets me on the ground but doesn't release me from his grasp. We're so close, I can see the small crow's feet lining the side of his brow. He smells like soap and peppermint. The collar of his pale blue T-shirt is frayed, adding to his boyish, innocent charm.

But he can't be all that innocent.

He's holding me.

While his girlfriend is sitting in the other room.

Lifting my chin, I clear my throat, trying to regain our professional boundaries. "I'll be out with the shoes in just a moment. You should head back out to your girlfriend Bonnie." I say her name, reminding him of his obligations.

One corner of his mouth tilts up. "Her name isn't Bonnie. You heard wrong." He inches closer. His breath whispers across my face, the sensation causing a tickle in the back of my throat. "It's Bunny."

My brow furrows and I frown. "Like a rabbit?"

His laugh surprises me. It almost seems genuine. Almost seems real. "Yeah."

"Merit?" The second I hear Kyra's voice, I push away.

His arms fall to his side, and an inexplicable shot of emptiness pierces my heart. In stunned silence, he looks down at his hands, like he honestly can't believe he was wrapped in an embrace with me for that long.

I try not to let that hurt my feelings.

Kyra peers around the corner of the shelving rack. "Y'all okay back here? I thought I heard something."

"Everything is fine. Kyra, can you please show Mr. Hill back to the front? Mr. Hill, I believe these shoes are for Anna's birthday, correct? I'll be happy to wrap them for you."

His face grows solemn and he bites his lip. "Yeah, that's right."

Nodding, I smile brightly. It's the same smile I always used at the work parties I had to attend with Edward. "Lovely. I'll be out momentarily."

Running his hand through his hair, he follows Kyra back out to the front of the store.

I can't believe she let him come back here in the first place. She may be my friend—the best one I've got—but she's also my employee; and we will definitely be having a conversation about this later. We only let customers back here in the event of an emergency. A parent with a four-year-old who is about to pee his pants kind of emergency.

Call me stupid, but I definitely think Holt Hill can hold his pee until he gets home.

I wrap the shoebox with purple tie-dye paper and decorate it with yellow and purple bows. When I make it back out front, Bunny is playing on her cell phone, and Kyra is showing some of the new sleeveless tops we just got in to Holt. I pretend not to notice him watching me. His gaze is different now than it was. It's softer, gentler. Not as... reckless.

I suppose he feels bad for... well, for doing whatever he was doing with me in the back.

And he should feel bad. It's pretty brazen to have your arms wrapped around a stranger while your girlfriend is patiently waiting on you to buy a birthday present for your niece.

I pull Anna's card from our database and write down the shoe information. "Will there be anything else, sir?"

He squints his eyes. I don't think he likes me calling him sir. "I was thinking of getting her something else too. Something to go with the shoes. This shirt, maybe?"

"When is her birthday?" Kyra asks.

"Tomorrow. I'm leaving from here to go to her party. We're having it a day early."

"Tomorrow?" I glance down at the card, searching for the information. We keep track of all the kids' birthdays. "You're right."

That makes him laugh. "I should hope I'm right. Or else, I had a three-layer pink velvet cake delivered to my house for no reason."

Kyra leans across the top of the clothes rack. "The party is at your house?"

He shrugs. "We always do family get-togethers at my house or my cousin's house. We have the most room." He pulls his phone out of his pocket. "I can call Raylee to see what size she wears."

"There's no need to do that." I wave the card in his direction. "I keep track of the kids' sizes."

"You do?"

"Yeah, and she was just in here last month picking out those tennis shoes from the catalog. Raylee bought her a new dress that day; so, unless she's been eating spinach for three meals a day, she should be the same size." I tell Kyra the size, and she searches the rack and pulls a shirt down. I come around the counter and quickly grab it from her. Not wanting to be left alone with Holt and Bunny, I don't give her the option of offering to wrap the new present herself. Plus, I want to add something special of my own to it, a little present from me to Anna. I keep a plethora of trinkets for just such an occasion.

When I finally make it back out front, Holt and Kyra are standing by the register making small talk. And Bunny? Well, she's standing in front of the full-length mirror, attempting to try on a cardigan.

Is she a moron?

This is a children's store. All we have are child-size clothes.

Normally, I'd call someone out for this. She might rip it or stretch it beyond repair. But I keep my mouth shut because I just want them out of my store as soon as possible. This whole visit has been very unnerving for some odd reason.

"Kyra, will you ring everything up, please?" I grab a bag from underneath the counter and slide the wrapped gifts inside.

He places his hand on top of the bag. "I need something else too."

I purse my lips in frustration. How much stuff is this guy gonna buy? Can't he just leave? And take his pet rabbit with him?

I must make a face because he lifts his eyebrow at my reaction. Taking a deep breath, I stretch that fake smile across my teeth, once again. "How else can I assist you?"

He nods to the small bookshelf of odds and ends to my left. "Are those bookmarks?"

"Yes, sir."

Again, with the squinty eyes. It almost makes me laugh.

Almost.

He points at one. "I'll take a pink one."

I shake my head. "Anna's favorite color is purple." I pat the wrapped shoebox. "Like the trim on her new shoes."

"I know. This isn't for Anna. It's for someone else."

"Who? Another niece?" Why am I engaging him in conversation when I just want him to take his things and leave?

He tosses his head back and forth. "For lack of better words."

Tired of waiting, Bunny finally makes her presence known with another whiny moan. "Seriously, Holt? How long does it take to buy one silly pair of shoes?"

Tossing the bookmark in the bag, I bump Kyra with my hip and take over checking him out. He barely has time to slide his credit card back in his wallet before I'm pushing the bag into his hands. "Thanks so much for coming. Come back anytime."

Or not.

I'm glad Anna's birthday is only one time a year.

He cocks his head to the side, and then he winks at me.

Really? I can't decide if he's a heartthrob or a womanizing ass-hole.

And then, for no apparent reason, he laughs.

Seriously, I think he can read my mind.

Well, if that's true, I hope he heard the womanizing asshole part loud and clear.

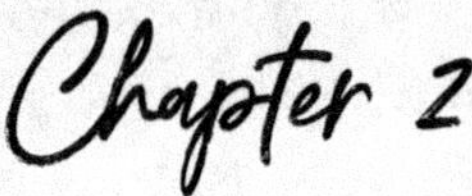

Chapter 2

Holt

I don't chase after women.

They come to me.

They flock. In droves.

So, why am I driving to this children's store to see her again?

Because it's been less than twenty-four hours, and I can't get her out of my mind. I badgered Raylee for all the information she had. Which wasn't much. She's been going to the store since it opened about four years ago, but she said that Merit doesn't really talk about herself. She did notice that she used to wear a huge diamond on her ring finger, but she said that discreetly disappeared a while ago.

I used my newfound obsession with this stranger as an excuse to break up with Bunny. Not that we really needed a breakup; last night was only our third date. It's not like I saw a future for the two of us. Hell, I didn't even really like her. I was just lonely.

I *am* lonely.

I turn thirty-one in a few months, and I'm more than ready to settle down. Start a life, make a family.

Shit, if Ella and Crutch can make it work, then there's hope for any of us.

It's the last day of July, and the sweltering, midday Alabama sun beats down, covering everything in an oppressive, smothering heat.

Sweat rolls down my back in the fifteen seconds it takes for me to walk from the parking lot into the store. Kyra's standing at the register, checking someone out. Her head pops up, and she acknowledges my presence with a quick smile and wave. And maybe even a look of surprise on her face. Standing in the corner, I scan each inch of the interior, searching for Merit.

The store is basically one big rectangle with the front door set nearly flush with the left wall. When you walk in, there's a couple of sales tables and racks. Then you have the register, and past that is a bookshelf filled with knick-knacks. That's where I bought Laura's bookmark. She loves to read and immediately fawned all over it. The entire back wall is covered with shoes. Planted high on the wall above the shoes is a big-screen TV. It looks like she's playing another old movie. The right wall and half of the front wall are dotted with clothing racks and shelving. There's one small display window on the right wall, where it meets back up with the front door. The middle of the store is lined with chairs, but it's mostly open around the chairs.

I don't see her.

Immediate disappointment floods over me.

Maybe she's in the back.

At that precise moment, I hear her. I hear her laugh. It's the very same laugh she did yesterday when watching the funny part of the movie. The same laugh that I dreamt about last night when my hand was wrapped around me, and I was trying to relieve the crushing pressure of constantly thinking about her.

The sound came from behind a shelf, over in the corner. I take a step in that direction but pause when I hear other voices. She must be helping a customer.

"Everything okay? Was something wrong with Anna's shoes?"

I turn to Kyra's voice and watch as her customer walks out the door.

"Hey." Stuffing my hands in my pockets, I walk over to the counter. "No, all is good. She loved them and the shirt."

She checks an old receipt and tosses it in the trash. "Perfect. Well, what can I help you with? You need to buy something else?"

I'll buy every damn thing in the store if it means I can spend more time with Merit.

"Uhhh...not really," I answer truthfully.

She opens her mouth and then closes it. Then opens it again. "Then, why are you here?"

Not exactly sure what to say, I nod my head in the direction of Merit's hushed voice. I still can't see her. She must be sitting on the floor.

Kyra's eyes grow wide and she grins from ear to ear. "Ahhh, I see." She nods, bending over the counter, drawing me closer to her. "She's beautiful, huh?"

Fucking gorgeous. "Is she involved with anyone? Husband, boyfriend?"

"Nope. No husband. No boyfriend."

Relief courses through me, filling my lungs with fresh oxygen. "Well, is she seeing anyone? Dating?"

Kyra snorts. "Merit? That would be a hard no."

"She doesn't date?"

She shakes her head.

I chew my lip in thought. "You mean she's not currently dating anyone? Or she never dates?"

"She never dates."

I lift my eyebrows. "Never?"

Kyra leans closer, exaggerating every single letter of the word. "Never."

I push back, letting that sink in. "Why not?"

She whacks me on the arm with an ink pen. "I'm not telling you that! She's my best friend." Kyra shrugs. "Plus, she's my boss. I need the paycheck," she jokes.

Despite her tongue-in-cheek answer, I can see she really cares about Merit.

About that time, three bodies stand up from behind the shelf. Merit is standing with her back to me, but I watch as a woman and her son meander around to another clothing rack. Kyra waves me on, wishing me good luck. By the time I make it to Merit, she's walking off in the direction of the back room. I know I shouldn't follow her, especially not after what happened yesterday, but I can't help myself. She's wearing an oversized green T-shirt and short gray gym shorts. Her hips sway back and forth with each step she takes.

And of all things, she's barefoot.

Standing in the doorway, I spend several seconds debating what to do. Giving in to temptation, I round the corner, stalking into the storage room like I'm the one who owns it. Not her.

Her back is still to me, and she's standing in front of one of those big steamers that irons clothes. I hear the gurgle of the water and watch as steam rises from the handle. She's hanging a boy's wrinkled dress shirt.

I guess she wraps presents *and* irons clothes for her customers.

"Hey."

Hey? I used to give fucking press conferences and the best I can come up with is 'Hey'?

She jumps, sucking a hiss of surprise through her teeth. When she spins around, I feel like I can finally breathe. Like I've been holding my breath since the moment she left my sight yesterday.

But that is short lived.

Her beautiful face is marred. And it pisses me off.

I cross the distance between us. My reflexes are super quick, so she doesn't even have time to react. No time to decide she doesn't want me to touch her, doesn't want me to invade her personal space. Gently grabbing her chin, I tilt her head up, giving myself a better look. She's tall for a woman, but still a good seven or eight inches shorter than me.

Too bad my reflexes weren't quick enough to save her from damage yesterday.

Underneath her right eye, her beautiful skin is swollen and colored purple and blue. "You have a black eye," I say, stating the obvious. "Anna's shoebox did this?"

She doesn't answer.

She just stares at me. I take the time to study her, memorizing every small detail. Her hair is pulled back in a loose ponytail. It was down yesterday, and I noticed it falls midway between her shoulders and her breasts. It's thick and looks like it would feel like velvet. It's a dark brown, but some of her strands look red and some look black. It reminds me of the redwood trees in California. Her eyes alone make my dick jump in my pants. They're the most unusual color of hazel I've ever seen. They're swirled with waves of brown, green, blue, and even yellow.

My eyes fall lower to the curve of her neck. I can see her heartbeat as it thunders in the artery underneath her soft skin. The collar of the green T-shirt hangs off her shoulder, confirming she's wearing a blue sports bra. It calls my attention to the line of her collarbone. It's summertime, and next to the strap of her sports bra, I see a thin, white tan line from a bathing suit.

Holy hell.

Even though I don't want to, I take a small step back. I don't need to scare her off even more by rubbing my massive erection all over her.

I *am* still a stranger.

I watch in awe as her pupils dilate. The reflex feels sensual and forbidden.

Fuck me. That's sexy.

Suddenly, and without warning, she gasps for air and steps even farther away from me. My hand falls to my side.

I didn't even realize she'd been holding her breath.

"What are you doing here?" Her whisper is caught in her throat.

I ignore her question and repeat again, "You have a black eye. Are you okay?"

She furrows her brow and shakes her head. "That's why you're here? Who told you I had a black eye?"

She's so freakin' funny.

"No one told me you had a black eye. I just saw it. Just now."

"Then, why are you here?" Her eyes grow wide in horror. "Oh no, the shoes didn't fit? They're supposed to fit the same as the other styles from that company. I'm so sorry. She must've been devastated."

I take a step closer to her. "No, the shoes fit great. She loved them and the shirt." I cock my hands on my hips. "And the surprise flowered notebook and glitter ink pen. She swore she was gonna save it for the new school year, but she was already writing in it before the party ended."

Her distress levels immediately drop, and her shoulders sag in relief. "Oh, good. I'm glad." Her eyes dart from side to side. I can see she doesn't want to ask the next question, but she does anyway. "And the bookmark?"

Intuition tells me she doesn't want to carry on a long conversation with me, but she can't ignore her curiosity.

Is she curious about everything? Or is she just curious about me? And if she's curious about me, why doesn't she want to have a conversation with me?

"The bookmark was a hit too. It was for Laura."

"And Laura is...?" Her face burns bright red and her throat makes a loud swallowing sound.

Yep. She definitely can't ignore her curiosity.

"Technically, Laura is the niece to my cousin-in-law, Crutch. He's married to my cousin, Ella. But Laura spends a lot of time with them, which means she spends a lot of time with me. It's just easier for me to call her my niece than to explain the whole situation to someone. And she calls me her uncle."

She nods, clamping her lips together to keep her mouth closed shut.

I can't help it. My eyes wander down her bare legs, absorbing and committing every curve to memory, and finally, landing on her hot pink toenail polish.

She clears her throat, snatching my eyes back up to her face. "If the presents were a hit, why did you come back?"

"To see you." Don't they always say honesty is the best policy?

She looks down at her feet. After a split second, she lifts her chin in the air and stares directly into my eyes. Granting me that fake smile she gave me yesterday, she folds her hands neatly in front of her. "I'm sorry, sir, but I have a lot of work to do." She tosses her head back to the hanging shirt, trying to give me evidence of her busy day. "If you'd like to browse the merchandise out in the showroom, I'll be happy to assist you when I'm done with my current clients. However, I must insist that you leave the storage room." She lowers her voice an octave, intent on conveying her seriousness. "Company policy prohibits you from being back here. It's for your own safety, sir."

There she is calling me '*sir*' again. Perhaps such language would be nice in the bedroom. Well, let's be truthful, if the word were tumbling from her lips while I buried my head between her legs, it'd be fucking stupendous. But here? The way she's saying the word...yeah, it's not so great. Diplomatically choosing when and where to fight the battle of her formality, I simply agree. "Of course. I'll just be out front waiting." Giving her a little wink, I walk back out into the main part of the store.

I'm watching the old movie on the big-screen TV when she comes out and calls over to the mom and little boy still looking at clothes. He looks to be about nine or ten. When he catches my eye, I politely smile. The second his face lights up, I know that he knows who I am.

He immediately tugs on his mom's shirt. "Mom! Mom!" Forcing her to bend down, he whispers in her ear. He points in my direction, and when I wave at him, his eyes grow wide and he starts bouncing on his toes. It takes a lot of effort on my part not to laugh—not to explode with pure happiness. I love seeing excited kids. It's the best part of my job and brings me so much joy.

Joy I used to find on the field.

Clearing his throat and manning up, he walks over to me. "Hi, Coach. Is it all right if I take a picture with you?"

"Absolutely. Does your mom have a camera?" I watch as his mom waves her phone in our direction. I squat down and wrap my arm around his shoulders. We smile, following his mom's prompt. "How about a funny one?" I offer. I make the classic muscle pose with my arms and hold back a snicker when he immediately follows suit, trying to make his little noodle-arms bulge. Before I stand up, I ruffle his hair. Little kid hair is the best. "So, do you play?"

"No, sir. I'm not allowed to. I have really bad asthma. But the doctor says I may grow out of it."

I nod. "I hope you do." I reach in my pocket and hand him a bright copper penny.

He stares at it like I just gave him the key to the city. "Thank you."

"C'mon, Jason," his mom waves him over. "We need to head home to get ready for the pictures."

He rolls his eyes, explaining to me. "We have family pictures today. I had to get a new shirt." He skips away before turning around for one last wave. "Bye!"

Merit mumbles to the mom, "Kyra can check you out. Thanks so much."

When they're out of earshot, Merit turns to me. She looks completely dumbfounded. And completely cute.

"What was that all about? What are you a coach of?"

"I'm a high school football coach."

She sighs, not really understanding how that makes me a star. "Okaaayyy."

I rub my fingers across my lips and drag them down my chin, giving myself time to study her. "You really don't know who I am, do you?"

She pouts, growing frustrated. "You're Anna's uncle. Raylee's brother."

"Yes, I am. But I also used to play football."

"Like in high school?"

"Yeah. And in college. And... in the NFL."

"The NFL?"

I nod.

She cocks her head to the side. Her ponytail bobs, and her shirt falls farther down her shoulder. "Like the NFL that's on television?"

Laughing, I say, "Yeah. That's the only NFL I'm aware of."

She narrows her eyes. She thinks I'm making fun of her. I would never in a million years do that. It's just... her innocence and naivety are a commodity for me. A welcome luxury.

She shifts to fold her hands in front of her, but instead drops them to her side. Her fingertips tap against her thighs. And cue the fake smile. "That's a wonderful accomplishment. Congratulations. Did you have a chance to look around? Is there anything I can help you with?" She waves her hand around the store. "What do you need today?"

You.

"Why do you do that?" I ask her.

"Do what?"

"Why do you switch midstream and act like you're having a conversation with a UN ambassador or a member of British royalty?"

She freezes. I don't know if anyone has ever called her out on that before.

She nervously straightens the collar of her T-shirt. Much to my chagrin, she hides her sports bra, but it doesn't stop me from imagining what's underneath. Her breasts look large and round and perfect.

"I'm sorry. What do you mean?"

I take a step toward her. I'm not sure why I do it, but I kick off my flip flops, matching myself to her bare feet. "Why do you switch your tone of voice and your mannerisms? Why act so formal?"

"I'm just trying to be professional, sir." She chuckles, trying to point out the obvious. "We're strangers."

I take another step. "Well, let's solve that problem. Go out with me tonight."

Her jaw falls open. "Excuse me?"

I take another step. She's close. I can smell her. She smells like raspberries. "Let me take you to dinner tonight."

Her hands curl into fists, and her beautiful face contorts in anger. "How dare you? How dare you ask me on a date when you have a girlfriend sitting at home waiting on you." Technically, it's a question, but she hurls it like a factual accusation.

"A girlfriend? You mean Bunny?" I shake my head. "She's not my girlfriend. Never was. Last night was only our third date, and I told her that I didn't wanna see her anymore."

She narrows her eyes, not sure whether or not she should believe me. "Are you lying?"

"No. I don't lie to people I care about. Ever."

She scoffs. Cynicism travels through the room like a heavy fog. "Everyone lies."

"Well, I'm not everyone."

We're both quiet for a moment as I give her time to think. She's choosing to selectively ignore my comment that I care about her.

I take another step. I have to make it a half-step, or I'd be embracing her in a hug. "So, what do you say? Date? Tonight?"

She shakes her head. "I don't date."

"And just why not?"

"I just don't."

"There has to be a reason," I urge.

My fingertips still burn from holding her chin earlier. I wanna touch her so badly I have to stuff my hands in my pockets just to play nice.

"I'm divorced," she says matter-of-factly.

I shrug. "So?"

Confusion etches across her face. "So, that doesn't bother you?"

"No, why should it?"

She opens her mouth to enlighten me with her great response. When she can't formulate one, she fumes. Her lips pucker, and the tip of her nose pinks.

I try a different tactic. "Let me ask you this—do you have a lot of work to do today?"

"I'm a small business owner. I always have a lot to do."

"Well, I'm gonna plant myself right here," I point to the chair on my left, "all day long and bug the ever-living-hell out of you until you agree to go out with me."

A giggle catches me off guard. For the first time, I notice that Kyra has joined our conversation. She's sitting in a chair right behind me, listening to every word.

Merit notices too. She frowns at her friend. "Don't you have something to do over at the register?"

"No. When I'm over there, I can't hear what y'all are saying over here."

She starts to argue with Kyra, but I wrap my hands around her arms instead, drawing her attention to me.

So much for keeping my hands in my pockets.

Her skin immediately breaks out in goose bumps. The air between us explodes with tension and electricity. "Say yes," I plead.

She looks down. Under heavy eyelids, her gaze follows the muscles of my arm. Her whisper is weak. "I don't date."

"I think what you meant to say is *I don't date just anyone.* But you can date me."

"I have to work. The store doesn't even close until six-thirty."

Kyra pipes up. "It's fine. I can handle it by myself. It's all good."

Slowly, she glances up. When she looks me in the eyes, her soul crushes my heart. It withers into dust and blows away. Someone has hurt her, that's for damn sure, and they hurt her bad. I only pray she gives me a chance.

Because that's all I need.

One small chance.

I slowly edge my right foot along the carpet, grazing the side of her sexy, little foot with mine. The action is so minor—so innocent—but it shoots a current of high-voltage need and desire and possessiveness through every molecule in my body.

What is happening to me?

I have never, ever felt like this before.

And honestly, I worried I never would. But here it is.

And when the innocuous touch creates an audible gasp in the back of her throat, I realize I wanna feel like this forever.

My voice is lower than I intend for it to be; it's dark and desperate. "One small chance, Merit. That's all you have to give me. I won't take anything more from you."

She blinks, her hazel eyes glistening with sparks of brown and gold. The war she's fighting is plainly etched across her face. She wants to say no; she's begging herself to say no. But somewhere—deep, deep down inside of her—hope is blossoming. A flower that was dying has just been given water. And just like me, she wants that feeling to last. "Okay, Holt. One small chance."

Yes. She said yes.

She said yes to my dishonesty.

I can't believe I just lied. I just broke my own rule. I lied to someone I care about. I lied when I said I wouldn't take anything more from her.

Because, the thing is, I already know I want to take everything.

Chapter 3

Merit

"Why are you wearing that?"

Kyra's voice echoes through the speaker of my phone. My best friend is brash and brazen and absolutely wonderful. A few years younger than me, she's working on her master's degree in graphic design, and she's one of the most talented women I've ever had the pleasure of knowing. I'd be completely lost without her.

"What do you mean? I know it's been a long time since I've been on a first date, but since when does a black dress not meet the standard?"

"Since your asshole ex-husband always made you wear a little black dress every single time you went out." She growls, "Emphasis on *little*."

Turning around, I stare at my closet and the fifteen little black dresses that take up nearly half the space. Kyra's right. That was one of Edward's rules. He always wanted me to look classy—yet sexy—in case we ran into one of his clients or work colleagues. It always made me feel like I was attending a funeral as a high-price escort on the arm of a mobster. Well, I take that back...all the mobsters in my old movies are sexy, debonair, and dangerous. Even the attorney consiglieres are usually strapping and charming. Edward's none of those things. So, I guess a better description would be I was the hooker draped across the arm of the mob's weaselly and whiny CPA.

I slam the closet door and walk over to my jewelry box. "This is the first time I've had dinner with a male—who isn't my dad—in two years. I have bigger concerns than what I'm wearing." I slide the dangly pearl earrings through my ear. Reaching over, I run my fingertips over my great-grandmother's diamond and ruby bracelet before closing the lid.

"Concerns? Like what?"

"Conversation, for starters. What in the world are we gonna talk about? What if he wants to take me for sushi? You know I hate sushi."

"Then tell him you hate sushi."

The doorbell cuts off my sarcastic, R-rated response.

Kyra gasps. "Was that the doorbell? Is he there?"

I still can't believe I gave him my address. I'm a complete lunatic. I should've just told him I would meet him somewhere.

"Lock up my store," I bark my order to Kyra.

"Yeah, yeah. Have a great time. Call and tell me all about it."

I end the call and stand in the small hallway, staring at the front door. My heart thunders in my chest and a small drop of sweat rolls down my back. I wonder what he'll do if I don't answer? Maybe if I'm quiet, he'll just leave. I hold my breath and tiptoe to the door. I lean closer to it.

All of a sudden, he knocks. Hard. "Merit? I know what you drive. I know you're here; I see your SUV. Just come to the door."

Holy shit. He's an actual stalker, and I invited him to my doorstep.

"How do you know what I drive?" I ask him through the door.

"It doesn't take a rocket scientist to figure it out. The same two cars were parked in front of your store yesterday and today. One has an Alabama tag, and one has a Minnesota tag. I've heard both you and Kyra talk. It's pretty easy to figure out that you're not the one from Minnesota. They do call it a southern accent for a reason."

I think about that. It's pretty smart and observant, actually. "And you're a high school football coach, and not a cop?"

"There are a lot of cops in my family, but no, I'm not one of them. Now, do you plan on letting me in, or do we have to spend all night talking through the door?"

Huh. That might not be a bad way to ease into my first date as a not-so-newly-single woman.

"C'mon, Merit. I don't think I've ever had to work so hard to go out with a woman before."

Giving in to his honey-and-gravel voice, I open the door, adding to his comment. "Maybe that's a good thing. Working hard for something, I mean."

My sudden appearance takes him by surprise. I watch in eager anticipation as his eyes roam my body. When Edward looked at me, I felt like he was critiquing me, judging me, never quite happy with what he saw. But this? I feel like Holt is appreciating me. Absorbing me. Soaking me up, like water in a sponge.

And it makes me nervous in a wonderful way. A wonderful *and* horrible way.

A way I haven't felt in such an incredibly long time.

He chokes on his words and has to clear his throat. "Something tells me I'm gonna have to work hard every minute of the day with you, Mer."

I'm not sure if that's a compliment. I'm also not sure if I like the nickname, but I don't get a chance to tell him that before he continues.

"You're beautiful."

Well, at least I know *that's* a compliment. "Thank you."

Discreetly I try to study him in the same way he studied me. He's wearing khaki pants and a pale blue button-up with the sleeves rolled up to his elbows. And flip flops. I bite my lip to stifle my bashful and heated giggle. The contradiction of his church clothes and stained flip flops does nothing but add sincerity to his already larger-than-life charisma.

He's so attractive it almost hurts to look at him.

He takes a step across the threshold, and for a brief moment, I think he's going to kiss me. I have no idea what comes over me, but I close my eyes. Instead, he grabs my chin and tilts it up, examining my face.

"You can barely see your black eye. If I didn't know it was there, I would never know you had it."

I can't believe I closed my eyes, thinking his intentions were less than gentlemanly...or at least hoping they were.

Taking a step back, I turn around. "Makeup. I may not wear it much at the shop, but I still have a little talent up my sleeve." I walk over to the kitchen island and drop my cell phone in my purse.

Holt uses that as in invitation to come inside. "I was surprised you lived here. I thought these condos were mostly student housing. College kids."

"They are." I don't elaborate, and he doesn't press.

He looks around, taking in the small living room and kitchen. It's pretty grandiose for the slight space. Expensive leather furniture, fancy appliances. I can't help it. This is the way Edward's mom decorated it.

He nods down the hall. "Just one bedroom and bathroom?"

I nod in return. He acts like he wants to keep walking through my place, and then it hits me. I'm so rude. "Did you need to use the restroom? I'm sorry, sir, I should've offered that."

"No, I'm good. And you have to stop calling me 'sir' before I go bat-shit crazy," he says with a throaty chuckle. Turning to me, with good humor still plastered on his perfect face, he holds out his hand. "Ready?"

I stare at it.

He wants me to hold his hand?

Yeah, that's not happening.

He smiles, tilting one corner of his mouth. Dropping his hand to his side, he walks over and holds open the door. "After you."

I'm glad I won that battle.

This hostess is flaunting her ass all up in Holt's face. She's not even walking us to our seats. She's *prancing* us to our seats. I'm waiting on her to dislocate a hip as she sways back and forth.

I know he's gorgeous. I see it; I'm not blind. I also know I have no right to be jealous, but I literally can't help it. These girls are just being obscene with their flirtation. First, there was Bunny. And now, there's Rosie, the hostess. And don't even get me started on that girl who made eyes at him in the parking lot just outside.

He holds out my seat for me before seating himself. I nearly barf on the table when Rosie uses grabbing the extra silverware as an excuse to dangle her cleavage under Holt's nose. When she finally leaves, I have to roll my shoulders to lessen the tension. Holt clears his throat, and I watch as he leans back in his chair, rubbing his fingers across his lips.

"It's cute, you know?"

I set my purse on the empty chair beside me. "What's cute?"

"Your jealousy."

My eyebrows bolt into my hairline. "Excuse me?"

"When you get jealous, you scrunch your nose, like you smell something bad."

Oh, he can't be serious. "I have no idea what you're talking about. I don't scrunch my nose."

"Yes, you do. Don't be embarrassed. Ella rolls her eyes every time a girl hits on her husband Crutch. He loves it."

"Let me get this straight...he loves it when other women hit on him." I push the menu out of my way. "In front of his wife."

Holt sits forward, leaning closer to me. His growl is low, and it rattles in his chest. "No. He loves it when his woman wants to bare her teeth and fight for him."

I don't know if he meant for his words to be so sexy, but they were. Heat coils low in my stomach. With super-heroic strength, I ignore it. "Well, it's a moot point anyway. Because I don't scrunch my nose."

He opens his mouth to rebut, but he's interrupted.

"Hey, Coach. It's great to see you." The teenage boy who just walked over turns his head to me, nodding. "Ma'am."

Holt shakes hands with the boy, slapping him on the shoulder. "Hey, Carson. It's good to see you too. I requested a table in your section."

Carson grins, standing an inch taller. "Thanks, Coach." He smiles at me, his eyes glistening with a little mischief, and says, "Everyone fights for him when he comes in. He's a really good tipper."

Holt reclines in his seat and folds his arms behind his head as he pretends to protest, "Hey, who said I was paying tonight?"

We're in one of the fanciest restaurants in town. It opened about two years ago, and people still trip all over themselves to get their name on the reservation list. So, needless to say, his boisterous behavior has a couple of stuffy patrons looking in our direction.

He winks at me.

Unfortunately, I'm starting to like it when he winks at me.

"Yeah, right," Carson rolls his eyes. "I've never known you not to pay for a date."

"Just how many dates have you brought here?" I can't believe I just asked that question. I clamp my hand over my mouth, and my face burns red.

Holt sits up straight and makes a knife-over-his-throat motion in exaggerated fashion. "Cut it out, Carson. You're ruining the mood."

Carson laughs. "I'll go get you some water while you read over the menu."

I shake my head. "I apologize. That was a rude thing to say."

Holt shrugs. "Why are you apologizing? I *have* been on a lot of dates here."

Oh.

I knew this was a bad idea.

He reaches across and grabs my hand. I'm too shocked to move it away. "And before you race out of here—because it's written all over your face that you wanna do just that—you should know that I'm not some player stringing you along. I've had a lot of dates because that's what people do when they're searching for the one."

"And that's what you're doing? Searching for *the one*?" I ask.

His calloused thumb circles around my skin, sending shivers down my spine. I should really move my hand.

"Isn't everybody?"

I shake my head. "Not me."

"That's the thing, though, Merit…maybe you are, and you just don't know it yet."

Carson walks back up to the table and sets crystal goblets of water in front of us. I pull my hand back, but not before Holt gives it a soft squeeze. Carson straightens the black bow tie on his waiter's uniform. "I'm sorry I didn't introduce myself earlier. My name is Carson, and I'll be your server this evening, ma'am."

"Carson is one of my students. He's also one of my players. He'll be a senior this year." Holt's face beams with pride. "He's got a very bright future ahead of him. He wants to be an aeronautical engineer."

"Wow. That's amazing," I say. "What made you pick that field?"

"I watched a documentary on it when I was in elementary school. It always stuck with me." He tugs at his bow tie again. "I'm working here over the summer and saving up money for college."

"That's so admirable of you, Carson."

"Thank you." Gifting me with a shy nod, he goes back to work. "Would you like to start off with an appetizer this evening?" He turns to Holt. "You wouldn't like the soup. Today is lobster bisque."

Holt makes a funny face.

"You don't like lobster bisque?" I ask.

"Ugh. I can't stand seafood. Or sushi."

I bite my tongue.

Holt waves the menu at me. "Did you want an appetizer? Or just stick with the main course?"

"Main course is fine with me." One, I don't want to drag this date out longer than it needs to be. Two, he doesn't have to spend the extra money on me. I can survive without a couple of overpriced stuffed mushrooms.

"What can I get you?" Carson eagerly awaits my answer.

"I'll just have the grilled chicken salad. House dressing is fine." Politely smiling, I hand Carson my menu. We both turn to Holt, waiting on him to order.

But he doesn't.

He cocks his head and narrows his eyes, staring at me. Eventually, he sighs. "Carson, can you give us just a minute, please."

"Sure thing, Coach."

I'm thoroughly confused about what is happening right now.

"You ordered a big salad," he says simply, firmly.

Oh. I fold my hands in my lap. "I'm sorry. I'll be happy to just get a side salad." Anger flies in the pit of my stomach. He's just like Edward. Well, screw him.

It's fine; I'll just treat myself and order take-out after I get home.

He snorts. "A side salad? That's the most pitiful thing I've ever heard. Listen, it's completely fine if you want a grilled chicken salad. Hell, I actually eat that a lot at home. I just wanna make sure that's what you really want. I know someone who always ordered a salad because that's what was expected of her. Like she had to be some prim and proper little thing. When what she really loved was Philly cheesesteak sandwiches."

"A woman you dated?"

His brow furrows. "What?" He shakes his head. "No, I'm talking about Ella." His face softens. "You remind me a lot of her, and I just don't want you ordering something because you think it's what I wanna hear. I don't want you to go home and have to order take-out because you're still hungry."

He. Can. Read. My. Mind.

"What's your favorite food?" he asks.

I take a deep breath. "My favorite food?"

"Yeah."

"Well, I have two. Steak and blueberry pancakes."

He bursts out laughing. "Well, I don't think blueberry pancakes are on the menu here, but we can definitely make steak happen." He waves Carson back over and nods to me, waiting for me to rise to the challenge.

I clear my throat. "You can scratch the salad. I'll take the filet. Medium-rare. With the loaded baked potato—extra cheese and bacon—and the grilled summer vegetables. And water to drink will be fine."

Holt smiles widely, proudly, like he just won a ballgame. "I'll take the exact same thing. And a beer."

After a bartender drops off Holt's beer, we settle back to wait on our food. I worry that we'll have an uncomfortable silence, but Holt doesn't let that worry come to fruition.

"How old are you, Merit?"

He asks the question like he has a secret. Like he knows something I don't know. "Oh my gosh. Am I older than you? Like cougar old? How old are *you*?" I blink.

He snickers, enjoying my anxiety. In fact, he seems to enjoy my anxiety a little too much, if you ask me. "Calm down. I doubt you're older than me. But it wouldn't matter even if you were."

"It would matter to me." I don't know why I feel the need to share honest answers with him.

He shrugs, intrigued with my comment. "Why?"

"Think of the optics. If you're some big football star, I don't wanna be seen as the older woman, chasing the handsome athlete around town."

The tilt of his mouth drives me crazy. Even the freckles on his nose drive me crazy. I had no idea freckles could be so sexy.

"*If* I'm some big football star? Are you telling me that you didn't google me this afternoon as soon as you found out I played in the NFL?"

I shake my head. "Half the stuff on the Internet may be true, but the other half is a blatant lie. Do you really want me learning about you from my laptop?"

"Point taken. And that may be the most refreshing thing I've ever heard on a first date." He takes a long pull from his beer. "I'm thirty, by the way. I'll be thirty-one in October."

"I'm twenty-eight. I'll be twenty-nine in March."

He grins over his bottle. "See. You have nothing to worry about, my little cougar."

Oh god. Let's hope that nickname doesn't stick. I'll take *'Mer'* any day over that.

"Why'd you stop?" I ask.

"Why'd I stop *what*?" His words are slow and lazy, like he knows what I'm asking but he's decided to tease me, nonetheless. "Why'd I stop spouting off cute little nicknames for you?" His teeth playfully bite into his bottom lip. "I can come up with a few more for you. Is that what you want, sweetheart?"

Agh! My parents call me sweetie and sweetheart. So, no, thank you. I definitely don't wanna picture the drop-dead sexy Holt Hill every time Mom asks if I need a new toothbrush head because they bought a huge pack on sale from Walmart.

"Uh...Mer is just fine," I concede, afraid of what name may stick if I fight the battle too hard. "I mean why'd you stop playing in the NFL?"

His lively demeanor fades just a smidge, and he twirls the beer bottle around on the table. Everybody else is drinking out of fancy, frosted mugs. Holt told the bartender he wanted to drink straight from the bottle. "Injured my knee and neck," he says, giving a little point to a barely visible scar in the crease of his neck.

I frown a little. He doesn't have a limp and doesn't seem to be in any pain when moving his neck, so I'm guessing he's mostly—if not fully—healed, depending on when it happened. "I'm sorry. I know football can be rough on the body."

He opens his mouth but freezes before any words come out. It's clear to see he's not exactly sure what to say. I'm guessing talking about his career-ending injuries is not high on his small-talk list. He leaves me with a simple, "Yeah. It is."

Our eye contact is broken by the hostess—and her swishy ass—announcing loudly in our direction, "A table for two." I watch as an older couple is seated two tables over from us. Rosie makes certain to take the long way back to the hostess stand, passing right by our table.

Holt stares at me, watching for my reaction.

I don't give him the satisfaction. I quickly stand from the table. "Please excuse me." I look around. "Do you know where the restroom is?"

Holt points down the back hall. He stands to escort me, but I quickly wave him down. "I'll manage. Thank you."

Edward always wanted me to excuse myself by saying I had to 'powder my nose'. I always thought that was the most ridiculous comment ever. People know that's code for peeing and pooping. It felt really good not saying that tonight.

On my way back to the table, I nearly have a heart attack when a huge crash and the sound of breaking dishes filters from the partially open kitchen door. Being the curious sort, I slow my walk and peer around the corner, checking to see if my steak is on the floor. Several people are standing around, and I see Carson bent over a couple of broken plates, picking up the pieces.

"How could you be so stupid! That china costs more than you make in a week!" An older guy with a small mustache and a white chef's jacket is shouting at the boy.

Carson nods at a box of laundered linen napkins sitting by the door. "I'm sorry, Chef. Someone left that box right in front of the door. I tripped."

"I left that box there. Are you blaming me? I'm trying to run a kitchen," he yells. "I can't be responsible for every little moron who doesn't have enough sense to watch where he's going." He tosses his hands in the air. "I told Luke he should never hire high school kids, but he doesn't listen to me. This is coming out of your paycheck. Clean up this mess and try not to ruin my night more than you already fucking have." He walks away, mumbling under his breath. "Imbeciles."

I watch as Carson's shoulders slump. He works silently, taking care to gather every last shard. Not one single person offers to help him.

Not one.

After a few seconds, another server cuts around him and bounds out of the door with plated food, making me jump. She, at least, has the decency to look somewhat embarrassed, assuming I heard her boss's outburst. When I look back, Carson is gone.

With a broken heart, I retreat back to the table. No kid deserves to be talked to that way. What makes me even sadder is there were a couple of times in our marriage when Edward called me stupid or made me think I was the cause of something happening when it was all him.

That's something you never forget.

Ever.

"Well, there you are. I was worried you'd ditched me." Holt takes another drink of his beer.

His joke falls on deaf ears.

Immediately sensing something is wrong, he reaches across the table and grabs my hand. Again. And once again, I wasn't quick enough to remove it. "What's wrong? Are you okay? Are you sick?"

I shake my head. "I'm fine."

"You're most definitely not. I already told you, Mer, you wear your emotions all over your face. And something is definitely wrong." When I don't answer. He squeezes my hand. His face is serious, his voice stern. "There is no choice here. You have to tell me what's upset you."

"Carson dropped a couple of plates in the kitchen. He tripped over a box that was blocking a doorway. I saw it on my way back from the ladies' room."

Holt's hand leaves mine as he looks behind his shoulder, searching for his student. "Is he okay? Is he hurt?"

"Not physically."

Holt turns back around, eyeing me suspiciously. "What's that supposed to mean?"

I bite my lip. "It's not my place to say."

"It *is* your place. Carson's my student, my player. If anything happens to him, I need to know about it."

I take a deep breath. "The guy back there—I guess he's the chef—he wasn't very nice to him. He said some things."

Holt's jaw tenses. "What things?"

I look down at the table. Gathering my strength, I look back up, staring Holt in the eyes. "He called Carson stupid. Said he was a moron. Told him that the cost would be coming out of his paycheck."

Holt's eyes grow wide, and his nostrils flare. He pushes back from the table with so much force I worry his chair might tip over and holds out his hand. "C'mon."

His tone leaves nothing up for discussion. Trying not to overthink it, I place my hand into his, and he pulls me behind him so quickly, I nearly trip over myself as I grab my purse. Stalking down the corridor, Holt bursts into the kitchen, not caring that he's not invited, not caring that he's not supposed to be back there. Everyone in the kitchen turns to look at us.

Glancing at me sideways, Holt growls. "Which one?"

I nod to the chef in the corner. He looks up from the grill at the same time Carson comes walking in from the back area.

"Coach? Is everything all right? I was just bringing your bread and butter to you." He holds up an overflowing basket in our direction.

"Come here, Carson." He leans down, getting eye level with the boy. "What happened? Are you okay?"

Carson doesn't know I saw anything, so he's completely confused. His innocent eyes look from left to right. "Sorry?"

"You dropped some plates?"

Carson lowers his eyes, once again slumping his shoulders. "Yes, sir."

Holt pats his shoulder. "Hold your head high, son." Focusing his attention back on the kitchen staff, Holt points a finger at the chef. "You. I've met you before. What's your name? Chef Asshat?"

The guy's eyes bug out of his face. "Chef *Ashman*."

Close enough.

"It makes you feel good about yourself to call other people names? Treat them like second-class citizens? No one deserves that."

He shrugs. "I don't know what you're talking about. We're fine, aren't we, Carson?"

Carson tugs on Holt's arm. "It's fine, Coach."

"No, Carson, it's not. No one is allowed to belittle you. Ever."

Asshat folds his hands across his chest. "I'll ask you politely to get out of my kitchen."

"Not until you apologize to him for calling him names."

"I didn't call him names."

"Liar." Holt flicks his head to me. "She heard you. She saw you."

Asshat points a finger at me. "Then, she's the liar."

Holt turns to me. His face—his whole body—is filled with anger and fire, but also a sweet passion. For a moment, it steals the breath from my lungs. I open my mouth to defend myself, but I don't have to.

"She doesn't lie. Not to me she doesn't."

I can't even wrap my head around Holt's assertion, his confidence in me.

Asshat flings his hands in the air. "Fine. I called him a few names. He broke some very expensive china. He needs to start paying attention to what he's doing. He acts like a dumb kid? He gets called a dumb kid."

"Sounds like you need to start growing some common sense along with that holier-than-thou attitude. Putting a large box right in front of a doorway is just begging for trouble." Oops. I didn't mean to open my mouth. How did I drag myself into this standoff?

Holt squeezes my hand, nonverbally thanking me for my words, for my support. Oh, that's right, he's still holding my hand.

Asshat screams at the top of his lungs. "Get the fuck out of my kitchen!"

Everyone in the restaurant had to have heard that. There's no way they couldn't.

Holt shakes his head in disgust. "You make me sick." He nods his head at Carson. "Go get your stuff. We're leaving."

Carson whispers, his eyes torn with anguish. "Coach, I really need this money for college."

Holt shakes his head. "Not this money. Not from him, you don't. We'll find you a new job—a great job—I promise." Holt grabs the bread basket from Carson's hand and sets it on the counter. "Go on. Get your stuff, son."

Carson reaches down and pulls out his cell phone and car keys, before taking off the black waist apron. "This is it." He looks down at his outfit. "Well, and the uniform. But I don't have clothes to change into."

Finally letting go of my hand, Holt reaches into his back pocket and pulls out his wallet. I watch as he peels three crisp, one-hundred-dollar bills from the money inside. He tosses it on top of the bread basket. "There. This should cover it." He pins Asshat with one last punishing glare, "And if this isn't enough to cover the plates, I suggest you start going to Costco and buy in bulk, you pretentious douche."

Pushing open the kitchen door, he ushers Carson out, and when he reaches behind, grabbing for my hand again, I don't think I've ever felt better.

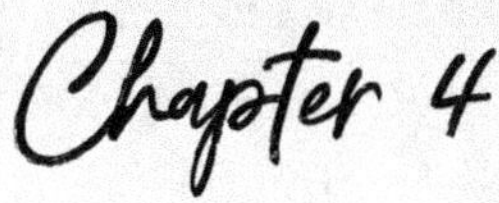

Chapter 4

Holt

I have the best family in the world.

Well, technically, Jeff is a friend. But that's just semantics.

"I can't believe you got him a new job that quick." Merit shakes her head in awe. "It was who? Your friend's dad?"

"My best friend's dad," I clarify. "We grew up together, so he's more like my uncle. Jeff owns The Elegant Taste. It's a catering company."

She sits up straighter in her seat. "I know them! They've catered a lot of functions I've been to." She leans back, automatically placing her hand on her stomach in appreciation. "Their food is amazing."

I side glance at her. The streetlights reflect through the truck, softly lighting her face like she's an angel. Her redwood hair fans across the tan leather of the headrest of my passenger seat. She blinks, waiting on me to agree with her.

"Try growing up next door to them. I'm lucky I don't weigh five-hundred pounds."

Grinning, she turns to the window, watching as we drive through town. She's definitely the curious sort, asking me three times where we are going—even after I told her it was a surprise. I actually had to pull the truck over and tell her I wasn't driving another inch until she promised she wouldn't ask the question again. She pretended to be mad, but seeing as she *does,* in fact, wear her emotions all over her face, I know she found my hijinks funny after the drama at the restaurant.

"So, he'll be part of their waitstaff at events? And they'll work around his football games and practices?"

"Yeah. Jeff and Cullen know that weekday practices end at five. Our school does a block schedule, so we get to start practice at one-thirty. For the first three blocks, I teach physical education, and then I have football athletics for the fourth block. And they know Friday nights are off-limits as long as it's football season. But, that's fine...they're so busy, Carson will probably work at least one event a weekend, if not more. It'll be good money."

"Who's Cullen? Is that your best friend?"

"Jeff and Dana have two sons—Ridge and Cullen. Ridge is my best friend. We're the same age. Cullen is a few years younger than us."

"Ridge doesn't work for The Elegant Taste too?"

"No, he's a firefighter. And Cullen splits his time between the catering business and the bar."

"The bar?"

"He and Will own a bar together. The Last Call. It's downtown. Cullen was just a bartender, but Will sold him part of the business this past spring. It gives him more time to spend with Raylee and the kids because he and Cullen divide the workload."

She nods, smiling brightly at the mention of my niece and nephew. "Anna and Ty are great kids. I love when they come in the store."

"Raylee said you opened the store four years ago?"

I wait on her to answer, but it just so happens that I pull into our destination so my question takes a back seat to her surprise.

She glances from me to the restaurant. "Breakfast?"

I wave my hand at the front of the twenty-four-hour breakfast diner. "Well, I didn't give you steak tonight. I figured the least I could do is blueberry pancakes."

Blushing, she looks down at her dress and picks at an imaginary piece of lint. "Thank you."

I nearly lost my shit when I saw her tonight.

She looks so beautiful in that short dress, heels, and makeup. Of course, she also looked beautiful in her T-shirt and shorts with her angry black eye. Her smooth, lean legs are driving me completely crazy. There's a deep muscle line on the outside of her thighs that flexes each time she walks, each time she shifts in the seat. Not to mention, the fabric of her dress falls against the curve of her large breasts. I'm surprised I've been able to drive us around and keep us in one piece. My eyes keep leaving the road and roaming over her gorgeous body.

There is one thing that bothers me, though.

It's black.

She doesn't really strike me as the 'black dress' type. When I think of Merit, I think of colors. Bright and airy. Innocent and fun. Black is way too serious.

Turning off the truck, I race around, opening her door. When I offer my hand, she stares at it. For some reason, she doesn't want to touch me now, but seeing as she held my hand during the shit show at the restaurant, she doesn't know how to decline. Lifting her head, she stares straight into my eyes, sliding her fingers against mine.

How can someone be so scared and so brave at the exact same time?

What happened to her?

The hostess quickly shows us to our seats. I think back, trying to remember if I've ever brought a date to a simple diner like this. I don't think I have. Not even in high school.

My fingers immediately stick to the menu. No matter how much cleaning they do, they're covered in permanent remnants of syrup and bacon grease. Now I definitely know I've never brought a girl to a place like this. The women I seem to date would definitely complain about something like that. The thought alone makes me angry. Why do I always attract women who live outside the simple box of normal? Women who have to have everything perfect in life? A perfect life served on a silver platter.

Hell, not even silver. It seems my women always want it on a platinum platter. And they want me to pay for it.

And although I'm perfectly fine paying for things, having a woman who only wants me for that reason is not what I want in a partner. In a girlfriend. In a wife.

The waitress quickly brings over glasses of water. She's plump with a frizz of gray hair. When she smiles, there's a dimple on her left cheek. "Don't you two kids look nice. Are you having a good night?"

I smile, watching Merit as she pretends to study the menu like she's having to pass a written exam on it later. "It's been wonderful, thanks." I look at her name tag. "We're just starving, Clara."

"Well, honey, we can take care of that. Do y'all need more time? Or do you know what you want?"

I thump Merit's menu with my finger, making her jump. "Blueberry pancakes?"

She blushes again, before quickly turning to Clara and politely nodding. "Yes, please."

"We'll take two of the biggest stacks of blueberry pancakes you've got."

Clara smacks her ink pen against her order pad. "Perfect. Anything else?"

I watch Merit, amused by her nonverbal response to Clara's question. She wants something else. I know she does. I can see it. "Better tell her now, Mer. I wasn't kidding. I'm fading away to nothing over here." I lean back in my seat and fold my hands behind my head. Her eyes dilate in pleasure and rake over my body, scalding me where I sit. I know exactly what I'm doing to her...and I like it—a lot.

She had the exact same reaction when I did this earlier, when we were talking to Carson at our table.

That's why I'm doing it again.

Because I really like having her eyes on my body.

Clara pushes her. "Well, sweetie?"

She lets out a little sigh. "Bacon and sourdough toast, please."

Laughing, I sit up straight. I hold up two fingers for Clara, letting her know I want the exact same thing.

"Sounds good. You kids holler if you need anything."

Merit watches her walk away. "She's really nice."

You're really nice.

"You never answered my question."

She cocks her head to the side. "Hmm?"

"About the store."

"Oh. Yes. I opened the store four years ago in May."

"And it's always been in the same spot?" I ask.

"Mmm-hmm. That small strip mall has been around for about twenty years. My store used to be a barbeque joint, so it took a ton of remodeling to get it ready. It's just me and three other stores." She holds up her fingers, ticking the places off one-by-one. "The place that sells men's suits, the beauty salon, and the coffee shop."

I take a sip of my water, wishing it were a beer. I like to drink when I'm nervous, and being with Merit makes me nervous.

Well, nervous and not-nervous all at the same time.

"I go to that coffee shop on the corner a couple of times a week."

"I know. Their stuff is addictive, right? I don't drink coffee, but I really like the smoothies," she says.

"I'm surprised I haven't seen you there before."

She shrugs. "I try to only go there once a week. I typically pack my lunch and snacks for work. You know, sandwiches and stuff. It saves money."

This is the first time one of my dates has voiced being concerned with saving money.

Minute by minute, that weird, fluttery feeling consuming my body grows. The feeling I'd never—in my entire life—experienced until seeing Merit yesterday. It's expanded through my heart and brain. Slowly, inch by inch, it's devouring my soul. It's eating away at me, ripping from me the desolate dreams of how I thought my future would go. And that feeling is replacing each void it creates with a new dream of Merit. Visions of her kissing me, falling in love with me, being by my side.

She's my own little mirage.

I clear my throat, trying to get back on track with our conversation. "Ella and her husband, Crutch, go there too. They sort of have a thing for that coffeehouse. I wonder if you've ever seen them there before."

"You talk about your cousin a lot. Are you close?"

"We all are. We grew up together. Me, Raylee, Ella, Ridge, and Cullen." I rub my fingers against my lip in thought, trailing them down my chin. "I had another cousin too."

"Had?" Merit's question is cautious. She's scared to ask, but too curious not to.

"Ella's sister, Carrie. She died." I never say she passed away. That indicates a natural death. Carrie's death was anything but natural.

Merit's hand flies to her face, covering her open mouth. She lowers her fingers just enough for the words to escape. "I'm very sorry." She leans forward, wanting me to see her sincerity. "I'm sorry you had to lose someone you were so close to."

I reach across the table, wanting to touch her. Wanting to feel her hand in my hand. Unfortunately, she's quicker than me.

Just this once.

She pulls her hands onto her lap, politely folding them. She reminds me of a porcelain doll when she does that.

Letting her think she's won this small battle, I switch topics. "So, what did you do before opening the store?"

"I worked at an attorney's office. I was an executive assistant and paralegal."

"Oh yeah? For which office?"

"Plott, Ezzell, and Crispin."

Un-fucking-believable. "You worked with Stanton Plott?"

"Yes. Do you know him?"

"And his son, Hudson?" I answer her question with a question.

She furrows her brow. "Well, Hudson is based out of the firm's Mobile office, but yes, I know him. Why? You obviously know them?" she asks again.

"Yeah, I know them. They're fucking grade-A assholes."

Merit's jaw falls slack in shock. Then, she starts to giggle uncontrollably, snorting in the process.

She's so freakin' cute.

I spread my hands across the table. "C'mon, you can't tell me you don't think the same thing about them."

She busies herself by unwrapping her silverware and placing her paper napkin in her lap. She's trying to bite back a smile, but I see it, nonetheless. "They can be...hard to take in large doses."

"Stop being so diplomatic, they're horrible. Please don't tell me you were Stanton's assistant."

She shakes her head. "No, I worked mostly with Charles Ezzell and his son, Edward."

"How in the world did you ever get hooked up with that place?" I hold my hands in the air. "Don't get me wrong, I know it's a prestigious law firm with lots of wins. But still...they're a bunch of pricks."

She looks down at the table, straightening her fork and knife. Eventually, she lifts her chin, focusing on my face. "Edward Ezzell was my husband."

Holy hell.

"Here we go." Clara pops between us, setting down a container of maple syrup and a pile of extra napkins. When she pushes the syrup to the middle of the table, the lid wobbles. "Uh-oh, looks like the lid is broken on this one. I'll get you a new one," she says, balancing the lopsided jar under her fingers.

I watch as Merit's napkin falls from her lap to the floor. She bends forward, reaching to pick it up.

Before leaving, Clara leans across the table, grabbing Merit's empty water glass. "Let me get you a fresh water, hon."

And then it happens.

I'm not sure how it happens.

Well, actually, I know *how* it happens. I just can't believe that it *does* happen.

After finding her napkin, Merit's head snaps up, and she rams herself right into the pitcher of syrup dangling from Clara's hand. The bottom of the container breaks off from the lid attachment. The glass jar clunks down, right on top of Merit's head, and bounces off her in slow motion. But not before a huge pile of warm, gooey maple syrup coats the whole left side of her hair.

The three of us freeze, too stunned to even move. My mouth hangs open, and I watch in fascinated disbelief as sticky syrup travels down Merit's hair like a slow-moving glacier.

Clara looks from Merit to me and back to Merit again, before dissolving in a puddle of panic. "Oh my gosh! Are you okay? I am so sorry!"

Flustered, Merit grabs a handful of napkins from the table and immediately runs them over her hair. The thin paper does nothing but stick in the syrup and break into small pieces.

This situation somehow got worse. It now looks like she got attacked by a duck and has a thousand small white feathers all over her head.

Clara huddles over Merit, trying to pick the pieces out.

Several customers snicker and whisper, and from the corner of my eye, I see a manager racing out of the kitchen to see what's happening. I'm about to burst out laughing when I see the tears start to well in Merit's eyes.

In that one short second, it becomes my life's mission to never see this woman cry. To never see this woman hurt.

I quickly step into action, rising from the table and picking up the jar of syrup from the floor. We're lucky it didn't break. But now, there's a huge swimming pool of syrup all over the tile. I hand it to Clara right as the manager comes rushing up.

"What happened?" she whisper-yells. "Clara!"

I use my on-field voice. Both women immediately turn to me, hushing and listening. "It's fine. It was a complete accident. No one's to blame. It'll take some time to clean up the floor, though. Why don't y'all work on that. Okay?"

Looking at each other, they both nod.

I lift Merit from the chair. Holding her by the arms, I stand right in front of her, grazing my body against hers. "Merit." Her eyes are glossy and unfocused, so I say her name again and take a small step closer. Her breasts rub against me. "The bathroom is right over there." I nod behind my shoulder, forcing her to follow my line of sight. "Why don't you clean up as best as you can? I'll take care of things out here, and I'll come check on you in just a minute."

Syrup slowly cascades down her hair, collecting against the straps of her dress and coating her naked shoulder. Blankly nodding, I watch as she disappears into the restroom.

It takes about ten minutes for me to finish up with the manager and Clara. They eagerly work to please me, quickly setting about getting a new table ready. Grabbing a chair, I pull it behind me and knock on the door of the ladies' restroom. I push it open, just a crack, and see Merit bent over the sink sideways, trying to rinse her hair and epically failing. The faucet is squirting everywhere, and half of her body is drenched. It looks like she got in a water balloon fight with a group of rowdy kids. Once again, I have to bite back a laugh. "Merit, I'm coming in."

"You can't come in, Holt. This is the girls' bathroom."

I swing open the door, carrying the chair over my back. "Does it look like I care?" I dangle the small gift in my hand. "Manager had a bottle of shampoo in her locker."

Her eyes light up and her fingers eagerly reach for it. I snatch it away and shake my head. "Nope." I position the chair in front of the sink and nod at it. "Sit down."

She pouts. "Huh?"

"Sit down and lean your head back. I'm gonna wash your hair."

"Oh no, Holt, that's not necessary. I can get it."

"You can?" I slowly drag my eyes down her body. Water is dripping from her arms. "It looks like you went swimming in the ocean." I lift my eyebrows, "And we're five hours from the beach."

Scowling, she spins around and plops down in the chair, gently laying her head back into the sink. Pouring nearly the whole bottle of strawberry-scented shampoo on her hair, I spend the next several minutes washing and rinsing all the suds and the breakfast condiment down the drain. I wring out her hair and pull a small white towel from my back pocket. "They assure me this has never been used." I sniff it. "Although it does smell like sausage."

For the first time since she became a walking breakfast burrito with feathers, she smiles. And it damn melts my heart. Yanking the towel from my hands, she eagerly towel-dries her hair and finger-combs it.

Eventually she stands up, turning to look at herself in the mirror.

And she stops smiling.

I have no idea why she stops smiling. Because I don't think I've ever seen someone sexier. Her damp hair falls in waves around her. Her mascara has smudged, and most of her eye makeup has been washed away. The previously well-hidden black eye is back in full force, no longer concealed by whatever cream or powder she used. Her face is flushed, and her lips are swollen.

I step behind her, breathing deeply.

Plus, she smells like strawberries and sausage.

Her spine stiffens, and she stops breathing. My crotch grazes against her. I take a small step back so she won't feel the jump of my dick. "You look beautiful." Stepping to the side, I hold out my hand. "Shall we?"

What can she say? How can she deny me? I just washed her hair in the sink of a public bathroom. Underneath the shadow of a dispenser selling tampons for a quarter.

Her fingertips barely touch mine, and I'm pulling her behind me. When we make it back out into the dining room area, she gasps. The few patrons who saw our fiasco gently clap, trying to give Merit encouragement to finish the night in style. I guess they don't know whether she's my date, my girlfriend, or my wife, but they're encouraging her to continue on with the night, regardless.

Clara and the manager set us up at a new table next to the window. They actually pushed three tables together for us. Just like I asked, they were able to dim the lights in this one small section and find a couple of candles. The soft, dancing candlelight really brings out the beauty of the blue, flame-retardant curtains.

More importantly, the table is filled with basically every single item from the menu. Pancakes, waffles, omelets, grits, hashbrowns, sourdough toast, bacon, sausage, ham, egg sandwiches, and more.

"Holy crap. Is that all for us?"

I lean down, whispering against the shell of her ear. "It's for you."

She shivers. "There's no way we can eat it all," she denies.

Right then, her stomach growls. Loudly.

This time, I can't help but laugh. "No. But we can sure as hell try."

I put the truck in park outside of her condo. "Let me walk you up."

She's already scrambling for the door. That's not surprising, considering nerves were getting the best of her the closer we got to her house. With every mile, the conversation became more one-sided, meaning I heard more of my own voice than I wanted to. "No, that's all right. I can make it," she says, rushing through the words.

My hand snatches out, grabbing her wrist. "Merit, that's not code for 'I wanna come inside'. I promise, our date will end by the front door."

Slowly nodding, she still climbs out of the truck on her own versus waiting on me to come around and get her. That's a damn shame, too, because I like watching the way her dress inches up on her thighs.

As soon as we're standing by the front door, she forces her key into the lock, and I notice her hands are shaking.

"When can I see you again?"

She bites her lip. "I don't think that's a good idea."

"Why is that?"

"Because I told you, I don't date."

I smirk. "I think we just proved that theory wrong, Mer."

She scoffs. "I think we proved exactly why I *shouldn't* date." She tosses her hands in the air. "Tonight, I got someone fired from the fanciest restaurant in town, and I lathered myself up like some gigantic French toast stick."

I chuckle, thinking back to our smorgasbord. "I wonder why they didn't bring us any French toast?"

She groans, rubbing her flat stomach. "Uhh. Don't even joke about food."

I shake my head in disbelief. "I still can't believe you invited every waitress and the whole kitchen staff to join us."

She smiles sheepishly. "I didn't know you ordered all that food. I thought they made it for free because they felt bad about my hair. I didn't want it to go to waste."

Granted, the manager did try to give me some free food, but I told her upfront that I would be paying for everything. What happened was no one's fault. It was just an accident.

She lowers her head, staring at her feet. "I'm sorry."

"What are you apologizing for?"

She shrugs. "For everything. For Carson. For the syrup. For inviting people to eat the food you paid for."

Why hasn't she looked back up yet? From what I've seen, she always steels herself, composes herself after a moment, and stares straight into my eyes. I like it. It gives me a chance to study all the colors in hers. My finger circles underneath her chin, tilting her face to mine.

"I'm accident-prone," she offers.

I wink at her. "I figured that out."

If I bent my head just a little, my mouth could be on hers. What would she taste like? What noises would she make? What would her tongue feel like sliding against mine. What would—fuck me, stop it,

Holt. Refocusing, I jump back to our conversation. "So, like I said, when can I see you again?"

"Are you sure you wanna see me again?"

Hell, yeah.

"Can I see you tomorrow?" I beg.

Her eyes widen and her pink lips fall open. "Tomorrow?"

"Yeah. We'll do something fun...that doesn't involve syrup."

"Like what?"

I shrug. "We'll figure it out."

She wants to say yes. I know she does. I can see it.

"Just one more chance," I prod her with my whisper.

She sighs so deeply, I'm afraid she's gonna crack a rib. I can literally hear the shaky breath as it tangles in her mouth, afraid to leave the sanctuary of her body. "O...okay."

I snake my hand around her neck, relishing the feel of her soft skin underneath my hand, and I gently kiss her cheek. And then I walk back to my truck, grinning like a damn idiot the whole way.

Chapter 5

Holt

"So, how was your date?" Ridge's voice echoes through my phone speaker while I run on the elliptical.

"Eventful."

He snorts. "What the hell does that mean?"

By the time I finish telling him about the events of last night, he's rolling, laughing so hard I can barely understand what he's saying. "Well, she certainly sounds perfectly imperfect."

"Hell, yeah, she is."

For a few seconds, he's quiet. "You really like this girl, don't you?"

When I don't respond, he already knows the answer.

"And you've known her for how long?"

I look at the smart watch on my wrist. "Forty-four hours, but who's counting?"

Ridge groans. "And she's not lying about knowing who you are? About knowing your fame? Knowing what kind of money you have?"

"I'm positive. There's just something about her."

He snorts, "You mean she's fucking beautiful."

I chuckle. "Well, there *is* that. But there's more. I just don't think she would lie to me."

"What makes you say that?"

"Because I wouldn't lie to her," I answer honestly.

Ridge is about to say something else, but he's cut off by the blaring alarm of the firehouse. "Gotta go."

"Be careful, man."

"Always, brother."

She's dressed in another killer black dress when she answers the door. Off the shoulder, formfitting, and sexy. With fuck-me heels. Her black eye was a little harder to hide today, but she still did a good job. The purple and blue is now mixed with that sickly healing-yellow color, and I can still see some of the bruise peeking from underneath her makeup. Her hungry eyes travel the full length of my body, from head to toe. When her breath catches in her chest, I know she likes what she sees.

What I wouldn't give to wrap her in my arms and spend the whole afternoon in bed, making love and fucking until we're so exhausted we can't even lift our bodies from the sweat-soaked sheets.

Blinking, she shakes her head and gathers her thoughts. "I'm overdressed." She pouts, staring at my ballcap, T-shirt, cargo shorts, and flip flops.

When I texted her, telling her I would pick her up at three, she asked where we were going. I told her it was a surprise. I guess she just assumed it would be a normal, intimate dinner date, replacing the one interrupted last night. Although, I don't know anyone—at least our age—who goes to a nice restaurant for a dinner date at three in the afternoon.

"This is why I don't like surprises."

I take a step toward her. "Don't lie, Merit."

"Mmmm?"

I take another step. My chest brushes against her. Gently grabbing her arms, I unfold them, placing them by her side. "You love surprises. It's written all over your face."

Her eyes glitter with emotion, and her tongue darts out, wetting her lips.

"Tell me the truth," I urge her.

My thumbs circle around her wrists. I can't stop touching her. I wanna touch her for the rest of my life.

Looking down, she takes a step back, removing herself from my grasp. Lifting her chin, she stares into my eyes. "Fine. I used to love surprises. But that was a long time ago. Now I'm not so sure how I feel about them anymore."

Oh well, I'll take what I can get at this point. Begrudgingly, I concede. "Okay, whatever you say." I nod at the darkened hallway. "Go change into something casual." Stepping into her condo, I shut the door with my foot. "I'll wait."

She's halfway down the hall when she turns around, pointing a finger at me. "And no snooping."

I lift my eyebrows, feigning innocence. "I would never snoop through your things."

She smirks. "Don't lie, Holt," she says, giving me a dose of my own medicine. Swinging her hips left and right, she disappears into her bedroom.

I like her like that. I like Playful Merit. Confident Merit. Busting-my-balls Merit. One day, she'll be nothing but those things.

Somehow, I think it's my job to get her there.

Because I'm not too keen on UN Ambassador Merit.

Well, I mostly keep my word. I don't pull open drawers or pilfer through the cabinets or anything, but I do look at the magazines and books on her coffee table and the framed photographs on the bookshelf.

No wedding photographs. No vacation photographs. No date photographs. I don't see Edward in any of these pictures. And I know what he looks like.

Unlike Merit, the dangers of the Internet weren't enough to keep me away. I did an online search for her. And him. And the two of them together.

I read a few articles about big cases that he won or lost. The university's law review fawned all over him on numerous occasions, no doubt trying to schmooze a big donation from him. I saw picture after picture of the two of them from the local society magazine showing them at different functions and fundraisers. Each time, they stood next to one another, smiling. No matter how many pictures I looked at, I saw the exact same things... One, they never touched. He never had his arm around her, never held her hand, never kissed her. Two, in every picture she wore a black dress. Modest, kind of sexy—snug and short—but still *somewhat* respectable attire. Just like the dresses from last night and today.

Three and most importantly, in every picture, her smile was fake.

She's given me that fake smile a couple of times, and I immediately knew that it wasn't genuine. How did I know? Because I've been lucky enough to have been on the receiving end of her genuine smile a few times as well. Trust me, the difference is night and day. And now that I'm looking at these pictures on her bookshelf, I see nothing but joy all over her face. I see her real smile, her true smile. I see people, that I guess, must be her mom and dad. Maybe her grandparents. There's a picture of her as a little girl, holding hands with a man. They're both laughing, in a big field of thick, green grass, with the sun setting behind them. There's a picture of her with casts on both her right wrist and her left arm, at the same time. She's sticking her tongue out, posing for the camera. It looks like she's in middle school. There's a striking black and white image of her and an older man sitting on a wooden porch. She's watching as he shucks corn. There's even a picture of her and Kyra standing in the store. She's grinning ear to ear, holding a dollar bill in the air.

"I thought I said no snooping."

"It's not snooping if it's out in plain view." I stand motionless, giving myself time to soak her in.

That's better. So much better.

She's wearing a pale pink blouse, short gray shorts, and flip flops with pink flowers on them. Her hair is pulled back in a messy ponytail. She looks radiant and fresh, and she even wiped off her red lipstick.

Clearing my throat, I reach up, turning my ballcap around backward, giving myself a better view of her legs. It only takes me a split second to realize she likes it when I do that. Her face flushes, and I can see the pebble of her nipples from across the room.

Holy hell.

I would crawl across glass to kiss her right now.

Screw that. I would go through all my surgeries again just to be able to kiss her.

She must sense her body's response because she nonchalantly lifts her arms, blocking her chest from my stare, and pretends to scratch her chin. "I'm ready whenever you are. I apologize for the wait."

I ignore her apology—and my growing erection—and point to one of the pictures. "Who's this? Your parents?"

Unable to help herself, she walks over, standing next to me. "Yeah."

"They look happy. What's their names?"

"Deke and Marie."

I look at her, studying her profile. "Tell me your full name, Merit."

She turns to me, squinting her eyes. "You're dating me and you don't know my name?"

I smirk, teasing her. "We're dating?"

Her voice lowers to a frustrated whisper. "You know what I mean."

"Of course, I know your name. But I haven't heard you say it out loud. And I don't know your middle name."

She cocks her head to the side and rolls those gorgeous eyes.

I knock my shoulder against her. "Humor me."

"My name is Merit Eliza Browning."

Doesn't sound quite as good as Merit Eliza Hill, does it?

That thought comes out of nowhere, hitting me like a thunderbolt and practically knocking me off my feet.

When did I become such a lunatic? I look at my watch. Forty-eight hours. I've only known her for forty-eight hours. I thought I would never experience this level of attraction with someone, this level of longing and desire—both physical and emotional. And here I am, after forty-eight hours, basically signing a mental marriage license.

She's like a magnet for my body and soul, constantly pulling me to her.

"What about you? You're not gonna tell me your middle name?" she asks.

Now I know she still hasn't googled me. "Holt Matthews Hill."

"Matthews? With an 's'."

"Yep. My mom's maiden name."

She softly smiles. "That's nice."

Turning back to the pictures, I point to the one where she's covered in casts. "What the hell happened here?" I say with a laugh.

"I broke my right wrist and my left ulna."

"At the same time?"

She purses her lips, her face full of mischief. "I told you I was accident-prone."

"How in the world did you do that?"

"I fell off the harvester."

"Harvester? Did you live on a farm?"

"My family owns a sod farm in South Alabama. We grow Bermuda grass."

Well, that's a new one. "Seriously?"

"Mmm-hmm. My great-grandfather started it after World War II."

I nod, wanting her to continue.

"After the war, there was a subdivision boom, and sod was in high demand. My great-grandfather came home and had to figure out a way to support his young family. He bought some land, borrowed money until he was eyeball deep in debt, and started planting."

"That's amazing."

Her smile is soft and genuine. "Thanks."

I can't help it. I inch my face closer to hers.

That damn and glorious magnetic pull. Inch. Inch. Inch.

Clearing her throat, she pushes away from the bookshelf. "So, I guess I'm ready to go."

I do my best to clear my lust-filled brain. That's a pretty tall order, but somehow, I manage. "You're not ready yet. You need a pair of socks."

Chapter 6

Merit

I side glance at him.

He's grinning, ear to ear. It's pretty obvious he's proud of himself.

I cock an eyebrow. "The family fun center?"

He tilts one corner of his mouth. "What? It's a great idea." He lifts the ballcap from his head and rakes a hand through the waves of his blond hair. I really like it when he raises his arms. It's like every muscle in his body is on high-alert, taut with movement.

Today has to be our last date.

I have to squash this growing crush.

Why? It's just not healthy for me.

I don't think I've ever masturbated so much in my life. I'm surprised I don't have trigger finger based on the last forty-eight hours. I'm embarrassed to admit I thought about him Friday night, back when I never even thought I would see him again. Back when he was just a one-time customer.

He shrugs, "It's either this... or we can go to my house. Play in the swimming pool? Soak in the hot tub?" His eyes roam my body, from head to toe. "I'm more than happy to see you in a bathing suit."

I roll my eyes. "And the family fun center it is." I grab my purse and jump down from his truck.

He races around to meet me and shoves a ball of socks underneath my nose. "Will you put my socks in your purse?" He's holding them so close to me, it tickles. I snort, scratching my nose, making him immediately laugh. Not waiting on me to respond, he drops them into my small handbag.

When his hand finds its way to the small of my back, I nearly fall on my face. I know it's a common occurrence for men to do that, but it feels so intimate. My spine stiffens, and I quicken my pace, trying to stay one small step ahead of his guiding fingers.

It takes a few seconds for my eyes to adjust to the dim lights of the interior. I've never been here before, so I have no idea what this place is all about. And well, it's a kid's dream. There's a big arcade with flashing lights to my left, a large room filled with billiard tables and shuffleboard in front of me, and a ten-lane bowling complex to my right. A sign above the front desk tells me miniature golf and go-carts are outside.

Suddenly, the socks make sense. "Bowling?"

"Yeah, what did you think the socks were for?" Not waiting for my answer, he heads over to the desk.

There's a teenage boy and a twenty-something woman working the counter. The boy is standing at the register, and I watch suspiciously as the woman pushes him aside, scrambling to be front and center. Quickly reaching up, she tugs the ponytail holder from her hair and finger-brushes her curls. "Holt. It's so good to see you. It's been a while. We were missing you."

He smiles, acknowledging her fawning comment with a head nod. "Hey, Jessica."

Has he dated this Jessica girl? Has he brought other women here?

"There's two of us. We'll do one game." He points to the bowling alley.

She tilts her head to the side, flirting. "And you're still a size thirteen?"

What a stupid question.

He's a grown man. I highly doubt his foot size has changed recently.

"Very good memory," he says, gifting Jessica a compliment. He turns, searching for me. "What size shoe do you wear?"

My stomach drops. "Oh, I'm fine. I'll just watch you."

His brow furrows. "You don't wanna play?"

I shake my head. "I'm good."

"Jessica, give us just a minute?"

I ignore the fact that she places her hand on top of his. "Sure, take your time."

Pulling me to the side, he lowers his voice, stepping closer so I can hear him over the noise of the machines and the laughter of screaming children. "You don't like bowling?"

"I like it. It's fun."

He squints his deep blue eyes, studying me. "Then why not do it? Do you have a phobia of wearing rental shoes?"

I can't help but giggle. Because he isn't kidding; he's being serious. "No, it's nothing like that. I actually haven't even been to a bowling alley in years, not since college. But I always just watched everyone else."

"But why?"

I bite my lip, looking down at the floor. "It's more fun to watch."

Well, that sounded like a sexual innuendo.

If Holt thinks the same thing, he doesn't let on. "Don't lie, Merit."

Our second date. And he's already driving me crazy.

I have no intention of telling him the truth, but somehow the words escape before I have the chance to catch them. "Edward and I used to go bowling with his law school friends. He hated the way I bowled. It embarrassed him. He preferred I just watched everyone else."

Holt's jaw tics, and a growl rumbles low in his chest. "He said that? He said you embarrassed him?"

"It's no big deal, Holt. The way I bowl would embarrass anyone. I can't do it the normal way." I lift my hand and twist it back and forth. "It hurts my wrist. Where I broke it."

Grabbing my right wrist, he wraps his calloused fingers around me. Staring deeply into my eyes, he plants a soft kiss on the sensitive skin, kissing away the pain of my long-healed broken bone. My heart thunders so violently in my chest, it hurts.

"He sounds like a bastard. Today, you bowl. I don't care if you throw the damn thing like a baseball or use the ramp like a toddler, you're playing. Got it?"

All I can do is nod.

"Now, what size shoe?"

"Nine."

He leaves me standing in a stupor.

He pays for our game and grabs our shoes. Jessica definitely seems sad to see him go, but I can tell by the look on her face she's fine with me leaving; she hopes she doesn't see me again.

Trying to be a gentleman, Holt insists I go first. I glance to my left and to my right. Only four other lanes are being used. Two by families, one by an older couple, and one by a dad with three young boys. The oldest is probably in middle school. If I'm gonna make a fool of myself, at least we're only at fifty percent capacity. Grabbing the pink swirled ball I picked out, I hold it in my hands and walk up to the dotted line. Squatting, I granny-bowl the ball as hard as I can. Clenching my fist in anticipation, I nearly faint when eight of the pins fall down.

My cheeks burn bright red when I turn around and see Holt laughing and clapping. His words of congratulation drown in my ears. I do my best to get a spare, but my ball rolls into the gutter halfway down the lane. When it's Holt's turn, I watch as he brings the heavy black bowling ball up to his chest, readying himself for a throw. He looks like a professional.

And then he surprises me. Unplugging his fingers from the holes, he crouches and does a perfect imitation of my granny-bowl.

My mouth falls open, and I watch in awe as all ten pins tumble down, bouncing into the black abyss. I jump up from my seat like my ass is on fire and clap. "Yay!"

He spins around on two heels, watching me with eager eyes. He throws his arms in the air. "Strike!" His shirt gloriously lifts. I catch a quick glimpse of the band of his black boxer briefs and the taut, tanned skin of his stomach.

Holy. Crap.

Thick cotton grows in my mouth, making it hard to swallow. I quickly stop clapping and pretend to busy myself with checking the electronic scoreboard above us.

Shoving his hands in his pockets, he lazily walks over, stooping to whisper in my ear. His breath makes me shiver. "Did I embarrass you?"

He doesn't step away, and I have to lean back to look him in the face. "Only if I embarrassed you."

Softly smiling, he shakes his head. "Never."

We're just finishing our last frame when the dad and three boys walk over to us, cautiously waiting until Holt's finished. Of course, he wins, but I don't care. I had a really fun time.

"Excuse us, Coach?"

Holt hands his bowling shoes to me and slides his flip flops back onto his feet. Giving me a playful wink, he walks over to them, shaking hands with the man.

"Interesting way to bowl, Coach," the man says slowly, unsure how Holt will take to his teasing.

Laughing, he nods in my direction. "I had a good teacher."

The dad and his oldest son spend the next several minutes talking to Holt about football. Before they leave, Holt reaches into his pocket and gives a penny to each of the boys. When they walk away, he joins me, grabbing both of our used shoes from my hands. "Why do you do that?" I ask him.

He lifts an eyebrow, silently asking for more information.

"Hand out pennies?"

He laughs, thinking back. "I started doing it after I was drafted. All of a sudden, all these little kids wanted my autograph or my picture. After that, they'd just stand there. It's like they wanted something more. Like they wanted me to talk to them or something." He shakes his head. "I was just a kid myself and was scared senseless. I didn't know what to say or do. The uncomfortable silence would drive me crazy. One day, I just pulled a penny out of my pocket and gave it to the little boy. It was completely random, but he flipped out." He shrugs. "Been doing it ever since."

I like that story.

I hang back a few steps, watching him return our shoes to Jessica. She tries her best to keep him engaged in conversation, even touching his hand again. I can't hear what she's saying, but I know I don't like it.

Holt's biting back a smile when he finally joins me. I vow not to ask any questions and keep my big mouth shut, but I just can't help myself. Apparently, I have absolutely zero self-control. "So... is she a good friend? Jessica, I mean."

Before I know what's happening, he's looming over me. Bending his head, fanning his whisper across the side of my face. And the bad part is, I can't even move. I was leaning against a wooden pillar when he walked up, and now I'm trapped.

Trapped. And entirely too close to him.

"You're doing it again." The low timbre of his voice sends a boiling heat through parts of my body that have long been cold and dead.

I lick my lips, trying to unstick them. "Doing what?"

"Scrunching your nose."

"I don't scrunch my nose."

The corner of his mouth twitches. "Don't lie, Merit."

He turns his face. His nose brushes against my cheekbone.

And then...

The doors behind us open, and a group of twenty rowdy children come racing into the fun center, followed by a small straggle of adults carrying a birthday cake, a bundle of balloons, and handfuls of wrapped presents. Taking advantage of the situation, I slide to the side, giving myself a wide berth from Holt.

He let me move, of course, because he's a gentleman. If he wanted to keep me there, he could've. He's built like a... well, like a professional athlete. A specimen among men. Hard and muscular and lean. But he let me go. He could see I needed some space.

Clasping my hands in front of me, I study a speck of trash on the floor. I can't believe how badly I wanted to grab his neck and force his lips to mine. To taste and touch. And we're not even alone. We're in the middle of a crowded building.

"Wanna hit some games in the arcade?"

Taking a pained breath, I look up, staring deeply into his eyes. Even in the darkened room, the blue color steals the breath from my lungs. "Sure. But only if it's my treat."

He snickers. "What?"

"You paid for bowling. And supper last night. That couldn't have been cheap; you ordered every freakin' thing on the menu. It's only fair I pay."

"How is that fair? I'm the one who invited you, that means I should pay."

Ignoring him, I stomp off in the direction of the arcade, looking for the coin machine. He reaches out, trying to grab my arm, but I speed up. I don't think it's appropriate to run inside here, so I kind of bounce away in a quasi-jog while pulling a twenty-dollar bill from my wallet. Holt lunges forward, trying to wrestle it from me, but I swat his hand away and feed the money into the machine. I smile triumphantly as the machine loudly dings, happy with my deposit, and shoots a waterfall of quarters from its belly.

He rolls his eyes. "Pretty proud of yourself, huh?"

I press my lips together, feigning innocence.

Playfully knocking me out of the way, he scoops the coins into a plastic cup. Leaving him be, I walk up the aisle, looking at all the games. I haven't been to an arcade since I was a kid. Everything looks so different.

"Some of the classic games are in the back, if you wanna hit those."

I nod, following him. "Do you come here often?"

He drops coins for us into two Skee-Ball machines. "What makes you ask that?"

"Well, you know your way around." I put my purse on the ground and grab one of the smooth brown balls. I toss it up the ramp and watch as it drops into a forty-point slot. "And you never answered my question about Jessica. She seems like a good friend."

"Is that your way of asking if Jessica and I have dated?"

I could lie.

But I don't want to.

"Yes."

He doesn't immediately say anything. He just reaches up and slowly turns his baseball cap around backward. My crotch tingles with electricity, making my clit vibrate and hum. I quickly pick up a ball and toss it. It doesn't even make it up the ramp. In pitiful fashion, it rolls back down to me.

"I have never dated Jessica. Nor have I ever wanted to." Smirking, he effortlessly throws a ball and rings one of the hard to reach hundred-point slots in the corner. "I bring the kids here sometimes. Anna and Laura love the mini-golf. Ty's too young to really do anything, but he still loves to try. They give him a little plastic putter, and he carries it around."

"So, you don't bring dates here?"

"No." He doesn't glance over at me; he just tosses another ball.

I know that shouldn't make me happy, but it does. Really happy.

We blow through our quarters, laughing and playing different games. By the end, we have a pretty good handful of tickets. On our way out, he hands the tickets to a little girl standing next to her mom. I'm surprised he didn't keep them.

"You didn't wanna save the tickets? Give them to your nieces for the next time they come? Let them save up for a big prize or something?"

He shakes his head. "Anna and Laura never keep their tickets. They always give them to someone else."

"Seriously? Most kids flip out over the junky little prizes at the arcade."

He shrugs, trying to appear nonchalant but clearly drowning in a sea of pride. "My nieces aren't normal kids."

On our way out the front door, his hand snakes around my back. I don't have a chance to slide from his embrace, though. The sudden brightness of the sun blinds me, making me sneeze. His fingertips trail up, caressing the side of my waist. "Bless you."

My heart stops pumping. Every nerve-ending in my body freezes, turning to stone.

All of a sudden, his hand shifts lower.

Holy crap. He's gonna grab my ass.

Instead of copping a feel, his finger hooks in the belt loop of my shorts and he spins me around. I stumble. Without thinking, I reach out, planting my hands on his chest. I can feel the hard lines of his body underneath the thin fabric of his shirt.

It burns me, scalds my skin.

It causes thoughts of indecency to swirl in my head like a tornado.

Like the kind of indecency you need to go to the altar and ask forgiveness for.

"Why do you do that?" he asks.

Gasping in embarrassment, I quickly pull my hands away. "I'm sorry." I look down at the concrete of the parking lot, fumbling for words. "I told you I was clumsy."

I don't point out the fact that *he's* the one who made me trip... even though I should.

"Not that. I mean, why do you freeze every time I touch the small of your back? And trying to hold your hand? Taking Anna's cat to the vet is an easier task than that."

My head snaps up. I try to count the freckles running across the bridge of his nose, but it's a losing battle; they're as numerous as the stars in the sky. "I'm just not used to public displays of affection."

His finger leaves my belt loop and traces the beads of my spine. His head lowers, giving his whisper an edge of privacy. "But I don't do it for the public. I do it for me."

I can't help myself. My mouth opens, and a small sigh escapes. I want him to kiss me. So badly. So damn badly.

But alas, apparently, the two college-aged girls in the parking lot want the same thing.

Their screeches nearly burst my eardrum. They waste no time racing over to us and grabbing Holt by the arms, yanking him around like he's their very own marionette doll. "I can't believe it's you!" one cries.

The more brazen one openly flirts, not ashamed in the least little bit. "You're even sexier in person. Pictures don't do you justice, but I'm sure you hear that all the time, right?"

What a stupid question.

What's he supposed to say to that.

Holt smiles and politely nods. "Thank you."

"We have to get a picture with you." The less feisty of the two pushes her cell phone into my hand. "Would you mind?"

Yes. I absolutely mind every minute of this torture.

Gritting my teeth, I take a few steps back and point the cell phone camera in their general direction. Immediately, they flank to either side, forcing their way underneath Holt's arms. He has no choice but to lay his hands on them. I just assume he would touch their backs—like he did with me—but instead, he lays a tentative hand high on each of their shoulders. Evidently, the girls took a full semester class on Selfie 101 because they know just the right way to arch their backs to accentuate their breasts. And they know just the right angle in which to hitch their legs to make themselves look taller. And they know just the right place to grab their waists with their hands to make themselves look like a size two.

It all really pisses me off.

I clench my jaw and center the three of them in the camera frame. Unable to control myself, I discreetly slide my finger over the lens, blocking Holt's face from the picture. I would block the faces of the two girls, but there's no way to do that since they're on either side of him. And seeing how he's a giant compared to them, it's pretty easy to cover his head. They'll still have the picture. They'll still be able to gawk at Holt's perfect body. They just won't be able to stare at his face and daydream.

"All good!" I shove the phone back into her hand, almost violently, and speed walk in the direction of Holt's truck.

My heart pounds against my ribcage like a freight train. I can't believe I just did that. I can't even turn around and look at them. A small ounce of shame worms its way into the pit of my stomach. Holt says goodbye to them and jogs up next to me, clicking his key fob to unlock the doors. I jump in the truck with lightning speed, silently begging Holt to hurry. Fortunately, he senses my anxiety and doesn't waste any time. I hold my breath, refusing to breathe, until we pull out onto the main road. When I see the girls far off in the rearview mirror, I finally exhale.

I'm surprised by his raspy chuckle. "I saw what you did."

I nervously bite my lip. "Mmmm?"

"You covered the picture with your finger."

I lie. "I don't know what you're talking about."

He smiles. A completely heart-warming and heart-breaking smile. "Whatever you say, Mer."

And then he winks at me.

Chapter 7

Holt

Sweat pours off me.

Literally.

There's even puddles on the floor mat of my truck.

School starts a week from this coming Monday, so we started football practice this past Monday. There's not too many things hotter in this world than Alabama in Asugust. So, that's definitely the one downside of practice.

If I were more polite, I would shower. If I were more thoughtful, I'd make myself smell better. If I were more considerate, I'd come bearing a gift. But that's definitely one pleasant thing I've learned about Merit over the past several days...she doesn't expect to be given something for nothing. She wants to work; she wants to earn.

And that's not the only pleasant thing I've learned.

I've been unable to stay away. I'm chasing after her like a lovesick schoolboy. I can't even function unless I see her once a day. Unless I spend time with her, unless I get my fix. Like a junkie.

She tried to avoid me on Monday, saying she had too much work to do at the store since it's closed on Mondays. I showed up anyway. Uninvited. Same thing with Tuesday and Wednesday. I met her other employees—Kim and Emily. They are nice girls, but you can tell she's not as close to them as she is Kyra.

Sliding out of my truck, I grab the towel I was sitting on and use it to wipe the rest of the sweat from my body. I toss it in the back seat and turn around, studying the strip mall, giving myself a second to cool down before putting on a fresh T-shirt. The steaming heat rising from the asphalt pales in comparison to the heat from my own heart when I see Merit standing in the storefront, working on the window display. Even from here, I can see her mouth fall open. I watch as her eyes travel the length of my body, eagerly ogling my bare torso. I'm sure she can't make out every line and muscle from where she is, but what she *can* see? She likes.

A lot.

I've done photoshoots. I've posed for magazines. Hell, I was even *May* in the annual team calendar. And none of that has ever made me feel the way I feel with her eyes on me, staring at me across a parking lot.

A car drives past, severing our staring contest. In perfect timing—that I've determined can only occur with Merit—the head of the child's mannequin she's holding falls off and bounces against the glass with a loud bang. Loud enough I can hear it from here. I nearly collapse in laughter. Embarrassed and frustrated, she drops the decapitated body and scrambles from the display window.

Tugging the shirt over my head, I head into the store, smiling when Kyra glances up from the floor. She's sitting on the carpet, surrounded by paperwork and a huge box of new clothes. I look around, not immediately seeing Merit. "Customers?"

Kyra shakes her head. "This morning was really busy, but it's been quiet this afternoon."

I know it's selfish, but I'm glad she doesn't have any customers right now. It means I can have a few uninterrupted minutes with her.

And I want every single minute I can get.

I'm charging to the back room, like I own the damn place, when Kyra's voice stops me. "I don't know if I would do that."

Her voice holds an edge of teasing good humor, but I'm scared, too, because there's also a heavy dose of realism. Cynicism. "Why not?"

"She couldn't resist the temptation any longer."

I lift an eyebrow. "What temptation?"

Kyra twists left and right, stretching her back. "The temptation to know more about you." She sighs. "She was glued to the computer for hours."

"Shit." I drag my hand across my chin. "I was really hoping to avoid all that."

Kyra shrugs. "You're the one who kept asking her if she looked you up on the Internet. You were poking the bear. What did you expect?"

Kyra's right. I know how curious Merit is. I knew this day was coming. I was a fool to think I could skirt by the inevitable.

I grab the back of a chair, running my fingers across the fabric. "How bad is it?"

She chuckles. "Well, it's not good, Holt. I did damage control the best I could, but she's definitely back on her *I don't date* kick."

Shoving my disappointment in the pit of my stomach, I hold my head high and round the corner to the back.

Kyra hollers after me. "You've been duly warned."

Nerves are a funny thing. I've played in front of crowds of a hundred-thousand fans. People on the other side of the world have watched me on TV. I've met the President of the United States. Multiple presidents, if we're getting technical. And yet, standing here, I can't immediately think of another time where I've been quite so nervous. The thought of her saying she doesn't want to see me again leaves me sick, physically in pain.

She's stacking shoes on one of the large shelves. Her hair is pulled high into a messy knot, and she's wearing pink cotton shorts and a tank top. Every time she lifts her arm, I catch a glimpse of her sports bra. Despite my best efforts, my body reacts. I accidentally bump a hanger, and she immediately jumps, locking eyes with me. Her black eye has finally faded to a pale yellow. Of course, it wouldn't matter if it marred her face for the rest of her life... she'd still be the most beautiful woman I've ever seen.

She's made for me.

She's mine.

I know it's completely idiotic and stupid to think those thoughts after just a couple of days, but they're there, nonetheless. Oh well, I've been called many things in my life, and extremely intelligent has never been one of them. I leave that title for my sister and my cousin.

She tries her best to keep her face devoid of emotion and returns to stacking the boxes. "You shouldn't be in the back, sir."

Anger flames through my veins. "Seriously, we're back to that now?"

"Back to what?"

I stalk over next to her. "Formalities."

She shrugs. "There's nothing wrong with being formal."

She's trying not to look at me, but I catch her stealing a glance. It gives me a small sliver of hope. "Mer, there's many things I want to be with you, and *formal* isn't one of them."

A bright red blush colors her cheeks. Despite that, her eyes hold a sadness. "You should leave."

A grunted sigh races from my lungs. "So, what exactly is it that you believe?" I take a step closer. "That I have triplets with a woman in Australia? That I threw the Super Bowl because I owed money to some gangster loan shark? That I went to jail for assault?"

Having put the last box on the shelf, she nervously glances around, searching for something to occupy her time. Finding nothing, she has no choice but to begrudgingly face me. "Well, I know you don't have children. If you did, you'd talk about them. Just the way you talk about Anna and Ty and Laura."

I nod, amused at the thought she's given it.

"And I know you would never cheat at football. We've not really talked about it, but I can tell you love the game." She looks down at her feet. "You don't cheat on something you love."

Huh. Why do I feel like there's more to that statement?

Bypassing it for now, I give her a crooked smile. "And the assault?"

Lifting her head, she captures me in the hazel maze of her eyes. "From what I can tell, you weren't *actually* arrested."

She's right. I wasn't.

I walk over to the fridge she keeps in the corner and grab myself a bottle of water. I down half of it in one swallow. "So, that's why you're acting this way? Because I punched someone? I'm not sure what you read, but the guy was a perverted creep. He grabbed a girl without her permission. Put his hands all over her ass. And by 'girl', I mean *girl*. She was only fourteen. She did look older, but I had just met her and her family at a fan event; I knew how old she was. Her parents were on a tour of the press box, so she and her friend were standing by themselves, and I saw the guy hitting on her. I warned him to back off. He didn't. And then he touched her. He's lucky a broken nose is all he got."

Her mouth drops open. "Holy crap. That's terrible. She's lucky you were there."

I put the bottle down on the small table and slowly make my way back over to her. "So, that's it? You understand why I did what I did? We're good? Me and you?"

"Yes. I mean no. I mean—" She growls and shakes her head. "I mean that's not why I was saying you shouldn't be here."

"Then what's the problem? What's the rumor you believe? I thought you were the one who told me the Internet was filled with lies and falsehoods."

She lowers her voice. "It's not a lie."

I fold my arms across my chest, standing tall. "Why don't you let me be the judge of that."

She tilts her chin, challenging me.

I love it.

She mimics me, folding her own arms across her ample chest. "Fine." She takes a deep breath, like she's truly hurt by what she's about to say. "You're *really* rich."

Well, that's completely unexpected.

I think I'd be less shocked if she believed the tabloid story that I was in cahoots with the cartel and transported drugs across the country in hollow footballs.

"And that's a problem because...?" I wait for her to fill in the blanks.

She looks left and right, like she's checking to see if someone is spying on us. "I mean, you're like *obscenely* rich."

I lift my eyebrow. "And just how much do you think I'm worth?"

"I don't know, but it said you were a Round One pick. And that your four-year draft contract was $30 million with a $20 million signing bonus. Is that right? And then, there was some craziness about a new contract at $20 million per year. That can't be right." She narrows her eyes. "Is that right?"

All the women I've ever dated, before now, have loved my money. Loved my money more than me, as a matter of fact. So, I can't understand why Merit finds this so troublesome. It's refreshing—don't get me wrong—I'm just worried about what her concern actually means.

Since I can't lie to her, I figure a simple one-word answer is the best solution. "Yeah."

"See? That's what I mean."

No, I don't see anything.

I bend my neck left and right, stretching it, giving myself a second to compose a response. "Well, granted, I don't know anything about your family's finances, but you married into one of the most successful attorney families in the state. I can't imagine you were eating potted meat sandwiches and picking up cans on the side of the road."

She dramatically rolls her eyes. "Of course not. And yes, Edward is very well-off, but he's a pauper compared to you."

This conversation is making my head hurt. Deciding to play dirty, I lift my arms in the air and turn my ballcap around backward. I watch in hungry delight as Merit's eyes roam my body, setting me on fire. "So, what exactly are you saying? I know I'm dehydrated and not firing on all cylinders, but I'm not really seeing any issues here."

Blinking the painted lust from her face, she cocks a hand on her hip. "How can you say that? It's a major issue."

"My money is a major issue? You're saying you can't date me because I'm too rich?"

She smiles widely, proud that my pea-size brain has finally put two and two together. "Exactly."

"You're freakin' kidding me, right?"

She frowns. "Why would I be joking?"

"Because it's absurd, Mer. Money is far from the most important thing in life. In fact, I can honestly say it has no bearing on my happiness. As long as my family is healthy and I'm gainfully employed, I'm happy. Don't get me wrong, I am completely blessed to have my money. And now that I have it, my goal is to help others and preserve it for my kids and grandkids and their grandkids. But you're acting like I earned my money by making a deal with the devil, like I walked into the bank making deposits wearing red horns and carrying a pitchfork."

She gasps. "I didn't say that. I'm sure you worked hard for every penny you earned. You don't strike me as someone who would take advantage of the system."

I step closer to her, tossing my hands in the air. "Then we can date."

"Oh no, we can't date."

I can't help but laugh. "Why the hell not?"

"Because you're rich."

"So?"

"So..." she draws out the syllable, mocking my last word. "You can do anything you want, whenever you want. You could fly to Hawaii right this second if you wanted. My parents went to Maui for their twenty-fifth wedding anniversary. They had to save for five years to be able to do that." She bites her bottom lip, drawing my attention to the pink fullness. "You go to parties with famous movie stars. You date supermodels."

Ah.

I take another step in her direction. "Who said I date models?"

"I saw pictures."

"I dated one model. Only one. And it was years ago. Right after my first Super Bowl win."

The pout on Merit's face literally makes me weak in the knees. It's infuriatingly sexy. "Yeah, but she's a supermodel. Everyone knows who she is. In the grand scheme of things, that's like dating four regular models."

Holy hell. She's cute when she's spiraling out of control. "Says who?"

"Says me."

I use the opportunity to take another step. "Well, as you can see, we're no longer dating. In fact, we were never even really together. It was only five or six dates. It just seemed like more because of the paparazzi pictures."

She rubs her eyes, wincing when she rubs her healing black eye too hard. "That proves my point. Paparazzi followed you. You're incredibly good-looking, rich, and successful. You're famous. You can date anyone you want."

"Then why are you making it so difficult for me to date *you*."

"You don't wanna date me."

"I'm pretty sure I do."

"No, you don't."

"Why would you say that?"

She looks down. Studying her body, she runs her hand across her stomach, straightening her tank top and tugging on her shorts. "Because I'm me."

Break my fucking heart.

I don't know what the hell this Edward guy did to her self-esteem, but I wanna beat the shit out of him.

I close the distance between us, wrapping my arm around the small of her back before she has the chance to escape. I nuzzle my lips against her hairline. I can still smell her shampoo and the cleanliness of her skin. "That's exactly why I want to."

She inhales, and her breasts push against my chest. My heart's beating so loudly, I have to stop breathing because I'm afraid she'll say something and I won't be able to hear her. She wiggles, halfheartedly trying to untangle herself from my embrace. Quickly giving up, she lays her hands on my biceps and gently traces my muscles with trembling fingers.

It's quite possibly the most erotic touch I've ever had.

Doesn't bode much for the supermodel, does it?

"So, what do you say? Go out with me tomorrow night? I wanna take you someplace special."

She shakes her head. Her whisper is strained. "I don't wanna go out with you."

"Don't lie, Merit."

"Mmmm?"

"You're dying to go out with me again. It's written all over your face."

Instead of answering, she looks off to the side, pretending to study my water bottle on the table.

"Tell me the truth."

Eventually, she grunts. "Fine. I wanna go on another date with you." She looks up into my eyes. "But I warn you, there's no caterpillar waiting to transform into a butterfly under all this. This is what you get. Brown hair, crazy brownish eyes. I'm completely average. Completely normal. I'm not even tall. Your supermodel is six-feet tall."

My laugh bounces off the walls. "First of all, she's not *my* supermodel. Second, you're what? Five-eight? The average height of the American woman is five-four. So, see? You're actually way above average."

Her teasing smirk makes my dick jump again. "I noticed you said *American* woman. Perhaps, you should be more concerned with the statistics of women in Australia. I mean, you do have triplets with one." She giggles at her own joke, covering her nose with her hand when she softly snorts.

It's then I realize...

After these two years of missing my football career... After craving the thrill of being right in the middle of the sport I love...

I'm in for the game of a lifetime with Merit Eliza Browning.

And there's no place else I'd rather be.

Chapter 8

Merit

"A bar? This is the 'someplace special'?" I ask. He points up at the sign. *The Last Call.* I break out in a wide smile. "It's Will's bar!"

He turns off the ignition to his truck and sits back, looking at me. "I can't believe you've never been here before. It's a really popular bar. Will and Cullen get the greatest bands."

"Since I work on Fridays and Saturdays, I don't really go out on the weekends." I watch as a couple walk through the bar's front door, hand in hand. "When I was married, Edward required me to go to functions with him, but he and his friends didn't really hang out at bars."

Holt lifts an eyebrow. "Required you?"

Wrong choice of words. I look out the window, pretending I didn't hear the question.

Holt refuses to let it go. He uses the opportunity to his advantage, grabbing my hand in his before I realize what he's doing. My head snaps in his direction. Underneath the ambient light of the streetlamp, I study his face. His cheeks are sunburnt from football practice. The spattering of freckles across his nose has darkened, and his wavy blond hair looks a shade lighter. His thumb rubs back and forth across my skin. Wet desire pools between my thighs.

"What do you mean, he *required* you?"

I halfheartedly attempt to pull my hand from his grasp, but he doesn't let me go.

Oh well, I guess I'll just have to keep holding his hand.

"Nothing. It was just a poor choice of words."

"Sounds like there's more to the story, if you ask me." His hand circles around, and he slowly traces his finger up my arm, stopping and caressing the inside crease of my elbow.

Nervous energy bounces around my body. I feel like a pinball machine is stuck inside my stomach. I chuckle. "Good thing I didn't ask you."

I like that I can tease Holt. I missed that. My family was always one for teasing laughter and sarcastic jokes. When I first met Edward, I thought he was like that. I was wrong. Very wrong. He had a picture-perfect vision of life in his mind, and it was my job to live up to that ideal scenario.

Smiling, Holt licks his lips.

His perfectly pink-brown lips.

The lips I keep seeing every time I close my eyes.

Anger pours over my heart like ice water. The lips I saw kissing that supermodel in picture after picture. Damn the Internet.

He gives my arm a soft squeeze. "C'mon. Let's go."

I sigh in satisfaction; glad I won that battle. Because I really don't feel like talking about Edward. Talk about an epic buzzkill.

I also sigh in satisfaction when Holt leads me through the front door with his hand on the small of my back. Immediately grabbing my hand, he weaves me through the throngs of people, making a beeline for the bar.

I could really get used to these public displays of affection. Apparently, I didn't realize what I was missing all those years with Edward.

Behind the bar, a tall, good-looking guy with dark brown hair waves at us. Two cases of beer are sitting in front of him, blocking two barstools from use. I watch as he reaches over the counter and hides them on his side. "Good thing you showed up when you did. The band tonight is going to be really good. I wasn't sure how long I could save your seats."

"You know better than to give my seat away. I can still pummel your ass." Holt winks at me, letting me know he's not serious.

The guy rolls his eyes and tosses a towel over his shoulder. "Oh please, the older you get, the softer you get. I even heard you were playing with dolls the other day."

Holt furrows his brow. "Will has the biggest mouth ever. And in my defense, it was mermaid dolls, and we were in the pool." He holds out one of the barstools, helping me sit down.

The guy leans across the bar, offering his hand. "You must be Merit. I'm Cullen. It's a pleasure to meet you."

"You too."

Without asking, he places a beer bottle in front of Holt. Holt scoots closer to me. "What would you like to drink? Cullen is a wiz and can make anything you want." He points behind Cullen to a large, handwritten menu hanging on the wall. "They also have a huge non-alcoholic drink menu if you want that."

"All of those are non-alcoholic cocktails?"

"Yep. They did it for Ella. She doesn't drink. It's actually been a huge success."

"Well, those look great, but I think I'll just stick with a beer." My eyes flicker down to his bottle.

Cullen is already helping the person next to us, but when Holt holds his bottle in the air, Cullen wordlessly places a fresh beer bottle in front of me. I smile, mouthing a thank you.

"You must come here a lot."

Amusement settles on Holt's face. "What makes you say that?"

"You have an unspoken language with your bartender."

He bursts out laughing. "I guess I do. But I'm sure it has more to do with the fact that I used to change his diapers than the fact that he's my bartender."

I lift my own bottle to my lips, letting the cold liquid slide down my throat, praying it loosens some of the humming tension in my muscles—the underlying tension that's always present when I'm with Holt.

The *calm* tension.

Again, I don't know how I can feel two opposite things at one time, but I do...

Now, I know what people are talking about when they say 'the calm among the storm'.

Taking a deep breath, I force myself out of my head and into conversation. "I'm sorry we couldn't go out until later tonight. I had some customers come in right at closing time. It threw me behind, but I tried to get ready as quickly as possible."

His blue eyes scan my face. "Well, you look beautiful. And just so you know, I would wait all night long if I had to." He rubs his fingers across his lips. "But I must say, I'm glad Kyra is closing the store for you tomorrow night. It will give us even more time together."

"Speaking of, don't you think it's a little presumptuous to schedule tomorrow's date before you even go on today's date?"

He pouts, pretending to be deep in thought. "Hmmm. I actually don't think we're being proactive enough. Why don't we go ahead and schedule all our future dates? What are you doing for the next sixty years?"

Ummm... Holy. Crap.

I'm not sure what look befalls my face, but it must be pretty damn humorous based on the way Holt is cackling.

I don't even have time to properly formulate a response because a very flirtatious—and tipsy—woman works her way between our barstools. She flashes a smile at Holt. "Sorry. I'm just needing to order a drink. You don't mind, do you?"

What a stupid question.

He tries to look at me over her head, but she wiggles around like a worm, blocking him from view. He politely clears his throat. Cullen is at the far end of the bar, so he turns to the other bartender, holds his hands in the air, and snaps his fingers, begging for attention. The other guy immediately comes over to us, and the girl orders some fancy-sounding drink.

Of course, she would order something that would require her to wait around.

"It's a nice night, huh?"

Holt nods.

Accepting that as an invitation to rub her breasts in his face, she inches closer to him. "We're celebrating tonight. One of my friends got a big promotion at work." She giggles. "I'm getting too old for all of this. I'm sure I'll be hurting tomorrow."

Holt takes a drink of his beer. "Mmmm."

She glances at his bottle. "Looks like you're running low. How about I get you a fresh drink and you can join us?"

I can't see much past her hips and ass, but what I do see infuriates me.

Infuriates the hell out of me.

She runs a red-painted nail up the inside of Holt's muscular thigh. Her voice lowers to a purr. "We could have a really good time."

The second her fingers start to snake underneath the hem of his shorts, he snatches her hand and pushes it away. Not violently. But definitely firmly. He leans closer to her, whispering, but I can still hear him. "I *am* having a really good time. With my girl." He lifts his chin, pointing in my direction.

She looks over her shoulder, studying me with an evil, judging eye. Deciding I don't measure up to her opinion of herself, she turns back to Holt. "Are you serious?"

"As a fucking heart attack."

By now, Cullen has come back over, eyeing our trio with suspicion. "Everything okay?"

"Put her drink on my tab," Holt orders. "We hope you have a good evening with your friends, ma'am. We'll let you get back to them."

Huffing, she grabs her free drink and scurries away.

I still can't believe how much Holt gets hit on. And this woman didn't even seem to know he's some famous football player. I think she just wanted him because he's super-hot. I watch as she weaves through the crowd. She's wearing really high heels and a short, tight red dress. It rides up her ass with every step. And her circular neckline is cut so low, a small breeze would probably cause her nipples to flop out.

I absolutely hated when Edward asked me to wear outfits like that. The black dresses were a compromise. He hated when I wore vibrant colors. So, I compromised with black. It was at least better than beige. He wanted me to wear dresses so short the common passerby could perform a gynecological exam on me. I preferred shorts and leggings. So, I compromised with the black dresses at mid-thigh.

Compromise, compromise, compromise.

Fucking compromise.

And the bastard still cheated on me.

"Are you okay?" Cullen's voice draws me back into the moment.

"Huh?"

"You look like you smell something bad. Your face is all scrunched up."

I feel the red heat of embarrassment shooting across my cheeks like a flare.

Holt immediately starts laughing. "That's the face she makes when I get hit on. She hates it."

I sit up in my seat. "What!"

Cullen chuckles. "Ahh, like Ella rolling her eyes."

My mouth falls open, and I stutter to find the right words. "I didn't... I don't..."

Holt scoots closer, closing the space between us so no one else can weasel their way in. "Oh, but you do." He playfully winks, making me angry and giddy at the same time.

We spend the next hour talking. Will eventually shows up, returning to the bar after sneaking home to tuck the kids into bed.

The area around us clears out a little when the band starts to play, and the majority of the crowd shifts over to the next room to hear them. Holt asks if I want to get closer to the band, listen to the music, dance.

I love music as much as the next person, but I'm quite content where I am— listening to Holt, Cullen, and Will hash out old stories. Their families remind me so much of my own.

After a while, I excuse myself to go to the restroom. Walking past the pool tables, I actually see the older, adult sister of one of the small kids who comes into the store frequently. Stopping, I chat for a few minutes. I'm surprised when I see Holt's large frame wandering to the back of the bar. He's scanning the room, searching for something.

Or someone.

Maybe me?

When he spots me, he breaks out into a massive smile. I hate the way it makes my heart thunder in my chest.

But I also love it. And that's damn scary.

He points at me, mouthing the question to ask if I'm okay. I smile and nod, letting him know that I'm good. He heads back to the bar while I say goodbye to my customer and continue on to the bathroom. After washing my hands, I'm heading out the door when a large group of hyper, college-aged girls come racing in.

And one slams right into me.

Spilling her bright red drink all down the front of my yellow blouse.

"Ah! My Hurricane!" The plastic cup tumbles to the floor and rolls underneath the first bathroom stall.

I stare down at my soaked top. The red liquid covers me from neck to stomach. My wet shirt clings to my chest, highlighting the valley between my breasts like a well-traveled road.

Freakin' great.

Her little doe eyes widen like saucers when she sees what's happened to me. "Oh no! I'm so sorry. Are you okay? Look at your shirt."

Grabbing a handful of paper towels, I wipe the rogue drops of liquor streaming down my arms. "Yeah."

Her friends gather around, studying the damage. Whispering, they wait on my reaction. "I'm really sorry. Was it expensive?"

I politely smile. "No, it's fine. It was an accident."

"Are you sure?" She scrambles down, fiddling with the zipper on her clutch. "Let me get some cash. I can pay for your dry-cleaning. I feel just terrible about this."

Like dry-cleaning stands a chance against this shirt. It officially just became a dust rag.

"Yeah, I'm sure. Don't worry about it. Have a good night."

I make my way back up to the front. I tug the purse from my shoulder and hold it in front of my body. I guess Holt can tell something is going on because he lifts an eyebrow, studying me with narrowed eyes. I ignore his look and give him a fake smile.

But he's not buying what I'm selling.

His arm darts in front of me, blocking me from sitting on my barstool. "What's going on?"

"What? Nothing."

His smile fades and his brow furrows.

Once again, I'm annoyed that he can read my mind.

Or my face.

I guess both.

He shakes his head. "I can tell something's wrong. You need to tell me because I won't let it go."

Growling in frustration, I drop my purse and stare up at the ceiling. Things like this should embarrass me. But... I'm me. Way worse things than this have happened. My head jerks forward when I hear more laughter mixed with Holt's rambunctious cackle.

Cullen and Will are both shocked by my current appearance. Not shocked enough to keep their chuckles to themselves, however. Holt swivels on his stool. Leaning back against the bar, he turns his ballcap around backward and folds his hands behind his head.

I follow his every move. My mouth grows dry and my body grows restless. He has no idea how sexy he looks when he does that.

Or maybe he does...which is possibly why he keeps doing it.

He clears his throat. "Get into a fight with a pitcher of fruit punch?"

"Nope. The fruit punch knows I can kick its ass. This," I touch my shirt, "is the work of a hurricane."

Holt shakes his head in good humor. "Only you, Mer."

Cullen rolls his eyes. "Oh man, don't tell me those college girls are already shit-faced?"

I shake my head. "No, they didn't seem drunk. This was just an accident. I was leaving the bathroom right as they were coming in. She bumped into me by accident."

Will taps Holt on the shoulder, grabbing his attention. "Take her in back. There's an extra box of bar T-shirts next to the whiskey order." He frowns at me. "It'll be too big for you, Merit, but at least it's clean."

"That will be great, Will. I really appreciate it."

Allowing Holt to grab my hand, I let him lead me through the bar, past a swinging door, and into the back room. There's shelves and boxes filled with liquor on the right—gins, tequilas, vodkas... anything and everything. To the left is a large, refrigerated room with beer and kegs. At the far end are two large wooden desks with computers, and overflowing with paperwork. Behind the desks is a shelf of whiskey and one lone box. Letting go of my hand, Holt opens it and pilfers through it.

I grip my purse with both hands, unsure what to do now that his fingers aren't wrapped around mine. It's unnerving how attached I've grown to that feeling in just a couple of days—the feeling of being connected to him.

"What's your favorite color?" Holt asks.

"Blue." Like your eyes. I keep that last part to myself, of course.

Tugging a blue T-shirt from the box, he proudly holds it out, waiting on me to grab it. I glance around, looking for a separate room for me to change in.

There isn't one.

Holt's voice is low and raspy. He tosses the T-shirt on one of the desks. "You change here." He walks past me, gently grazing his body against mine. "I promise to be good." He leans against one of the shelves, watching the doorway, standing vigil.

My mouth drops open, and I slowly exhale, doing my best to keep my panting breath silent, lest I sound like a dog in heat. Setting my purse on a stack of purchase orders, I pull the alcohol-soaked shirt from my body. The pink liquid even soaked through to my bra. Grabbing the fresh T-shirt, I flip it around, trying to grab the hem. Right then, my elbow hits the table lamp on the desk and sends it flying to the floor. The plastic lampshade cracks.

"Merit!"

I don't have time to tell him to stop. I don't have time to tell him not to look. His reflexes are too fast.

I mean, he did win two Super Bowls.

For a second, he doesn't see my body. He only looks at my face and the cracked lamp, rolled halfway under the shelf stacked with the whiskey. "Are you okay?"

"I... I think I broke the lamp."

And then he looks at me.

All the air is immediately sucked from the room. The filtered noise of the crowd disappears. The pounding music from the band evaporates. Even the beating of my own heart stops. Silence falls, creating a thick, soupy wall between us.

His eyes slowly cascade down my body, absorbing the sight of me, standing there, in my bra and shorts. His chest heaves, searching for the oxygen that I can't find.

Looking down, I'm ashamed by what he must see. My plain, nude-colored bra is tie-dyed with splotches of the spilled cocktail. If Edward were standing in front of me, he would probably be yelling by now. Or pouting like a spoiled little brat. He refused to let me wear *normal* undergarments. No simple white cotton panties. No plain, nude-colored bras—even though they are the most practical (outside of my sports bras for work) because I can wear them under anything without the color bleeding through. He wanted *sexy* at all times. According to their husbands, the other high society wives wore sexy lingerie, so that meant I had to as well. Unfortunately, it wasn't a lie. The couple of times I got roped into shopping with some of them, it's like I was in the middle of a soft-core porn movie. Push-up bras, thongs, garter-belts. And everything was black. Black lace, black satin, black silk.

And see-through was a must.

It's actually pretty gross when the seventy-year-old wife of the eighty-year-old law firm partner is wearing see-through panties and wants *you* to help her try on a leather and suede dress in Saks.

Before Edward, I liked to take the most practical approach to my underwear. I'd wear all of my crazy, happy colors on the outside, and put the tame ones on the inside. I can wear taupe underwear with a white outfit, but I can't wear black lace with it. It shows through. Plus, the lace is bumpy. Why spend the money on something I can't wear all the time?

And don't get me started on the see-through part. Why would I want the grocery boy to see my nipple hard-on while I'm buying ice cream?

But no one could 'beat' Edward.

So...that meant I had to wear thongs. Thongs that made my asshole raw.

I could've said no.

But yelling Edward and pouting Edward were both equally hated by me during our time together.

He wasn't worth the effort.

But now?

Now, I really wish I was wearing some sexy black number. With lace trim. With push-up cups, that make my large breasts perk like they did five years ago.

"I'm sorry," I mumble under my breath, apologizing for my lackluster appearance.

Holt takes two steps forward. My body feels scorched by his stare. "I'll buy them a new one."

Huh?

Oh. He thinks I'm apologizing about the lamp. I look down at the floor, wondering if I should pick it up first, or put the T-shirt on first.

I side glance at him. He cocks his head, absorbing me to memory. "But that's not why you're apologizing, is it?"

My mind can't be that easy to read? Can it?

Looking back to the lamp, I blink several times, take a deep breath, and force my head back up. I'm surprised to find him standing right in front of me. His body looms over me, shadowing my nakedness from the rest of the room. Nerves quiver in my stomach. My thundering heart pumps scalding blood through every nook and cranny of my body, making me feel on fire.

My brain swims with only one thought.

Him.

I need him to extinguish the inferno consuming me.

"Why are you really apologizing, Mer?" His whisper is so low, if he were any farther away from me, I wouldn't be able to hear it.

I lick my lips. "It's not important."

"It's important to me. Everything you do is important to me. Everything you think, everything you say."

I swallow. My throat makes a weird gurgling sound. "But why?"

He shrugs. "I don't know. Or maybe I do, and I'm too afraid to say it. Too afraid to scare you away. But I feel like you're the truth after a lifetime of frauds. I finally feel like a believer. And not a skeptic." He reaches up and grabs the backward ballcap from his head, tossing it over on one of the desks.

The flex of his muscles deprives me of all common sense, and before I know what's happening, I'm dropping the shirt to the floor, and my trembling fingers are brushing across his tight stomach, traveling up the ridges of his ribs.

Holy shit.

I'm really glad he wore his shirt untucked tonight.

He sucks in a sharp breath between his teeth. His eyes dance across my face.

And lower.

He studies the mounds of my cleavage.

His eyes hood with desire, mimicking my own, I'm sure. "Do you want me to kiss you?"

I shake my head. "No."

A smile tugs at the corner of his mouth. "Don't lie, Merit."

"Mmmm?"

"You want me to kiss you. It's written all over your face."

When I don't say anything, he slides his hand across the bare skin of my back and presses his body against mine. His calloused fingers trace my spine. The steel length of his erection digs into my stomach. It feels more erotic, more sensual, than anything I ever did with my husband.

And my body responds. My nipples harden to the point of pain, and wetness soaks my core.

"Tell me the truth."

I'm not sure how he expects me to even form an answer. My brain has no blood flow; it's all in my clit. "What do you think, *sir*?"

His chuckle is short-lived as he turns almost feral.

He crashes his mouth to mine. Our kiss isn't innocent. It doesn't start as some closed-mouth peck and then morph into something more.

It's already something more.

From the very first second.

His tongue pushes into my mouth, tangling and tasting. My hands leave his chest and circle around to his back. My nails scratch against him, begging him to hold me tighter, kiss me deeper. With wild abandon. And he listens. With a firm, yet gentle tug, he pulls my hair, snapping my neck, exposing my throat. He trails kisses around my jaw, down the length of my neck, and across my collarbone. I can't decide if I want him to keep kissing lower or come back to my lips.

My breasts throb with the need to be touched, but my mouth is so lonely.

So damn lonely.

He must hear my silent plea as he races back up, plunging his tongue into my mouth once again.

I feel like I'm walking on air, walking through time and space with more happiness and joy than I ever thought possible.

With more passion. More desire.

More... everything.

And then, reality slides the carpeted air right out from under my feet.

"Oh! Sorry!" Cullen's voice echoes through my brain and bounces around like a marble.

My vision is blurry, and I have to blink several times to clear the heated fog from my head.

Good thing Holt has fast reflexes. He quickly spins around and blocks my state of undress from Cullen's shocked eyes. "Really, C? Whatever you need couldn't wait five fucking minutes?"

Cullen doubles over in laughter. "We need beer, man. It's a bar. What do you expect me to do?" I peek around Holt's shoulder and watch as Cullen looks from us to the lamp on the floor. "Fun times?"

I stand on my tiptoes, grabbing Holt's waist for balance. There's a low rumble in his chest that makes it hard for me to focus. I clear my throat. "I accidentally broke your lamp. I'll be happy to replace it. Or reimburse you."

Cullen opens the door to the fridge and grabs a case of beer. "Trust me, the look on Holt's face is more than payment enough." His good-humored laugh resonates through the room even after he leaves.

I bury my head between Holt's shoulder blades and let the burn of bright red embarrassment drown my face. My lips tangle against his shirt. "I'm sorry," I say, for what feels like the umpteenth time tonight.

He spins around. Trying to ignore my swollen and heaving chest, he rubs his hands against the chill bumps that have suddenly covered my arms. "For what?"

"For embarrassing you in front of your friend."

His face breaks out into a wide smile. "Embarrassing *me*?" He lifts his eyebrows. "When Cullen was in middle school, Ridge and I once caught him taking a shit behind a bush in the backyard because we were throwing a party, and he didn't want the girls to smell him. I think *he's* the one who should be embarrassed."

The image makes me giggle so hard I snort.

Holt picks up the discarded bar T-shirt and clicks his tongue, motioning with his head for me to lift my arms in the air. He slides the T-shirt over my head, and my body shudders at every single spot where he touches me.

He gently grabs my face and caresses his thumb across my lips. "Just so you know, there's nothing you could ever do that would embarrass me."

"You obviously don't know me well enough."

I watch in heated passion as Holt licks his lips. "Let's resolve that problem, shall we?"

And when his mouth slants over mine, sending visions of a lifetime of perfect kisses—just like this one—flooding into my brain, I have no other option but to kiss him harder. Fuck reading my face and my mind. I need him to read my heart.

Chapter 9

Holt

I lift my head, searching for Merit on the other side of the store. When she catches my eye and smiles, I turn into nothing but a big ol' pussy. If I weren't surrounded by people right now, I'd collapse on the floor and crawl to her on my hands and knees.

I've seen a lot of tits in my life.

Some I didn't even wanna see.

You'd be surprised what women will do to try and get the attention of a professional football player.

But Merit? She has the most perfect chest I've ever seen. And I haven't even *really* seen it yet. I've only laid eyes on the parts not covered by her modest bra.

But what I *have* seen? That much is tattooed to my memory for all eternity.

Plump and full and meant for me.

And don't even get me started on her kiss.

If I even think about it, I'll get a full-blown erection. And that would not be good, considering I'm currently surrounded by several kids and their parents, taking pictures and passing out shiny pennies.

I don't mind. It's nice to see Merit's store so busy. I want her to be successful.

An unusual feeling of pride swirls in my stomach.

I'm proud of her. I don't really think I could say that about any of the other women I've dated—even counting the supermodel, the actress, and the politician's daughter.

It's an hour before the rush at the store dies down. As soon as the last customers walk out the door, I collapse in one of the chairs.

Kyra immediately starts laughing. "Why do you look so tired? Aren't you some sort of bionic, super-human athlete?"

I fling an arm over my eyes. "It's mental exhaustion. That one boy spent twenty minutes trying to explain his Pokémon cards to me." I sit up, shaking my head. "I swear it's more complicated than our playbook for the Super Bowl."

Merit's sultry giggle tickles my ears. "So, you're not used to playing with that kind of stuff?"

"Absolutely not. Just give me Felicia Stinkbottoms, and I can happily entertain myself for hours."

The look on Merit's face is absolutely priceless. Her jaw drops open, and she turns white as a ghost. Those hazel eyes widen. Her whisper is low and filled with accusation. "What?"

She obviously thinks I'm talking about a sex doll.

"Get your mind out of the gutter, Mer." I playfully wink at her. "Felicia Stinkbottoms is what Laura named her baby doll. Anna liked the name so much she bought a doll just like it. Now, we have Felicia One and Felicia Two."

Relief courses over her body like a waterfall. "Well, what am I supposed to think with a name like that?"

I think about that. Hard. "Well, if I were to buy a sex doll, I definitely wouldn't buy one with the word Stinkbottoms in the name. I'm a clean bottom kind of guy."

Merit immediately bursts out laughing and snorts.

She grabs a couple of display shoes from Kyra and starts putting them back on the shelf underneath the large TV. Once again, it's playing an old movie. One I don't know. "What movie is this?"

"*An American in Paris.* It's absolutely wonderful." She stops and stares at the screen for a minute before heaving a content sigh. "Kyra, I'm going to put these others in the back."

I eagerly watch her as she walks away. The swing of her hips has my mouth watering. But what's even more fascinating is the way she discreetly looks over her shoulder to see if I'm following her. She doesn't realize I see her doing it. But I do and immediately stand to follow.

In the back, I help her put things away. "So, you haven't told me why you play the old movies. It's obvious that you love them. Is that why you play them? So, you have something to watch if the store is slow?"

"Well, I do love them. Old movies are my favorite, but I don't really have a lot of downtime when I'm working."

I stretch my arms above my head, playing with my hat. I bite back a smile when her eyes dart to the waistband of my shorts, eagerly devouring the small section of skin showing above my boxer briefs.

Blushing, she wiggles her head back and forth. "Where was I? Oh, right. I play the movies for the kids. Most of them will never watch the classics. A world without *An Affair to Remember*? I would die. And you'd be surprised at the kids who've never even seen *The Wizard of Oz*."

"So, you've always liked old movies?"

She nods, keeping something from me.

"What is it, Mer? What aren't you telling me?"

She smiles sheepishly. "Nothing."

I fold my arms across my chest and lift my eyebrows.

She slaps my bicep and immediately rolls her eyes. "Fine." She leans closer, readying herself.

I love that she gets so serious when she's about to tell a story.

"Growing up, I wasn't allowed to be gone with friends for the entire weekend. I had some friends who said bye to their parents on Friday morning, on the way to school, and didn't see them again until Sunday night. My family wasn't like that. My grandparents lived with us at the farm." She cocks her head. "Or I guess we lived with them. It was their house first." She shrugs, "Anyway, I could go out with my friends on Friday night, but I always had to stay home on Saturday night. They were afraid I'd stay up too late and then fall asleep in church on Sunday. So, on Saturday nights, my family and I always watched a movie. And it was always an old movie, a classic. In the summertime, Dad would set everything up outside with a projector, and the movie would play on the side of the barn. My Granny would always make fresh popcorn with real butter. It was awesome."

She looks so innocent. It literally takes my breath away. Reaching forward, my fingertips graze her cheek, and I tuck a strand of her redwood hair behind her ear. "That does sound awesome."

A thick silence engulfs us. It's wonderfully unbearable. Charged with emotion and fire and desire.

And need.

She takes a step back, giving herself room to breathe.

"Why'd you step away?" I ask, honestly wanting to know.

She swallows, trying to force the words from her mouth. "Because you're suffocating me—without even touching me." The passion in her voice is tangible.

And hot as fuck.

I shuffle forward, taking back the distance she gained. "And that's a bad thing?"

"I don't know. Is it?"

My fingers snake up her arm, and I tug her body against mine. Hard. She sighs in reflex, like she's been waiting for me to do that all day long.

Fuck, I know *I* have.

Her body fits perfectly against mine. It's like we were cast together in the same mold, and some unfortunate twist of fate broke us apart long ago. But we're together again. Matched. Aligned.

I grab the back of her neck and lower my mouth to hers. Her lips instantly part, wanting more. And I immediately give it to her.

And then I'm forced to immediately take it back.

"Merit! Can you bring a new paper roll up front for the credit card machine? It's about out."

A frustrated growl rumbles from the depths of my stomach. Merit blushes and turns her head to the side so her scream doesn't deafen me. "Yep. Be right up."

We stare at each other. Her pupils are dilated in passion, her cheeks are flushed, and her lips glisten with moisture.

Moisture from my tongue.

"I guess our friends have a master plan to keep us from kissing?" I ask.

She smiles. "Maybe that should tell us something. You think?"

"Yeah, we need new friends," I say with a wink.

Laughing, she grabs what Kyra needs and heads back out into the main store, stubbing her toe on the doorframe in the process. She curses underneath her breath and hobbles around. And of course, I follow her, making sure her toe's not broken.

Leaning across the front counter, I watch as Kyra fiddles with the credit card machine and Merit looks over some receipts. "I really appreciate you locking up the store again tonight, Kyra. Your eagerness to work some overtime is really helping my dating life," I joke.

"Hey, I'm just glad the words *dating life* are back in this one's vocabulary," she says, poking Merit in the ribs.

Merit makes a face. "Hardy-har." She glances over at Kyra. "In all seriousness, I do appreciate it. It's not fair for me to keep asking you. I started showing Emily the shut-down procedures. It'll take me a few more times to get her trained, though. I just hope she can remember everything."

Kyra shrugs. "What you really need is another part-time worker. I've told you time and time again, that one more person would make all the difference. It would help you have a real life again." Kyra points straight at me, not feeling the need for discretion. "And from what I can see, it looks like you have a really good life starting, if you catch my drift."

I can't help but laugh. "Gee, Kyra. Are you sure NASA can crack that code?"

Merit thins her lips. "Kyra, you know why I can't hire another person."

Now, I'm curious.

"Why can't you hire another person?" I ask. I wonder if it's a money thing.

"It's a money thing," she says with a shrug, jiving with my own thought.

"But the store seems to be doing really good. It's busy, right?"

She nods furiously. "Oh yes, it's doing great. I'm definitely blessed. It's just... I have a business loan that I'm eager to pay off."

Kyra pops the gum in her mouth. "Yeah, to her douchebag ex-husband."

What? "You owe money to Edward?"

Merit throws eye daggers at Kyra, slicing her in two. "Well, technically, I owe my ex-father-in-law. But, yeah."

"How in the world did that happen?"

"When I decided to open the store, my in-laws offered to loan me the money instead of me going to a bank. It seemed like the safest thing at the time. Charles and Scarlet loved me." She cocks her head to the side. "Or so I thought. Anyway, I told you this place needed a ton of work to it. And there was a one-year lease payment due up-front. And inventory and computer systems and employee salaries. It didn't take long for everything to add up."

I shake my head. "And you didn't have to pay them off when you got divorced? That doesn't make sense. Usually, people wanna sever all ties if they can. I mean, it'd be different if you had kids, but..." I furrow my brow. "Mer, you don't have any hidden children, right?"

She smiles, biting back a laugh. "No. I don't have any hidden children."

Even though I wasn't really serious, it's still nice to know she's not hiding a tiny lawyer toddler from me. "So, yeah, that's just weird then. Edward didn't want you to get a loan from the bank and pay his parents back as part of the divorce settlement?"

She bites her lip. "It was an interest-free loan. Plus, there were... extenuating circumstances. Edward and his parents were a little more lenient in some ways. Especially considering I signed an iron-clad prenup before we got married."

"Extenuating circumstances? What the hell does that mean?"

Kyra slides the credit card machine back in its rightful place next to the register. "It means he put his dick in another woman."

"Kyra!" Merit's mortified scream echoes across the room.

Neither Kyra nor myself have time to react before the front door swings open and the little bell chimes announcing the presence of a customer. Merit darts around the counter. She leaves a mumble of words in her wake, "You can handle this customer. I have something to do in the back. Excuse me."

We watch as she scuttles out of view, her shoulders slumped like a little kid who just lost his dog.

Kyra tells the customer she'll be with them shortly and turns back to me. "I guess I'm not one for discretion, huh?"

Disbelief circles my brain like a wet, soggy fog. "He did that to her?"

Kyra chews on her lip, nodding. "I shouldn't have said anything. The whole situation just pisses me off."

I pat her hand. "I'll go check on her."

I find Merit sitting at the small table in the back, tearing at the crust of a peanut butter and jelly sandwich. She wasn't kidding when she said she typically brings her lunch to work. "Don't you get tired of eating sandwiches?"

She pins me in place with her kaleidoscope eyes. "I thought we just established that I'm saving money to pay off a loan."

I hold up my hands in defense. "You're right."

I sit down next to her. Leaning back in the chair, I toss my ball-cap on the table and drag my hands through my hair. Despite her best intentions to ignore me, she can't help it. She watches my every move underneath the camouflage of her thick, black eyelashes. She nervously scratches her bronzed shoulder, drawing my attention to the strap of the black sports bra peeking out from the wide neckline of her oversized store T-shirt.

She's breathtaking.

Beautiful and strong and smart.

Curious and funny and alluring.

The thought that someone would leave her, cheat on her? It makes me so damn angry. If she were mine, I'd never stray, I'd never leave. More importantly, I would never do anything to make *her* leave *me*. That's for damn sure.

And my goal in life is to make her mine. Forever.

I'm not exactly sure when I made that decision. I guess it was the second she popped her little head up from behind the register talking about zipping her panties in her shorts.

"That really happened? He cheated on you?"

Merit folds her hands in her lap, taking comfort in the motion. I wonder if she always had this habit—folding and clasping her hands. Did she do the same thing as a child? Somehow, I don't think she did. After a few seconds, she lifts her head, steeling herself and forfeiting her meek demeanor. "Yes."

Black rage constricts my heart. "Just once?"

"Well, it started about a year and a half before we separated, but it was always with the same woman. His secretary." She lets out a small, cynical chuckle and tears another piece of crust from her mutilated bread. "They're actually still together. At least he's a monogamous cheater."

"I'll tell you what he is...a son of a bitch."

I reach across, searching for her hand. She quickly moves it back to her lap.

Hell, no. That's not happening.

I push against the leg of her chair with my foot, scooting her back from the table. I twist to the side and grab the seat of her chair, pulling her across the floor. My actions are so quick, she doesn't have time to react. She just widens her eyes and holds on for the ride.

Spreading my legs, I settle her chair right in front of me, so close, her sigh feathers hot air across my face. I wrap my hands around hers.

"No more. There's no more of that."

She swallows. "No more of what?"

"You know what. *Pulling away from me.* I thought we'd gotten past that. But I guess we need to have the actual conversation, huh?"

She opens her mouth to answer but quickly shuts it. There's a gleam in her eye and a small smirk to one corner of her mouth.

I can see it. Plain as day.

She wants me to fight for her.

I guess he never fought for her.

Well, that makes one difference between Edward and me.

I'll never stop fighting for her.

"When I reach for your hand, I wanna hold it. Got it?" My mind wanders, thinking of all the things I want—I *need*—to do. "I wanna trace my fingers down the small of your back. Down that sweet, sexy curve that leads the way to your ass. I wanna hold your body against mine. Whether we're by ourselves or in the middle of a crowded store, it doesn't matter. You said you weren't used to public displays of affection, but that doesn't matter. Everything I do is for me. And for you. No one else. So don't pull away from me." I lean forward and whisper against the shell of her ear. "I know you like my touch. Don't deny it, Mer."

Her body shudders.

She turns her head. Her soft lips graze against the stubble of my jaw. "Why would I deny it? Didn't you say that I don't lie to you?" She gently nips at me with her teeth. "And the truth is...I dream of your touch, of your hands. Every single night." She turns my right hand over and caresses the fresh callus running the length of my thumb. With football practice starting back, my body is following suit with the normal gamut of blisters, bumps, and bruises. I guess you could say I'm more of a hands-on coach than most in my position. I watch with bated breath as she brings my thumb to her soft, pink lips and rubs it back and forth. "Want me to kiss it better, *sir*?"

Holy fucking hell.

My dick just hardened into steel. True, part of me realizes that she may be dabbling in the art of seduction to distract from the fact that I'm pissed as hell that her ex-husband cheated on her and that she's still indebted to his pissant father, but...in this moment, I don't think I really care.

Because in this moment? I wanna fuck her mouth with my tongue.

And it's not just the all-consuming desire driving me to kiss her. It's the fact that—even though she may be intentionally misdirecting me—she's showing me a small glimpse of her true self, the *real* Merit.

And I'm loving every minute of discovering the real Merit, of pulling her out of her shell.

Because the *real* Merit is a damn pistol.

Dragging my thumb across her jawline, I bend forward, ready to devour her.

"Merit! Can you come out front, please!" Kyra's voice shatters our intimacy.

Merit blinks, her eyes dazed and fogged. My hand is still cradling her face when she shoots up from her chair, grumbling underneath her breath. "I'm gonna shove a shoehorn up her meddling, little ass."

Chapter 10

Holt

The second she opens the door she folds her arms across her plump chest and pouts. "This is getting really old, sir." The sarcasm dripping from her makes me laugh.

"I think it's pretty funny." She's so damn hot it makes my groin painfully throb just to look at her. Of course, she'd be even hotter if the dress weren't black. It's a short little number with one strap.

And I'm dressed in cargo shorts, flip flops, and a T-shirt.

"I specifically asked, and you said we were going out to eat." She looks down at her high-heeled feet. It looks like her shoes are rubbing her skin raw across the bridge of her toes.

"We are going out to eat. We're just not going to a white-table-cloth kind of place."

Despite her best efforts, the relief on her face is easy to read. Well, every emotion on her face is easy to read, but even a blind person could see she's relieved to hear that news. "Do you like wearing dresses and high heels like that? Because it sure doesn't look like you enjoy it."

She presses her lips together, working her red lipstick. "I'm a girl, Holt. Girls like playing dress-up every now and again." She turns and walks into the kitchen.

I've been here several times now, so she doesn't think anything when I follow her and grab a bottle of water from the fridge. "Ah, but that's the key phrase, isn't it? *Every now and again.*"

Her smile morphs into a shit-eating grin. "You think you know me so well."

Setting my bottle on the countertop, I slide my hands around her waist. She sucks a small breath into her lungs. And holds it. "I do know you. Now, tell me more." I press my fingertips into her skin, wondering how great it would feel not to have the fabric of this black dress between us.

"Well, let's just say the idea of not having to wear makeup and heels and life-squeezing fat-suckers was one of the major draws for me opening a children's store. I think I would collapse in a pile of tears if I still had to work at a job where I had to dress up every day. And when your bosses are your husband and your father-in-law, you have to make sure you always look perfect. Not a hair out of place, not a smudge of lipstick on your face."

Leaning forward, I softly place my lips against hers. Her body sinks against mine, and her mouth parts, already wanting more.

I absolutely love it.

She smells like toothpaste and almonds.

But instead of kissing her, I rub my lips back and forth, smearing her brick red lipstick across both her face and mine. "You mean like this?"

She tosses her head back and belly laughs, shaking in my arms. "Yes. This would've been completely unacceptable."

I stare into her eyes. The white light of the kitchen makes the greens and blues more prominent. "Well, fuck them. Because I think you're completely acceptable."

This time she catches *me* off guard. When her fingertips grab the waistband of my shorts, she catches my skin on fire, sending burning chill bumps across my abdomen. She places one soft kiss on my lips before stepping away. "Thank you, Holt."

Under normal circumstances, I'd laugh. I mean, her chin and nose are covered in red splotches. She looks like she hooked up with Rudolph the Red-Nosed Reindeer.

But... it's not so funny.

It's breathtaking.

Clearing my throat, I point down the hall to her bedroom. "Now, go put on something different. We don't wanna be late."

"Be late for what?"

"Go change, woman, or you'll never find out."

Mumbling under her breath, she stomps down the hall. I quickly wet a paper towel and clean the makeup from my face. A few minutes later, she races back into the living room. Her curiosity always gets her excited. "Okay, I'm ready. Where are we going?"

That's much better. She's dressed in shorts, a sleeveless blouse, and flip flops with sparkles all over them. She's pulled her hair into a messy bun. She also tried to take off a little bit of her eyeliner when she was removing her rogue lipstick. The smudges make her eyes look seductive and sultry. I reach for her hand and tug her next to me.

And then, I sit down on the couch. "Turn around," I order.

Her eyebrows lift into next week. "Excuse me?"

I pull out a spray bottle from the leg pocket of my cargo shorts and dangle it in front of her face.

"Bug spray?"

"Yep. Now turn around. I'll get the back of your legs first." When she doesn't move, I threaten her. "Now, do you wanna see what your surprise is or not?"

Her face immediately perks up. "You didn't say it was a surprise."

"Well, I'm saying it now, Mer. Stop being difficult and let me cover you in this," I turn the pump bottle toward me, reading the label, "aloe-scented, family-friendly, no-stain bug repellent."

"City Hall? Why are there so many cars here?" Her brow furrows. "I'm not really into politics, Holt."

"Well, I can assure you, I'm not taking you to a city council meeting on a Saturday night." I point to the alleyway leading behind the building. "You know what's behind there, right?"

"Yeah, City Hall Park."

"Well, did you know that they play movies in the park on Saturday nights during the summer?"

She leans across the console of my truck, trying to stare down the alley. "Yeah, but they always play kids' movies. Cartoons."

"Well, not every kid movie is a cartoon."

She smiles widely, flashing her white teeth. "What's playing tonight?"

"*The Wizard of Oz.*"

She jumps, making the leather seat squeak. "I love that movie!"

I smirk, damn proud of myself. "I know. You already said."

She cocks her head, studying me. "Wait a minute. Did you have something to do with this? Was *The Wizard of Oz* supposed to be playing tonight?"

She's really starting to read between my lines.

And I like it.

I shrug. "I didn't do much."

"But you did something, right?" She sits back in her seat and eyes me suspiciously. "I'm not getting out of this truck until you tell me what you did."

"It was nothing big. They had *The Wizard of Oz* scheduled to play at the end of the month, for the last movie. I just asked them to switch it to tonight."

"And the powers that be just agreed. Simple as that?"

"Well, a donation to the new public library might have been involved."

"Holt!" Merit shakes her head and stares at the floorboard. "You shouldn't have done that; there's no need to spend that kind of money on me."

"Hey," I reach over and slide my hand around the back of her neck. She immediately arches, rolling her head backward against my hand, basically pinning me to her. I don't think she even realizes she does it. It's so mild-mannered on the scale of sexuality, yet it may be one of the most sensual things I've ever seen.

And that includes the time a fan delivered a homemade apple pie to me, wearing nothing but an apron and fishnet stockings.

The fan, not the pie.

She turns to look at me when I don't finish my sentence. I'm so distracted it takes me a minute to even remember what I was in the middle of saying. "I was already planning on making a donation to the library. I promise." I massage my thumb against the edge of her collarbone. "This idea just popped in my head, and I couldn't stop thinking about how excited you would be. So, please, don't ruin my moment by worrying about money."

After a minute, she snorts, trying to rid herself of the lust drawn across every inch of her face before busting my balls. "Spoken like someone who has tons of money."

"And if I have tons of it, why does it matter if I spend a little bit for a good cause? It's not like I built a bonfire out of hundred-dollar bills, Mer; we're talking about a public library. Laura's in there nearly every single day checking out books. You want my niece's brain to wither away?"

She bites her lip, trying not laugh. "No, definitely not. I'm a firm believer that children need constant stimulation to thrive and grow."

I jump from the truck, growling under my breath. "I'm the one with constant stimulation over here."

She giggles, shutting the passenger door behind her.

I grab the blanket and large picnic basket from the back seat. Holding them in one arm, I usher Merit down the sidewalk with my free hand on the small of her back. Several large groups of people are walking near us. Some of them even glance our way, obviously recognizing me.

Despite the scrutiny of the public eye, she doesn't try to move away from my touch.

And I like that too. A lot.

I catch her glancing at the picnic basket. One. Two. Three times.

Finally, she can't stand it. "I didn't see that in the back seat."

"I know you didn't. I covered it with the blanket."

"What's in it?"

"Well, I promised we would eat out, didn't I?"

Excitement blooms across her face. "You packed us a picnic supper?"

I have to bite the inside of my cheek to keep from grinning like a damn moron because you can tell she's never had anyone do this for her before. That realization makes me feel like I'm on top of the world.

We settle in the middle of the park, close to the front where the stage is, with Merit helping me spread the blanket. She neatly stacks her flip flops in one corner and crawls across the fluffy white fabric. She looks around, absorbing her surroundings. There are some vendors set up selling different snacks and drinks and trinkets. I open the basket and hand the items to her one at a time. Paper plates, plastic silverware, napkins, and water bottles. I stop for dramatic effect before I get to the food.

Merit leans forward, eager to see what's on the menu.

"Chicken salad on croissant. Shaved prime rib with Swiss cheese and horseradish sauce on garlic-herb focaccia. Fettucine pasta salad with pesto and alfredo. And miniature sugar biscuits with honey butter."

I don't think I've ever seen someone so shocked before.

"Holy crap, Holt. You made all this?" Her eyes dart from side to side as she mumbles, her train of thought going off the rails. "How can you be so good at everything? It's unnatural."

I toss my hat to the side. "Well, I can hold my own in the kitchen, but I definitely can't take credit for this. Jeff and Cullen are catering a wedding tonight. They let me steal some food." I hold my hand up before she can protest. "And before you say anything, I got permission from the groom. Took a couple of photographs with him, and I even signed their wedding photo."

"Oh. Is Carson working with them tonight?"

I wasn't expecting her to ask that question, but the genuine concern on her face warms my heart. "Yeah, he is."

"Oh, that's so nice. I still feel horrible about the whole restaurant thing. He's a good kid."

When she catches me staring at her, she blushes. I love it when she's flushed. Pink cheeks, flustered smile. It's the way she looks after I kiss her.

And I *always* want to be kissing her.

In fact, if we weren't surrounded by forty families with little kids, I'm pretty sure I'd have my tongue in her mouth right now.

Food be damned.

I think she can read my mind, though, because she coyly smiles and starts plating the food. "Let's eat. I'm starving."

I lean forward, tucking an errant hair behind her ear. "Good idea. Let's eat and continue talking about how I'm *so good at everything*. Does that include kissing, Mer?"

She snorts. "Absolutely not."

"Don't lie, Merit."

"Mmmm?"

"You love my kisses. It's written all over your face."

When she doesn't answer, I press her. "Tell me the truth."

Suddenly, the speakers come to life, and the big screen hanging from the stage flashes with a picture. "Shhh. The movie's starting." She immediately faces forward, focusing all her attention on the screen, and takes a huge bite of her prime rib sandwich, promptly ignoring me.

It doesn't take long at all to see Merit takes her movie-watching very seriously.

There's a strict no-talking policy. Of course, she couldn't stop the whispers, yells, and tomfoolery of those around us, but the rule was strictly enforced within the four corners of our blanket island.

And when she had to use the bathroom? She ran so she wouldn't miss much. Well, sprinted is more like it.

And when I saw some guy hitting on her while she was standing in line for the porta potty? I nearly lost my mind. I bolted from the blanket and made a beeline straight for her, pretending that I needed to ask her a question that couldn't wait. In return, she scolded me for leaving our first-class seats and expensive basket open for stealing. Like we're in the middle of a biker bar and not in a park surrounded by a bunch of first-graders.

All in all, it's the best time I've ever had watching a movie.

When it's over, we gather our stuff and get ready to leave. For the hundredth time tonight, I watch Merit stare at someone walking past us with a funnel cake from one of the food vendors. It's plain to see she wants one. She's craving it. "Why don't you get one before he shuts down for the night?"

"Get one what?"

"A funnel cake."

She looks down at the ground and folds her hands in front of her. After a second, she lifts her head. "Oh, I'm fine. But thank you for the offer."

I squint, trying to stare past the façade she's projecting. A sliver of cold fury worms its way into my heart. "What did he do to you?"

She frowns. "Who?"

"Your dickhead ex-husband."

"Edward?" She furrows her brow, looking around. "He's here?"

If I were in a better mood, I'd chuckle. Sometimes talking to her is like running around in circles. Like a dog chasing its tail. "No, he's not here. I'm asking what he did to you to make you act like that?"

Her eyes widen. It's finally clicked, and she knows exactly what I'm talking about. She chews on the side of her beautiful, pouty lip. "Like what? What are you talking about?"

"Mer, you know damn well what I'm talking about." I cock my hands on my hips. "Formal. *Too* polite. Meek." Fear rips at my gut, making it hard to breathe. "Scared."

Her face softens, and she reaches for me. Quickly rethinking her decision, she grabs the hem of her shorts and twists the fabric. "It's not what you're thinking, Holt. He didn't hit me. He never raised a hand to me."

I feel like someone's injected adrenaline straight into my heart, releasing my tension in a powerful wave. "You promise? Because I swear, Merit, that thought blinds me." I pause, searching for my words. "It fills me with fucking blinding, violent rage."

She nods, telling me the truth. "I promise."

I suck air into my lungs, thanking God. "Then what? Why do you act like that?"

She takes a step forward. This time I don't give her a chance to rethink her decision. I grab her hands and lay them on my chest. The heat from her fingertips immediately sinks into my skin. Warming me, filling me with longing.

"How about we save that conversation for another day? I really don't feel like talking about my ex-husband right now."

"What do you feel like doing?"

She smiles brightly. "Eating a funnel cake."

I can't help but smile back. "Well, I was really hoping you'd say you felt like kissing me. But I suppose eating a funnel cake is the next best thing." I reach around, grabbing my wallet. "Here, let me give you some money."

She jumps back like a scalded cat. "Oh, no. You just did all this. I can't let you pay for that too."

I roll my eyes and shove a ten-dollar bill at her. "It's just a funnel cake. Here, take it."

She vehemently shakes her head. "Nope. You finish getting the stuff together. I'll be right back." She turns away, calling over her shoulder. "Do you want one too? Because I don't share funnel cakes."

Now, there's the Merit I like. *My* Merit.

I carry the blanket and picnic basket on our walk back to my truck while she happily eats her dessert. I've never seen a funnel cake with so much powdered sugar on it. She must've asked for extra. The little moans she makes when eating are driving me to the brink of utter madness.

It's better than the last porno I watched.

We're almost to the truck when a really big gust of wind comes out of nowhere. It's so strong, it nearly blows the blanket out of my hands because I wasn't prepared for it. I duck my head against the breeze and hit the unlock button on my key fob. Suddenly, I hear Merit's horrified whisper behind me. "Oh, no."

I immediately stop in my tracks. "What's wro—?"

I can't even finish my sentence. I nearly collapse on the sidewalk in laughter. I'm laughing so hard I can barely breath. She's covered from head to toe in powdered sugar. She looks like a snowman.

Like she rolled in flour.

Like she got caught in a cocaine explosion.

It's even in her eyebrows.

She sticks her tongue out and tries to lick the side of her face. She snorts and giggles. "Do I have any on me?" she jokes.

I wrap my arms around her. "No, baby. You're just fine."

Chapter 11

Merit

I lean forward, unable to control my shock. "*This* is your house?"

Holt gives me one of his sexy side glances. "Yeah."

I sink back on the leather seat of his truck, all pissed off. "See? Just like I said, obscenely rich."

He chuckles. "I thought we already went over this, Mer."

"We did," I say, pouting. "That doesn't mean I like it, though."

We come from two different worlds. When will he realize that? I've already been through this with Edward. And we all know how that turned out.

I feel like I'm constantly waiting for the other shoe to drop. For Holt to show his real colors. I'm ready to bolt the second that happens, but for now, he keeps reeling me in. He really has me thinking he's different.

Different than Edward and all his rich and powerful friends.

But I spent eight years with Edward. Eight long years between our first date and the time we separated. Eight years in his world, trying to get along with his family and his friends, and trying not to continually piss him off or embarrass him. And from what I've seen, as soon as people hit six digits in their bank account, they become complete A-holes.

And Holt has *way* more than six digits in his bank account.

He turns into the long driveway and stops, pointing at the beautiful mansion. "This house actually belonged to Ella's parents. Ella and my other cousin, Carrie, grew up here. When my aunt and uncle passed away, Ella sold the house to me. So, I got it at a really fair price. In fact, I refused to go as low as she wanted. Her only contingency was that I completely remodel and redecorate it. That's what I've spent the last year doing. In fact, construction just finished before Anna's birthday party a few weeks ago."

So that's why he mentioned always having parties at his house—because he has the most room. But all those juicy details spark my attention, even though I don't want them to. "Remodel it? Why would she want you to completely remodel it? Was it ugly before?"

Holt's eyes dance in good humor. He knew that comment would spark my curiosity.

Damn him.

"Ella had a very complicated relationship with her parents, my aunt and uncle. Let's just say they weren't the best parents. Or the best people. Plus, this is where Carrie lived." He somberly blinks a couple of times and runs his fingers across his chin. "This house had too many bad memories, and we wanted nothing but happy memories from here on out—for Ella and her new family, for my whole family, for Ridge and Cullen." He shrugs. "A fresh slate."

Without thinking, I reach over and touch his thigh. "I saw it online. When I finally searched your name, articles about your cousin pulled up. I should've waited for you to tell me about her. I'm sorry I snooped. And I'm sorry your family had to go through that."

Holt's cousin, Carrie, went missing fourteen years ago this past Fourth of July. Apparently, she got hooked on prescription opioids after a knee surgery and eventually started selling drugs. Let's just say, things didn't end well.

He stares at my hand, and I suddenly realize I'm still touching him. Before I have a chance to remove it, he wraps his fingers around mine, tethering me to him. "It's not snooping if it's public knowledge." He smiles softly, and I can see his mind literally traveling back to a happier time. After a minute, he shakes his head, clearing his thoughts. "Anyway, it won't be long, and you'll be able to read about the true story. Some of those internet articles have the 'facts'," he uses his free hand to make air quotes, "all mixed up."

"The true story?"

"Ella just finished writing a book. Finished it today, as a matter of fact."

"She wrote a book? To tell the story of her sister? What a wonderful accomplishment. There's no better way to fight for someone than to tell the truth."

He bites back a smile and puts the truck in drive again. "You should tell her that."

I frown. But it's not like I know Ella. Shrugging, I don't bother to point out the obvious. "Uh. Okay."

We round the corner, and what shocks me even more than the beauty of the massive house is the line of cars. "Holy crap, you own a lot of cars." I snatch my hand away from his. "Holt, this can't be healthy. You have an obsession. Why on earth do you need so many cars?"

He snakes around the huge driveway and pulls into one of the garage bays. He laughs. "All I have is this truck and my old truck over there." He points to a pickup that's several years older with a few dings on the side. "These other vehicles aren't mine."

I furrow my brow. "Then why are they here?"

He licks his lips. "Because they belong to my family."

"Why is your family storing their—" All of a sudden, my brain starts to function, making me feel like a complete idiot. My eyes widen in horror. "Your family is *here*? Tonight? Your family is here at your house? *Tonight*?"

"Yep."

I cover my face with my hands, mumbling unfiltered words through my fingers. "Holy shit, Holt. Why didn't you tell me your family was gonna be here? You could've invited me to see your place a different night."

"Well, that would defeat the purpose of having you meet my family."

He wants me to meet his family. "You want me to meet your family?"

Holt leans back against his door, watching me in amusement. "Why are you acting so shocked?"

"Because that's a shocking thing."

"Why? You already know Raylee and Will. And Cullen."

I look out the window at the line of cars and nibble my lip in anxiety.

Wait. That's a very good question, and a fair point he's made.

Why am I nervous?

He obviously brings women home to meet his family all the time. Just take Bunny, for example. She was his date to his niece's birthday party. And something like that is a huge deal.

Or it's a huge deal to most people.

I guess it's not a huge deal to him.

Not huge enough to stop him from bringing that little whore around the people he loves most. Granted, I don't actually know if Bunny is a whore, but I like to think she is...when I'm punching my pillow at night, pretending it's her face...and the supermodel's...and all the other women I saw him 'dating'.

And now? Now, I'm disappointed. I think I liked the feeling of nervous apprehension better. At least, that feeling blossomed from a genuine fear that this dating thing might actually be turning into something—something real.

And now? Now, I don't feel special at all. I feel like one *of* a million instead of one *in* a million. It's the same way Edward always made me feel.

I've really got to end this...whatever this is between us.

Just make it through tonight, and then you can end it, I tell myself.

Looking down at the floorboard, I sigh. I reach for the handle and climb out of the truck. "You're right. It's no big deal. I'm sorry for being a pain."

"Hey!" He reaches for my arm, but I'm already shutting the door behind me. It doesn't take long for him to race around to my side. "What's that all about?"

"What's what all about?"

He rolls his eyes. "Don't pretend you don't know what I'm talking about. Something's wrong."

"Nothing's wrong," I say, trying to sound chipper. My efforts fail, and my voice sounds fluttery, like a drunk ballerina.

"Don't lie, Merit."

This mind-reading/face-reading shit is getting old. I push past him. "C'mon, let's just get this over with." This time there's no hiding the indifference in my tone.

"Hey!" He snatches my arm, spins me around, and pins me against the truck. His firm body looms over me, making my anger and frustration cloudy with desire. "What the hell is that supposed to mean?"

His bright blue eyes grow murky with concern and displeasure. There's a twitch in his jaw.

His sexiness is irksome.

I stiffen my spine, lift my head proudly, and stare straight at him. "It doesn't mean anything, Holt. I just want you to know that I understand the situation. This is just another date for you, I get that. Don't worry; I won't make more of it than it is."

His face softens. "That's what this is about? You think this is just some average thing?" He looks at the house, like he can see through the walls. "I want you to meet my family, Merit. I wouldn't call that an ordinary date. Would you?"

"Yeah, I would. I think Bunny would say the same thing." I shrug, "Her and all the other women you bring home."

He leans closer. When he opens his mouth, I can smell his mouthwash. "It's not what you think. Bunny wormed her way into an invitation to Anna's birthday party through Raylee. I didn't invite her. I promise. I don't introduce my family to the women I date. Not unless I'm serious about them."

He's serious about me? I beg myself not to ask, but apparently my tongue has free will over my body. "You're serious about me?"

He bends down. His hot whisper tickles my jaw, sending a quaking shiver down my spine. "As a fucking heart attack."

How am I supposed to respond to that? Am I supposed to say that I'm getting serious about him too? Two seconds ago, I was telling myself I would stop seeing him after tonight.

But the sad truth is... I know what I want. And what I want is *him*.

I'm just scared.

Scared shitless, to be exact.

I don't think I could handle being hurt again.

Not only that, but I don't wanna lose myself again. I always liked who I was.

Before Edward changed me.

Before he molded me, shaped me.

When I met Edward, I was a pile of raw clay. Unkempt and messy. I was a fool to let him change me.

Not wanting to say all of that, I say the other thing occupying my thoughts. "So, who *has* met your family? The supermodel?"

He snorts on a chuckle. "Again with the supermodel?"

"You're the one who dated her," I say with another shrug.

He dramatically sighs. "No, the supermodel did not meet my family. And yes, they have met some of the women I've dated, but it's never been because I actively wanted to introduce them. It's just been at functions where they all happen to be—football games, public events, autograph signings. That kind of thing. So, if they happen to be standing in the same room together, I'm kinda forced to introduce them."

"So, you're telling me you've never brought a girl home with the sole intention of introducing her to your family?"

His eyes roam across my face, searching me, exploring me. It always feels so intimate when he does that. Like he's reading my heart.

We already know he can read my mind.

He smiles softly. "Never. Not until tonight."

I swallow, and my throat makes a weird noise because it's so dry. I swish my spit around, trying to wet my mouth. "Good to know."

He lifts his eyebrows. "Am I gonna have to go through this kind of interrogation when I meet *your* family."

"I was raised in the woods. By a pack of wild wolves. They're not much for meeting strangers." Getting carried away by my own stupid and corny joke, I snort. "But they sure as hell can have a good time during the full moon."

Holt just smiles and gives me a sexy little wink. Grabbing me by the hand, he leads me into the house. And I use that term loosely. Like I said, it's a mansion. Across from where we come in is a massive gym. It's humongous. With tons and tons of expensive equipment.

I point to something in the corner. "Uh, is that a tanning bed?"

"Yeah, but my butt's never been in it. I'm in the sun more than enough." He's right. His golden skin is mouthwatering. "It belonged to my aunt. Raylee wouldn't let me get rid of it. She and mom use it some."

"Do you use all this equipment? It's huge."

"I use most of it. I switch things up so it doesn't get boring. I did make the gym bigger." He points to the far side of the room. "That part was actually a guest bedroom, but the house had enough bedrooms. So, I changed that during the remodel."

"How many bedrooms do you have?" I can't help it…I blush when I say the word 'bedroom', you know, like the mature woman that I am.

"After taking this one away, there's still two bedrooms down here and four upstairs."

"Dang, you have six bedrooms? And it used to have seven?"

He nods. "And that's not counting the Children's Wing. It has two bedrooms."

The scent of money wafting through the air makes me feel faint. I lean my hand against the wall to steady myself. "Excuse me?"

His laugh bounces around in my head. "That's what we've always called it. Don't worry, I'm not planning on banishing my future kids to a secluded wing of the house to fend for themselves. It's more like a small apartment." He tilts his head, "A mother-in-law suite."

"Why is it called the Children's Wing, then?"

"Because that's what my aunt and uncle did—they exiled their children. They built a two-bedroom addition to the house for Ella and Carrie. It has a living room and a full kitchen. It even has a washer and dryer. Everything so they didn't have to come over to the Big House and interrupt the lives of my aunt and uncle."

Acid churns in my stomach. "Are you serious? That's terrible. How old were they? Teenagers?"

"They were in elementary school."

Shock pours out of me. "That's disturbing on so many levels."

He nods in sympathy. "I know." Gently tugging me away from the wall, we walk down the hall. He points out a bathroom and an office, and then we come to the kitchen. Gourmet doesn't even begin to describe it. There's high-end appliances and granite and marble. Inside the pantry, there's even a craft ice maker that spits out shaved ice. It pairs perfectly with the soda fountain machine.

"No wonder your family always wants to come here," I say. I wander over to the kitchen island. It's covered in food. My stomach instantly growls.

Right then, a guy with brown and gray hair walks in, whistling. "Oh good! You're here."

Holt introduces us. "Jeff, this is Merit. Merit, this is Jeff, Ridge and Cullen's dad."

"Pleasure to meet you."

His smile is genuine. "Oh hon, the pleasure is all mine." He turns to Holt. "I'm just checking on the potatoes and the mac and cheese." He peeks in one of the ovens. "Perfect timing. Ridge and Cullen said the ribs lack about fifteen minutes. These should be ready by then."

Holt slides his hand down my arm. I notice Jeff watching us from the corner of his eye. He bites back a smile. For some strange reason, it makes me do the same.

"You wanna continue the tour or go ahead and meet everyone?" Holt asks.

My anxiety returns. What if they don't like me. A fireball of nerves erupts in my body. I tug on him, forcing him to bend his ear to my lips. "Is there still time to leave? Is that option on the table?"

Before I can move, Holt jerks his head to the side and plants a soft kiss on my lips. "Nope."

Not giving me a chance to make a run for it, he wraps his hand around the small of my back and walks from the kitchen into the living room. My mouth falls open in awe. I can't even focus on the beauty of the room or the comfy furniture or the world's biggest TV screen. All I can focus on is the wall of glass windows and doors that opens to the back patio. Where all of his friends and family are milling around, waiting to meet me.

Little ol' me.

Chapter 12

Merit

I choke on my words. "Something's wrong here."

Holt's voice holds an edge of concern. "What do you mean? What's wrong?"

I can't even swallow. My throat is uncomfortably thick. "Why is everyone here so good-looking?"

Holt chuckles. "Excuse me?"

My eyes scan the crowd. It's like I just walked into a scene from a soap opera. Not even a soap opera—these people look better than that. It's like a telenovela of sexy.

"I knew you were impossibly hot." I can't help but take the opportunity to check him out. He smirks, liking my hungry eyes on him. My heart stops beating when I see the large bulge in his shorts twitch. I try to ignore the heat it stirs in my own body. "And I knew Raylee and Will and Cullen were all perfect-looking." I wave my hand over to the side where three people are huddled together in conversation. "But all these other people are hot too. It's…" I shake my head, thinking, "inhuman."

He leans into my personal space. "Well, first of all, I like it when you look at me like that. Feel free to do that anytime, anyplace. Second, the fact that you just called Cullen and," he nods to the two guys standing to the side, "Ridge and Crutch hot? Well, that makes me want to violently strangle them all. So, it's fine with me if you keep that opinion to yourself."

Then he winks at me. That make-me-weak-in-the-knees, sexy little wink.

I don't have to look around to know everyone is watching us. I can feel their eyes on me, burrowing little holes into my armor. "Maybe you should back up. Everyone's watching us."

The side of his mouth tilts up. "So?"

"So, I don't really think having our bodies pressed up against one another, like we're trying to stave off hypothermia, is the best way to make a good first impression with your family."

"Hmm. Maybe not. But it sure as hell is a lot of fun."

I raise my eyebrows, begging myself not to snort in laughter. "Really, *sir*?" Fortunately, I win this battle. Growling under his breath, Holt takes a step away, giving me some breathing room.

First, we head over to the large patio area. At the center, there's a gigantic, from the looks of it, custom-made, round dining table. I've never seen one so huge. There has to be fifteen seats. Next to it is a smaller picnic table. I guess that's the kids' table. The men all stand to greet me.

"Merit Browning, I'd like you to meet my parents, Ray and Teresa Hill."

I pray they can't see the tremble of my hand or feel the cold sweat pooling on my palm. "Pleased to meet you, Mr. Hill. And it's good to see you again, Mrs. Hill."

Holt cocks his head. "You know my mom?"

Teresa affectionately squeezes Holt's shoulder. "Son, I *have* gone shopping with my grandkids before. Of course, I've met Merit." She turns to me, smiling widely. "I'll say it again, Merit, your store is beautiful. Just like you." She gives me a little wink.

Must be where Holt gets it.

"And please, call us Ray and Teresa," Holt's dad says.

Not knowing what to do, I simply nod and fold my hands in front of me.

Holt clears his throat and points across the table. "You met Jeff inside. This is his wife, Dana Conway."

We're too far away from each other to shake hands, so I just wave.

"And this is Patrick Marcum and his wife, Nancy. You can just call Patrick, 'Marcum'. We all do."

I don't think I've ever heard him mention these people before. Who are they? Relatives? Neighbors and best friends like the Conways?

My curiosity has me opening my mouth to ask, but I realize that would be rude so I shut it, using my willpower to clamp it in position.

My willpower is easy.

I just pretend I'm with Edward.

Holt bumps my hip. "You wanna know who they are, don't you?"

Everyone at the table chuckles. My face turns hot, spewing red heat like a flare gun.

"Oh honey, don't be embarrassed," Nancy says kindly. "We *are* kinda hard to explain."

"Marcum was the original detective on my cousin's case," Holt says. "As you can imagine, we all grew extremely close over the years. They love Carrie just like the rest of us, even though they've never met her."

"A rose among the thorns." My own voice catches me off guard. I chastise myself. So much for keeping my mouth shut.

Teresa smiles. "My mother used to say the same thing. Something good from something bad."

I nod. "Yes, ma'am."

Nancy reaches over and squeezes Dana's hand. "Well, Carrie definitely shined her light on Patrick and me when she brought us all together, that's for sure."

"C'mon, let's meet everyone else." Holt tugs at my folded hands, boldly grabbing one and leading me around.

We bypass the large grill, causing Cullen to raise his hand and yell out. "What about me!"

"She already knows you, dumbass."

We walk over to the two guys I don't know. The woman has walked away and is talking on the phone. Adonis Number One is taller than everyone else. He has light brown hair, and his eyes are the palest color of green I think I've ever seen. It's like they're translucent. Adonis Number Two is just a smidge shorter than Holt with dark brown hair—the same color as Cullen's—and dark brown eyes, rimmed around the edge with a light brown color.

Holt nods to Adonis Number Two. "This is Ridge Conway. And the best day of his life was when his parents moved next door to my parents."

Ridge rolls his eyes. "Keep telling yourself that, brother. I was only six months old. If I could've walked, I would've hightailed it right out of there." He's so handsome, I actually get nervous shaking his hand.

"And this is Ryland Crutchfield," Holt says, talking about Adonis Number One. "You can call him Crutch. Poor bastard fell in love with Ella. Now, he's stuck with us."

Crutch's voice is all gravel and seduction. I'm pretty sure I blush when he talks. He glances over at the woman with her back to us, whom I can only assume is Ella. "Lucky bastard would be the better definition." His stare is so full of emotion, it almost feels like we're invading their privacy. Eventually, he turns back to me and shakes my hand. "Nice to meet you, Merit."

"It's really nice to meet both of you. If I remember correctly, Ridge, you're a firefighter and Crutch, you're a detective with the sheriff's department, right?"

They both nod, taking a drink from their beer bottles.

Holt pretends to whisper in my ear. "They're being modest." He uses the opportunity to snake a hand around my waist. Both Crutch and Ridge notice right away. I hold my breath, afraid to breathe. "Ridge is a firefighting badass. He's a paramedic *and* he's trained to fight wildfires. And Crutch is a sergeant." Holt's voice gets stuck in the back of his throat. "Without him and Ella, we wouldn't have justice for Carrie."

Holy crap. Who are these people?

All I do is sell shoes and clothes.

A sweet voice captures my dumbfounded attention. "I'm so sorry about that. It was work. I promise that is my last call for the night."

Ella looks like a model. She's super tall with honey and caramel-colored hair. The setting sun frames her body like she's an angel as she walks back over to join us. And what makes her even more beautiful is the perfectly round pregnancy belly leading the way.

Holt didn't tell me she was pregnant.

I study her graceful movements. She also has really good posture I think to myself.

"Ella Crutchfield, this is Merit Browning."

"It's nice to finally meet you, Merit. Holt has told us so many wonderful things about you."

"Oh." I freeze. I can't think of a single thing to say. She's so beautiful and intimidating, I'm completely tongue-tied.

After a moment, I watch in horror as Ella's lips thin. She lifts her chin in the air and gives me a tight, fake smile. "At least the weather is pleasant tonight. Not too hot."

I look down at the ground, trying to gather my thoughts.

She hates me. "Yes. There's a nice breeze tonight," I respond stoically.

Huh.

This may turn into an 'Edward-like' party before you know it. Fucking lovely.

I'm caught by surprise when Crutch growls. The noise is low and dangerous. He leans across and traces his mouth up and down Ella's jaw. Settling against her ear, he orders, "Stop it." She visibly shakes.

The moment seems intimate. Too intimate. We shouldn't be watching it.

I'm surprised even further when Holt sways against me. He knocks my hands loose—from where I subconsciously folded them—

and they fall limply to my side. Rubbing his lips against the shell of my ear, he whispers, "The same goes for you."

Now, it's my turn to visibly shake.

Once I've recovered, my face scrunches in confusion. "Huh?"

I'm less tactful than Ella, no matter how hard I try.

Her laugh plays like music. "I'm sorry, Merit. It's my fault." She shakes her head back and forth and rolls her shoulders to loosen them. "Sometimes, it's hard for me to talk to new people. Unless it's about work, that is. I can be a little... stiff. I revert back to old habits and use the same talking points I learned from the gazillion boring parties I had to attend throughout my life. You know—talk about the weather, the stock market. Boring stuff."

I chuckle. "I know exactly what you mean," I say rhetorically. "I used to watch the Weather Channel for hours before a party just so I would have something safe to talk about. I mean, when it was finally my time to talk."

Ridge licks beer from his lips. "Well, that certainly sounds ominous."

I can't believe I'm always sticking my foot in my mouth.

No wonder Edward kept me on such a tight leash.

Holt's deep blue eyes search my face. "I know. She's said stuff like that to me too. I fully plan on getting to the bottom of it, but I don't think I'll have to dig too hard. Her ex-husband is a real asshole." He nods to Ella. "An asshole you know, as a matter of fact."

Her eyes widen. "Who?" she asks me.

I take a deep breath. "I was married to Edward Ezzell."

Her chin lifts in the air. "As in, Charles Ezzell's son? Of Plott, Ezzell, and Crispin, Attorneys at Law?"

I nod, swallowing the bowling ball-size lump in my throat. "How do you know him?"

"I actually went to school with Edward when he attended North and Camden Academy. He was a few years ahead of me. Something happened when he was a freshman, though. I don't know the whole story, but he transferred to some boarding school in New England.

I've seen him at a few business functions over the years, but I never sought him out for small talk." Her beautiful face contorts into an emotionless statue. "But that's not what Holt is talking about."

Crutch wraps an arm around her waist, binding their bodies together. She exhales, like what she's about to say is painful. "Hudson Plott is my ex-husband."

Oh hell, yes, being married to him would definitely be painful.

I can't believe Ella was married to someone besides Crutch. I've only known them for two minutes. Literally. And I can't picture them with anyone but each other.

"Holy crap. Seriously?" I ask, completely dumbfounded.

Despite the seriousness of the conversation, my face must look pretty funny because Ridge immediately snickers. He tries to cover it with a fake cough, but fails. He holds up a hand in his defense, apologizing. "I'm sorry, I... It's just... your face..." His voice trails off, unsure how to finish.

Fortunately, Ella starts giggling too. As soon as she relaxes, Crutch loosens up and smiles.

She clears her throat. "Let's just say I was young and stupid."

I snort. "Must be a prerequisite for marrying an attorney in that firm."

Everyone bursts out laughing at that revelation, including Holt.

Even though I was being completely serious, I laugh, nonetheless.

Once we settle down and Ridge wanders away to check on Cullen at the grill, I nod to Ella's stomach. "Congratulations."

Her hand protectively rubs her baby bump. "Thank you, Merit."

"Your first?"

All of sudden, it feels like the oxygen is sucked out of my lungs. The world around us falls silent.

Something's wrong with the question I asked.

I can feel it.

We all can feel it.

I'm startled when Holt's fingers scratch against my thigh, searching for my hand.

Shit. I've really said something wrong this time.

I'm so embarrassed; it feels like my blood is on fire. Like steam is pumping through my body—not liquid. Needing Holt's touch to calm myself, I sigh in relief when his hand wraps around mine. He immediately circles his thumb against the soft skin of my wrist.

He doesn't jump in and say anything, though. Watching Ella and Crutch, he patiently waits to see what they'll do.

The silence is killing me.

I'm completely sucking at making a good first impression.

Ella's staring at her stomach, like she's trying to see past her own skin, to the baby growing inside of her. Crutch steps behind her and wraps her in his firm embrace. His hands splay across hers, and together they hold their unborn child.

His words chill my soul, making the heat of my embarrassment feel like an iceberg. "This is our second child. Our daughter passed away a few hours after she was born."

My heart shatters. "Oh, Ella. Crutch. I'm so sorry for your loss. That's devastating."

"Thank you, Merit," she says simply with a small smile. And I'm touched that the soft turn of her mouth is genuine. Not fake.

Holt nudges me. "C'mon, Mer. We'll give them a minute."

I don't mean to ignore him. But I do.

My whisper is raspy. "My baby brother died."

Ella blinks and swallows. "What?"

A tear races down my cheek, making the back of my throat tickle. I wipe it away. "I know it's not the same as losing a child. But I saw what my parents went through, and I just want you to know that I really am sorry for your loss. I'm not just trying to be nice."

Holt's hand leaves mine, but it doesn't go far. It slides up the curve of my spine and lands on my neck. Pulling me closer to him, he bends down and kisses my temple. He murmurs my name.

A murmur of sweet, unspoken adoration.

"He was two months old. Exactly two months, to the very night. He was fine when my parents put him down." I wipe another tear. "The doctors weren't sure what happened. They just called it SIDS."

I grab Holt's waist, holding him tightly.

I just... need him. There's no simpler way to explain it.

So much for not wanting my body pressed against his in front of his family.

This entire conversation has stirred up memories from long ago, memories that I'd shuttered while married to Edward.

"His name was Daire."

Ella looks like she's about to cry, but she doesn't. Her bravery is damn impressive. "Our daughter's name was Reality."

I'm about to open my mouth to comment on the beautiful and unusual name when we're interrupted by the excited screams of children. Two little girls in swimsuits round the opposite corner of the house, through a gate in the wrought iron fence. I recognize Anna right away. I assume the other girl must be Laura. A teenage boy lags behind them, dragging two large pool floats, each shaped like a unicorn.

The girls race up to us, and Anna immediately tucks herself against Holt's free side. I step away giving them a little space. "Uncle Holt!" She points at the unicorns. "Thank you so much for the floats. Don't they look beautiful?"

Holt squints his eyes and pretends to study the creatures really hard. "Well, now that you mention it, I don't reckon I've ever seen an ugly unicorn."

Ella lovingly strokes the hair of the other little girl. "Are you sure you wanna swim before supper? I thought you said you were hungry?" she asks her.

"I *was* hungry. *Until* I saw the float," she answers. "Just thirty minutes, and then we'll take a break to eat. Is that okay, Aunt Lulu?"

That's cute. *Lulu.* Must be a nickname.

Ella pretends to think about it, even though we all know the answer is yes. "Okay. Deal."

"I was about to send the search party after you guys. What took so long?" Crutch asks.

She looks up at Crutch and pushes a small pair of glasses up on the bridge of her nose. "Well, Uncle Ry, that's Nate's fault. It would've gone quicker if he let me help. But he wanted to do it all by himself." She cocks a hand on her hip, staring at the boy in accusation.

The boy sighs in frustration and blows a strand of hair out of his eyes. "She kept pulling the hose out of the air pump. It nearly hit her in the head three times."

Crutch just laughs and tips his chin at the boy. "Thanks for looking out for her, Nate."

Holt uses the opportunity to introduce me. "Merit, this is Nate Marcum. He's Patrick and Nancy's grandson."

Nate politely nods and excuses himself to dispose of the unicorns in the swimming pool. Anna chases after him, but not before giving me a quick hug.

Holt reaches for Laura's shoulder. "And this is—"

Laura abruptly cuts him off, loudly clearing her throat. He throws his hands in the air. "Sorry. Sorry."

Her back straightens, and she walks forward, perfectly mimicking Ella's good posture. She sticks her little hand in the air. "Hello, my name is Laura Margaret Crutchfield. Pleasure to meet you, ma'am."

Being around kids every day, I'm quick on my feet. There isn't much they do that shocks me. I even had one little boy drop his training pants and take a poop right in the middle of the store.

I gave Kyra hazard pay that day.

I squat down on one knee and shake her hand. "My name is Merit Eliza Browning. And the pleasure is all mine."

She leans closer, studying my face. Like she's judging everything about me in this first ten seconds. Her scrutiny makes me vulnerable. It leaves me feeling naked. Eventually, she steps away.

Holt's gaze darts between the two of us. "Well?" he asks her.

She smiles brightly and nods. Holt laughs and gives her a high five. Spinning around, she hands her glasses to Crutch and then runs away, full speed, diving into the swimming pool.

Holt helps me stand back up. "Well, that was…intense," I say, honestly.

Holt grins. "You passed the test. She took it pretty easy on you. Just wait until she meets one of Ridge's dates. She's made some of them cry before." Holt points at Crutch. "I swear you're training her in the art of interrogation."

"Hey, man, that's all her."

My mouth falls open. "She's made grown women cry before? Seriously?"

"They're being a little dramatic. I've never seen tears." Ella wobbles her head back and forth. "Maybe sniffles," she jokes.

"Why is she so hard on Ridge's dates?"

Holt smiles and tucks a hair behind my ear. My skin tingles in his wake. "Because she has a crush on Ridge."

I bite my lip, trying not to giggle or blush in giddiness. "Really?"

Crutch growls. "Yeah, it makes me pretty damn furious to know she's already boy-crazy. And she'll be only eight in a couple of weeks. I'm gonna fucking lose my mind when she turns sixteen."

Ella wraps a hand around her husband's arm and kisses his neck. "She not boy-crazy. She has two crushes. That's completely normal."

"Two?" I ask.

Holt snorts and nods to the corner of the pool. "Nate."

I raise my eyebrows. "Aghhh. Gotcha."

Right then, Raylee and Will walk out of the house. Ty's squirming around in Raylee's arms. "C'mon! Food's ready!"

Ella and Crutch urge us to go ahead and fix our plates while they stay outside with the kids. We're walking back up to the house, hand in hand, when I pull away and fold my arms across my chest. My eyes narrow into small slits.

Holt furrows his brow. "What?"

"You said I passed the test. How many other women have passed the test?"

He rolls his eyes. "I told you I don't bring women home."

"Uhh. Bunny?"

He chokes on a laugh. "Okay; well, she did meet Bunny."

"And?"

"Let's just say Laura is a very good judge of character." His arms wrap around me. His fingers find the hem of my shirt, and he traces a line across the sensitive skin of the small of my back. "Now, c'mon. I'm starving."

Me too.

Just not for food.

Chapter 13

Holt

"So, tell me about your store, Merit." Nancy leans forward in her seat. "I wish there had been a children's shoe store in town when Nate was little. It was a pain trying to find church shoes for him."

Merit lights up like a Christmas tree. Her hazel eyes sparkle underneath the lights of the patio. I love watching her talk about the store. I guess it's like me and football.

"What's the name of it?" Jeff asks. "Jump something?"

"Run and Jump and Twirl."

My mom shifts a sleeping Ty on her lap. "That's so unusual. How'd you come up with it?"

"My grandma. When I was growing up, there was a children's store a couple of towns away, and my granny was always the one who took me shopping for new shoes. Every time I would try them on, she'd say, 'Now, run and jump and twirl. Make sure they fit.' It always stuck with me."

My dad smiles. "That's such a nice sentiment. Is your grandmother still with us?"

Merit softly clears her throat. "She is. My grandfather passed away when I was in high school, but Granny is still in very good health. She lives with my parents."

Cullen opens a fresh beer. "They must be very proud."

Merit turns bashful, looking down and politely folding her hands in her lap. I can't help myself. I reach across, grab her hand, and bring it to my mouth, planting a gentle kiss on her skin. When I return her hand to her lap, I use the situation to my advantage. I plant my palm on her upper thigh, tethering myself to her. It doesn't go unnoticed by me that she stops breathing. It also doesn't go unnoticed by me that her eyes dart around the table to see who's watching us.

And when she sees that everyone is watching us?

Well, she squeaks underneath her breath like a baby bird and tries to discreetly wriggle from my grasp.

She doesn't have any luck.

Why? Because I don't have any plans of letting her go.

Observing our interaction, Crutch chuckles and pushes away from the table. "I'll go check on the kids."

After they swam and ate, Nate started a movie for them in the theater room. He was supposed to come back out and join us, but if I had to guess, Laura guilt-tripped him into watching it with them.

Ella stands up and reaches for him. He's not looking in her direction, but he immediately senses her and turns back to his wife. She whispers in his ear, and he nods. "I'll go with him. We'll be right back."

After about ten minutes, they all come out of the house, kids included. Anna rushes over, worms her way between me and Merit, and hops up on my lap. I kiss the top of her head. For some strange reason, I love it when she smells like chlorine. "We had to stop the movie. Smelly Ellie has something to tell us."

"She does?" I ask, looking over at my cousin.

"Well, we actually have something to give Laura. And we wanted you all to be a part of it."

Crutch sits back down and pulls Laura onto his lap as Ella places a small box in front of her. It's decorated in shiny silver wrapping paper.

Anna bounces. "Ohhhh, a present. Open it!"

Laura studies the box. "There's still a couple of weeks before my birthday."

Crutch laughs. "It's a present, Little Girl. It doesn't have to be your birthday or Christmas for us to give you a gift."

Laura's not like most kids. She thinks. A lot. And we can clearly see she's thinking the entire time she unwraps her gift. Eventually, she pulls a silver bracelet from the box and gasps. "It's beautiful."

Ella leans over Crutch's shoulder and spins the bracelet for Laura. "It's a charm bracelet. You put little charms on it that remind you of special things. Or people or events. That way, you can always remember them. The older you get, the more charms you add."

Anna leans forward, blocking everyone's view with her head. "What are your charms?" she asks. I tug on her waistband, forcing her to sit back down.

Laura meticulously and methodically works her way through the bracelet. "This one is shaped like a baby. It has my name on it. *Laura Margaret Crutchfield.* And this one's a book." She smiles kindly. "Because I love to read." She waits for us to nod and say how beautiful it is. "And this one's a seashell."

Crutch kisses her head. "To remember your first vacation to the beach."

Anna basically screams in my ear. "Hey, that was with me! I was with you. Yay!"

"And this one is shaped like two hearts together. One inside the other."

Ella points at it. "Your Mom picked that one. She said it's always supposed to remind you of how much she loves you."

When she gets to the last charm, Laura pushes her glasses up on her nose. She searches the table, making sure everyone's eyes are on hers. When she sees Nate on his phone, she not so subtly clears her throat. He rolls his eyes but quickly puts his phone away. It makes Ridge chuckle. "Smart man," he says.

"And this one is a baby too." She looks up at Crutch.

"Why don't you check the other side," he suggests.

She puts the charm so close to her face it nearly scratches her glasses. "Harlan Michael Crutchfield." She gasps, just a half second before all the other women do.

Well, everyone but Merit. And that's just because she has no idea what the hell is going on.

"It's a boy!" Laura squeals. "You found out it's a boy?"

Ella wipes her eye before a tear can escape. "Yes, this morning. I had the jeweler add the script as a rush."

Everyone showers them with congratulations, including Merit. And the smile on her face tells me her words are sincere. Sincere and heartfelt. *That* smile is definitely not her fake smile.

"What a wonderful name, strong and perfectly unique," she says.

Crutch smiles. "Thanks." He steals a glance at Ella. "It's a family name."

We're all excitedly talking about the baby when Merit's phone vibrates with an incoming call. She checks the caller ID, silences it, and turns it face down on the table. It happens two more times. Eventually, she sighs and whispers an apology to me before excusing herself. She's gone just long enough to pique my curiosity, and I'm about to go in search of her when she walks back to the patio table and sits down next to me.

I lift an eyebrow. "Everything okay?"

She leans close, trying not to garner everyone's attention, but that's hard to do because there's a slight lull in the conversation now that the kids have gone back inside and Raylee is trying to explain the different bottle types to Ella via a very complicated article on the Internet.

"I'm so sorry. It was one of my delivery guys. There was a mix-up with his route, and he needs to drop-off my order at seven tomorrow morning instead of eleven."

Dana leans forward in her seat, not even pretending she didn't hear what Merit said. "From what Raylee and Teresa tell me, you're always at your store, Merit. You must work some crazy hours."

I watch Merit's face turn a sexy little shade of pink. "But I love it."

I lean back in my chair and fold my arms behind my head. Merit's eyes widen in hunger. I bite back my smile, doing my best to ignore her gaze. Because if I don't? I might just toss her across this patio table and have my way with her.

In front of my parents.

And that's just fucking gross.

"What she needs is more help. She needs to hire another part-time worker," I add.

And now... Merit's fiery little attitude is back.

I love it.

"Well, as I've explained to Holt, I'm trying to pay off a business debt, so every penny I save is a penny less I owe."

"That's certainly admirable," says Jeff. "But take it from one small business owner to another, you have to be careful of burnout. You work too many hours and think you have to do it all yourself? You may very well turn your dream into a nightmare."

Will nods. "Exactly. Having Cullen come in as my partner at the bar? Best decision I ever made."

Needing to feel the heat of her body, I reach over and run my hand across the smooth skin of her thigh, leaving chill bumps in my wake. "See? That makes perfect sense."

She watches intently as my fingers squeeze her supple skin. Her head lifts, and her kaleidoscope eyes bore into me. "Perhaps your concern is more self-serving?" she questions me, her comment laced with seriousness and a slight edge of anger.

I answer truthfully. "No, not *more* self-serving. I'm *equally* self-serving. I want more time with you, yes. But I do worry about burn-out. And you being in the shop alone at night."

"I'm safe."

"Until you're not."

She doesn't answer, but she does furrow her brow. She's absorbing the information, really thinking about it. And that's all I can ask for at this point.

After a few moments, she snorts in disgusted resignation and sits back, shifting her leg in just the right way so my hand falls away. It takes only a split second for her to remember that we're not alone. And it takes only two split seconds for her to cringe in embarrassment.

My whole family is sitting on the edge of their seats watching us, inhaling every last detail of our conversation, like they're starved for air. Merit is mortified. Of course, I think it's damn funny. Well, funny except for the part where she moved my hand away from her.

Ever the hero, Ridge comes to her rescue. "Well, speaking of early mornings, I have to report for shift at seven a.m. myself, so it's about time for me to call it a night."

Everyone else nods and begins to clear the table.

Merit snatches my wrist and pulls me close. "Oh no," she whispers, "are they all leaving because of me?"

"Probably," I say with a playful wink and stand up to carry some of the leftover plates into the kitchen.

It's an hour before everything is cleaned up with everyone headed home, and now we're in my truck making our way back to Merit's condo. I catch her reflection in the darkened passenger window, and a soft smile curls on her lips. She's thinking about something happy.

She looks content.

But that doesn't mean I'm letting her off the hook.

I turn off the radio. "You got mad at me."

Her smile quickly morphs into a frown. "No, I didn't."

That's almost damn comical. "Mer? Seriously? You realize I can still see your face, right?"

She turns in her seat, ready to accuse me of lying, when I nod to the window. Realization dawns that I was looking at her reflection. She snorts and rolls her eyes, laughing at herself.

"So, care to answer that question again?"

"Yes, I did get mad at you. But it was just for a second. I can't believe I did that in front of your parents, in front of everybody. It was so embarrassing." Closing her eyes, she leans her head back against the seat. Her strands of brown, red, and black fan across the leather.

And I can't help but think how fucking great it would look fanned across the pillow of my king-size bed.

She mumbles under her breath. "Now I understand why he said it was easier when I just kept my mouth shut."

My ears perk up, and the hairs on the back of my neck stand straight. "Excuse me? When *who* said *what*?"

She nonchalantly shoos me with her hand. "Oh, it's nothing. I didn't mean anything by it."

My eyes scan the road, looking for the nearest place to pull over. When I throw the truck into park, she opens one eye and looks around. "Why'd you pull over?" Sitting up, she squints, looking at the building in front of us. She points to the darkened medical clinic. "Are you sick? The doc-in-a-box is already closed." She furrows her brow, studying me like she has X-ray vision. "What's wrong? Do I need to take you to the emergency room?"

I toss my ballcap onto the back seat and drag my hands through my hair. "Yep. There's something wrong with me."

Her eyes widen like saucers. "There is?" She blinks. "What's hurting?"

"My heart."

Her face pales. "Oh my god! Are you having a heart attack?"

She's so damn funny.

I can't help but laugh. "I'm not having a damn heart attack. I'm in agony because there's too much you aren't telling me. Those little comments of yours make me crazy. And I'm not driving another inch until you talk to me. Until you tell me what happened with Edward. What he did to you."

Her excitement level drops like a lead anchor. "It's just your imagination running away from you. I promise you're making it out to be way more dramatic than it is." She grunts, "I mean, than it *was*."

I unbuckle my seat belt and get comfy. "Why don't you let me be the judge of that."

She looks around, stalling for time, and spots a no parking sign on the side of the building. "You can't just park here. It's private property. We'll get in trouble."

She smiles triumphantly, like she's actually won this battle.

Isn't that cute.

Scrolling through the numbers on my phone, I find just the right one. He answers on the second ring.

"Hello?"

"Hey, Steve. It's Holt Hill."

"Coach! Good to hear from you." He rustles around on the other side. "It's a little late. Everything okay?"

"Yeah, everything's good. I'm sorry for calling so late. I'm actually pulled over in your parking lot right now. I know you probably have security cameras, so I just wanted to let you know so you wouldn't worry if you saw a truck parked out front."

"Something wrong with it? You need a jump? I've got cables."

"No, my truck is running fine. I just needed a quiet place to talk to my girl."

The good doctor pauses, trying to digest the information. "Oh. Okay." He takes a deep breath. "Well, we'll see you on Friday night. Jake is really looking forward to the first game."

"We all are. Thanks, Steve. And again, sorry for the late hour."

By the time I hang up, Merit's scowling at me. "So, I assume you know the owner of this fine establishment?"

"Yep. The doctor actually volunteers as our team athletic trainer. His son, Jake, is a junior. He's our punter."

"Oh," she pouts.

I clear my throat, not giving her any leeway. I think I've made it more than clear that I've won this round.

Moving at a sloth's pace, she unbuckles her own seat belt and leans back against the door, mimicking me. "Fine. What do you wanna know?"

"That's a bullshit question. I wanna know everything."

She folds her hands in her lap and circles her thumbs around and around. I'm on the verge of chastising her when she interrupts my thoughts. "He was my first boyfriend," she says with a simple shrug. Her head cocks to the side in thought. "Well, I guess he's been my only boyfriend."

Burning cold anger swirls deep in my stomach.

If she thinks I'm not her boyfriend, she's wrong.

Fucking dead wrong.

"I went to a small private school. Our county is pretty rural, and the public schools aren't the best. My graduating class only had forty-eight. It was all the same kids I've known since kindergarten. The boys were more like my brothers. Dating one of them never even crossed my mind. It never crossed theirs, either. I mean, we didn't even have a senior prom because it would've been just too weird. Instead, we had a big party at someone's house."

She shakes her hands, freeing them of their captivity and smiles softly. "Everything was so different when I came here for college. I mean, there were people everywhere. My American Civ class had more people in it than my entire high school. Everything was...big and overwhelming.

"I met Edward on my second day in college. I was in the campus bookstore. My arms were loaded down, and I couldn't see what was below my feet. I tripped on a box. Books went flying everywhere, and I nearly busted my face on a metal shelf. But...he caught me. He asked me out, right then and there. My second day of college and someone had *finally* asked me out on a real date." She purses her lips. "So, I said yes."

I hate that she met him. I hate that she said yes.

I hate that he was her first date, her first boyfriend.

If only she had gone to a different university...

Then, it could've been me. It could've been us falling over each other in the bookstore. It could've been us all these years. I could've had an actual healthy relationship, instead of the useless, mindless shit I had.

The shit that made me skeptical of ever finding love. Love like my parents. Love like my sister. Love like my cousin.

Love like the one I now feel.

Fuck me... yeah, it's there. My love for her is like a living organism, growing and thriving and multiplying every single day. In my blood, in my bone marrow. With every passing minute, Merit is feeding off my soul, replenishing my cells with more of *her*.

In high school and college, girls wanted the conquest of bedding the star quarterback. And once the NFL came calling, girls wanted the conquest of bedding the star quarterback who had a fat bank account. A bank account with more zeroes in it than the majority of the world will ever see. Hence, the lies that have been poured like molasses across my feet by other women, making it so heavy and sticky I can barely walk sometimes.

But Merit's different. Isn't she?

When I don't immediately join the conversation, she lifts her eyebrows, silently asking me if I want more.

I'm not necessarily looking forward to hearing about her life with her peckerhead ex, but I need to know.

To *know* her, I need to know *what* happened to her.

What turned the goofy, happy girl with two broken arms into the woman who fake smiles and orders side salads?

I nod.

The corner of her mouth tilts up. "I was so excited. He was handsome and nice. And so mature. I mean, there I was, fresh from high school, and he was starting his second year of law school. I was completely shocked when he asked me out." She softly chuckles. "We had our first date that night. From then on, we were together."

"You never dated anyone else? I mean, y'all were exclusive?" I ask.

She snorts. "Well, *I* was exclusive. But now, I wonder if *he* was exclusive with me? I mean, looking back now, I wonder if he cheated on me back in college." She sadly shakes her head. "I guess there's no way to really know."

"So, you're saying he was a mega asshole back then too. It's not just a recent development."

She gifts me with a smile. "You could say that. An asshole gene embedded in his DNA, maybe?" She laughs at her own joke and accidentally hits her head against the truck window. "Ow," she mumbles and rubs the back of her head. "Anyway, we got married the summer before my senior year." She looks out the windshield, emotionally distancing herself from the next comment. "I caught him having an affair two years ago. I walked in on them. In our bedroom. We immediately separated and finalized the divorce about a year and a half ago."

Well, that's certainly a condensed version of events. "That doesn't answer my question. What did he *do* to you?"

"I told you, he didn't do anything."

"Don't lie, Merit."

"Mmmm?"

"He might not have done something physical to you, but he sure as hell did something to your spirit, and more than just criticizing your bowling game. It's written all over your face."

She turns and stares out the windshield again.

"Tell me the truth."

She looks down at her hands. She slowly lifts them, studying her fingers for a moment. Scoffing, she shakes them out and slides them underneath her thighs. "It happened slowly. I didn't even realize it was happening. It was just small stuff, you know? I mean, he was my first boyfriend. I thought maybe all relationships were that way. Well, I mean, I knew my parents and grandparents were different, but I thought maybe you only reach their level of love and fun and comfort once you had been together for a really long time." She swallows. "I guess that sounds silly, huh?"

It doesn't sound silly. It sounds damn heartbreaking. "What started small? Tell me."

"Suggestions. That's the best way to describe it. Little suggestions here and there. *'Why don't we go here to eat instead? Why don't we do this instead of that? Let's hang out with so-and-so to-night instead of your new friends.'* Before I knew it, he was politely telling me which classes to take. What to wear. Who to talk to. It got worse when we married and he passed the bar. He immediately started to work at the firm, and I had to be the perfect little wife to match with his perfect new career."

My fist is clenched so tightly my muscles twitch. I drag my hand across my chin, scratching my facial hair and trying to loosen the tension coursing through my body. I give her an encouraging nod, not wanting to break her train of thought.

"My hands, for example. He said I move them too much when I talk. I accidentally knocked a drink out of his hand one time when we were at a bar in college. That's when he told me to start folding my hands in front of me. He said it made me look refined."

She shifts in her seat. "Black dresses. I always had to wear black dresses. I've always loved bright colors, but Edward said that wearing yellow to a business dinner made me look flippant. It always had to be those sexy, little black dresses. He said they made me look sophisticated. But some of them made me uncomfortable."

Her eyes flare with anger, just thinking back on the past. "And every year, we had to go on vacation to the beach with some of his friends and their wives. Of course, he wanted me to look like all the other *perfect* women there. I had to wear a skimpy bikini with full hair and makeup. And jewelry! I had to wear full jewelry—to the beach; can you imagine? Let me tell you...it sucks to have a gold and diamond necklace stuck to your neck fat with sweat and sand."

I nearly laugh.

Nearly.

"He didn't want me to talk unless someone spoke to me. He said my accent made me sound like a country bumpkin. He didn't want me to drink beer. He said it was uncouth for a woman. So, I had to drink wine. I freakin' hate wine. It all tastes like it needs a cup full of sugar poured into it. Anytime we went out for dinner, I couldn't order a big steak. All the other women in his life ordered salads and grilled fish. Well, grilled fish stinks! So, that only left salad. I couldn't even clean my own house or mow my own yard. He always hired people to do it because manual labor was beneath me," she says with air quotes. "I guess he forgot I spent my whole childhood playing in dirt and sod."

She leans forward, scooting closer to me. "I never even had a chance to make real friends in college. We always had to hang out with his friends. I lost touch with all of my high school friends because he didn't want me to talk on the phone. He said *he* wanted to be my best friend."

Her lip trembles just a small fraction before she steels it. "He always made excuses for why he couldn't go with me to visit my family." She takes a defeated breath. "And he had a rule about children. We couldn't even start trying to have a baby until I was thirty-four and he was forty. He was terrified that pregnancy would ruin my body. He said he needed to reach his sexual peak before I got all..." her voice trails off to a whisper, "fat and stretched out."

That lowlife piece of shit.

I'm irate.

I'm blinded by rage.

Shaking her head of bad thoughts, she leans her elbows on the console of my truck, propping her chin in her hands. "You know what else? After the first year of dating, we didn't even watch TV in the same room." She tries to smile. "He couldn't stand old movies."

I study her face and the myriad of emotions hidden behind her curtain. And I read each one of them like a book. Pain, sadness, anger, annoyance. They're all there, making Merit even more beautiful.

She blinks, waiting on me to say something.

I take a deep breath. "So, he tried to change you?"

"No. He tried to break me."

Chapter 14

Merit

I stare at the phone. "You're kidding, right?"

"Do I sound like I'm kidding?"

No.

No, he does not.

I pick up my cell and turn the speaker off. "But that would be weird, right?"

"Why would it be weird?"

I feel like the reasons should be obvious. "Well, for one, I don't have a kid playing."

His laugh is low, and it vibrates seductively through the phone line. "Well, once again, I'm definitely glad to know you don't have a secret child. Mer, you're overthinking this way too much. It's a community event. People come from all over."

"But I haven't been to a high school football game since...well, since high school."

"All the more reason to come."

I won't know anyone there. I'll be sitting in the middle of a bunch of teenagers. A colonoscopy sounds more appealing right now.

Just like always, he reads my mind. It doesn't matter that he can't see my face, he still does it. It's unnerving.

And wonderful.

"You won't be alone. Everyone always comes. Unless they have to work, I mean."

"Everyone?" I ask.

"Well, Will and Cullen are usually at the bar, but Raylee and Ella bring the kids. My parents come. Ridge and Crutch come if they aren't on duty. And everybody else." There's a noise on the other end of the line that sounds like metal on metal, like he's working out on a weight machine. "You'll have plenty of people to sit with. And it'll be more packed than normal since it's the first game of the season."

"You really want me there?"

He pants into the phone, slightly out of breath. Before he can answer, I interrupt him. "What are you doing?"

"Working out."

"But I thought you met your players at the school for a workout this morning?"

"I did. We meet at six-thirty, four days a week all school year for an hour-long session. It's not required, but most of the kids show up. I always tell them I'll be there working out and they're more than welcome to join."

I grab another sweater from the large cardboard box in front of me and fold it. "And then you had actual football practice this afternoon?"

I hear him swallow a drink. "You know I did."

"And now, you're working out again?" I close my eyes. My mouth waters just picturing him shirtless and covered in sweat.

"Well, maybe I wouldn't have so much energy to burn if a certain someone let me hang out with her tonight. Correct me if I'm wrong, but wasn't that you shooing me out of your store just two hours ago?"

I did shoo him away.

And it was one of the hardest things I've ever had to do. He was flushed and sweaty and sexy. He even had a piece of grass sticking out of his tousled blond hair.

What I really wanted to do was lie flat on my back with my legs spread open wide and let him have his sweaty way with me.

But alas, that would've been completely counterproductive to my resolve to protect my heart and take things slow.

Painfully slow.

Because I don't think my heart could take another beating. And the sad truth is, I don't even think my heart was that devasted by Edward.

It was mainly my brain. And my pride.

I snort. "Well, maybe I wouldn't have had to shoo you away if you weren't so distracting. You've seriously thrown a kink into my work ethic lately, and now I'm having to play catch-up."

"Well, maybe you wouldn't have to play catch-up if you hired another part-time worker."

I roll my eyes. Truth is, I've been thinking about it. Well, I was thinking about it even before Holt came into the picture. It's true I want to pay off the loan to my ex-father-in-law as quickly as humanly possible, but when I crunch the numbers, it looks like I can add another body for just fifteen or twenty hours a week and it will only add twelve more months to my payout. That's assuming business stays good and I can keep sending in extra on the payment. Really, in the long run, an extra year isn't all that bad if it means I can finally start having a little bit of a personal life.

Now that there's a reason to have a personal life, that is.

"About that...I've been thinking that maybe, just *maybe*, I could start looking for a part-time associate."

When he doesn't say anything, I pull the phone away from my face to make sure we didn't get disconnected. "Holt? Did I lose you?"

His mocking voice shatters my eardrum the second I put the phone back to my ear. "I can't believe I won that battle."

I fight back my smile, refusing to give him the satisfaction. "I said *maybe*. That doesn't necessarily mean I've waved the white flag."

His chuckle rumbles like thunder, making my body tingle. "Don't lie, Merit."

I've seriously underestimated high school football.

Well, to be fair, I'm sure it has something to do with the fact that the coach is a former Heisman winner. A guy who's made three Super Bowl appearances. A former quarterback who's actually won two of those appearances.

Hell, he's been on the cover of a cereal box.

Plus, everyone's saying he's going to lead this team to a state title this year.

Regardless of the reason, there's more people here than all of my high school football games put together. All four years. Granted, my school was small, and the coaches had to scrape the bottom of the barrel to even get enough boys for the team... but still...

This is madness.

It's halftime and I'm standing in line at the concession stand, quietly minding my own business and people-watching. Raylee just went to the restroom, and Ridge walked over to the paramedics on duty to say hello. Everyone else is watching the band's halftime show and visiting with friends.

Strangely enough, it's been a great night. My nerves were on a violent rampage, shredding my stomach into knots when I walked to the front gate. Tickets for the game were already sold out, but Holt said he left my name with the front workers. Sure enough, he did. I only walked a few steps when Crutch waved me over. He was talking to some of the officers working the event and pointed me in the direction of everyone else. Of course, they were sitting at the fifty-yard line.

Prime seats. Front and center.

The royal family of football on display.

The line moves up, and I pull some dollar bills from my pocket, counting out the money for a bottle of water and a candy bar. A screech of excitement from somewhere behind me catches my attention.

"Aghh! Callie! It's so good to see you." I watch two girls wrap their arms around one other. They both look to be in their early twenties. One has brown hair and the other strawberry-blonde. They're both wearing booty shorts and cropped tops.

The late summer mosquitoes must be in heaven.

"It's great to see you. I didn't think your little brother was playing this year," the blonde says.

The brunette waves her hand in the air. "Oh, he's not. He graduated last year. I brought some friends so we could get our daily dose of eye candy." She laughs, "You know what I mean."

"Hell, yeah, I do. I could not care less that my brother is out on that field. I only have eyes for the coach."

The brunette sighs, "No shit. I brought my college friends with me tonight. No one believed me when I said he looks even better in person. I read that he hangs out at a bar downtown. I think we're gonna go there tonight and scope it out. You should come with us."

"I do love a challenge," the blonde says with a wink.

"The hot-millionaire-husband challenge," the other girl says with a laugh.

I'm so engrossed with their putrid conversation that I jump a mile when Raylee touches my arm. "Are you okay?"

I blink, trying to focus my wandering attention on her and Ridge. "Yeah, why?"

She sniffs the air. "Does something smell bad?"

I shake my head. "No, why?"

"Well, you're making a funny face. Like you smell something."

Ridge looks around, taking inventory of the crowd. It only takes a nano-second for his gaze to land on the two partially dressed trollops a few people behind me. They must say something because Ridge snickers before turning back to us. He bumps Raylee's shoulder. "She does that."

"Does what?"

"Makes that face when women hit on Holt."

"What!" My scream is way louder than I mean for it to be. The guy in front of me turns around and waves his cell phone in my face, warning me to be quiet because he's on a call.

It's a freakin' football stadium, dude.

Take the call in the bathroom like a normal person.

"Really?" she asks Ridge.

He smiles wickedly. "Yep. He told me."

Frowning, I fold my arms across my chest. "Well, he doesn't know what he's talking about."

Raylee completely ignores me and scans the sea of faces around us. "Who's hitting on him?" Ridge nods his head in the direction of the two girls. "Ahhhh…" Raylee doesn't even have the decency to hide her laugh.

"Hey!" Taking a play from cell-phone guy, I waft my dollar bills under Ridge's nose to get his attention. "I don't make a face."

"Holt thinks it's cute," he says with a knowing smirk.

Fiery heat scorches my face in embarrassment. I immediately look at the ground, trying to find the right words. "Well… that's completely beside the point," I mumble in a strained whisper.

Raylee wraps her arms around me, her voice tinkles in my ear like fairy dust. "It's completely the point. Don't you see that, Merit?" She bumps me with her hip. "Besides, you totally make a face. I really thought someone farted."

I can't hold it in anymore. My laughter shoots out of me like a rocket, immediately making me snort.

It's my turn at the order window, but Ridge nudges us out of the way. "Here, let me. Call it my amends." He orders a variety of snacks, and we help him carry everything to our seats.

The second half passes, ending in an easy win for Holt's team.

I'm not exactly sure what happens now. I just tuck myself behind everyone as we make our way out of the stadium. It takes a while, though, because everyone is stopping Holt's family to offer congratulations. At the front gate, they all turn, walking down a gravel path that leads to a big building. I'm not sure where it goes, or if I'm even allowed to go with them. Out of the humongous crowd, only Holt's family and a small spattering of others are headed that way. The majority of the people are migrating back to the parking lot.

My car is there.

I guess that's where I'm supposed to go.

Maybe Holt's family has special parking somewhere else or something.

I open my mouth to tell them goodbye when a little hand tugs against mine. "C'mon! We get to wait for Uncle Holt outside of the field house," Anna says.

"Me too?"

Did I really just ask a seven-year-old that?

I'm so damn pathetic.

Teresa turns around and smiles, waiting on me to catch up. "Of course, you too. He'll want to see you."

My heart blossoms at the thought, but I'm quick to squash that feeling. Or, at least I try.

But based on the shit-eating grin plastered across my face, I don't think I'm very successful.

A couple of beefy security guards are posted around the building. They nod here and there as people walk past. One guy eyes me suspiciously and opens his mouth to say something when Ray cuts him off. "It's okay. She's with us."

His suspicion fades, and he gives me a polite nod instead.

Ella walks beside me, her hand protectively spread across her stomach. "There's a list," she says. "Only certain people are allowed to wait by the field house. You have to be a family member of a player or a coach."

"They don't let the other students come out here?"

She shakes her head. "That stopped after the second game last season. Too many people saw it as an easy way to get next to Holt. Reporters. Fans." She gives me a soft smile. "Women."

I bite my tongue to keep from growling.

I should probably buy the security guards a fruit basket. Entice them to keep up the good work.

My eyes dart to the side where a woman with auburn-colored hair and glasses snaps pictures of me and Ella. I watch as Ella's spine stiffens. "One reporter still gets access, though. And I use that term loosely."

I wipe under my nose to make sure I don't have anything on my face. "Why is she taking our picture?" I ask out of the corner of my mouth. I have no idea why I'm pretending to be a ventriloquist, but it's definitely unusual to have a stranger take your picture.

I always hated it when people did that at the events I had to attend with Edward.

"Because she's a paparazzi."

My eyebrows lift into my hairline. "Excuse me?"

Ella nods, a frown on her face.

"Paparazzi? Here? In Alabama?"

"She's one of the few who covers the South. She's stationed out of Atlanta. She comes over a couple of times a month to keep tabs on Holt. Sells his picture, makes a little cash."

Her voice holds a dislike, which piques my curiosity. "I thought you worked with reporters and TV people all the time? Holt told me you do reports and interviews for all those true crime documentaries on TV."

"I do. And I'm very selective on who I work with. My colleagues are true professionals, real investigators. She," Ella says with a pickled tartness, "sells an image to the highest tabloid bidder and doesn't care what they write in the end. Truth, lies. It makes no difference to her as long as she gets paid. Don't get me wrong, there are some good ones out there. Chloe just isn't one of them." Ella cocks her head and stares at the woman. "Maybe that'll change one day."

"Why does Holt let her come back here then? Why give her a pass?"

"They have an... agreement of sorts."

My throat makes a weird noise. I should mind my own business, but I think we all know that I can't. "What kind of agreement?"

"Holt poses for a few pictures and she agrees to leave the kids alone. The first time she tries to sell a picture of one of the kids—Anna, Ty, Laura, even Nate—Holt will cut off her access. Well, at least as much as he can."

That's intense.

What am I supposed to say to that?

We clap as one by one, the players and other coaches come out. Crutch, who joined us a few minutes ago and notices my fidgety movements, leans over and nods at the building. "He's always the last one out." After what seems like an eternity, Holt emerges. Everyone cheers and hollers in congratulations.

And me?

I nearly lose my shit because he looks so good.

And because he catches my eye and winks at me.

Humbly nodding his head, he rakes his hand through his soft blond waves and fits his baseball cap back on his head. His polo shirt clings to his sweaty body, tugging against his skin in all the right places. The crowd descends on him, and I watch in jealous envy as he shakes hands and slaps shoulders, mumbling words of appreciation for supporting the team. He even hands out a few pennies to some of the kids fighting for his attention. The flex of his arm muscles alone is enough to drive a virgin into the whorehouse.

Weaving through the bodies, he walks over to us, quickly hugging Ray and Teresa before reaching into his pocket where he pulls out two lollipops and hands them to Anna and Laura. Every step he takes puts him closer and closer to me. My fingers ache to touch him. My mouth yearns to taste him.

Since I can't do either of those things here, I simply fold my hands in front of me.

"I'm glad you came. I was afraid you'd back out," he says.

I shrug. "I had to see what all the fuss was about."

His chuckle is low and breathy. I can smell mint on his breath. "And?"

I frown and grunt. "Ehh. Nothing special."

He takes a step closer, erasing the distance between us. His whisper crawls across the shell of my ear, draping me in intimacy, despite the crowd. "I think you forget that you wear your emotions all over your face."

I can barely swallow. I turn my head, hoping that no one can see me. In my haste, my lips graze against his neck. He smells like grass and tastes like salt. "And what does my face say?"

"That you can't wait for your mouth to be on mine."

Damn. Straight.

An impatient voice interrupts us. "Holt! C'mon, Holt. I have to drive back to Atlanta."

Holt takes a step back, grinding his teeth. Turning around, he tosses his hands in the air. "Sorry, Chloe. I'm just a little caught up. First game, first win. It's a good night." His fingertips rest against his waist and he smiles for her.

Her camera chatters into the night air with every picture she takes. Tap, tap, tap. Click, click, click. "And who's this?" she asks with a nod in my direction.

Holy shit. Don't tell her who I am.

Holt turns to look at me, gauging my reaction. I must look like a deer in the headlights. He bites back a laugh. "A friend of the family."

"Based on the way you're looking at her, I'd say she's *your* friend, Holt. I've never known you to be one to make googly eyes."

"I didn't know you charted my eye movement through that lens of yours."

She hangs the camera at her side, taking a moment to enjoy the banter. "I chart everything you do. You're my assignment."

That comment chafes him a little bit, and I watch Holt's jaw twitch.

Chloe immediately smirks.

Ridge laughs and strolls into the frame. "I still don't know how pictures of him buying eggs and toilet paper at the grocery store constitute a newsworthy piece of information. Chloe, I have to run into the drugstore on my way home tonight to buy toothpaste. You think you could get any money for a shot like that?" He lifts his arm and flexes his impressive bicep. "I'm not too shabby of a subject."

Chloe rolls her eyes. "C'mon, Ridge. You know I save all the pictures of you just for myself. Well, you and that delicious brother of yours." She quickly sidesteps him and plants herself in front of me. "Care to give your name?"

"All right, time to wrap this up, Chloe," Holt says. "You should have plenty of shots."

"Let me just get one of you and *your friend*, and I'll be good to go."

Holt quickly tells her to mind her own business. From the corner of my eye, Crutch takes a step forward. Crutch, the police detective, may be one hell of a sexy man, but he's also kind of scary. I don't really feel like causing a scene, so I shake my head, letting him know it's okay.

I nod, giving her the go-ahead. "It's fine. One picture."

Holt's face falls into a portrait of concern. "Mer, you don't have to do this," he whispers.

"Holt, the kids are watching, all these people are watching. Let's just take the picture and get on with our night."

He shakes his head. "You don't know what you're doing."

He's right. I don't.

What if a picture of me ends up in a magazine plastered across every newsstand in America? I'd be mortified.

Completely mortified.

But... he was right when he read my face.

I can't wait for my mouth to be on his.

It's all I think about.

All. The. Time.

I want more. So much more.

True, he saw me in my bra that night in the bar. But since then? There's been no physical intimacy but kissing. Granted, we've been making out like two horny teenagers who just got their braces off, but I want *more*. I've never been so anxious to get to second base. And I can't quite do that with a paparazzi following our every move.

I can't believe these thoughts are even swirling through my brain. Two years ago, I packed a bag and left my cheating husband. I never thought I would want another man.

What's even crazier? It's not just a *normal* man. It's a man who has multiple websites dedicated to detailing every attribute of how sexy he is.

One even rates his shirtless pictures on a scale of one to ten. It's called the 'Holt Hotness Scale'. Yeah, I've scoured more of his internet fandom than I care to admit.

When I don't answer, he just assumes I didn't hear him. He leans even closer and whispers again, "You don't know what you're doing."

I look into his gorgeous blue eyes, and the emotion there cements my decision. "Yes, I do. I'm making her leave. So we can be alone." I lick my lips. "Don't you wanna be alone with me?"

Clearing his throat, he folds an arm around my shoulder and turns back to Chloe. "Say cheese."

Chapter 15

Holt

I won a game. Not just any game—the season opener.

And I got to second base.

I'm one lucky bastard.

Just thinking about last night…her soft breast underneath my fingertips, her peaked nipple between my teeth. It's almost more than I can handle. And when I think about the noises she made when I was lapping at her skin? Well, that makes me wanna jizz in my pants like a pubescent fifteen-year-old.

Fucking sonnets should be written about her tits.

They. Are. Epic.

Full and heavy. Round and soft.

Kissable, suckable, and sensitive.

Hell, I've said it before, and I'll say it again, I'd go through all my surgeries again just to be with Merit. Just to see her smile. Just to taste her lips. And now? Just to watch the way her back arches when my thumbs graze over her bare-naked chest.

Quickly adjusting the growing erection in my pants, I knock on her door and glance at my watch. Technically, the party started at seven, so we're already an hour and fifteen minutes late. But that's fine by me. The less time I have to spend with these people, the better. When Merit told me she had to do some extra work after closing the store, I counted it as a blessing.

The second she pulls open the door, the glowing smile fades from her beautiful face. She looks me over. Once. Twice. Her eyes flare in desire; although, she does a pretty good job masking it with her scowl.

"Seriously!" She folds her arms across her chest. The chest I spent hours mapping and exploring. "This shit's really getting old, Holt."

I lean against the doorframe. I can't help but laugh.

She tries to stay mad at me. Really, she does. But it's a losing battle. She spins on her heels and heads back inside the condo before I see her smile. Of course, when I hear the soft snort of her giggle, I know she's already forgiven me.

She'd never admit that, though.

Not my Feisty Merit.

She props against the kitchen counter, studying my white button up and black slacks. I'm even wearing expensive leather dress shoes. She fans her hand down her blouse and simple cotton skirt. "I can only assume I'm underdressed for whatever you have planned."

Lazily closing the distance separating us, I slouch my body, grabbing the hem of her skirt. Rubbing the fabric between my thumb and forefinger, she gasps when my knuckles graze against her thigh. "Well, I can cancel the plans and strip down. Then you can join me. I'd hate for you to be underdressed alone," I say with a wink.

A pink blush colors her cheeks. "Where are we going?" she asks, ignoring my request for nakedness.

"It's a surprise."

Offering me a little smirk, she plants her hands on my chest and gives me a gentle shove. When my fingers disconnect from her leg, I frown, pouting like a scolded child.

She walks down the hall, gifting me with a consolation prize—the sway of her perfect ass—and hollers behind her. "I don't like surprises."

"Don't lie, Merit. You love surprises." I watch her turn into her bedroom. "And no black. Wear anything but black!"

I sit on the couch, dreading what's coming.

Typically, I do anything and everything possible to avoid these people.

But...I have to go. I gave a pretty sizeable donation to the new public library—especially for *The Wizard of Oz* movie switch. But I didn't mind. Laura is addicted to reading. The donation was basically my love letter to my nieces and nephew. Unfortunately, that means I have to attend the obligatory *kiss-your-ass* reception with the other donors.

My plan is to make an appearance, do a little small talk, and steal Merit away.

I really hope all goes according to plan.

But when you're in a mansion filled with assholes, you never know what may happen.

If you think about it, there's about four really rich neighborhoods in our town. Like really rich.

I live in one of the neighborhoods. The mayor lives in another.

The closer we get to his house, the more sullen Merit gets. I can only assume, by now, she knows where we're going. Ben's been the mayor for several years, and I happen to know he's a client of Plott, Ezzell, and Crispin. So, it stands to reason that Merit has been to his house before.

When I pull up in the driveway and Merit makes no move to gather her purse, I motion for the valet to give us a minute.

I clear my throat. "Surprise."

I watch her reflection in the window. Her beautiful face is marred with a grimace. "I'm not going in there."

"We'll look pretty weird trying to small talk with everyone through the cracked windows of my truck."

She spins in her seat. "The mayor's house? A party with the mayor? You thought that would be a fun surprise?"

"I didn't say it would be fun. I just said it was a surprise. And I didn't tell you because I knew you wouldn't come. And I refuse to spend a free night without you. You don't work tomorrow, so that means I can keep you awake all hours of the night."

She's thinking about last night. My mouth on her, on her body. It's written all over her face.

Making me want more.

Making me want forever.

"Well, I may not let you keep me up all hours of the night. Not after this stunt."

She's too cute to make idle threats.

"I didn't wanna come either, but I didn't have a choice. I gave that donation to the new library, so I have to make an appearance at this reception. It's for the donors and supporters." I reach out, taking her hand in mine. "I'm sorry I didn't tell you. But I'm not going in without you. I meant what I said, I'm not giving up any free time with you."

She sighs. "You have to go in. It's a reception for you. You'll look ungrateful if you don't."

"I know." I cock my head to the side. "So, we better go in. The sooner we go in, the sooner we can leave."

She gnaws on her lip. "The people in there know me."

"Yeah."

"I mean, they know me as Edward's wife. I haven't been around these people since before the separation." She folds her hands in her lap and looks down. "Aren't you worried about what they will say? When they see you with me?"

"I don't give two shits what these people think." I lift her chin. Sliding my finger down her throat, I caress the lines of her collarbone. "Mer, from the day I started playing college ball, I've had everyone giving me their opinions. They write about me. They do interviews about me. They have press conferences about me. Everyone has always wanted to tell me what to do. Tell me how to act, how to play, how to lead a team." I have to stop touching her, or I'm going to lose my mind. I sit back and rub my hand across my jaw. "None of that matters to me. Outside of the Lord above, there's a very small group of people whose opinions actually matter. It's my family," I swallow, "and now, you."

She blinks, the brown and green swirls more prominent in her eyes tonight. "I used to live here. In this neighborhood. Our house was two streets over." Hearing the word *our* rips my heart out. She corrects herself without me saying anything. "Edward's house, I mean."

I'm not sure what to say, so I just nod.

Opening her purse, she fishes around and comes back up with a five-dollar bill. She waves it in the air as she reaches for the door. "I've got the tip." She jumps out of the truck, slapping the bill into one of the other valet's hands before I can even make it around to her side.

Sliding my arms through my jacket, I soak in every single inch of Merit.

Holy hell.

I still can't believe how beautiful she is.

Heeding my warning, she's wearing a form-hugging red dress with cap sleeves. It's still short, but several inches longer than her selection of black dresses—I mean, than *Edward's* selection of black dresses. And trust me, the modesty does nothing but enhance her beauty. Her hair is curled and styled back in a simple ponytail. My eyes travel the length of her bare legs, absorbing every curve and muscle.

And I'm not the only one.

The remaining valets are eyeing my woman like she's a community birthday cake, just waiting on everyone to have a slice.

Over my fucking dead body.

Clearing my throat, I shoot them a death glare, silently declaring the woman in front of us is mine.

All mine.

Reaching for her hand, I tug her body next to mine as we walk up the stone steps to the ornate front door. My fingers graze across the bracelet on her wrist. A very expensive bracelet. Looks like rubies and diamonds. "This is nice. A gift?"

Please don't say it's from your ex-husband.

Her lips curl into a soft smile. "Yes, but not to me."

"Any kleptomania I should know about?"

"It's from Europe. My great-grandfather bought it at a small antiques store in Belgium when he was in the service. He brought it home for my great-grandmother. I only wear it for special occasions."

I guide her into the house with my hand on the small of her back. She doesn't freeze or shy away. In fact, she takes a small step closer to me. "And tonight's a special occasion?" I ask.

She turns her head, whispering against my neck. "I figured it had to be. I mean, you *are* wearing church shoes."

What I wouldn't give to kiss her right now.

Of course, that desire is placed on hold the second we cross the threshold and are thrust into the lion's den of the rich and privileged and entitled.

The next hour moves at a snail's pace.

And I hate every second of it.

I can survive the boring small talk. I can survive the handshakes and attaboy shoulder slaps. I can even survive the lingering stares from the unhappily married searching for their next extramarital affair. But what I can't survive is making Merit uncomfortable. I hate her fake smiles and her folded hands. I hate that she never talks unless specifically asked a question, and even then, she either agrees with whatever was said or makes some non-committal, non-controversial comment.

I'm standing out of the way, waiting on Merit to return from using the restroom, and checking my watch, wondering if we've made enough of an appearance to satisfy the masses when the mayor's wife corners me.

Literally.

I have to basically shove myself into the corner of the room like a toddler in timeout to avoid having my hand graze her chest.

I'm not looking forward to this. I met the mayor and his wife right after I moved back home. Saying she's a shameless flirt is like calling a mountain lion a cute little kitten.

"Holt. It's great to see you. I was wondering when you would show up."

"Georgia." I dip my head, greeting her. "I've been here for a while, actually."

"Well, I've been out back. I just had the veranda completely remodeled last month. All new landscaping too. We have the full bar set up out there. Come outside," she purrs. "Let's get you a fresh drink." She leans forward, tapping my chest with her fingernail. "Something hard. Just like you," she says with a small giggle.

I shuffle to the side, trying to avoid the temptation to roll my eyes. "Well, I'm not exactly sure how your husband would feel about you plying another man full of liquor."

"Oh, Holt. Everyone's entitled to a little fun. Don't you think?"

"Well, I've never been a liquor person. Beer's more my speed." I make a big show of checking my watch again. "Besides, it's starting to get a little late. We were just about to leave."

Her perfectly manicured eyebrows lift in surprise. "We?"

"Me and my date."

She cocks a hand on her surgically minimized waist and laughs. "And what fine female specimen did you bring this time? Are you still dating Bunny? She's nothing but flash. Her family is new money, and from what I hear, her father's company is already having financial difficulties."

"It's not Bunny, no."

Her brow furrows. "Who then?"

At that exact moment, the crowd shifts, and we can see Merit on the opposite end of the massive living room politely maneuvering her way through the throng of people.

Well, we can't actually see all of her through the masses, just her top half. Regardless, the look on my face must speak for itself.

Georgia gasps, "You're kidding me. Merit Ezzell?"

My angered heartbeat ricochets against my eardrums. "That's not her name anymore. She's Merit Browning."

For now.

"Oh, Holt," she cackles. "You can't be serious. Edward's ex-wife? She's a heathen, some country bumpkin. Completely uncouth. Edward even had to pay for etiquette classes so she wouldn't make a fool of herself at business functions."

My fists clench and my teeth grind. I have to remind myself over and over that hitting a woman is wrong—no matter the circumstance.

A guy with a really bad toupee blocks Merit's way. He's not even talking to her. He's reaching around her trying to grab a flute of champagne from a passing waiter. Craning her neck to see me, she rolls her eyes and pretends to tug his hair.

She's so freakin' funny.

Once he finally moves, it takes only a split second for her to realize that I'm not alone. When she sees Georgia, her face falls into a somber frown. Quickly recovering, she lifts her head and dons her fake smile like a Halloween mask.

Georgia growls. She actually growls. Turning to me, she lifts on her tiptoes and whispers in my ear. "She's pretty, I'll give you that. But she's not worthy of someone like you. Of all that you have to offer. You need someone of a certain pedigree. A certain breed. A purebred. Someone who can actually keep her husband content." Her hand darts between us, and her fingers tug on my belt buckle.

Fuck you, lady.

I grab her hand, forcing it away from my crotch. "And I need someone single, Georgia. That's a pretty standard request."

"Single can be arranged. Just let me know." Taking a step back, she straightens her dress and glances over at Merit. She scoffs, "And why does she have that look on her face? She looks ridiculous." Georgia sniffs the air. "Does she smell something?"

Merit's fake smile has faded in favor of her jealous look. Her nose is scrunched up, and she looks like she smells a rotten egg.

I love it.

Merit steps around another large group of people, and her full body comes into view. And she looks gorgeous, don't get me wrong. Right down to the toilet paper stuck to her high heel. It trails behind her like the tail of a kite.

Georgia laughs like a hyena and walks away, mumbling underneath her breath. I can't hear what she says, but I can guarantee it's not nice.

"So," Merit says, "I see Georgia kept you company while I was in the restroom."

"I'd rather have a rattlesnake as a companion."

"Hmmm." She looks around the room, thinning her lips, pretending she's not interested in what happened between me and the mayor's wife. But it doesn't take long before she gives in to her curiosity. "What was she laughing at?"

I stomp the floor next to her foot, kicking the toilet paper to the side. Merit's eyes bulge and her face turns crimson. She groans, laying her forehead on my chest in embarrassment. "Oh my gosh. I can't believe that just happened."

Her hot breath steams across the fabric of my shirt. The sensation sends a chill down my spine. I wrap her hair around my hand and tilt her head to the side. I kiss the soft skin of her neck. "C'mon, let's get out of here."

She stands straight and sheepishly glances around, seeing if anyone witnessed our stolen moment together. Satisfied that our private moment stayed private, she nods, eagerly waiting on me to lead the way. I should feel bad for leaving, but I don't. I think they're actually giving out plaques or some shit to us donors. Oh well, they waited too long. They can just stick mine in the mail.

We make it to the front stoop when Merit's cell phone starts ringing. Looking at the caller ID, she says, "It's the alarm company." She answers, and after a minute of talking, she covers the phone, telling me what's going on. "The power flickered off at the store right when they were doing a software update. They want me to stay on hold while they reset everything."

"Stay here and take care of it. I'll have them pull the truck around. I'll be back in just a minute." I'm halfway down the steps when I realize that I'm a complete fool. Spinning on my heels, I jog back up and plant a soft kiss on her lips.

I catch her by surprise, and she jumps. Her hand darts up, hiding her face from the two older women who just walked by. "Holt?"

"How else am I supposed to get you used to public displays of affection." I wink and leave her smiling on the steps.

Maybe this party wasn't such a bad idea after all.

Chapter 16

Merit

This party was a terrible fucking idea.

I'm gonna kill Holt.

The four eyes staring at me right now are making my skin crawl. Every blink is giving me murderous tendencies.

My heart is roaring so loudly in my ear, I can barely hear the alarm company rep talking to me. "Everything should be set now. Thanks so much for your patience. I'm sorry for the late hour, and I hope you have a good rest of your evening."

I pretend to be on the phone for a few seconds more just so I don't have to engage with them. When it's painfully obvious that the other person already hung up, I slowly drop my cell phone in my purse.

"Interesting to see you here," Edward says.

I nod. "You too."

His brow furrows. "Why would that be interesting?"

I fold my hands in front of me. "This reception honors those who donated to the new public library. I'm surprised you gave a donation." The whole time we were married, Edward refused to give money to any charitable cause. No hospitals. No schools. Not even the Girl Scouts for cookies.

He scoffs. "Of course, I didn't donate. The old library is good enough for people. I'm here because Ben and Georgia are dear friends."

Oh, please. Edward is not *dear friends* with Mayor Ben and his overly flirtatious wife. He's social-climbing acquaintances with them. And that's only because the law firm represents them.

I glance down at the ground, trying to keep my composure, silently begging for this to be over. And silently begging *her* to keep quiet. "Of course."

But I'm not that lucky. *She* talks. "What about you, Merit? Did you donate to the library? Is that why you're here?"

Taking a deep breath, I look over at Delaney. Her blonde hair is sleek and perfectly styled. She's wearing a black dress that's so short and tight, it would constitute a swimsuit to some church denominations. A former cheerleader, she's extremely petite. I bet she's barely over five-feet tall. One thing has changed since her cheering days, though, and that is her breast size. In fact, she took sick leave during her first month of work at the law firm to have them done. I still have my suspicions that Edward paid for them. But, since he required us to have separate bank accounts, there's no way to know.

"Merit?" she asks again. The look of superiority etched across her face tells me all I need to know.

She thinks I'm a total idiot.

An idiot who couldn't keep her husband happy.

An idiot who didn't even know her husband was banging someone else. For nearly two whole years. Before catching them in the act. And then fainting.

"No, I didn't donate anything."

"Then, why are you here?"

"Well," I clear my throat. "I'm here on a date."

Edward cocks his head to the side. "A date? With whom?"

Right at that second, Holt appears, taking the steps two at a time. Great. This should be torture.

"Hey." Sliding his arm around the small of my back, he doesn't even look at the couple in front of me. "They are pulling the truck around." Finally realizing he's being rude, he turns to introduce himself. "I'm sorry to interrupt, I'm—" He abruptly stops. His fingers tighten on my back. His voice shifts to a dead tone. "Delaney."

I blink.

Excuse me.

I watch in stunned fascination as Edward's eyes widen in surprise. I'm sure Delaney's would bug out, too, but she's had too many fillers to show that much shock.

She takes a small step forward. "Holt."

That pounding in my ears just got a whole lot louder, like a damn tropical hurricane pounding against a tin roof. "Ummm. Y'all know each other?"

Holt's jaw twitches. His body tenses. "Delaney was a couple of years behind Ella at North and Camden Academy."

Delaney smirks. Like the Devil. "Come now, Holt. That's a very simplistic way to describe an ex-girlfriend."

What. The. Hell.

What did she just say?

I beg myself to stay quiet, but my brain doesn't listen. "Ex-girlfriend?"

Holt looks between Delaney and Edward, before glancing back to me. "We went on a few dates."

He's actually lying to me.

I can tell he's lying.

But Holt doesn't lie. Not to those he cares about. Not to me. At least that's what he said.

I don't have to call him out, Delaney does it for me. Her high-pitched cackle makes me cringe. "A few dates? Is that what you call it? We used to live together, Holt."

Holy crap.

I'm gonna die. Or faint again.

I feel like my lungs are being crushed by a giant boulder. I move to step away, but Holt refuses to let me go. His hand clamps down on my side, his fingers gripping the fabric of my dress. If I keep trying to pull away, I'm afraid I'm going to trip.

So, what do I do?

I give up.

I give up and stand there, staring at my feet. I wiggle my toes, silently counting them. Silently begging for everyone to leave me alone.

"What are you doing here, Delaney?" His finger taps against my side, trying to draw my head up.

"I should ask you the same thing," she pops back.

"I donated to the library."

"And the two of you came together?" Her voice lifts at the end, like she really can't understand why someone would choose to be with me. Willingly, that is.

"We did." I can feel his eyes on me. "Merit and I are dating." Under normal circumstances, the possessiveness in his voice would make me swoon. But these aren't normal circumstances, and I'm just doing my best not to throw up in my mouth.

"Really? Well, I guess I can speak for both Edward and myself when I say, we're really glad to see you're finally moving on with your life, Merit."

Holt snorts in shock. "Edward." His voice is cold and icy. "My apologies, I should've recognized you. I'm Holt Hill." He holds out his hand, offering a handshake to my ex-husband.

I finally look up, unable to avoid the encounter anymore.

Edward's glaring at me, pinning me to the ground with a disapproving stare. Trying to prove he has more class than us, he eventually shakes Holt's hand. "Ah, the football player." He puffs his chest out and stands taller. But it doesn't matter how hard he tries, he's still a shrimp compared to Holt. When wearing my heels, I'm actually an inch and a half taller than Edward. "Delaney has mentioned you."

"Yeah, I'm sure she has," Holt says with a scoff.

Delaney reaches over and traces her hand across Edward's chest. "Oh Holt, don't let your feathers get ruffled." She smiles up at Edward, pretending to be engrossed with him. "Edward and I talk about everything. We have no secrets. Isn't that right, love?"

Edward brushes her hand away and straightens his collar. He doesn't even answer her. I used to hate it when he would do that to me.

Ignore me in a crowd.

Well, I guess I preferred being ignored to being criticized. Maybe if he just ignored me the entire time, I would've been happier.

Edward narrows his eyes. "You don't even like football, Merit. You've never watched a game."

Stay quiet. Stay quiet. The mantra doesn't work. "You're the one who didn't like football. I watched college ball with my dad and grandfather all the time."

That's true, I did. But I stopped after my freshman year of high school when my grandfather passed away. It made me miss him too much. That's why I honestly had no idea who Holt was. It's also why I don't really know that much about football. I was too young to grasp the rules and the stats and the terminology. After that, my experience was limited to our small-town, high school games—which, as we all know, were more of a social event than a true athletic event given the size of my school. I wanted to go to our college games, but Edward didn't want to.

So, we didn't.

Holt leans down, whispering low and secretive against my ear. "Really? I didn't know that."

I softly clear my throat, silently begging him to stop. I can't have him so close. I can't have his hot breath sending comforting and forbidden chills down my spine. Not when my ex-husband is staring at me. And not when my mind is clouded with visions of Holt and Delaney.

Dating.

Living together.

Playing house.

I straighten my spine and fold my hands again, trying to regain my composure. It's plain to see that Edward didn't like my comment.

And it's even plainer to see that Delaney didn't like Holt's intimate gesture. Her face reddens in anger.

Needing to gain the upper hand over me again, Edward decides to cut me where he knows it will hurt. "Well, I suppose it's good we ran into you. I can tell you that Dad and I are going to be out of town for the next two weeks for a trial. I think your next loan payment comes due on Thursday. You can leave it with Jill, like normal, at the front desk. I just wanted you to know it will be a few days before we cash it." He reaches around and grabs Delaney's ass. He cocks his head to the side and makes a humming noise, like he just came up with a really good idea. "Actually, that may help you out some. Giving you a few more days, I mean. Dad did mention your last payment was two-hundred dollars less than what you had been paying."

A low growl reverberates through my chest. "You know I always pay way more than my required payment, Edward." I'm gritting my teeth so hard I'm not sure how he can even hear me.

"Oh, I'm aware," he feigns innocence. "I just wasn't sure how the store was doing this month." He chuckles, making my brain shudder in fury. "Like we talked about, at some point, the novelty of a small-town children's shoe and clothing store will wear off."

Holt pulls me tighter against him. Despite my displeasure with him, I can't force myself to step away. Edward still has that power over me; he is pushing me down, chopping away at my strong roots, like someone cutting a pine tree from the forest.

I need Holt's strength.

Just for a few more minutes.

And then? Then, I think it's pretty obvious I can't have him in my life anymore. The threads tying him to my old life are wound too tight, suffocating me with their complexity.

Holt's voice rings out loud and firm. "The store's doing great. Busier than ever. In fact, it's so busy that Merit's gonna hire another part-time staffer in the next few weeks."

Edward's eyebrows shoot up. "Really?"

What the hell am I supposed to say?

I nod. "Mmm-hmm."

"Well, that's good. And I see you're at least making enough discretionary income to buy some new clothes." He nods at my red dress.

"This dress is seven years old. It just looks new because you never wanted me to wear it."

Delaney gasps. "Seven years!" She laughs, "Geez, Holt, can't you afford to buy your date some new clothes."

"Delaney," he warns.

She immediately cuts him off. "As fun as this has been, we should head back inside before someone misses us. Right, love?" She leans her head against Edward's shoulder and actually forces a red-painted fingernail inside his tux shirt, nearly popping a button. "Our attempt to sneak outside for a little alone time has backfired."

Nodding, he gives us a quick goodbye and leads Delaney into the house.

The second they're out of earshot, I sigh, exhaling the breath I didn't even know I was holding. My shoulders sink, and my spine curves.

Holt eyes the door. "Your ex-husband is even more of a dickhead than I imagined. How is that possible?"

The relief I feel being out of Edward and Delaney's shadow is short-lived. Extremely short-lived. Hurt and anger curl into my soul like smoke climbing out of a chimney. Finally, I walk away, giving myself space from Holt.

Guess what? There's not *enough* space.

Even if he were on the moon, there still wouldn't be enough space between us.

I trot down the stairs, doing my best not to fall.

"Merit, wait."

Holt grabs my arm. I snatch it away, hissing like a snake. "Don't touch me." I turn my gaze so I don't have to see the hurt in his eyes. Instead, I busy myself, digging for my phone in my purse. He rushes ahead of me, opening the passenger door to his idling truck. I sidestep and plant myself in front of a bush landscaped to look like a spiral.

When I start pecking around on my phone, he groans and slams the door shut. "What are you doing?"

"Ordering a ride." I really don't feel like paying for a ride-share, but it's too late to call Kyra. And I'll be damned if I get in that truck with him.

He folds his arms across his chest. The same chest that only ten minutes ago, I couldn't wait to wrap my arms around. I had every intention of lavishing the same attention on him tonight that he lavished on me last night.

A lot of shit can happen in ten minutes.

A lot of shit *did* happen in ten minutes.

"Why?" he grunts.

My voice hitches up like a middle school girl. *"Why?"*

What a stupid question.

He flaps his hand behind him. "My truck's right there. I know you, I know you don't wanna pay for a ride. Let me drive you. We obviously need to talk about this, talk about what happened."

The three valets stare at us, slack-jawed and intrigued.

I glance at my phone. It says the nearest ride is fifteen minutes away. Well, I guess they better pull up a chair and enjoy the show.

"There's nothing to talk about, Holt."

"Bullshit."

I hike my purse higher on my shoulder, trying to ignore him. My whole body feels irritated, like even my blood cells are scraping across sandpaper. I can't believe I started falling for him. I'm a fool. A complete and total idiot. I should have kept to my *no dating* policy. "Go," I whisper. "Leave me alone."

"No. I'm not leaving. We need to talk."

"Fine. You wanna talk?" I swallow, trying to keep my all-consuming sadness at bay. "Did you know?"

His brow furrows. "Know what?"

"That Delaney was the mistress. That my husband left me for her?"

"Of course, I didn't know. If I did, don't you think I would've mentioned it."

I toss my hands in the air. "I don't know what to think!" I scream. "We've only known each other for a month. How can I know you?" My lips are so dry they crack with each word. "I don't know you at all."

He takes a step forward, casting his body in the glow of the streetlamps. I can see the freckles on the bridge of his nose. He shoves his finger into his chest. *"You know me."*

"No, I don't. But I can learn about you, can't I? You want me to learn, Holt? Fine. How long did you and Delaney date? How long did you live together? Did you sleep in the same bed? Share the same shower? Did you prefer morning sex or night sex? Was she at your beck and call?"

His head falls back. He stares at the sky, mumbling to himself. Lifting his arms, he drags his hands through his hair.

A fumble of noise catches my attention, and I see all three of the valets shuffling to get their cell phones in position. They aim and hit record. Two bright camera lights shine in our direction. The third guy curses and tilts his phone, trying to figure out why it isn't recording.

Fear and anxiety crash over me like a tsunami.

The last thing I need is for this fight to be plastered all over the Internet.

And despite my anger at Holt, I would never want his privacy to be invaded like that. I feel the need to protect him.

I *want* to protect him.

He deserves better than some tabloid lies.

As much as I hate to admit it... he deserves better.

"Mer, it wasn't like that. You have to beli—"

I cross the distance separating us, stopping him before he can say anything else. Blocking their view, I lower my voice. "Stop talking. They're filming us."

Holt looks over my head and frowns. Turning back, he gazes into my eyes. "I don't care. I need to explain everything to you."

I shake my head. "Just go."

"I'm not leaving you here. Not in a million years."

I close my eyes and take a deep breath. I can't believe this is happening. The last thing I want is for this moment to be preserved on video. I lick my lips, wishing I didn't have to give in, but there's really no other choice. "Fine. You can take me home. I'm just ready to be done with this."

It doesn't take a rocket scientist to see he's hurt by my choice of words. He opens the door for me, and then hands the closest guy a tip, the whole time pretending he doesn't even care that they're trying to film us. As soon as I'm in the truck, I cancel my ordered ride. I make a move to fold my hands in my lap, but as a fuck you to Edward, I rebel against the trained habit and instead rapidly tap them against my thighs, pounding a quick rhythm to match that of my racing heart. Quickly, we drive through the winding streets of my old neighborhood.

Holt plays his own finger percussion against the steering wheel. "Are you ready to talk?"

"If you say one single word, I'll open this door and throw myself out."

I guess he reads my mind.

Or my face.

Either way, he doesn't make a sound for the entire ride.

Chapter 17

Holt

"So, what happened?" Ridge's voice cuts through the speakers of my truck. I can hear the confusion in his tone.

"Delaney's the mistress."

"Whose mistress?"

"Edward's mistress. Edward left Merit for Delaney. She's the one he was having an affair with."

Ridge sucks in a breath. "No shit?"

I nod in the dark. "No. Shit."

"Does Merit know about you and Delaney?"

"Well, she does now," I say. "I tried to downplay it, but you know Delaney. She still wants everyone on God's green Earth to know that I was with her. Despite my better judgment," I mumble.

"I think we can all agree that you had *no* judgment during that time period. It's like your brain went on sabbatical. In fact, I think Raylee still refers to it as the 'dark age'."

Despite my sour mood, I smile. "Try to be the one living it. It was darker than dark. It was... the inner ring of Hell."

"Well, how's Merit taking it?"

"I don't know."

"What do you mean, you don't know."

Anxiety makes my heart pound. "She refused to talk to me last night. I barely had the truck in park when she raced inside her condo like an Olympic sprinter and deadbolted the door. After twenty minutes of me begging and pleading—and when her neighbor threatened to call the cops—I left. On top of that, she's refused to answer any of my phone calls today."

"Huh. That's not good."

Ridge. A man full of wisdom.

I keep my mouth shut so I don't say something I'll regret. My girl's mad at me; the last thing I need is for my best friend to be mad at me too.

"So, what are you gonna do?" he asks.

"I'm headed over to her condo now. I'm gonna stand outside like a fool until she agrees to talk to me. Let the cops come. Let the fucking army come. I'm not going anywhere until she talks to me."

Ridge's voice lowers, growing serious. "And she's worth making a fool of yourself?"

"Ridge, I'd become a fucking court jester for this woman."

"Welp, that tells me all I need to know, man. Good luck is the only thing I can tell ya."

"Thanks, brother."

We hang up the phone and ten minutes later, I'm banging on her front door. After a few minutes, I call out to her. "Merit, I know you're here. I see your car in the parking lot."

Of course, she refuses to answer.

I brace myself against the door, leaning closer. A warm feeling courses through my body, calming the worry swimming through the pit of my stomach. "Mer, I can *feel* you. Leaning against the door, looking at me through the peephole. I know you're there. And you know I'm not leaving until we talk. Please don't ignore me anymore. Let me in. Please."

After a few beats, I hear the turn of the deadbolt and the slide of the chain lock. She doesn't open the door, but at least she's unlocked it. I assume that's the only invitation she's going to give. Holding my breath, I open the door and walk into her condo. She doesn't even turn around to acknowledge me.

But that's okay.

Just the sight of her alleviates some of the pounding pressure in my head. And my heart.

A pressure, a need.

A need to make her understand. To make her forgive my horrible decision from the past.

And trust me, that's what Delaney was.

A horrible decision, so full of regret.

And the pathetic thing is I knew the outcome before I even opened my own condo door to Delaney that night.

Poor judgment doesn't even come close to describing it.

I stare at her backside, gazing at her body as she slowly meanders her way back to the couch. She's wearing gray cotton shorts that are so short I can almost see the fold of her ass cheeks. Knowing Merit, there's no way she would wear this outside of the house. Her hair is tangled in a lopsided ponytail, and her baggy sweatshirt falls down her shoulder, giving me a glimpse of her green tank top.

I don't see a bra strap, and that thought alone makes my mouth dry.

She plops down on the sofa, dragging a white blanket across her legs, still avoiding my gaze.

I lift the bulging fast-food bag in the air and shake it. "Hungry? I brought double cheeseburgers and fries."

She sniffs the air like a hungry little hound dog. She wants to ignore me; I know she does. But...Merit is curious. As always. She turns her head just a millimeter and discreetly looks at me from underneath her dark lashes. She's trying to see what store name is on the food bag, but she's out of luck—it's plain white. When I tell her where it's from, I can almost hear her stomach growl from across the room.

"I'm not hungry."

I take a look around. Based on the yogurt container sitting on the kitchen counter and the protein bar wrapper on the coffee table, I'd beg to differ. After pulling two bottles of water from the fridge,

I make my way over to the couch, and I pretend it doesn't fucking shred my heart into small bits when she pulls her legs away, scrunching against the corner so she doesn't have the slightest chance of touching me. I spread the food out—placing hers gently in front of where she's sitting—and start eating my own.

I eat like my life depends on it, praying that she gives in. Praying that she makes it a little easier for me. Eventually, she sighs dramatically and starts devouring her own meal.

We eat in complete silence.

Even the television is muted, frozen on whatever movie she was watching. I can't tell what it is, but I know it's an old one, of course. And even though it's still a hundred degrees outside, there's a Christmas tree on the screen.

I toss my trash in the empty bag and lean back. "Are you watching a Christmas movie?"

She grabs the remote and turns off the TV. "It's my favorite movie." She has a little bit of burger and fries left, but instead of throwing them away, she carefully wraps them up and takes them to the fridge.

"What movie is it?" I ask.

She spins around, leaning against the counter. Her face is hidden in the dim light, but I see her shoulder shrug. "It doesn't matter."

"It matters to me."

She stands a little straighter. "What do you want, Holt? Why did you come over?"

"You know why I came over. We need to talk."

She's standing like a statue. It's probably the same way she stood next to Edward a thousand times over.

And I hate it.

She looks down at the floor. "There's nothing to talk about."

"Mer, if you think I'm giving up that easy, then you've got another thing coming."

After a second, she growls and holds her head high. The Merit I know is in there finally making an appearance. "Fine. You wanna talk? I'll listen. Only because I have nothing better to do." She stomps back over and flops down, once again sitting as far away from me as humanly possible. The leather makes a sticky sound against her thighs as she shifts. "Just say what you have to say and get out. *Sir.*"

For the first time since my arrival, she looks at me head-on, and what I see rips the breath from my lungs. I'm not even sure I'll ever be able to breathe again.

Her eyes are bloodshot and swollen. Her cheeks are ruddy, and the tip of her nose is raw from blowing it. Glancing behind her, I see the side table is covered in tissues.

She's been crying.

Over me.

Over us.

My hand darts out, eager to pull her into my arms, but she tsks me, hissing like a snake.

I tug the ballcap off my head and twirl it around on my fingers before setting it on the coffee table, stalling for time, trying to figure out how to get the jumble of words and emotions from my brain to my mouth. I guess I'll start with the simple stuff first. "Have you checked out the Internet today?"

"You mean have I seen our pictures from the football game plastered all over every tabloid blog and social media account? Yep. My family called. Their phones have been ringing off the hook. Even my granny's sewing club from church called her and wanted the scoop." She grabs at her blanket, fiddling with the fringe. "At least Chloe's pictures didn't make me look like some kind of troll."

She looked beautiful. She always looks beautiful.

"I'm sorry."

She shrugs. "I knew it would happen. You warned me. I was just surprised that Chloe didn't give my name." She snorts, "Although, it didn't take long for people to figure out who '*local area family friend*' was. People are posting my name in the comments. They're writing about me—my customers, Edward's old friends, even my middle school English teacher."

"And that bothers you? People knowing about you? Knowing about us?"

She stares at me. Her eyes are void of the vibrant greens and yellows that I've come to love. They're dull and lifeless. The only streaks of color are the red blood vessels branding her.

A roadmap of her tears.

She shakes her head. "Funny thing is, Holt, it doesn't bother me near as much as you and Delaney." Her lips thin. "That's what bothers me... you and her."

"There is no me and Delaney."

"But there was. And you lied. And those two things break my heart."

And those words break mine. My voice is thick in my throat, choking me. "I'm sorry."

"Sorry for being with her? Or sorry for lying to me?"

"I didn't—"

She sits up straight, raising her voice. "And don't say you didn't lie! Downplaying it and not admitting what it was is the same."

I open my mouth, but she cuts me off.

"And I'm not saying you should've told me everything about your past. But, c'mon! You lived with the woman! I mean, she's *here*... in the same town as you. Plus, she used to work for Edward. Couldn't you put two and two together? You have a college degree, damn it. Think!"

A small flurry of excitement blossoms in my chest. I'm crushed that Merit is upset; I'm beyond devastated knowing that I've hurt her.

But...

Her fire? Her passion?

Even though it's in anger, a small part of me is so glad to finally see it. To be the one who brought this energy out of her.

The Merit I met a few weeks ago kept this part of herself hidden. And she sure as hell never would've shown this side of herself to Edward.

"I had no idea she worked for Edward. I had no idea she was the one he had an affair with. I promise. If I had, I would've told you." I sigh. "We don't run in the same crowds. Believe it or not, we haven't even bumped into each other since I moved back home. I've been home almost two years now, and last night is the first time that I've seen her."

"You didn't know?" she asks, her eyebrows lifting up in suspicion. "No one posted anything about her? She didn't try to *tag* you in something or whatever the hell you call it."

I can't help it. I laugh.

Which Merit doesn't like.

I scrub my hand across my mouth, literally wiping the smile from my face. That's definitely one of the things I love about Merit. She's oblivious to social media. Sure, she has stuff for the shop, but Kyra actually does all the posts. Merit has nothing personal out there.

Well, she didn't. Until today.

I confess, I did read some of the comments on the tabloid pages. I'm thrilled to report that her middle school English teacher found her bright and eager, with a wonderful aptitude for diagramming sentences.

"Mer, you know I don't have social media. You know I quit all of that stuff the second I could." When I was in the NFL, I was forced to keep up with all the latest technology. I was even required to create a certain number of posts each week, and that quota increased if I didn't meet the magical number of likes and reposts that the bigwigs wanted to see.

"She didn't call you?"

"When things ended, I changed my phone number."

She chews on her plump bottom lip. "Who ended it?"

"Me."

"Why?"

"You want the long answer or the short answer?"

She thinks for a few seconds, weighing the heaviness of my question. "I have to know, Holt. For my own sanity, I have to know everything."

I nod, wishing I didn't have to rehash the worst time of my life. And trust me, it was bad. Much worse than injuring myself and ending my whole football career.

Bile rises in my throat. My body physically tortures itself when I have to say her name. "Delaney. We met back in high school. I went over to Ella's school to see her for something, and Delaney was there. She was a year younger than me. She flirted, so being a male teenager, obviously I asked her out. I think we went on three dates before I cut things off. I told her I needed to focus on football. The truth was, I could see the writing on the wall. Her true colors started to show after just the first date. Calling and texting all the time, even when she knew I was in school or at practice. She seemed normal enough, but something was just *off*. I couldn't really put my finger on it, but I could definitely sense she had a manipulative side."

My mind swirls with a memory, like water running down a drain. "She was a snob. Her dad is a big-time financial advisor, and he's also a State Senator. So, of course, they never hurt for money. I remember taking her to a movie, and this girl Beth was working as an usher. She went to the same school as me. I didn't really know her because we hung out in different crowds. She was really smart, but also really shy. Well, we were late to the movie because Delaney took so long getting ready. Beth held a flashlight for us so we could make it up the stairs. I remember Delaney making a comment about how old and stained and ugly Beth's shoes were." I look down at the floor, shaking my head in shame. "I know Beth heard her. And I didn't say a damn thing. I kept my mouth shut." I lift my head, searching for Merit. "Later, I overhead some teachers talking. They were talking about donating money so Beth could pay for an overnight field trip. Her parents had filed bankruptcy because of medical bills. Her mom had cancer."

Merit's already sad face frowns. "That's so sad."

"I know. I never forgave myself for not saying something." I swallow, trying to move on. "Anyway, Delaney wasn't too happy that I didn't want to date her anymore. She called and texted so much after I ended things that I had to block her number. She showed up at my practices and games, telling everyone she was my girlfriend. I made the mistake one time of telling her she looked nice in her cheer uniform. She wore the damn thing everywhere after that. After a few months, she finally gave up. She started dating someone new. But I still did my best to avoid her whenever I could."

Merit's brow furrows. "I don't understand. You lived together? You went on one date, maybe a few, and then moved in with her? Your parents let you live with a girl while you were in high school?"

She's so freakin' funny.

"Mer...do Ray and Teresa really seem like the kind of parents who would let their seventeen-year-old son move in with a sixteen-year-old girl?" I ask, referring to my parents by their names and chuckling.

Instead of answering, she folds her arms across her chest and pouts, casting daggers my way.

More like steak knives.

Very *large* and very *sharp* steak knives.

"Sorry. I'll finish." She nods curtly, and I pick up where I left off. "After college, I was drafted to the North Carolina Bearcats. I moved up there and bought my condo. I was midway through my first season and going through a little bit of a depression. So much had changed in my life in such a short time. I was vying for play time with the veteran quarterback. And I missed the fun of the game."

I drag my hand through my hair, scratching my scalp. "Don't get me wrong, college ball was hard. My coaches worked us. They took me from childhood into manhood. But through it all, it was still *fun*. But all of a sudden, I wasn't having fun anymore. I had a job. Knowing that my whole livelihood was riding on how well I performed was a tough pill to swallow. I mean, I wanted to be able to support my parents when they retired, the rest of the family, you know?"

I take a deep breath. So deep my lungs burn. "One night, Delaney just showed up at my door."

"Uninvited?" Merit asks.

I nod. "I don't know how she found out where I lived, or how she made it to North Carolina from Alabama, or how she even got past the doorman."

Her eyes flicker to the darkened television. "But you didn't send her away?"

I wish I could say yes. But that would be a lie.

And I don't lie to Merit.

"No, I didn't. I was so relieved to see someone from home. Someone who knew me before I was an overnight millionaire."

"So relieved you immediately gave her a key and her own toothbrush?" Despite the anger in her tone, her voice quivers. It reminds me of a plastic bag shaking in the wind.

There's no point in sugarcoating it. "I guess you could say that."

"Seriously? I was joking."

"I didn't know me inviting her in would lead to a relationship, would lead to us living together. If I had known that, I would've slammed the door in her face."

Merit pretends to scratch her eye, but really, she's wiping at a tear.

"She came in…" I shrug, trying to find the right words, "and she just didn't leave."

Merit shakes her head, a grimace of disbelief etched on her face. "I don't even understand what you're saying. Why didn't you just ask her to leave?"

"Well, at first, I skirted around the subject, trying not to be rude."

She closes her eyes. Her eyelashes fan across her face, granting her a look of calm in the midst of her sadness and fury. "You mean, you didn't wanna throw the woman you just slept with out to the curb."

I try to play it smart and not specifically answer that question. "Every day I would leave for work, and she would come up with some excuse as to why she needed to stay, saying that she would just lock up for me when she left. But when I came home, she would still be there. With more of her stuff—clothes, shoes, toiletries. Everything."

Her eyes slowly open. The swirls of brown shift, dancing in her watery eyes like falling ribbon.

Despite the seriousness of our conversation, my body reacts to hers. I shift in my seat, trying to adjust my growing problem, because I don't think Merit would necessarily appreciate me sporting an erection while I'm talking about living with Delaney.

"I could've put a stop to it if I really wanted to. But, like I said, I was lonely and depressed. It felt good to come home to someone. Someone kind and gentle and attentive. It felt good to have a friend. I knew she was putting on an act. Delaney's been a lot of things to a lot of people over the years, and *kind* has never been one of them. But I ignored it. I knew she was lying, and I ignored it so I could pretend to be blissfully happy."

"So, what happened?" Merit reaches for the box of tissues. When she sees that it's empty, she lifts her shirt and wipes her nose.

Definitely not something anyone else would've done. Not Delaney. Not Bunny. Not the supermodel.

And I fucking love her for it.

Chapter 18

Merit

I think I just wiped a booger on my shirt.

Oh, well.

Not like I care. Holt should just be glad I didn't wipe it on him.

I lift my chin in the air and grunt, letting him know he hasn't answered my question.

"She did what Delaney does. She went bat-shit crazy." He shifts on the couch, adjusting his position. "At first, she insisted on traveling with the other wives and families to all my away games. I didn't really want her to go, but how could I tell her no? I mean, she *was* my live-in girlfriend. She continued to call and text constantly, every single time I left the condo. I mean, like every thirty minutes. It didn't matter if I was working or just going to the grocery store. She accused me of never answering the phone because I was cheating on her. Even when things were going somewhat easy, she would pick a fight for no reason. Then, I found out she was stealing my money."

I nearly choke on my own spit. "She did what?!"

He licks his lips and nods. "I was so busy during the season that I hired an accountant to pay my bills for me. I didn't want anything to slip through the cracks. I had to sign a power of attorney form for him to handle all my finances. He could basically do anything. Well, he knew we were dating, and she sweet-talked him into believing that I wanted her to be added as an authorized user to my credit card. I have no idea how she spent the amount of money she did. It was outrageous—clothes, purses, jewelry, spa packages, a new laptop. Each month the accountant paid off everything she bought. I had no idea. Once the season finally ended, I was going through all my paperwork and ran across the bills. I flipped out. I told her we were done and that she needed to move out."

He growls under his breath, just the memory of it has him shaking with anger. "She basically collapsed, cried, and begged me to let her stay for a few more weeks. Our team was hiring a couple of new cheerleaders, and tryouts were in three weeks. She wanted to do that. Like a fool, I agreed to let her stay until then."

Bitterness and bile swirl in my stomach like a fire-breathing dragon. "She stole from you, took your hard-earned money, and you *still* let her stay with you? In your house? In your bed?" My head falls back, and I stare at the ceiling. "What is it with this woman? Why does every man want her? Is her crotch filled with magic fairy dust?"

He chuckles and squeezes my knee, immediately drawing my attention. His calloused fingertips scorch my skin. I can't help but notice that one of his knuckles has a small cut on it. I wonder how he got it.

Who the hell cares, I scream at myself.

I shouldn't.

I shouldn't care.

So, how come I do?

Noticing my scowl, he takes his hand off my leg. "Same house, yes; but not the same bed. She went to the guest room. When I ended it, I meant it."

"So that's it? She tried out for cheerleading, didn't get it, and then moved out?"

He cocks his head to the side. "Not exactly." He takes a deep breath. "She tried to ruin my career. She nearly cost me everything."

"How? What happened?"

"She was in the facility for a tryout and busted in on a very serious team meeting we were having. She went berserk. Yelling, throwing things. She even threw a crystal trophy across the room, trying to hit me. She told everyone that I was a liar and that I cheated on her—with several of the coaches' wives, nonetheless. Then, she claimed that I hit her. She actually took off her shirt—in the middle of the room—and showed this huge bruise on her shoulder and chest."

My mouth falls in my lap. "She what?"

No matter how mad I am at Holt, I know that he would never hit a woman. That's not in his heart, in his soul.

"Yeah, she said that I had hit her at breakfast that morning. Punched her."

"Wh-what happened?" I stutter over my words.

"They immediately investigated. Fortunately, it only took a few hours to get to the truth. Of all things, Raylee was actually in state for a work conference about two hours away. I made plans to go and see her, have dinner, and stay with her at her hotel before she flew out the next morning. I didn't share my plans with Delaney, of course. She actually spent the day drinking and passed out really early. She had no idea that I had left for the night, no idea that I was two hours away having dinner and watching a stupid hotel rental movie with my sister. Fortunately, the next morning, I drove straight in to the team meeting from out of town. No stops at home. They had me on surveillance tape leaving my condo the evening before and not coming back. And of course, I was all over the hotel video that morning, eating breakfast with Raylee, walking her to her car, everything. When our team security pressed Delaney, she admitted she made it up to get me in trouble. She bruised herself on purpose by slamming her shoulder in the bathroom door." He snorts, "I guess I should be glad Delaney was only a subpar student and not some mad genius. I can't believe she actually thought she could get away with something like that."

I can't help myself, I lean forward, closing some of the distance between us. "Holt, I can't believe you went through that."

He scoots a little closer. "Yeah, it wasn't my finest hour, that's for damn sure."

"But everything was okay? After they cleared you, I mean?"

"It was. I worked my ass off to prove to everyone I wasn't anything like the man Delaney was talking about. I just wanted them to forget her, forget she was ever a part of my life. I worked myself into starting position. By the end of my third season, everyone had a Super Bowl ring on their finger. And I helped put it there. My five months with Delaney weren't even a blip on anyone's radar anymore."

"Why isn't she in jail?" I ask. "I mean, I didn't see anything about this when I searched you on the Internet. People should know about this. I mean, I don't care about Edward, but she was working at his law office. His clients might've been in jeopardy."

"I was a freakin' idiot, Merit. I mean, I had more sense as a seventeen-year-old kid when I dumped her after a couple of dates. Here I was, this successful man," he says with air quotes, "this famous football player, and I let myself get conned. I was completely embarrassed that I let my loneliness and insecurities put me in that position. I just wanted it to go away. I promised not to press charges if she just left and kept her mouth shut."

I sit, absorbing all the information he just bombarded me with. My body was tense and rigid when he got here. And then he told me the truth. And with every minute he talked, my resolve broke down a little more.

And now?

Now, I feel like a pile of warm jelly.

Unsettled and uneven. Unbalanced and unsure.

"Mer?" He reaches out and gently brushes my cheek. "You believe me, don't you?"

This time, I don't shy away from his touch. My whisper chains the two of us back together. "I do."

His body relaxes, and he rolls the tension from his shoulders. "I'm sorry for putting you through this. I can't stand to see you hurting."

I press my lips together, thinking about what I want, a little of the old me bubbling to the surface. "Then don't ever hurt me again."

It's an irrational request; I know.

Holt smiles softly. "Never." A blond curl falls down on his forehead, adding a boyish charm to his heartbreakingly handsome face. "And you'll never hurt me, right?"

Holt's a strong man. Tough and rugged. To hear him ask such a real and vulnerable question makes me want to shelter him even more. I push the hair from his forehead, allowing my fingertips to graze down the side of his face. I trace the line of stubble against his jaw. "Are you scared? Worried about my intentions? Skeptical of me?"

He swallows. "I've always been skeptical when it comes to women. Ever since that first paycheck deposited into my account. But now? The only thing I'm scared about is losing you."

My voice barely comes out. It's so strained, I'm surprised he can even hear it. "I'm scared I'm gonna be lost."

The gasp that leaves Holt's mouth is low and guttural. In a split second, he's wrapped his hands around my face and lovingly pulls my mouth to his. His lips taste mine, tenderly erasing the painful memories of last night and today. His mouth opens, eager to deepen the kiss.

Pulling back, I lovingly cover my lips with my fingertips, etching to memory the emotion and power of the moment. I shake my head. "No more kisses tonight."

His brow furrows in confusion.

I continue, "Delaney is still hanging over us. Tomorrow's a new day. Everything from today will be washed away. I don't want her to steal any more of our passion."

Holt leans back and opens his arm, nodding for me to join him. Immediately, I snuggle against his side. Snaking my arm around his firm stomach, I settle in his embrace. We spend the next hours talking. Laughing, joking, telling stories of our past. And when he finally says goodbye at 11:30, it takes every ounce of willpower coursing through my veins not to stick my tongue down his throat and tell him that I love him.

After he leaves, I'm brushing my teeth with one hand and grabbing a fresh bottle of water from the fridge with the other when a soft knock at the door scares the crap out of me. It's a weird, eerie kind of knock, like a criminal quietly testing the waters before busting the door down and asking for all your money. I shut the fridge and look at the clock on the microwave. It's after midnight. Holt left over thirty minutes ago, and the only person I know who would knock on my door at this time of night would be Kyra. But Kyra would call first.

The person on the other side of the door knocks again. Looking around for a weapon, I pull a large knife from the butcher block before sliding it back in place. I really don't think I could stab someone. I need to rethink my weapon of choice. Opening a kitchen drawer, I quietly snag a steel meat mallet. It should get the job done if needed. I once hit my own finger when pounding on a chicken cutlet. I nearly lost a fingernail. It was black and purple for weeks.

Tiptoeing to the door, I pray the other person can't hear the beat of my pounding heart. It's so loud in my brain, it feels like I'm front and center with a marching band. I pull the toothbrush from my mouth and swallow the foamy paste. Gathering my courage, refusing to cower in fear, I hold my breath and look through the peephole.

My jaw falls open and my thundering heart immediately quiets to a flutter. I fling open the door and stare at his intimidating frame. "Holt! What's wrong? What are you doing here?"

His eyes fall to my hands. Cocking his head, he studies my pink toothbrush and meat mallet. "It's an odd time to be tenderizing meat, don't you think?"

"It's an odd time to be showing up at someone's door when you left half an hour ago," I say with raised eyebrow and sarcasm. I sigh, wondering what's happened. Has he changed his mind about us? About me? "You have to be at school for workout in six hours. Are you okay? Did something happen?"

He takes a small step forward. "It's tomorrow."

"Huh?"

He takes another step and kicks the door closed behind him. There's a predatory look on his face. His voice is lower than normal, dangerous and intense. "You said no more kissing until *tomorrow.*" He dramatically looks at his watch. "It's now tomorrow."

Immediately, my panties dampen and my vision blurs, growing hazy with the strain of desire. My lips part. I want to say something, but I can't; the ache to have his mouth on mine is too great. Speaking just seems too damn painful right this second.

It doesn't really matter if Holt can read my mind or read my face. Either way, he gets the point.

Hoisting my body against his, he slams his lips against mine, instantly melting me.

I'm glad Holt can do two things at once. Because I sure can't. Fortunately, he grabs the steel meat mallet from my fingers, catching it before it clatters to the floor and bounces across my foot, just like my toothbrush did.

Chapter 19

Holt

Kyra looks up from her position on the floor where she's lacing tennis shoes for a little boy. He's completely engrossed in whatever classic movie Merit is currently playing on the big screen. An older woman with bright red reading glasses nods hello in my direction. Not seeing Merit in the front part of the store, I immediately make my way to the back, not even asking permission. We're past all that now.

I do give pause, though, when Kyra chuckles. Slowly turning around, I lean against a rack of pink dresses with silver stars on them. "Well, that laugh sounded mischievous."

She smiles and nods at the little boy, telling him to get up and test his shoes. "I just think I need to wish you good luck again."

She can't be serious. Not again.

We already went through this on Tuesday. Of course, who could really blame Merit for feeling overwhelmed then. She had Chloe and three other paparazzi trying to snag pictures of her when she showed up to open the store that morning. Taking a cue from my playbook, she made a deal with Chloe that she would pose for some pictures if Chloe could make the others go away. And if she promised to blur the name of the store and never take pictures of children coming or going. Once the other vultures found out Chloe would have the advantage, they cut their losses and headed out of town.

And that's how new pictures of Merit made their way online by Tuesday afternoon. Chloe told her that people like candid shots best. There are pictures of Merit walking across the parking lot, pictures of Merit pulling a sale table out to the sidewalk, and pictures of Merit walking back into the store with one shoe off because she'd stepped in gum.

My spine stiffens, and a small river of anger flows through my veins. "They were back?"

"Oh no, not that."

"Then what?" I ask.

She laughs, boxing the shoes back up after the little boy decides he wants them because they make him fly like a superhero. "It'll be best if you see for yourself."

As soon as I walk in back, I'm glued to the shit show in front of me. It really cements the fact that I'm falling in love with Merit Eliza Browning.

Hell, I'm *in* love with Merit Eliza Browning.

She's in the small bathroom sitting backward on the toilet like she's riding a horse, with her elbows buried deep in the toilet tank. Her phone is balanced on the sink across from her, and she keeps glancing up, trying to follow along with the plumbing tutorial playing on the screen. She doesn't hear me, doesn't even know I'm behind her. Blowing hair out of her face, she curses under her breath. After another minute, toilet water starts squirting everywhere—the clean water, at least—splashing across her face, and making her squeal.

Racing into the bathroom, I yank her from the toilet seat—out of the line of fire—and turn off the water at the shutoff valve on the wall. I grab a hand towel from the side shelf and wipe down my soaked forearms. Walking over to her, I do my best to hide my shit-eating grin, but based on Merit's scowl, I can tell I'm not doing a very good job. I dab the towel across the bridge of her nose.

Snorting, she tugs it out of my hand and tries to dry herself, eventually tossing it on the wet floor and discreetly cleaning it with her foot.

I lean against the doorframe and study her blushing pink cheeks. "Sooo... whatcha doing?" I ask, drawing out my syllables.

She blinks, keeping a straight face. "The toilet was running. I was changing the ball and that flappy thing."

"And you didn't turn the water off beforehand?"

She glowers at her cell phone, where the random video is still talking her through everything. "*He* didn't say to do that."

"*He* might not even be a plumber. *He* might not even know how to use a toilet, let alone fix one."

She turns off her phone, setting it on the shelf out of the way. "Well, I was doing fine until I had an audience."

"You didn't even hear me come in." I laugh and point at the toilet. "That was all you."

Her pout is so damn cute; I can't stay away from her. Digging my fingers into her waist, I pull her body close to mine. It doesn't go unnoticed by me that she shifts herself even closer, fitting to me like a glove. "Why didn't you just ask me for help?"

"It's simple plumbing. I need to know how to do that stuff by myself."

"But I would've fixed it for you."

She looks down, studying her hands as they splay across my stomach. "You won't always be here," she says in a timid, hushed tone.

Wanna bet.

"Hey," I nudge her chin up, "I'll always be here."

She cocks her head, searching my face. "I thought you said you wouldn't lie to me."

"Mer..." I can't stand to see her hurting, to see her questioning our growing romance. Not sure how else to comfort her, I lean forward and gently graze my lips across hers. My tongue flickers out. With a low and husky sigh, she wraps her hands around my neck, deepening the kiss. Her fingers tangle in my hair, just the way I like.

If she doesn't believe my words, maybe she'll believe my body.

"Well, my plumber didn't do *that* the last time he fixed my toilet." Kyra's voice booms through the room, making Merit jump away from my embrace.

I growl in good-humored frustration. "See, I told you we need new friends," I say with a wink to my girl.

"Hey!" Kyra yells in protest.

Merit chuckles. Completely ignoring both of us, she bends down and starts cleaning the water from the floor. I don't have to see her face to know that her cheeks are bright red. Even her gorgeous tan can't hide her scarlet skin when she's embarrassed.

I think it's funny that she gets embarrassed. Kyra is her best friend; she knows we kiss. Hell, Ridge has walked in on me having sex before. More than once, as a matter of fact. Then again, Merit's still getting used to public displays of affection. Fortunately, the front bell dings and Kyra disappears to help a customer.

Merit leans against the wall when she's done cleaning, watching me as I fix her plumbing masterpiece. "Practice was good today?" she asks.

"Yep. I like the shorter practices on Thursdays. We stop an hour early. It helps build the anticipation for Friday nights." I glance at her reflection in the mirror. "You can come, right? Emily is going to close the store?"

She rolls her eyes and puffs out her cheeks. "Things aren't going so well in that department. Don't get me wrong, Emily is super sweet, and she's good with the kids, but...she's not the sharpest knife in the drawer. She keeps forgetting certain steps in shutting down the point of sale for the night, and she's accidentally set the alarm off more than once."

My heart sinks, like a balloon low on air. "So, you can't come?"

"No, I can," she grins. "Kyra agreed to shut down for me again. I wasn't even going to ask her, but she volunteered. Her boyfriend is having dinner with his mother, and she can't stand his mother. Work is her excuse. So it's a win-win."

"Uh-oh. Sounds like trouble. What if they get married? Then, she'll hate her in-laws. Doesn't sound like the recipe for a long-lasting marriage. Holidays will be torture."

She snorts, "You got that right."

It doesn't take a genius to discern that she's talking about her own situation and not Kyra's. "Mer, I'm sorry, I didn't mean anything by that."

She waves off my concern. "Oh, I know." She shrugs. "But what you said is true."

"You didn't like Edward's parents?"

"Well, I thought I did. Just like I thought I liked Edward," she says. "I was talking about my parents, though."

"Edward didn't like your parents?"

"I don't really think Edward felt *anything* about my parents. He was...indifferent. Polite but not engaged. Respectful but not loving. My mom and dad, though? They freakin' hated Edward. Couldn't stand him." That actually makes her smile widen.

Mine too.

I can't stand the little shit.

"And you stayed with him, even though your parents hated him?"

"They didn't come out and tell me they hated him until years after we started dating. At first, they kept their mouths shut because they honestly didn't think it would go anywhere. They thought I would come to my senses and break up with him. By the time we were engaged, I was already in too deep. I was a completely different person, and when my parents tried to voice their concern, I did my best to convince them he was the love of my life." She frowns. "I think I broke their hearts a little bit. That still haunts me."

I take a look around, making sure I've done everything correctly. Turning on the water, I flush the toilet. Merit leans forward, watching in awe, like she's never seen a working commode before. "So, when do I get to meet them?" I ask as I wash my hands.

"Meet who? My parents?"

"No, the outfielders for the Yankees," I tease. "Of course, your parents."

She flitters out of the bathroom, like a nervous cat, avoiding me. "I'm not sure. I haven't given it any thought."

Bullshit.

She's lying. It's plain to see.

I could press her and get the truth, but there's something else I really want to talk to her about. Something that's going to raise her hackles like a hound dog on the hunt. Letting her think she's won that small battle, I drop the subject. She's pulling some clothes out of delivery boxes, unwrapping them from the plastic packaging. When I join her, mimicking her work, she softly smiles. She watches my every move, like she's committing me to memory, especially the movement of the muscles in my forearms. Her stare makes my dick jump.

"So, you worked here all day?" I ask.

"Of course. Why?"

"You make your loan payment today?"

She freezes, her arms tangled in a red shirt. At first, I don't think she's going to answer me, but she finally does. "Yes, this morning on my way to work. Whyyyy?"

My attempt to fold a boy's polo shirt goes awry, so I just toss it on the shelf. "How much do you owe?"

Her plump lips thin into a small line, and her sparkling hazel eyes harden. "I don't see how that's any of your business."

"Everything about you is my business. And I think it's bullshit you're still paying your ex-husband. After what he did to you? He cheated on you, Mer. And he kept the house. You shouldn't owe him a damn thing."

"I don't owe him. My loan is with Charles."

"We both know that's just a technicality. Besides that, what does it matter? They're both weaselly little fuckers."

She skirts around me, grabbing the polo shirt and re-folding it. "That's beside the point. I still owe them money."

"How much money?" I ask again.

She shakes her head, ignoring me. When she grabs another shirt, I take it from her. I'm trying to force her to focus on me. Instead, she just grabs another shirt. I take that one from her, too, and toss them over my shoulder into the abyss of the room.

She scoffs, flapping her hands in the air. "Seriously?"

I take a step closer. "How much do you owe?"

She tries to take a step away from me, but I'm much quicker than she is. Hell, I still do quick hand ladder drills for fun. My hand snatches out, grabbing her waist. My fingers tangle in her tank top. It's still damp from the toilet water.

She folds her hands in front of her and looks down at the floor. I nudge her hip with mine. "Mer?" I urge her with a gentle voice.

She finally looks up, locking eyes with me. "If I tell you, will you drop it? Will you leave it alone?"

"Yes." Technically, I'm not lying. I'm just leaving the words *'for now'* out of my response.

She nods, "After this morning, I owe $71,620.38." Her eyebrows lift into her hairline, and her face inches closer to mine. She wants me to know she means business. "But it's fine. If the store keeps doing good and I keep watching what I spend, I'll be able to pay them off two years from this coming February. So, about thirty months. And that assumes I hire another worker to do fifteen to twenty hours a week. Then, I can move out of his condo, and I won't have to see him ever again."

What the fuck?

Did I just hear what I thought I heard?

"Excuse me? What do you mean, *his* condo?"

Her eyes widen and her mouth falls open. She looks like one of those porcelain dolls pretending to sing. "Oh, I didn't mention that?" She uses my shock as an opportunity to break away from my embrace. "I should go help Kyra. I've been back here for way too long."

My coach's voice comes out, booming across the back room, forcing her to stop mid-escape. "Merit Eliza Browning, you aren't going anywhere." I rub my jaw, waiting for her to slowly turn around. "You live in your ex-husband's house?"

She lifts a finger in the air, tsking me. "Not his house. His condo. They're two completely different things."

Smartass.

Not to get sidetracked, but I love it. The Merit I met a month ago wouldn't have acted like this.

"Fine. You live in *his condo, not his house*?"

She nibbles on the side of her lip. "Yes."

I lift my arms and drag my hands through my hair. The movement must raise my shirt because she's suddenly focused on my stomach.

"It's not as bad as it sounds," she offers.

"I don't even know what to say." I shake my head in disbelief. "How? Why?"

"Edward lived in the condo during college and law school. He never sold it. It just sat vacant. When we divorced, we agreed that I would stay there rent-free until I could pay off the business loan. That's part of the reason I've been able to pay so much extra each month. I don't have rent or a house payment looming over me."

"He didn't sell it when he bought that big ol' house for y'all? You realize that probably means he kept it so he could use it as a place to meet women, right? Delaney and whoever might've been before her that you don't even know about."

She blinks. "I know."

"Then why?"

"I already told you, the sooner I can pay the loan off, the sooner I can be done with them all." Her shoulders slump. "I'm so ready to be done with them, Holt. They've taken enough of me."

I wrap her in my arms.

Because she's right. And I might be getting myself into trouble, but I'm not letting them take another damn thing from her.

Chapter 20

Merit

My boyfriend's parents are driving me home from the football game.

Yep.

I'm twenty-eight and doing something a high school sophomore would do.

And *boyfriend*? That's a new development. Very new and something we didn't even discuss. After the game, Holt just introduced me to the opposing coach as his girlfriend.

I should be scared. Hell, I should be terrified. But I'm not. When he said it, my stomach fluttered, and a warm heat ballooned in my heart.

I'm listening to Ray and Teresa talk about buying new flowers for their back porch when my phone dings with an incoming text.

Holt: You'll get home earlier than me. The bus is nearly back at school, but I have to wait for all the kids to get picked up. My parents can let you in the house. Wait for me?

I smile, typing out a teasing response.

Me: I should really get home. Tomorrow is the monthly 20% off sale. It'll be a busy day. I'll just see you later?

I doubt he's even had a chance to read the whole text message before he's calling me. I'm chuckling under my breath when I answer. I don't even say hello. "I was kidding."

The celebration and noise on the bus drowns him out. "You were kidding?"

"Yes. Of course, I'll wait for you."

I literally hear him smiling across the line. "Good."

When we pull up in Holt's driveway, I just assume Ray and Teresa will come inside, but they don't. Ray uses the keypad to open the door and disarm the house alarm while I put my rain jacket in my parked car. I was worried it was going to rain during the game, but fortunately, the skies cleared. After waving goodbye to his parents and thanking them for driving me to and from the out-of-town game, I meander my way through my boyfriend's empty mansion.

"Hey." Holt's voice pours over my skin like melted butter. It takes me a minute to crawl off the couch. It's so comfy I nearly fell asleep. "What are you doing just sitting here? You didn't wanna turn on the TV?" His strong arms circle me.

I love the way Holt hugs me. His hugs are never quick; they're long and sincere. His large, muscular hand massages the small of my back, and slowly travels up the length of my spine, settling on the nape of my neck. I lean back, looking into his eyes. The blue sparkles with the excitement of his win. His body is sticky with sweat. Even the curls peeking out from underneath his ballcap are damp.

"I was afraid to turn it on. What if I break it?" I look over his shoulder at the world's biggest TV screen.

"You don't need to worry about that, Mer. There's nothing in this house that can't be fixed if it breaks."

He hasn't let me go yet. My fingertips trace the veins in his forearms. "Speaking of the rest of the house, we never finished the tour. I wanna see the rest of it."

He cocks an eyebrow. "You've been here by yourself for an hour. You didn't snoop around?"

Trust me, I wanted to. I'm super curious, and just sitting around has been killing me. But with my luck, I would've broken some priceless Ming vase or some crap like that.

When I shake my head, he laughs. His voice is slightly hoarse from yelling on the sidelines. "I tell you what, I'm jumping in the shower. You snoop around all you want. I have nothing to hide." He winks, planting a salty kiss on my mouth, leaving me standing in the middle of his living room as he takes the stairs two at a time.

I walk down the hall, peeking into the rooms as I pass. There's a theater room with a huge movie screen and two rows of reclining seats. I smile much larger than a sane person would at the thought of watching old movies in there with Holt. Then, two large guest bedrooms with a massive bathroom between the two. There's one last room, much smaller than all the others, in what looks like the 'normal' area of the house. Beyond that, there's a small hallway. I can only assume that leads to the Children's Wing. When I flip on the light switch in the last room, I have to take a step back to catch my breath.

Crystal and gold and silver and diamonds are everywhere.

And I mean...everywhere.

It's a trophy room. With literal trophies.

There's so much stuff stored in the small room it almost looks comical. Framed pictures, newspapers, and magazine covers adorn the walls. And everything in here has two things in common—it's all about football and all about Holt. There are cheap plastic trophies from when he was younger. The older he got, the fancier the awards got. And then there's a glass case filled with diamond and gold rings. The biggest ones, declaring him a Super Bowl winner. Two times over.

Most people would have this stuff on display in their living room or something. Someplace where anyone and everyone could see it. But Holt? It's in a small, non-descript room, far out of the way.

I run my fingers over a magazine cover from one of his many college National Championship wins. The picture is so crisp, I can see the freckles on his nose.

Carefully shutting off the lights, I turn and walk down the darkened hallway to the isolated wing. My heart beats faster as I open the door at the end of the corridor. It feels like I'm doing something I shouldn't be doing. But he gave me free rein. Free rein to look, and I can't curb the desire to know more, see more.

This is where his cousins lived.

Ella, whom I've grown to like so very much over the past few weeks. With her honey-colored hair, extreme posture, and round belly. And who can forget the stolen glances she shares with her husband? It's like the world is theirs, and the rest of us are just living in it out of the kindness of their hearts.

And Carrie, whom I will never meet.

The wing is bigger than my condo. There's a small laundry room, an open kitchen and living room, and two bedrooms each with their own bath. One bedroom is decorated in pale blues and greens. The other in beige, dark brown, and bright coral. Lots of colors. I remember Holt saying that Ella required him to redecorate everything after buying the house, especially the Children's Wing. From what I understand, it was nothing but creams and grays and whites—professionally decorated without a thought to it being children's living quarters.

I think back to my own room growing up. My furniture was mismatched pieces Mom and Granny refurbished. And I think I changed the color of my bedspread every single year.

Instead of shutting the door, blocking the wing back off from the rest of the house, I leave it wide open. I make my way back to the living room and up the marble staircase. My flip flops pound against the polished stone, echoing through the house. The first room I come to upstairs is a large laundry room. The ironing board is standing in the middle of the floor, yet I can still spin around with my arms wide open and not knock it over. Now, that's a big laundry room.

Two of the upstairs bedrooms share a bathroom. The third guest bedroom has its own bathroom. It's a large bedroom, and I can tell right away that it's a bedroom for the kids—Anna, Ty, and Laura.

My heart melts a little at that realization. There're two twin beds piled high with pink and purple comforters. In the corner, there's a toddler bed on the floor with a superhero blanket on it. The bookshelves are filled with toys, books, and games. There's even a white porch swing dangling from the ceiling, with another pile of books and notebooks stacked on its puffy cushion.

The last bedroom door is partially closed. By process of elimination, I know what's behind that door, and it makes my mouth dry and my stomach fold in knots.

Holt's bedroom.

My feet feel like weighted concrete as I take a step closer to his room. I glance to the side when I hear the telltale ping of an incoming text message and see his cell phone plugged in and charging on a side table. Leaning in that direction, I flip it over and check the home screen, wanting to make sure there's not an emergency. What if something happened to Ray and Teresa on their drive home? The first line of a message blazes across a picture of him and Anna.

Nope. Not a text message...just an alert from some sort of sports app. I quickly flip the phone back over and close the distance between me and his bedroom.

His. Fucking. Bedroom.

I gently push against the door, trying not to push too hard because I don't want to slam it against the wall. I take a step forward right at the same time Holt jerks the door open. I run slap dab into his chest.

"Whoops," I say with a stumble. His arm darts out, catching me.

All of a sudden, I can't breathe.

And it's not because my funny bone hit the doorframe.

He's standing in front of me, wearing nothing but low-slung gym shorts. Beads of water drip from his hair onto his chest and travel along the paths of his muscles, down his stomach. My eyes eagerly trace every drop...down, down, down. His love handles are indented, chiseled with years of exercise. More importantly, I don't see the band of his boxer briefs.

I. Cannot. Breathe.

The thought that he's naked underneath the gray shorts makes it hard to swallow. Hard to think. Hard to stay on my feet.

He smells like soap and toothpaste.

I'm ogling his body like I've never seen a man up close before. And I haven't. Not a man like Holt. Edward, most assuredly, is not the same as this man before me.

Even the other night when we made out after our fight and I stripped the shirt from his body and scraped my teeth across his nipples, I didn't have the opportunity to fully appreciate what he looks like. Every time I tried to pull away, he pulled me back in, acting like he couldn't survive without his mouth on mine.

Without thinking, my fingers reach forward, wiping away a rivulet of water before it reaches his belly button.

My gaze is drawn up to his face the second he sucks a sharp hiss of air between his teeth. His eyes are dilated, nearly drowning the blue in black.

My heart stops beating.

"You finished the tour?" he asks.

I have to wet my lips to even get enough traction to talk. "Mmm-hmm. Yep. Saved the best room for last," I say with a nod behind his shoulder.

"Well," he steps to the side, giving me a wide berth. "Don't let me stop you."

I can't believe I find the strength to cross the threshold, but I do. The room is very large. Should I expect anything less from this house? On one side of the room is a small sitting area—a plush loveseat and two chairs, with side tables and lamps. The king-size bed is made, but lacks the fluff and decoration of the other beds. It's covered in some kind of fake fur comforter marbled with shades of black, gray, and white. There's two nightstands, two armoires, a dresser, and a super big TV on the wall. A light shines behind the door in the corner. I'm guessing that leads to the bathroom.

I close my eyes, doing something that I know will get me into trouble.

I picture myself on the bed, writhing beneath the scorching heat of Holt's touch.

As if on command, his hands grab my hips, and he nuzzles against the side of my face. I can feel the bulge of his erection pressing into my lower back. "Stay with me tonight," his whisper is low and gravelly, and the essence of my wet dreams.

My swallow is audible. "I can't."

"Why not?"

"I don't have my stuff."

His chuckle sends a shivered heat down my spine. "What stuff?"

"My toothbrush."

"I have a whole bucket filled with toothbrushes. I save every free toothbrush the dentist gives me."

Huh. Me too.

"Well," I stammer, "I... I don't have my shampoo and conditioner."

"I have plenty. And if you don't like what I have, the girls' strawberry-scented kid's shampoo is right next door."

My brain churns, trying to think of another excuse, when all my body wants to do is strip him naked and lick him from top to bottom.

He spins me around, holding my face in his hands. "Stay with me."

"I don't want to." My voice sounds so pathetic even I don't believe it.

"Don't lie, Merit."

"Mmmm?"

"You wanna stay. It's written all over your face."

I nibble on my lip, not answering. I turn back around. Maybe if I turn around, I won't have to confront the emotions swirling in my mind and body.

He drags my ponytail to the side and kisses the nape of my neck. "Tell me the truth," he urges softly. The tenderness of his actions and my own need soak my panties even more.

"I wanna stay. But I don't think we should have sex yet."

"I'm okay with that."

I twist my neck and kiss the stubble on his jaw. "You are?"

He chuckles again, nodding. "Yes. We have every day for the rest of our lives. There's plenty of time."

Oh, he shouldn't say things like that. He shouldn't promise me a lifetime of happiness unless he plans to deliver.

His lips kiss a slow path down my neck. It sends pure electricity coursing through me, from head to toe. His left hand finds my breast, eagerly teasing my nipple through the fabric of my shirt and bra. His breath hitches, and it's like I can literally hear his hand shaking as it snakes down my stomach, down my pelvis. Cupping my groin, he firmly strokes the mound of my sex through my panties and shorts. Clothes be damned, he finds my clit right away and circles his thumb around it.

Holy shit. I want him.

His whisper is sticky and sweet. "But, how do you feel about heavy petting, baby?"

My voice is so loud it rivals a full-blown scream. "Oh god, I'm completely for it."

Spinning around, I jump into his arms and crash my lips to his.

Chapter 21

Holt

"Are you sure you wanna do this, son?" Dad's voice booms through the speakers of my truck. "You're opening yourself up to a whole new group of people. Showing them the real you. The actual person behind the fame, the money. You don't need to do this unless you're serious about it. You're gonna expose your heart, and there's always the chance someone will try to hurt you, make it about the money. Like they always do."

"I'm sure about it." I try to wipe the grin from my face, but I can't. "She's the *one*."

He snickers. "I know."

My eyebrows lift. "You know?"

"Son, I knew the second you walked her out on that back patio. You gave her the look."

"What look?"

"The look that says *I'll never need another thing in life. Only you.*' Plus, you've been flitting around like a giddy schoolgirl who just got asked to prom." He bellows at his own joke.

"Thanks for that, Dad," I say with sarcasm.

"It'll definitely be odd not having you with the family for a Labor Day cookout, but we all understand."

I can't believe I'm actually nervous. "What if her parents don't like me?"

"Does her dad like football?"

"Yeah."

"Well, I think you're probably good, then. Be safe. We love you."

I pull up in front of the store. I've barely thrown the truck into park when I see her come out of the shop, trying to carry her overnight bags. One snags in the door, and she trips, busting ass. "Dad, I gotta go. Love you guys too."

I get out and jog over to her, but Emily is already helping her up. Merit's cheeks are rosy with embarrassment. Merit and I both thank Emily as she heads back into the store to help with a customer. I search over her body, looking for injuries. "Are you okay?"

"Just my knee." She lifts a leg in the air, and we watch as some blood bubbles around a scrape.

"We need to go in and wash it off."

She shoos me away, waving her hand in the air. "Oh, it'll be fine. C'mon, let's go." It's clear she's super excited.

She tries to pick up both overnight bags, but I playfully slap her hand away and throw them over my left shoulder. "But you're bleeding."

"Oh, it'll stop. It's no big deal." She takes a step in the direction of my truck and freezes mid-step. And for just a second, the old Merit takes hold. She turns back around, folding her hands in front of her and staring at the ground. "Holt, I'm sorry. I didn't even think about your truck. I don't want to get it dirty with my blood. That was inconsiderate of me. I'll go wash up."

She moves to walk right past me, but I snatch her up. I dip down and sling her over my empty shoulder. Her upside-down laugh is contagious, and she has to push against my butt to keep from flopping around. My hands are tucked securely under her ass cheeks, holding her in place. I can't help myself—I graze my thumb across the elastic of her panties. When we get to the truck, I don't immediately put her down. I open the door and unload her bags first. Smacking her on the ass, I finally put her down. Her hazel eyes sparkle, the blues are really prominent today.

We both look down at my T-shirt. The front of it is smeared with blood. She cocks her head. "That might not come out, you know."

I shrug. "I've worn dirtier things."

She's about to lean in for a kiss when we're interrupted.

It was gonna be a good one too. I could tell.

I want to be mad at whoever decided to intrude on our moment, but it's hard to do when I hear a little boy's voice. "Excuse me, sir? May I have a picture with you?"

I turn around and see a young kid and his mom. "Hey, there. Absolutely. What's your name, son?"

"Aiden."

"Aiden, that's a good name. How old are you?"

"Eleven."

"Eleven. That's great. Do you play football, Aiden?"

He nods proudly, sticking his chest out. "I just started this year. Special teams."

I squeeze his shoulder. "That's a tough job. Be sure to listen to your coach." He nods enthusiastically. "And this is your mom?" I ask, nodding to the woman beside him.

The buxom brunette giggles. "Oh no, I'm his aunt." She drags a fingernail across her cleavage before ruffling his hair. "Just spending some quality time with Aiden. Children are a blessing. I'm just soaking him in until my time comes."

The look on Aiden's face nearly has me rolling on the pavement in laughter. You can tell by his shocked frown that this has to be a babysitting situation and that she never spends time with him unless absolutely necessary.

She offers her hand, and I quickly shake it. "Stephanie. You can call me Steph."

Why would I call her Steph? I don't even know her and most assuredly won't see her again after she leaves.

Ignoring her, I nod at the phone in Aiden's hand. "Got the camera ready?"

Without my prodding, Merit immediately steps up. Bending down, she tells Aiden that she'd be happy to take the picture and listens intently as he gives her detailed instructions on how to use the camera, like it's something that was just invented last week.

After my picture with Aiden, Stephanie announces that it's time for a picture with both of them, and she quickly tucks herself against my side. Her manicured nails scratch down the back of my shirt. I discreetly shift my legs, pulling out of the way, when her fingers dip beneath the band of my shorts, right above my ass.

Eager to be done with the meet and greet, I reach in my pocket for a penny but come up empty. "Shoot." I nod at Merit. "Can you check the console? I keep extras in there."

She climbs into the truck, grabbing a shiny copper penny. She's a little too quick for Stephanie's liking, though. Stephanie barely has time to tuck the piece of paper with her cell phone number on it in my breast pocket. Pretending to ignore what she just saw, Merit bypasses me and hands the penny directly to Aiden.

He smiles wide. "Thanks so much."

Standing tall, Merit folds her arms across her chest, glaring at Stephanie. Stephanie stares at Merit and then mimics her face, scrunched nose and all. "Yeah, I smell that too. I think some workers hit a sewer line somewhere down the road."

I try to drown my laugh with a pretend cough, but I'm not a very good actor.

We climb into the truck the second Aiden and Stephanie walk away and start the drive to her parents' house. "Emily's working today?" I ask, questioning the obvious since I just saw her.

"Emily and Kim are both working the rest of the day. Kyra's going to come in and close up for me." Her voice is much more stoic than it should be.

She sits on her hands and stares out the window. Her leg, with the now-dried blood, bounces up and down.

Reaching into my chest pocket, I pull out the piece of paper with Stephanie's phone number on it and hold it under Merit's nose. "Care to do something with this?"

That brings back her wide smile. The one that makes my dick jump in my pants.

She lowers the window, and she's about to toss the number out when she realizes that would have her littering. Raising the window, she looks around the truck, trying to decide what to do with the vile piece of paper. She spots an old, half-empty water bottle in the bottom pocket of the door. Opening it, she drowns the number inside. Quite satisfied with herself, she smugly sits back in her seat. "And by the way, I *do not* make a face."

Merit talks the whole time.

And I mean the *whole* time.

I love it.

"Oh, I can't believe I nearly forgot to tell you. I think I found the right person to hire."

"Really?"

"She's a high school senior, valedictorian of her class. She gets out of school each day at lunch, so she can work half-days any day, Tuesday through Friday, and she can work any Saturday I need her. Right now, she works at a women's boutique downtown. They use the same point-of-sale system as me. Obviously, she's really smart, so it should be a breeze teaching her how to shut down the system, set the alarm, and close up." She looks over at me, lifting her eyebrows. "I think Emily is relieved."

"That's so good. When is she supposed to start?"

"She's turning in her two-week notice at her other job today." She points to a side road. "Turn here."

Doing as she says, it's clear to see we're on the right road. As far as the eye can see, there's fields of Bermuda grass, bright and green and thick. After a couple of minutes, we turn into the driveway, parking in front of a remodeled farm house. There's a quintessential red barn next to it, and a few other buildings about a quarter of a mile away. "Mer, this is gorgeous."

She smiles brightly, dulling my senses with her beauty. "Thank you."

Right as we turn off the car, two women race out the front door. A second later, a man walks around the side of the house. The process of elimination is pretty quick; it's her parents and her grandmother. The women hug and kiss and chatter, leaving me alone to greet Merit's father. He's wearing jeans and a dirty T-shirt with the company name on the pocket—Browning Sod Farm.

I remove my ballcap and tuck it in my back pocket. "Sir," I immediately shake his hand. "Pleasure to meet you."

He flicks his own ballcap up, giving himself a better view. "Ah, you must be the ball player."

"Yes, sir. Holt Hill."

"Well, Holt, I'm Deke Browning. And this," he nods to his wife and mother, who both wrap me in hugs, "is my wife Marie and my mother, Gertie."

"Ma'am." I politely nod at them. "Pleasure to meet you both." I look around at the property. "You have a beautiful home."

Gertie speaks up. "My husband's father built it. There was a small one-bedroom cottage they lived in for years after he bought the land." She points to a section of yard, closer to the road. "Eventually, he built this house. Of course, Deke and Marie really outdid themselves with a remodel a few years ago." She smiles at her son. "His daddy would've been proud of him."

I nod, eagerly agreeing, "Yes, ma'am, absolutely."

"Y'all made such good time. I'm so glad you're here!" Marie reaches over, giving Merit another kiss on the cheek.

Deke clears his throat. "Girl, you don't have a hug for your own father?" Laugh lines crinkle around his eyes.

Merit laughs loudly, snorting. "You're the one ignoring me, old man." She wraps her arms around her father, hugging him with all her might. Deke soothes her hair and kisses her forehead.

It's beautiful.

I have to say…there's definitely a special bond between fathers and daughters. On more than one occasion, I've been jealous of Raylee.

Irrational, I know.

"Well, come on in. Get settled." Marie waves her hand at the house.

"Actually, we've got a couple of hours before the game comes on," Deke says.

By *'the game',* he means the team from where Merit went to college—the college in the town where we both live. My alma matter already played today. In fact, I tried to listen to the game on the drive down, but I found myself more interested in Merit's constant stories.

Like I said, she was really excited.

He looks at me, lifting his eyebrows. "Feel like doing a few chores?"

"Deke! He's our guest! You can't put him to work." Marie chides him.

I chuckle. "I don't mind. Really. It'll be good to stretch my legs after the drive."

He looks me over. Luckily, I have on tennis shoes instead of flip flops. "You need to change?"

I look down at my blood-stained T-shirt. "No, sir. I'm good."

Merit rolls her eyes and bounces over to me. "You don't have to do chores, you know that, right?" She doesn't bother to lower her voice, letting her dad hear what she says.

I love this Merit. The Merit comfortable in her own skin and her own surroundings.

My head tilts toward hers. I can't help it. It's like there's a magnet drawing me to her. Constantly. Obsessively. I should back up, put some space between us. I suppose being this close to his daughter might be construed as a sign of disrespect.

But…it's her own damn fault for being so irresistible.

"I reckon you're worth a little hard work," I whisper with a wink. My fingers tangle with hers, and I discreetly pinch her thigh. At least,

I think it's discreet. "And don't try to carry the luggage, you'll hurt yourself. I'll unload everything after I get back. Okay?"

She nods, biting back a smile. "Whatever you say, *sir*," she whispers back, teasing me.

∝

"So, you're dating my daughter?"

I pick up two fifty-pound fertilizer bags from stacked pallets and lay them in the bed of a work truck. Nothing like slinging bagged manure for the woman you love. "Yes, sir. We've been dating for a little over a month."

Deke moved a couple of bags himself, but now he's content to lean on the truck and watch me. Size me up. And who can blame him? I'm dating his daughter.

Well, more than dating her.

In fact, I had my fingers inside of her again last night after the football game, making her writhe against me, making her come. She's the sexiest little creature I've ever seen when she's coming. And I can't get enough of it. Her body, her moans. The way she tangles her fingers in my hair, pulling it almost to the point of pain. Just as promised, though, we are taking things slow. I haven't even gone down on her yet. In fact, I've only finger-fucked her with her *panties on*, obsessively committing to memory what I can while I have her panties pushed to the side. It's been fucking torture. Her pussy is pink and perfect and ripe. It smells like heaven, and what little bit of her I've licked from my fingers tastes like sugar and spice and fucking everything nice.

I also haven't let her touch me. I want it. Trust me, I want it so fucking bad, I can't see straight. But... I'm afraid I'll lose control. I don't want to move too fast, don't want to scare her. She's slept over just twice, last Friday and Saturday nights, and each time, when she was fast asleep, I snuck into the bathroom and jerked off until I was shooting nothing but sand.

"You gonna change her too?"

I wipe the sweat from my brow—even though it's a losing battle—and balance my forearms on the back of the truck. "Pardon?"

His voice lowers. "He changed her." He reworks the hat on his head. "You know from the minute Merit was born she was silly and loud and independent. And he changed all that. Before we even knew it, he had molded her into a completely different person. She was a shadow of her former self." He looks down, and I hear him kick the dirt with his boot. "And he forced her to dress like some high-priced escort. I knew what he was doing. He wanted other men to envy him. He wanted to prance her around like a prized filly."

I breathe through my nose, trying to calm the rage coursing through my body. Pictures of black mini-dresses flip through my brain. String bikinis and jewelry. Layers of makeup and stiletto heels. Visions of other men hitting on my woman make me sick to my stomach. Deke's right. That's exactly what Edward did, and I want to pummel his fucking face for it.

"So," he cocks his head, "do you plan on changing her too?"

"No, sir, I don't wanna change her. I wanna be the one who finds her."

He stands straight, studying me for several long seconds. When he doesn't say anything, I push off and grab another two bags. "Holy shit, you're in love with her."

My hand slips, and my thumb breaks the bag, sliding right into the rich, black dirt filled with shit. I toss the bag in the truck and wipe my hand across the front of my shirt.

Well, I guess there's no point in lying to the man.

"Yes, sir, I am."

"You tell her yet?"

That makes me laugh. "Definitely not. I just now got her to stop saying '*I don't date*'. I don't think she's ready for a conversation that heavy."

"Smart man." He shuts the tailgate of the truck.

I guess that means we're done loading it.

His lips thin into a small line. "You know, it doesn't matter whether or not you love her...you're still sleeping in separate bedrooms when you're under my roof."

I nearly choke on my own spit. "Well, sir, you'll be happy to know that the thing married people need a bed for? Yeah, that hasn't happened with us."

Yet.

Of course, I keep that last word to myself.

He waves his hand in the air, telling me to get in the truck. He tries to hide his smile, but there's no way to miss it.

I just earned her daddy's respect, and I smile right back.

Chapter 22

Merit

I reach for another handful of popcorn, carefully making sure I don't shift the blanket. I don't want Daddy to see Holt's hand caressing my thigh. Although my dad's not stupid, so I'm sure he knows something's up. I mean, the thermometer on the side wall of the screened-in back porch shows it's still seventy-six degrees outside, despite the late hour. And we're covered in a blanket. Needless to say, we're suspicious as hell.

It's been a great two days. Better than great, actually. Fabulous.

My family loves Holt. It's plain to see. Last night, after whatever 'chores' Holt and Daddy did, we all watched college football together. It's the first time I've really done that since my grandfather died, and I forgot how much I missed it. Best of all? Daddy really enjoyed it. He and Holt talked until after two in the morning.

Today, after church, I took Holt all around the property and showed him everything about the farm. And now, we're on the porch, watching a movie together. Well, everyone except Granny, who went to bed a while ago. Daddy is actually taking tomorrow off, too, which is almost unheard of for him. Farmers don't get holidays. But a couple of the employees volunteered to work because they want the double-time pay. The plan is to drive to the coast for an early lunch and spend a few hours on the beach before Holt and I head back home. Mom loves the beach and used our visit as an excuse to guilt-trip Daddy into a day trip.

I dropped a kernel of popcorn down my shirt, and I'm trying to fish it out when my phone buzzes with an incoming call. A ball of dread forms in the pit of my stomach when I glance at the screen. I quickly hit the decline button. I wish there was a 'flip the bird' button, but decline will have to work for now. After a couple of minutes, it happens again.

I do my best to avoid eye contact with Holt, but he nudges me with his elbow. "Kyra?" he whispers.

I shake my head no.

"Alarm company?" he whispers, louder than last time.

I give him a side glance, pretending to be engrossed in the movie. "It's no one."

He frowns when I don't offer an explanation. He's about to ask another question when my phone buzzes for a third time.

I'm gonna kill the bastard.

Yanking my phone from the table, my legs tumble off Holt's lap, and I mumble an excuse to my family, telling them I'll be right back. I speed walk through the house and race up the steps to my bedroom. By the time I get there, the phone's done ringing. I stare at the screen, daring it to ring again. Daring it to give me a reason to fling it across the room like a Frisbee.

Sure enough, the vile device dares me again.

"Yes," I answer. There's plenty of other greetings I'd like to extend to my ex-husband, but I'm trying to remember I'm still a lady.

"Well, that's an interesting way to answer the phone."

I never would've answered the phone like this when we were married. Just the thought of defying his expectations of politeness makes me smile a little bit. "Edward, it's late. Why are you calling me?"

"I know it's late. So, imagine my surprise when I stopped by the condo for a visit and found you weren't home."

"Why on earth would you stop by the condo?"

"I need to discuss something with you. Are you coming back soon?"

"No," I growl, already perturbed this conversation has lasted as long as it has. "I'm at my parents' this weekend."

"Ahhh, how are Deke and Marie? Please give them my best."

He's got to be kidding. He knows my parents despise him. "Edward, we're in the middle of something. Can this discussion wait until I get back? If it's about the loan—"

He cuts me off midsentence. "I'm selling the condo. You'll need to be out by next Sunday. One week from today."

All the blood rushes from my brain, down my body, and pools in my toes. For a second, I feel like I'm about to faint. I grab onto the edge of my bed. Unable to hold the phone up to my ear, I put the speaker on and drop it on my white and green-striped comforter. "Excuse me?"

"I'm selling the condo."

"What do you mean you're selling the condo?"

He sighs like he's disappointed that I don't comprehend what he's saying. "I've held onto it for way too long. It's a drain on my resources. Appraised values have really increased, and I have a motivated buyer lined up. It's a cash offer and they'll be taking possession in two weeks. I need you out so I can have everything professionally cleaned. It's the courteous thing to do. We both know you were never the best housekeeper."

My voice raises. "The courteous thing? The courteous thing! The courteous thing would be giving me some notice." I shake my head violently, giving myself a headache. "No! No. What about the divorce settlement? That says I can stay there, Edward. I have the right to stay there."

"The condo is mine and mine alone. The divorce decree specifically says that, and you know it. You were a legal assistant, Merit. Or did you forget everything I taught you." He starts his car and the phone switches over to Bluetooth. "I was letting you stay in the condo out of the kindness of my heart. I was giving you a break so you could make the business loan payments to my father. I wouldn't want my father to pay for your poor financial mistakes. But," he sighs again, this time more dramatically, "the time has come for you to stand on your own two feet. I can't support you anymore, Merit."

Support me? He thinks he's supporting me. Oh, that's just fucking ridiculous. There's not even a word to describe how big of an asshole he is. "I have to work when I get back! How do you expect me to work at the store, find a new place, and move—all at the same time and in less than a week? I need more time, Edward."

"Hang up the phone, Merit." Holt's voice catches me off guard.

I spin around to find him standing in my doorway. If I weren't about to throw up, I'd find the whole intimidating vision of him incredibly sexy.

"Hang up the phone, Merit," he says again. His voice is low and predatory. I've never heard him speak that way before.

"What? Who's there? Deke?"

Holt stares at the phone like Edward's about to emerge from it like a genie from a bottle. Fury etches across his face, and his hands curl into fists. Before I can say anything, Holt crosses the room and grabs my phone from the bed.

"She'll be out by Saturday."

"Holt? Holt, is that you?" Edward cackles into the phone. His high-pitched laugh sounds like nails on a chalkboard. "Ah, man. You realize she's only after you because of your money. That's all she cares about. Her *and* her family. They have everybody fooled. You know that sod farm has been close to bankruptcy more than once."

I open my mouth to defend my family, but Holt's already answering. "Shut the hell up, Edward. Like I said, she'll be out by Saturday. And don't worry about the professional cleaning. We'll take care of that. Consider it our parting gift." He hangs up on Edward. His grip on the phone is so tight his knuckles are white.

What the hell just happened? Holt just agreed to Edward's demands, and in the process made me homeless. "What did you just do?" I gasp.

Holt shrugs. "You'll just move in with me."

"Absolutely not," Daddy and I both say at the exact same time.

We're all sitting around the kitchen table trying to digest what just happened. Correction, Holt, Mom, and I are sitting at the kitchen table. Daddy is pacing back and forth, wearing a hole in the floor.

"It's not like that, Deke. There's an apartment connected to my house. It's completely separate living quarters. It even has its own entrance from the outside."

I shake my head. "We can't move in with each other. That's totally crazy."

Holt cocks an eyebrow. "Why is that crazy? It's no crazier than living in your ex-husband's condo."

Touché.

Daddy finally sits down, chugging from the beer bottle he grabbed from the fridge. "It's a little soon to be talking about living together, don't you think?"

Mom tilts her head and makes a tsking noise with her teeth. "Deke, I think you may be forgetting that we met each other and within two months were married. Compared to us, the kids are taking it slow."

He chides her underneath his breath. "Marie? Really? You think *now's* the appropriate time to talk about that?"

She lovingly rubs his arm. "They're not even talking about living together. Good grief, he just said it's a separate apartment."

Daddy snorts like a horse and lifts a furry eyebrow. "And you expect me to believe these two..." he nods in our direction, "will let some walls and doors keep them separated? They can't even keep their hands off one another for two seconds."

Eww. Gross. My dad is about to have a sex talk with me and my boyfriend. I shake my hands in the air, interrupting before the conversation goes any further. "Where I put my hands is a moot point because I'm not moving in." Well, that's not exactly how I planned to word that. "What I mean is…I'm just going to find my own apartment. I'll rent."

Holt leans back in the chair. Reaching up, he grabs his baseball cap and turns it around backward. He lazily folds his hands behind his head. "Really?"

I scowl at him. He knows I like it when he moves like that, flexes his arms like that. It stretches his shirt across his broad chest.

He's playing dirty.

"Yes, really. If I find someplace cheap enough, I can budget other ways and still pay the loan off early." When I tell them my thoughts on a price range, Holt bursts out laughing and Daddy chokes on his beer.

Mom pats my hand. "Honey, you live in a city. Sure, it's not a gigantic city, but it's still a city. Even I know you can't find anything for that price range in a decent location."

"I don't need a decent location. I'll be fine with anything."

"Mer, you'd have better luck finding housing on Skid Row for that price," Holt says.

Why does he have to look so good when he's being so irksome. "Oh, will you just put your hands down and turn that hat back around!"

And what does that get me?

A playful wink.

That jerk!

When I don't smile, he rolls his eyes. But at least, he finally puts his hands down. Ignoring me, he turns back to my parents. "The apartment has two bedrooms, two full bathrooms, a kitchen, a living room, and a laundry room. It even has its own separate driveway on the opposite side of the house. It's already furnished." When my parents exchange a look, Holt uses that opportunity to dig even deeper. "Let me do this. Please. I'll do anything and everything for Merit. Let me help her. I'm begging you."

My anxiety makes everything move in a fog of slow motion. Turning to Daddy, Mom nods her agreement. He takes one last swig of his beer. "I guess it's settled, then."

Holt smiles, wrapping his fingers around mine. "It's settled."

I smack my free hand against my forehead. "What the hell just happened?" I mumble.

Chapter 23

Merit

"I can't believe we got everything in one trip," Ridge says, carrying a box inside my new apartment—aka the Children's Wing.

We were able to load up all my possessions in his truck and Holt's truck. He sets it on the kitchen counter, and Ella immediately opens it and starts unloading some cooking utensils. Crutch, Ray, and Teresa are here helping too. I think it surprised everyone to find out that none of the furniture in the condo was mine. Not the couch, not the bed, not even the TV.

"Merit, I love all these movies. You have a great collection." Ray looks at the covers of some DVDs and Blu-rays as he stores them in the living room cabinet.

"You play them at the store, right?" Teresa asks. "Both Holt and Raylee said something about it."

I peek inside a box labeled bedroom and see my panties. I quickly shove it underneath my arm. "That's right. Whenever the store is open, I have some type of old movie playing. Children nowadays have no exposure to that kind of stuff. I mean, when I see a child get completely engrossed in the dance scene between Gene Kelly and Jerry Mouse in *Anchors Aweigh*? It's just breathtaking."

Crutch leans against the counter, taking a break from installing a new faucet. He absentmindedly and possessively rubs his hand across Ella's pregnant belly. "I'll have to admit, when you made me watch *Singin' in the Rain*, it was better than I thought it would be."

She smiles. "So, what you're saying is...you should always listen to your wife."

Instead of answering, he leans forward and kisses her.

Passionately.

Heat blossoms across my cheeks. No one else seems to mind their public display of affection. I guess they're used to it. Not knowing what else to do, I turn to carry the box into the bedroom. I stop at the threshold to the hallway, unsure which way to go.

"Which bedroom are you taking?" Ridge asks. He's got another box in his hands marked bedroom.

"Oh... I... uh..."

Holt slides his arm around my waist. His touch sends a tingle down my spine.

I love that feeling.

"You can choose either one," he offers.

I nuzzle against his jawline, whispering so everyone doesn't hear me. "I shouldn't be in *her* room. I don't wanna be rude or disrespectful. I don't wanna tarnish her memory."

He doesn't ask who. He knows I'm talking about his cousin, Carrie.

Ella's soft voice catches me by surprise. "You won't tarnish her memory." She gently laughs. "She would've liked you, you know. All she ever wanted was for all of us to be happy. And you make Holt happy. It's as simple as that." She nods to the two bedroom doors. "Just choose. It's only four walls. Nothing more."

Holt kisses my cheek and nudges me forward. Swallowing loudly, I walk into the bedroom on the right.

Thankfully, no one tells me whose bedroom it is that I chose.

I'm about to throw up.

If I put one more bite of pizza in my mouth, the other five slices will come spewing back out. I guess moving makes me hungry.

Holt checks the time on his watch. He promised Ridge he would meet him at the bar to watch football. Normally, Will and Cullen have a band playing every Saturday night, but apparently, they forgo that during the fall so everyone can watch college football instead. "You better head out before you're late," I say.

"You sure you don't wanna come?"

I nod, looking around at some of the mess. "I wanna finish getting everything unpacked." He growls his displeasure, making me giggle. "I'll be fine. I promise."

He pushes away from the table and stretches. His pale blue T-shirt draws out the color of his already gorgeous eyes. His bronzed skin stretches across the hard lines of his muscular body. Even, the sun-bleached hair on his arms is sexy.

Holt is all man. Masculine and hard and confident.

"Like what you see?" he asks with a wink.

"Huh?"

His cocky smile curls one side of his mouth. "You're staring at me."

I plant my hands on my hips. "Well, that's because I'm just wondering when you're gonna leave so I can get my work done."

He licks his lips, crossing the distance between us. "You forget I can read your face." He lifts his eyebrows. "And according to you, your mind too." His hands tug at my hips.

I lean forward. Lifting on my tiptoes, I squint my eyes together and fake a grimace. "So, what am I thinking now, *sir*?"

He laughs, nodding his head, playing along with my game. "You're ready for me to leave you alone." Tugging me behind him, he leads me over to the alarm panel. "Let me show you how to use the alarm and electronic door lock. There's a panel connected to every outside door." He shows me how to arm and disarm. It looks fairly simple. "So, it's the same number for everything—1102."

I furrow my brow, nonverbally questioning the importance of the number.

"It's the date I found Mr. Hard Knock."

"Mr. Hard Knock?"

"He was my pet turtle."

"You had a pet turtle?"

"Hell, yeah. I loved that thing."

We end up talking about childhood pets while we gather the trash. Holt heads out to the bar, and I spend the next several hours putting away the last of my belongings. It's midnight before I finally lie down in my new bed. It's quite possibly one of the most comfortable beds I've ever laid on. Despite that, I can't fall asleep. After an hour of tossing and turning, I finally get up.

I'm not sure why I open the door that connects the Children's Wing to the Big House. And I'm definitely not sure why I walk down the marble hallway, tiptoeing, listening for sounds of Holt. I shouldn't be out here. I shouldn't be exploring. I made Holt promise that we would respect each other's space and privacy when I moved in.

Here I am breaking the promise on the very first night.

I stop walking. Holding my breath, I listen again.

I don't think Holt's home. Surely, he would've called or texted when he made it home safe. He hasn't done either. In fact, our last text was a couple of hours ago. Where the hell is he? Aren't all the football games over by now?

Turning into his trophy room, I slowly look around. There's no window in here. Holt told me it doubles as a safe room, so that makes sense. Fortunately, there's a nightlight in the corner, giving my eyes just enough light to focus on the trinkets in front of me. Well, I don't really think a Super Bowl ring can be called a trinket, but you know what I mean. Opening the glass case, I trace my fingers across the diamonds.

"Lost?"

Shitting my pants, I jump in the air and spin around, knocking over a box of newspaper clippings in the process. Holt's leaning against the doorframe, watching me.

"Shoot." I quickly bend down and try to gather the thin pieces of paper without ripping them. "I'm sorry, I shouldn't be in here."

"Why not? Everything in this house is yours. You can go anywhere you like. Do anything you like. Take anything you like."

I put the box back on the shelf and carefully lower the lid to the glass case. "I thought you were a cynic of women, scared we were all out to poison your chalice, plotting to steal your riches. Yet, here you are, already turning over the keys to the kingdom? I guess my spell on you is working," I joke.

He doesn't say anything. It's too dark for me to even see if he's smiling. All I know is that the air grows thick with tension. Is he angry?

"Sorry, it was a joke," I say in a rush. "I was watching *Court Jester* when I was putting things away. It has that whole bit about the poisoned chalice. You know how much I love Danny Kaye. And he—"

"Merit, stop talking, baby." He swallows with a gulping noise. "What are you wearing?" His whisper is low and pained.

I glance down at my simple, white sleeveless nightgown. The lace edge barely covers my bottom. I've slept in the same bed with him—twice, as a matter of fact—and each time I was in my bra and panties. And he wanted more nights than that, but I made excuses about work and then packing up my condo. In reality, I've been scared. What if I'm on borrowed time with Holt? What if our happiness has an expiration date? As stupid as it sounds, I didn't wanna exhaust all of my bliss. In my mind, if I didn't spend the night with him, then it didn't count. If I woke up in my own bed—alone and without him—then I still had all of my 'Holt' tokens in my pocket. I still had time to kill, money to spare, candy to eat, seeds to plant. Maybe that's why I was so hesitant to move in. Why I made him promise that we would give each other space and privacy, despite only being separated by some walls and doors.

Because if I'm on borrowed time, I wanna savor it. I wanna make it last. If I could drag it out forever, I would.

Because I don't want this to end.

"Mer," he urges, begging me to answer his question.

I run my hand across my stomach, feeling the material. This gown might be a smidge skimpy from shrinking in the wash, but it covers *way* more than just my bra and panties... so I'm not exactly sure where this line of questioning is going. "It's a nightgown."

"I can see your silhouette through it. The lines of your body. Every single curve. The fullness of your breasts. The hardness of your nipples. The flower print on your panties." He drags a staggered breath through his lungs. "You. Are. A. Fucking. Goddess. Just waiting to be worshiped."

Holy shit. I guess the nightlight gives off more light than I thought—from where he's standing, at least.

And from where I'm standing, I might not can see his face, but I sure as hell can hear the liquid sex in his voice, fucking my eardrums senseless.

It's like I just had phone sex... in person.

"Oh." Well, that's original. I'm trying to think of something sexy to say or do when Holt beats me to the punch.

He stands straight and grips either side of the doorframe. He seems larger tonight. More masculine. More intense.

More Holt.

"Do you know how long it's been since my fingers have been inside of you? Since I heard you cry out in orgasm and soak my hand in your cum?"

My mouth dries, and I can't even swallow. Afraid I might choke, my hand snatches up and massages the base of my throat. All I can do is shake my head.

He makes a big show of checking his watch. The face of it lights up with his movement. "Seventy-seven hours."

"Well, that seems like a long time," I croak.

"Come here, Mer." His order is laced with longing and urgency.

My heart pounds in my chest, beating louder and faster with every step. When I get within arm's reach, he pulls me close, pinning me against the wall. His lips rub against mine. He doesn't kiss me, though; he teases me. My mouth parts. His breath mingles with mine, intoxicating me with scents of beer and mint-flavored gum. He skims his hand across my thigh, instantly breaking me out in chill bumps as his calloused fingers expertly caress my skin.

He draws the want and need from me, stoking me slowly like a fire.

A fire about to engulf everything in its path.

When he dips beneath the elastic of my panties and drags his thumb through my wetness, I buck against him, unable to control the movements of my own body. His growl cuts through me like a knife, filleting my resolve. "Mmmm. Such a sweet fucking pussy. So wet, so perfect." Moaning, I beg for more.

I suddenly feel abandoned and forgotten when his hand darts away.

But I'm not forgotten.

Not by a long shot.

He lifts me with ease, and my legs wrap around his waist. My damp crotch rubs against the erection tenting his cargo shorts. Without saying a word, he leads me back down the hallway, into the Children's Wing, into my new bedroom. Lying me down on the bed, he kisses me.

And I mean *he kisses me.*

Like he hasn't seen me in a month.

Like he just realized he can't live his life without me.

His tongue pushes against mine. He draws the breath from my lungs and into his own. I suck his bottom lip, biting him, just wanting to make sure he's real. In a tangled fury, he wrestles my panties down my shaking legs.

This is new.

Every other time, he's worked his hands underneath my panties. I've never been bare for him before. He stops kissing me and stares at my body, committing to memory what he can see between the moonlight and the living room lamp, filtering down the hallway and into the open bedroom. "Fuck, Merit. You're gorgeous." When his fingers press into my core, everything I thought I knew about desire is upended. He stretches me, marking the deepest part of my body with his touch. His words are panted and breathless, tumbling through the darkness between our wild kisses. "So tight on my fingers I can barely move." Twisting, he strokes the swollen ridges of my G-spot and presses his thumb against my throbbing clit. "Enjoy my fingers now, baby, because once my greedy tongue gets a taste of you, you may never see them again. I'm gonna be a hungry bastard."

Instinctively, I grab his hair, tugging his face closer to mine so I can kiss him more forcefully, more violently. It feels like only mere seconds pass before my stomach clenches. My heart stops beating. My brain fogs with a flood of euphoria.

And just like seventy-seven hours ago, I come all over his hand.

Grabbing my ass, he folds me against him, holding me tightly as I float down from my high.

My Holt High.

He peppers kisses in my hair, and I can feel the sticky residue of my passion coating his fingers as he draws a lazy line down my shoulder and arm. I lower my hand, gliding it across his firm muscles and dipping my fingers beneath the waistband of his shorts. He jerks away from me.

Leaning up on my elbow, I stare down at him. Even in the dark, I can see the dilation of his eyes. The hunger, the want, the need. "I've seen you. I know what you do." My voice is raspy and strained.

Grabbing my hair, he brings it to his nose and inhales deeply. "What?" he asks with a soft smile.

"You go into the bathroom. You shut the door. And you touch yourself."

He swallows. Loudly.

"Why don't you want me to touch you? To do the same things to you that you do to yourself?"

His eyes dart to my lips and down to the gap at the front of my twisted nightgown, where my breast is halfway showing. He licks his lips. "Because I want you to touch me."

I blink, trying to absorb and comprehend his nonsensical words. "You don't want me to touch you because you *want me to touch you*?"

He nods, sucking air deep into his lungs.

"That doesn't make any sense." I pout.

"You're my everything, Merit. And I know that once you touch me, I'm done for." He cradles my face. "I wanna give everything to you. And I wanna *take everything from you*." His voice is a rumble of thunder, animalistic and possessive. "I'm afraid..." he pauses, trying to gather his thoughts. "The things I want from you..." his voice trails off again, overcome with the power of his declaration, the truth of it. "I wanna own you—your body, your soul, and your heart. I wanna fucking consume every inch of you. In my mind, there's no world in which we are two."

He slides his hand into my gown, fondling my left breast. His fingers circle my hardened nipple, and then he pinches it. Hard. A shot of electricity pulses through me, making my pussy throb for more. "From the minute my heart formed in my chest, it was destined to beat for you."

Slowly, he pulls his hand away, dragging his fingers up my sternum, up the column of my throat, where they settle against my lips. I can smell myself on his fingers as he traces the outline of my lips. "I'm afraid you'll run. I'm afraid I'll scare you. So..." his sigh is so heavy it's almost tangible, overflowing with equal parts of adoration and sexual frustration, "we'll take it slow. As slow as you want." He halfheartedly chuckles. "Why do you think I haven't tasted you yet? Because once I do, it's game over."

In my entire life I never imagined a man could make me feel the way Holt makes me feel—physically, emotionally, mentally.

And these words? These confessions of his soul? Now, that I've heard them, can I ever live without them?

My tongue snakes out of my mouth, licking his fingers. A half-moan, half-sigh rattles deep in his chest before he leans up and crushes me back down to the bed. But instead of ravishing my mouth with his tongue, he plants one long, lingering kiss on my swollen, needy lips as he gently nuzzles my nose with his own. Slow and steady, this is the kiss reserved for couples who have been lovers for a thousand years, mates since the sun first rose over the horizon.

"Holt?" My lips move against his.

"Yeah, baby?" His words push oxygen into my lungs.

When I don't immediately respond, he stops kissing me and looks into my eyes.

"You're right. I'm scared." His face immediately falls, filled with dread that he's taken, not only our conversation too far, but our physical intimacy as well. He makes a move to roll off me, but I grab his waist, fusing his body to mine. The steel length of his erection is so hard I wouldn't be surprised if it bruises my side. "But if I run, I want you to follow me."

His eyes dance across my face. His gaze is so intense it literally leaves tingles in its wake. His whisper is calm and chaos wrapped into one. Flight and fight. Permissive and domineering. Love and hate. "I'll chase you to the ends of the earth, Merit."

I wrap my hands around the back of his neck, weaving my fingers through his curls, tugging and pulling. There's a good chance I pull too hard because he hisses between his teeth. I hook my left leg around his waist. My bare pussy opens wider and scrapes against the fabric of his cargo shorts. My whisper is barely audible. "But I'm not running tonight."

Shifting my body, I force him to roll us over so he's spread across the bed and I'm on top of him. I grab the hem of his T-shirt. Pushing it up, I leave him no option but to take it off. I drown in the sight of him. Holt is all man. His hard lines look like chiseled marble in the blue-white glow of the moonlight. Leaning down, I take his nipple in my mouth, lightly nibbling the pebbled skin, before I kiss my way down his stomach.

His palm reaches out, instantly massaging my scalp. "Talk to me, baby. Tell me what you want."

"What I want is to feel you in my hands." I look up at him from my position on my hands and knees. "And then I want you to fuck my mouth with your cock, *sir*."

Holy shit. Did I just say that?

Hell, yeah, I did.

Quickly working his shorts, as soon as the button falls open, I latch onto the soft skin right above the band of his boxer briefs. I suck hard, leaving no doubt in either of our minds that my goal is to mark my territory and bruise him with a hickey. His hips thrust forward, bucking against me. "Oh, fuck me. You're branding me, baby." He hisses again, slithering against me like a snake.

"Yes," I answer, my hot breath bouncing back in my own face. Satisfied with my damage, I lick and kiss the now-tender spot.

He doesn't say anything, but I can't help but notice that his hands are shaking when he helps me lower his shorts and his boxer briefs. His dick immediately jumps under the perusal of my stare. It's so much larger than I thought it would be. Massive, huge. A fucking giant compared to Edward. Well, a fucking giant compared to any man. His throbbing skin is pulled tight, begging for release. Pre-cum glistens on the tip of his thick, mushroomed head.

For a second, I wonder what it would feel like to fully take him inside my own body. My eyes fall closed, picturing the moment.

Tenderly, he caresses my face. "What are you thinking about?"

"Just thinking about the future."

Satisfied with my answer, he just nods. I straddle his legs, curious if he can smell the desire still weeping from my naked crotch as it spreads open wide. His intake of breath tells me that he obviously can. Sliding my hand between our bodies, I grab his cock, relishing the feel of his velvet skin over his hard length. His back arches, making him bow off the bed like a man possessed. It's erotic and passionate. And completely gives me the confidence I need to pleasure him. I quickly find the rhythm he likes—tight and fast and intense.

"Oh, Merit..." His moan alone makes my pussy drip. Unable to stop myself—because I'm about die without some friction—I shift so that I'm straddling only one of his legs instead of both of them, and I start grinding myself against his kneecap, giving my clit the attention it so desperately needs. How in the world, I have enough brain power to remember to hump his right knee instead of his scarred and previously injured left knee, I'll never know.

He strangles on his words, spewing them into the night, disguising them as heaving breaths. "My baby has a hungry little pussy. Spin around, and I'll give her the attention she needs."

There he is... reading my mind again.

I decide to reward him for his telepathy.

By taking him in my mouth.

He screams wildly into the night, driving me mad with desire. "Oh shit!"

I shove his dick into my mouth like I'm trying to swallow the damn thing whole. With every bob of my head, his tip pokes the back of my throat, making my eyes water. He's not only long, but wide. I can feel the corners of my lips cracking. Like when you're sitting in the dentist's chair and have your mouth open for too long. His fingertips dig into my scalp. My forearms are braced across his abdomen, and they begin slipping around against his sweat. Giving up on chasing my own orgasm—because I want to solely focus on his pleasure—I scoot a little higher and sit on his thigh. His mumbled words tell me he's getting close. Sucking his cock with the same fury of my pumping hand, I bring him to orgasm, eagerly swallowing every last drop. I drain his body, making damn sure there's no possibility of him going to the bathroom later to jerk off.

After his shuddering body calms down, I sit up, eager to see his handsome face. And I can't stop my smile.

Digging his fingers into my hips, he chuckles. I think it's the most loving sound I've ever heard. Simple, but filled with emotion and intensity.

I tilt my head in curiosity. "What?"

"You forget you wear your emotions all over your face."

"Oh, yeah? And what does my face say?"

His lopsided smile is the sexiest I've ever seen. "That you never want me jacking off in the bathroom again."

Nailed it.

Chapter 24

Holt

"I can't believe this is happening." Merit's downtrodden voice echoes in my ears.

The football game ended a couple of hours ago, but I had to stay late to get caught up on some paperwork. My school grades are due by midnight. I glance at the clock on my computer before I shut it off. Twenty minutes to spare.

"She just said she decided to stay at her current job? That's it? No other explanation?" Holding the phone against my ear, I lock the exterior door to the gym.

"She said that her current job came back today offering her three dollars more per hour. I can't match that." She sighs into the phone. "She was supposed to start tomorrow. What the heck am I gonna do?"

"You'll just have to start looking again. You need another employee, there's no way around it."

I'm surprised to see my truck isn't the only vehicle in the parking lot. Parked a few spots away from me is a beaten-down car with a girl standing outside. "Hey, Mer, let me call you back. I think someone's having car trouble."

"Who?"

I chuckle. Curious Merit, as always. "It looks like a student."

"Okay. Call me back."

When I get closer, I realize I recognize the girl. I think her name is Heidi. She was a flyer on the cheerleading team last year, but she had a terrible fall during a competition around Christmas time. Broke her ankle and needed surgery. She was in a cast for months, and her recovery must not have gone as well as expected—she's not on the sidelines with the team this year.

"Heidi, right?" Engrossed in texting or playing a game on her phone, her head whips in my direction.

"Oh! Hi, Coach."

I look around the parking lot, but I don't see anyone else. "It's pretty late to be out here alone. Is everything okay?" I unlock my truck and open the door.

She pats the trunk of her car. "It's my car. It won't start."

I sling my bag into my back seat and walk over. "Let me take a look." I take the key from her and try to turn the ignition. "The battery is dead. Did you leave your lights on during the game?"

She shakes her head, staring at me with big brown eyes. "No, this car always has problems. I'm trying to save up for something better." She kicks the ground with her shoe. "But that's a slow process."

I pull my truck around and connect the jumper cables. We try several times, but it doesn't work; there's no life left in the thing at all. "Have you called someone to pick you up?" I ask, packing the cables away in my toolbox.

"Yeah, I called my uncle about an hour ago, but he's not the most reliable person. I have no idea when he'll actually show up."

"Anyone else? Parents?"

"It's just my mom, and she can't drive at night because of the fibromyalgia medicine she has to take."

"Friends?"

She giggles. "It's Friday night. After a massive football win. All my friends are three sheets to the wind."

I should chastise her classmates, but there were a few times I celebrated a high school win a little too hard myself. In fact, it's how Ridge's favorite T-shirt got ruined. Cheese balls and cheap wine coolers don't mix.

"Could you take me home?"

I vehemently shake my head no. "Oh, Heidi, students aren't allowed to ride with teachers unless there's written permission from your guardians and the school ahead of time."

"Oh..." Her face falls, and she studies a crack in the asphalt.

It reminds me of Merit. Well, the old Merit.

Looking down, uncertain and unsure.

"But don't worry, I'm not leaving you here. I'll wait with you." Lowering my tailgate, I nod, giving her permission to sit down. She jumps up and we small talk about school and her classes. We wait another twenty minutes, and there's still no sign of her uncle, despite her calling and texting him. She also talks with her mom. I do my best to hide my yawn, but I'm unsuccessful.

"You should go. It's really late, and you're probably exhausted. I'll be fine. I'm sure he'll be here soon."

I stand up and walk closer to the road, taking a look. No cars, no headlights. Everything is abandoned. I really shouldn't take her home, but I don't see any other choice. I can't leave her alone in the middle of the night in an empty parking lot. There's not even school cameras in this section. If something happened to her, no one would even know, and it would be completely my fault. "Maybe I should just go ahead and drive you home," I say against my better judgment.

She jumps down from the truck, clapping her hands in excitement. "Really! Oh, that would be awesome."

"I need to call your mother for permission."

She holds out her phone. "Yeah, that's fine."

"No, I need to call the official number listed for her in the school system." I start walking back toward the gym. "C'mon, we'll call from my office."

Once I get her on the phone, Denise, Heidi's mom, nearly bursts into tears. I have to interrupt her waterfall of thank yous to tell her we better get on the road before it gets even later. When we're walking back out to the parking lot, Heidi tells me where she lives, and I'm relieved it's somewhat on my way home because I'm dog-ass tired. All I wanna do is wrap Merit in my arms and pass out. If I had to guess, she's already asleep. She's having a season closeout sale on summer clothes tomorrow, so the store will be flooded with customers.

Five minutes into the drive, I hear a barely audible sniffle. In the reflection of the passenger window, I watch as Heidi wipes some tears from her eyes. "Heidi, is everything okay?"

She gasps, shocked I noticed her crying. "Oh, I'm okay. It's just been a really bad day."

"Your car?" I ask.

She nods. "That, and I lost my job."

"You lost your job today? What happened?"

"I had a disagreement with my boss." When I lift an eyebrow, she continues. "I'm a half-day student. I get out at noon every day and go to work at a daycare. Today, a little boy from the four-year-old class had an accident and wet his pants. My boss forced him to stand in the corner for timeout. I disagreed with the punishment. It was an accident. He was playing outside and having so much fun... he just didn't wanna take a break for the bathroom. It's something every little kid has done." She shrugs. "Anyway, I really needed that job. Like I said, I'm saving money for a new car. After graduation, I plan to move to the beach and live with some of my friends who graduated last year. They go to nursing school at the community college during the day and work in the restaurants at night. You can make really good tips from all the tourists. Plus, since they would already have a year of school under their belt, they can help me if I have any trouble with the classes."

Holy shit. This could be the answer to all our problems.

"You work in a daycare? You like kids?"

Her face lights up. "Oh, I love kids."

"Have you ever worked in a store or a restaurant with a point-of-sale system?"

She cocks her head, answering slowly. "Last summer I worked at the snow cone stand. They had a POS. Why?"

I drag my hand across my face, wondering how much I should say. Considering I don't want Merit to work herself to death—like she's been doing over the past several years—and considering I want more of her to myself, I dive in, head-fucking-first. It's not like I don't know Heidi. Plus, I saw her grades when I was looking up her mom's phone number. She's in the top ten percent of her class. Learning how to shut the store down should be a breeze for her. "Listen, I'm not trying to get your hopes up or anything, but my girlfriend is looking to fill a part-time position at her store."

"Her store?"

"It's a children's store—*Run and Jump and Twirl.*"

Her face brightens up, and she bounces in her seat. "Are you serious! That would be so amazing! I swear, I would be the hardest worker ever." She looks out the windshield, covering her mouth with her hands in excitement. "It's gonna be so much fun. Oh my god, I can't wait!"

I can't help but laugh at her innocence and joy. "Hey now, this isn't a done deal. Who she hires is completely Merit's decision." Heidi holds her breath, waiting for me to say more. "But why don't you come by the store tomorrow night after it closes? About seven? I can introduce you."

"Yes! Absolutely! And tell her I can work whenever she needs. Every single afternoon and night and all day Saturday. Whenever she wants."

We pull up in front of Heidi's house. It's a small brick home with peeling paint on the front door and a cracked window off the porch. A couple of the shutters dangle, about to fall off. They're dangerously close to being lost in the overgrown bushes. If it's just Heidi and her mom—and her mom is sick—it's not like I can really fault them for not having time to tackle deferred maintenance.

I think I see movement at one of the window curtains when Heidi catches me completely off guard, wrapping her arms around my shoulders. Her breath drags across my neck. "Thank you so much, Coach!"

I immediately press back against my door, trying to ease away from her embrace.

Her cheeks turn bright red, and her eyes widen. "Oh crap, I'm sorry. I wasn't thinking. I'm just so excited."

Nodding, I take a deep breath and smile, trying to diffuse the awkwardness of the situation. I know her action was totally innocent, and it just sucks that as a teacher you can't even high-five a kid without worrying about what other people think. Let alone give a kid a hug. "It's fine." I brush it off as a non-event. "So, we'll see you tomorrow night at the store?"

She jumps from the truck. "I'll be there! Thanks so much for the ride, Coach."

Fifteen minutes later, I'm tiptoeing down the hallway, trying not to wake Merit. Turns out, she's somewhat of a light sleeper. Not me. I sleep like the dead. I'm fairly certain I could sleep through a hurricane. Literally. It's a by-product of years of football camp—hundreds of loud, snoring guys all sleeping in the same dorm. I slide my cell phone out of my pocket and leave it on the side table outside the door to the Children's Wing. When I get to her room, I lean against the doorframe, studying the curve of her body. Lit by the soft moonlight, she looks like an angel.

"Are you planning on standing there all night and watching me sleep? Because that's kinda creepy." Looking over her shoulder, she tosses back the covers, inviting me into her bed. Stripping down to my boxer briefs, I crawl in next to her. Pulling her against me, I ignore my growing erection. I know she can feel it against her ass because she stops breathing. Her reaction always makes me chuckle. Nuzzling against her neck, I whisper, "I think I solved the problem."

"What problem?" she yawns. "By the way, you never called me back."

I'm too tired to even answer her. We can talk tomorrow. For now, I hold her against me, determined to never let her go, and I fall into a deep, soundless sleep.

Chapter 25

Holt

I call a few more guys over to the huddle and point out some play changes that I think will make a difference tomorrow night. We'll be playing our toughest opponent yet. Not to mention the coach is a douchebag. I'm really not a vindictive guy, but after some of the stuff he said during my first season of coaching last year, it'll be nice to wipe the smug smile off his face.

I'm right in the middle of my speech when Carson nudges my arm, nodding behind my shoulder. "Uh...Coach?"

Turning around, I follow his line of sight. Standing at the top of the hill, looking down on the field is Merit. Her hands are planted firmly on her hips, and she eagerly scans the people, obviously looking for me.

There's something else that's pretty obvious too...

She's pissed.

Maybe pissed doesn't even properly describe it. I can literally feel the anger pulsating in the air.

I can't say I'm surprised, though. I knew this was coming. I just thought I had another week. Catching my eye, her scowl deepens, and she takes off, stomping down the hill like a rampaging bull.

Well, this isn't going to end well.

She's not even taking the sidewalk. There's a sidewalk for a reason.

The lawn maintenance guy won't be cutting the grass until to-morrow so everything looks pristine for the game. But for now, the ankle-deep grass is a landmine of ant beds and sticky weeds. Tossing my clipboard down on the bench, I cut across the field, trying to get closer so I can tell her to stop and use the sidewalk and concrete stairs instead. She glances down at her feet, twisting to the side as she takes a few more steps. All of a sudden, she screams and plops down on the ground. I see a flip flop fly through the air as she tosses it off her foot.

"Shit," I mumble under my breath and take off in a sprint.

I don't realize Carson is behind me until I hear him cutting to the side in the other direction, telling me he's going to get ice for her. By the time I reach Merit, most of the ants are gone, but she's still swatting at her left foot and leg.

"Get 'em off! Get 'em off me!"

Squatting in front of her, I lift her foot in my lap and smash the last four ants still crawling around. Her soft, tanned skin is already angry, flared in red and white splotches. Scooping her into my arms, I carry her back up the hill to the parking lot. The whole time she's squirming like a little kid, trying to pull her foot close to her face to check the damage.

"Ow. Ow. Ow. Ow. I stepped in an ant bed. They bit me. Oh my gosh, I got bit so bad." She gives me a play by play, like I wasn't just right there with her. Lowering the tailgate to my truck, I gently set her down. She's already itchy. She turns her foot to the left and right, violently scratching the inflamed skin. "Little fuckers," she mum-bles, barely loud enough for me to hear.

I can't help but laugh. She's so freakin' funny. "Try not to scratch, Mer."

Her face snatches up, staring at me like she can't believe I would have the audacity to even speak to her.

Fortunately, Carson jogs up with an ice pack and her missing flip flop. "Here you go."

Her face instantly melts. "Oh, thank you so much, Carson." She shows him her swollen foot. "I stepped in an ant bed. I got stung."

Carson nods. "Yeah, those ant beds are brutal. The guy only has time to mow one time a week so he does it on Friday mornings."

She sighs, "It's my fault. I should've taken the sidewalk." Her eyes narrow in my direction. "But I was in a hurry."

"Yeah, I saw that." Carson glances between the two of us. "Everything okay?"

"It's fine," I tell him. "Head on back down. Keep going with practice."

"Yes, Coach." He cocks his head, studying Merit. "My mom always has me soak my foot in baking soda and lemon juice."

Merit smiles softly, "Maybe I'll try that. My granny always had me do vinegar, but it never really worked. I'd think everything was good, and then it'd start itching again like three weeks later."

I wait until Carson's out of earshot, and I close the distance between us. Lifting the ice pack, I run my finger across several of the ballooned bites.

She slaps my hand away. "Don't touch me."

Instead of saying anything, I lift an eyebrow.

She doesn't like that.

Anger flares in her hazel eyes, making the colors dance back and forth. "You!" She leans forward, pointing her finger in my face. "How dare you!"

I fold my arms across my chest. "You'll have to be a little more specific."

"Don't play coy with me, Holt. You know exactly what I'm talking about. How dare you pay off my loan?" Her voice is so loud she's basically yelling.

I reach up and turn my ballcap around. My shirt must ride up—like usual—because her eyes dart to my stomach before traveling back to my face. "I did it to help," I say.

Her brow furrows. "What are you talking about? It's not your debt to pay. It's mine."

When I don't say anything, she starts in again. "Do you know how embarrassing that was? I went to make my loan payment, and Edward waltzed out in the middle of the crowded lobby and announced to everyone that my millionaire boyfriend had paid off my loan." She tosses the ice pack to the side and jumps off my tailgate. "And then, he asked what I was trading for your generosity." She tosses her hands in the air. "He basically called me a whore."

Outrage. Pure hatred and outrage crawl from the pit of my stomach to the back of my eyes, blinding me. I've never wanted to hurt someone so badly. "I'll fucking kill him."

"Why?" Her scream is muted by the break in her voice. "I mean, it's true. He may've called me a whore, but you're the one who made me feel that way."

My chest splits open. "Mer…" I reach for her, but she sidesteps me.

"Why did you do it?"

"I was just trying to help. I wanted us to be done with him. Wanted you to be done. Finished."

"But it was my responsibility!"

"It's fine; I promise. It's no big deal. It's just money. I have plenty of it."

It catches me off guard when she gives me a look of utter disgust. It's like she doesn't even know who I am. Like she's staring at a stranger. It suddenly stabs my heart. Without saying another word, she climbs in her car and drives away.

I never want to see that look on her face again.

Whatever I do, I have to fix this. Now.

It's a few hours before I make it home.

Terrified of what Merit may say or do, I go to my parents' house, seeking my dad's advice. He, of course, confirms that I'm a dumbass and never should've paid off her loan. Not because he's worried about me wasting my money, but because he sides with Merit. He explains to me that I took away her empowerment. Her ability to conclude her business with her ex-husband on her own terms with the money she earned from her own two hands from the store he never thought would be a success.

After leaving, I stop by the store, but she isn't there. I have to say I'm more than relieved when I see her SUV parked in the driveway of the Children's Wing. My worry starts to escalate, though, when I can't find her. She's not in the Children's Wing or outside by the pool. Room by room, I search the bottom floor, eventually taking the stairs two at a time, praying she's upstairs. My mind runs rampant with thoughts of her abandoning me, leaving me. My only saving grace is all of her stuff is still in the Children's Wing—clothes in the closet, toiletries in the bathroom, diamond and ruby bracelet in her jewelry box. Merit would never leave that stuff behind.

I slow when I see a light coming from beneath the door of the large bathroom attached to the kids' room. I lean forward, listening. "Merit?"

"Don't come in. I'm naked."

Every muscle in my body relaxes. I'm so damn relieved to hear her voice, nothing has ever sounded so sweet. "I've seen you naked before. I'm coming in."

I slowly open the door, unsure about what I'll find. She immediately shifts in the bathtub, folding her arms over the side, shielding her nakedness from me. "Not all of me at one time," she says.

I take a step forward. "What do you mean?"

She points to a dressing bench on the far back wall. "You can sit over there. I don't want you close to me."

That sentence nearly makes me collapse. I've fucked everything up. I feel like my lungs are crushing in on themselves. In a fog, I sit down. There's a towel with a picture of a dinosaur draped across the edge. It's Ty's.

Her voice swirls in my head. "What did you mean by that?" I ask again.

"You've not seen all of me naked at one time."

Oh. She's right. I haven't.

I've seen her perfect breasts. I've seen her perfect pussy. But not all together. And when she sleeps? She's either in her bra and panties or one of those flimsy nightgowns. And now? I glance up, catching her reflection in the large mirror on the wall behind the tub. Her bare back is on display. I follow the alluring curve of her spine down to the top of her ass. And the rest of her is hidden beneath the water and bubbles.

If I stare at her anymore, I'll get an erection. I'm already in dire straits just being in the same vicinity knowing she's wearing nothing. It's just the way my body responds to her. I don't really think my giant erection will make her happy, considering she doesn't even want me to sit next to her. So, I glance around the room, trying to clear my mind. A large bowl is sitting on the counter next to a box of baking soda and some spent lemons. "Did it help?" I ask, nodding at her home remedy.

"It did." She looks down at the tiled floor. Her voice is meek and somber. The old Merit. "I apologize for invading your space, but this is the largest bathtub in the house. I just wanted some time to myself to relax. And I know you sometimes like to get in the hot tub after practice. I didn't want to use it and interrupt you."

What she means is she didn't want to see me.

And she's right. This bathtub is huge. The girls call it their indoor swimming pool. It's actually close to the same size as the hot tub.

"It's fine. You know everything in this house is yours."

She glances up, studying me. "Don't say that."

I open my mouth, but quickly close it. She has to know I'm telling the truth, there's no point in adding more fuel to the fire by trying to defend that one comment.

She sighs. When she talks her voice quivers. "Why did you do it?"

"I told you. To help you."

She shakes her head. "Don't lie to yourself, Holt. You did it to help yourself, not me."

I shake my head. "What are you talking about?"

"You didn't like me being tethered to him."

I think about what's she saying. Once again, she's right. "You're right. I hated that you lived in his house, that you were beholden to him—or his parents—for that loan. He's had you in purgatory all these years, and I wanted to free you. I wanted to free *us*."

"And you didn't think to discuss it with me beforehand? Before writing this huge check?"

I hang my head in shame. "I knew you'd say no."

"And what about all those other women?"

I lean forward, resting my forearms on my knees. "What other women?"

"The women who wanted your money? The women who tried to steal from you, swindle you? And here you are, just throwing money at me. Why? We barely know each other. We've been dating, and I'm your tenant. That's it."

My throat is raw and swollen. I can't even swallow. "Don't, Merit. Now, you're the one lying to yourself. You know it's more than that. It's been more than that since the second I walked in that store."

She turns her face, thinking I can't see her wipe her tears in the reflection of the mirror. "Maybe." After several long seconds, she twists back around. Water splashes around her waist. Her tone is somber and serious—dead. "Could you close your eyes, please."

Silently nodding, I do as I'm told. I hold my breath just so I can hear everything she does. Sliding out of the tub. Wrapping herself in a towel. When I hear her feet shuffle past me, I snatch her, gently grabbing her wrist. Wet strands of hair fall from her bun and stick to her shoulders. Her eyes are red and glassy.

She's heartbreakingly breathtaking.

"Are you leaving me?" I finally ask the question I've been scared of since the minute she pulled out of the parking lot this afternoon.

"What are you asking, Holt? If I'm leaving you for the night? Or if I'm leaving you forever?"

"Both. Because both of those outcomes are unbearable."

Chapter 26

Holt

She doesn't respond.

She just pulls away and walks out of the room.

I'm not exactly sure how long I sit here, but long enough that my eyes grow blurry with worry and sleep and dread. Pulling the drain on the tub, I turn out the light. No matter how I feel, I have to force myself to get some rest. Tomorrow's a huge game, and everyone is counting on me. Most of the time schools play a cushion team for Homecoming. But this time? It's a tough rival, that's for sure. Laying my cell phone on the hall table, I round the corner into my bedroom.

There she is.

Sitting on my bed, wearing one of my T-shirts.

With her redwood hair fanned around her shoulders.

"Mer?"

"I don't wanna leave."

I feel like a crater of ice just melted away from my heart. "Good."

"And I don't want you to be skeptical of me."

I shake my head, taking a step closer. "I'm not."

She bites the corner of her lip and picks at a spot on the comforter. "But you're lying to me."

I hold out my hands, pleading, "I'm not, I promise. I know you're different. I know there's no hidden motives, no masked agenda, no ploy to get money and bleed me dry."

"That's not what I'm talking about." She stands, facing me. Her fingertips worry the hem of her T-shirt, snaking it up the firm skin of her thighs. It's super fucking distracting, but I do my best to focus on her face instead. "Is that the only reason?"

"Is what the only reason?"

"You wanted me to be free of Edward, is that the only reason you paid off my loan?"

Tossing my ballcap on the loveseat, I drag my hands through my hair. "No."

She swallows. "What's the other reason?"

I take two more steps, closing the distance between us. "You know the other reason."

"Tell me." Her whisper is strained and broken.

"Because I love you. Because I'm *in* love with you."

There we have it. I was worried I would never feel this way, never say those words. And here we are, I'm throwing them out first and not even regretting it.

Her face pales and then immediately flushes. The only light in the room is the soft glow from one of the lamps and the slanted moonlight cascading in from the blinds. But I can still see everything. I can see the peak of her nipples as they strain against the fabric of her shirt—my shirt. I can see the irregular fall of her chest as her breathing hitches. I can see the tremble of her hand as she lifts her shirt and tosses it to the floor.

The heaviness of her breasts. The soft curve of her lower stomach. The lean lines of her legs. The tan lines on her collarbone. The bare beauty of her pussy.

Her heart. Her soul. Her love.

She's not saying it back, she's not proclaiming it, but it's there.

And I see it all.

Kicking off my shoes and socks, I yank my shirt over my head. My belt buckle clinks together as my fingers fumble. I refuse to take my eyes off her perfect body, even for one second. By the time my shorts and boxer briefs hit the floor, I can feel the moisture from pre-cum sliding down the length of my erection.

Her eyes dilate and she licks her lips.

We're standing so close our bodies are touching each other in all the right places.

"What do you want from me, Merit?" My voice is a growl, basic and demanding.

Her hands reach up and tangle in my hair, tugging and pulling, drowning me in her passion. "I wanna take everything from you. Every fucking thing."

We crash into each other, wild and feral. Her tongue slides against mine. She jumps into my arms. The feel of her naked crotch against me drives me to the brink of utter madness. She sinks her teeth into my neck, marking me as her own. Fighting for me, the way I've always wanted. Needing me, the exact same way I need her.

Falling to the bed, I explore her body, slowly building the desire between us until there's so much tension, I think I'm about to break in two. I lavish her with sweet, tender kisses. And then punish her with my teeth, determined to imprint my lust on her soul. Trailing my tongue down her stomach, gliding my chest over her crotch, I lick her from hip to hip. "Open wide, Merit. Show me my new home."

Moaning, her legs fall apart even wider, gifting me with the sight of her spread-open pussy. I can feel the heat radiating off her skin. She's plump and pink and perfect. And soaking wet.

Her fingers dig into my scalp, impatiently pushing my face into her cunt. I flick her clit with my tongue. Just that one small movement has her moaning again, and I watch in eager fascination as a bead of wetness leaks from her tunnel and travels down to her ass. "Fuck me, baby. You're so wet I could go swimming."

"Holt. Now." Her pleas fill my soul with a passion that's so vivid, so real, so tangible, it resets the pattern of my beating heart. My rhythm isn't my own anymore; it all belongs to Merit. She's my defibrillator, my pacemaker.

"You can't rush me, Mer. I'm gonna love every part of you to-night. With my fingers, with my tongue, with my cock. I told you we would take it slow, and we have. I've never tasted you before, and I'm gonna fuck this tight pussy with my tongue over and over and over. Until I'm drowning in your cum, and there's no doubt that you'll be able to ride my cock without one ounce of pain."

Because let's be real... I have a big dick.

She sighs, her body shaking underneath mine. "Then, show me how much you love me, Holt."

I bury my face in her. Literally.

Fuck me. It doesn't get much better than this.

My body floods with sensation. My stubble scrapes against the insides of her thighs, turning them red with heat and friction. Her pink and swollen clit rubs against my lips, begging me to suck it. And when my fingers push inside her, her pussy clenches around them like it's been starved for days.

The smell of her arousal making me dizzy with need...

The texture of her soft skin underneath my mouth...

The taste of her nectar covering my every single taste bud...

I wasn't kidding when I told her to show me my new home.

I work her body, lavishing devoted attention on her with my mouth and fingers, eagerly licking her clean when she comes un-glued underneath me. After her second orgasm, I can't take it any-more.

I have to be inside of her. Before I cease to exist.

Reaching into the nightstand, I grab a condom. She watches in eager fascination as I roll it on. She doesn't ask me to turn the lamp off, and I'm glad. I don't think I could, even if she asked me to. I *have* to see her. I have to see her face when my body is inside of hers.

"Are you sure?" I whisper, positioning myself between her legs. The tip of my dick slides against her soaked entrance. My forearms frame her face, and I stare into her eyes. The yellows and greens are on fire, dancing back and forth in excitement.

Her answer is a moan. "Yes."

"There's no going back. You're mine. You understand?"

"No Holt, you've got it all wrong. *You're mine.*"

Holy hell.

I slip into her slowly, savoring every damn inch. When I think I can't go any farther, I pump into her, spreading her more, exploring her depths. Her head falls back, and her body grows limp in pleasure as she adjusts to me. She's tight and perfect and made for no one but me.

If I ever had any doubt in my mind that Merit was my endgame, it's been erased by this one simplistic motion—of me sliding my cock into her throbbing and weeping pussy. One straightforward and fluid movement of my body has sealed my fate. For all eternity.

There's nothing dishonest or artificial about our relationship, about her feelings for me.

Her love for me is authentic. Packed with an intensity so powerful it's like I feel it shattering my bones, crushing me to dust. It's decimating me. And then immediately putting me back together, assembling my pieces around the cornerstone of her love.

It might take her longer to admit—out loud—that she feels the same way.

But that's okay.

Because she's telling me with her body everything she might be scared to say with her mouth.

I lower my lips onto hers, kissing her slow and lazy—relishing the moment that our bodies have joined as one.

When her hips start moving back and forth trying to frenzy our momentum, I slide her hands above her head and pin them to the bed, elongating her body and taking control of her actions. I refuse to rush. I refuse to neglect her.

I refuse to treat this like sex. Because trust me, it's so much more.

It's the start of forever.

We make love slowly, perfectly in sync, perfectly in rhythm, until she nips at my neck and wriggles beneath me, nonverbally telling me she's done playing nice. I loosen my grip and murmur against her ear. "Tell me what you want, baby."

"Harder. Faster. Give me more, *sir*." Her hands drop down, and she immediately claws at my back, pleading for my rampage.

And then... all fucking bets are off.

Wanna see me possessed? Out of control? Out of my mind? Just let me fuck Merit Eliza Browning—the love of my life—and you'll see it.

Even her orgasm doesn't slow me down. When her screams leave her breathless, I kiss her, breathing my life into her own. Only a few seconds later, I can feel her body building again, strangling my dick, and I pray for yet another orgasm to hit her so I can let go. The instant her body freezes and her throat chokes on a scream, I lose my shit.

I literally come until my vision tunnels and white starbursts cloud my eyes.

Holy fucking hell.

It takes several minutes for each of us to recover. Eventually, I carry her to the bathroom where we both clean up. She's quiet so I don't press her to talk. It doesn't take a genius to know she hasn't been with a man since her ex-husband. Even if I didn't know it, the blood staining the outside of my condom would tell me. She digs in 'her drawer' of my dresser and pulls out a fresh pair of panties. Forgoing the T-shirt or her white cotton nightgown, she jumps back in bed and pulls the sheet up to her chin. Her eyes follow me around the room as I pull on a fresh pair of boxer briefs and then grab my discarded clothing, tossing them in the laundry basket. Turning out the light, I crawl into bed. She immediately tucks her body next to mine. Wrapping my arms around her, my hand cups her bare breast. The heat pouring from her is comforting, relaxing.

Unable to bear the silence any longer, I nuzzle my lips against her ear. "Well?"

She talks through a yawn. Her syllables are drawn-out and sleepy. "I told you. You're mine."

A few hours later, my alarm wakes me, blaring at a volume loud enough to make people in California shit their beds. I'm fucking exhausted.

And I've never been so happy.

Chapter 27

Merit

I had sex with your brother last night.

Every time I glance up at Raylee, that's what I'm thinking.

Ella leans over, grabbing a tennis shoe from the display, and in the process her belly knocks down another one. She curses underneath her breath.

I had sex with your cousin last night.

I can feel heat prickle my cheeks. Heat of embarrassment.

The heat of my memories.

"What about this one, Little Girl?" Ella turns around and holds up a gray sneaker with blue and silver trim, showing Laura. "It looks like it has a lot of cushion. It's pretty too." Her eyes divert to me, and she lifts a questioning brow. "Merit, are you okay? You look feverish."

Raylee snickers. "I think you call that afterglow."

I choke on my own spit.

Teresa smiles, chiding her daughter, though the scolding lacks any real threat behind it. "Raylee, stop it. Mind your own business."

I had sex with your son last night.

Fortunately, Heidi comes to my rescue. At least she's more professional than Kyra, who happens to be sitting on the floor next to me, laughing her ass off. "I'll be happy to pull the size you need from the back," she says, her eyes flickering between me and Ella.

"Thank you, Heidi." I tell her the size, and she disappears around the corner.

Anna leans forward, forcing herself into the conversation. She pats my cheek with her pink-painted fingernails. "I think you look pretty with afterglow."

Of course, everyone bursts into a fit of laughter. Even Ty, who only laughs because everyone else is laughing. Well, everyone except for Laura, who cocks her head in question and stares at all the adults. And me... I don't laugh. I shoot up from the floor like my ass is on fire and pretend to busy myself with searching for shoes.

Right then, the bell sounds on the door and every head swivels to the front. Holt walks in, grinning ear-to-ear and juggling three drink carriers in his arms. He stops as soon as he sees their faces. "Uh... hi."

They immediately start howling, laughing like old hens with nothing better to do. Rolling my eyes, I race over, carefully grabbing one of the carriers from him. I'm completely surprised to see him at this time of day. He's a sight for sore eyes, and my heart immediately skips a beat. He smells like mint gum and soap. Give him a few more hours, and he'll smell like sweat and grass. "Hi."

His eyes flicker down to my lips and back again. "Hi." He nods at his family. "What's up with them?"

I look behind me, scowling at the lot of them. Leaning forward, I whisper, "They know."

He frowns. "They know what?"

I wiggle my head back and forth. "About last night."

His eyebrows shoot up. "You told my mom we had sex?!"

"What!" I jump, slapping him on the wrist and nearly making him spill one set of drinks. "Oh sorry." I sigh, making sure my body is angled away so they can't hear me. "They figured it out."

"How?" he asks.

Looking down at my feet, I shrug, wondering if he's mad. "I guess... I guess I look happy."

He nuzzles my chin with his own, forcing me to look up. His eyes look darker today. More vibrant, more fulfilled. He smiles sweetly, flashing his white teeth. "*Are* you happy?"

I nod, biting my bottom lip, trying to contain my cheek-busting smile. "Very happy."

"Just so you know, I wouldn't mind making you happy every night for the rest of our lives. Even multiple times a night," he says with a drop-dead sexy wink. Kissing my cheek, he skirts past me and holds the drinks in the air. "Ladies, how about some strawberry-banana smoothies." He sets the drinks down on one of the shelves, and the kids immediately race forward, trying to grab one. Raylee reaches Ty in the nick of time before he accidentally spills one all over a blue jeans display.

"Son, what are you doing here? I thought only the elementary school had half a day off today," Teresa says.

"They do. But the entire high school is watching a play in the auditorium before the big pep rally, so I decided to run home and get some things I need for the game." He looks over at me. He slowly lifts his arms and turns his ballcap around backward, egging me on. He knows I love the way his muscles flex when he does that. "I was a little distracted this morning and forgot some stuff."

Kyra snorts, trying to disguise her laugh with a cough.

"Anyway, I was stopping by to check on Merit and saw all of y'all through the window. I thought the kids could use a snack."

Heidi finally makes it out of the back room, carrying a couple of boxes in her arms. Her smile widens when she sees Holt. "Hi, Coach."

"Hey, Heidi."

I take one of the smoothies over to her. "Heidi, you didn't tell me there was a big pep rally today. Don't you wanna go?"

She looks from Holt to me and then back again. "Oh... well, I mean, it's no big deal." She takes a sip of her smoothie, politely thanking Holt.

She's not very convincing. "Heidi, it's okay if you wanna go." I toss my hand around the room, "We all did that stuff in high school. It's your senior year; I don't want you missing out on something because of work."

"Well..."

"C'mon, Heidi," Holt encourages her. "Merit says you've worked every single day since starting. Go enjoy the pep rally with your friends. It's the big game—it's Homecoming. There won't even be another pep rally until the last game of the season."

She stares at me with big doe eyes. "Are you sure? I can be back in time to help Kyra close up and then go to the game afterward. Remember, just five more times, and then I can start closing by myself."

Kyra bumps her with her hip. "I'll handle tonight. You enjoy the pep rally and football game."

"And I'm here all day tomorrow," I add. "You and I can do the close-down together tomorrow night."

Grinning, she nods. "Are you sure?"

"Of course."

Holt tosses his hands in the air. "Perfect. It's decided." He looks at his watch. "And if we're gonna make the pep rally, we both need to leave right now."

Hugging his mom, he tells everyone he'll see them tonight at the game. Wrapping his hand around the back of my neck, he kisses my lips. "Goodbye, my happy little Merit."

"And goodbye to you, too, *sir*."

His laugh trails both him and Heidi out the door. I watch as he walks her to her car and opens the door for her, acting as a gentleman and making sure her car starts without any trouble.

I appreciate the kindness he's shown to Heidi. She doesn't talk much about her homelife, but from what little bits and pieces I've learned, she's been dealt her fair share of hardships. She's mentioned that her dad's not in the picture and that her mom suffers from a permanent medical condition. I know she found joy in cheering and tumbling but had a terrible fall that injured her ankle and effectively killed her cheerleading career—something she was hoping would provide her with a scholarship to attend college. On the rare occasion she does speak about her family, she mostly talks about her uncle. I think he's intervened in her life, in a positive way, more than once.

Of course, when I heard that, my mind immediately correlated their relationship to that of Crutch and Laura's. But then, she made an offhand comment that he sometimes gets angry with the world and the cards he's been dealt. We were watching an old movie at the time.

Even though the temperature outside has barely dipped low enough for a light sweater at night, I was feeling Christmas-ey the other day and started *It's a Wonderful Life* while we were unboxing new inventory. After the scene where George tears apart the living room and yells at his family, Heidi said George's whole life reminded her of her uncle. When I tried to press her for more information, she shut down.

Not wanting to enlarge a gaping wound—or irritate a healing one—I dropped the subject.

I know how it feels...to want to keep some parts of yourself hidden, buried from those around you. Some days, you feel like shoveling your past off you with a commercial-sized backhoe. And other days? Other days, you wanna have a panic attack if someone tries to remove a small sliver of dirt—one small memory—using nothing bigger than a teaspoon.

Not to mention, I'm her boss. I have to tread that thin line between professionalism and camaraderie. I'm not worried about it, though. We'll find our way.

Holt climbs in his truck, following her out of the parking lot. When he drives off, I can't help but think of how funny life is.

My old Friday nights used to consist of cocktail parties. I'd sit around in a slutty black dress and watch Edward smoke cigars and drink whiskey.

And now?

Now, I'm going to a high school Homecoming.

And hopping into bed with the coach afterward.

Chapter 28

Merit

I jump up from the couch the second I hear the knock on the door. I'm immediately rewarded with Crutch's sexy smile. "You ready?" he asks.

"Yep." Setting the house alarm, I follow him out to the driveway. He opens the door and offers his hand, helping me climb in his truck. "Thanks so much for coming to get me," I say. "It just didn't make sense for us to have two vehicles there."

Holt's been at the bar for the past few hours, watching football with the other guys—Ray, Will, Ridge, Cullen, Jeff, and Marcum. He had an autograph signing at a PeeWee Football Jamboree today. They all ended up going. Cullen and Jeff handed out homemade granola bars; Ridge's firehouse brought a fire truck for the kids to see; and Marcum brought the old paddy-wagon the sheriff's department uses for publicity pictures. Holt arranged for Crutch to pick me up and meet them at the bar.

"It's no problem. I'm sorry I'm a couple of minutes late. My last call ran long."

"You worked today?"

He chuckles. "Someone had to. My partner was out taking pictures and passing out plastic badges all day long."

He can joke, but it doesn't take a super-smart person to see that Marcum holds a special place in his heart. Holt told me he was a great mentor to Crutch.

"Ella's not coming out tonight?"

"She and Laura told me not to come home. Apparently, they've kicked me out of the house to gorge on junk food and watch romance movies all night long." He sighs contently, obviously thinking about his wife. "I think she's just wanting to give Little Girl some special attention before the baby comes."

"She's with y'all a lot, huh?"

He nods. "Every weekend. Her mom, Brooke, is one of our department dispatchers. She got a big promotion earlier this year, and now she's dispatch lead for the weekend shift. She works seven p.m. to seven a.m. every Thursday, Friday, and Saturday night. So, that means Laura is at our house."

"And her father is your brother?" His face falls and his lips thin. I silently curse myself. One of these days, I'll learn to keep my big fat mouth shut.

"My brother's a lost cause. The only thing he ever did right in his life was make her." He looks over at me. "I couldn't love her more if she were my own."

"She's lucky to have you."

We spend the rest of the ride pleasantly chatting. When we get to the bar, he leads me through the crowd of people on the outdoor patio with his hand on the small of my back. There's a group of young twenty-somethings who immediately spot us. Well, they immediately spot Crutch, I mean.

He's definitely hard to miss, with his pale green eyes and gigantic stature. And while Holt's all lean, firm muscles, Crutch is built like a brick shithouse. Half the girls blush, and the other half stare, slack-jawed like babies waiting to be spoon-fed.

I snort on my giggle.

"What's so funny?" he asks.

I motion for him to bend down with my finger. "Those girls over there are having a come apart. They think you're hot."

He looks over my head. "Good thing Lulu's not here." He cocks an eyebrow. "Her pregnancy hormones have amplified her jealousy. She nearly threw a drink at our waitress the other night."

Laughing, I pat his arm. "Well, it's not too much longer. What is it? A month?"

"Three weeks and some change," he answers, opening the door for me.

The indoor noise drowns my senses. Not only are the TVs blaring the football game, but there's still background music pouring out of the speakers overhead. It's completely packed tonight. Body after body bump into us. Sensing our presence, Cullen glances up, waving us over.

The closer we get to the bar, though, the angrier I get.

Apparently, there's an open casting call for whores tonight, and I missed the memo. Trust me, if I received it, I would have done my best to keep the Hill Family Men at home—especially *my* Hill Family Man.

Ridge is flanked by a blonde and a brunette, both vying for his attention. The blonde reaches up and runs her fingers through his hair. One girl with pink underwear showing underneath her skirt is hanging over the bar, trying to flirt with Cullen. He's doing his best to weave around her and keep up with the drink orders. Right then, a girl with massive boobs bumps into Crutch on purpose and tries to introduce herself. He flashes his wedding ring in her face and keeps pushing me toward the bar.

And then, there's the famous Holt Hill.

My Holt Hill.

He's sitting on a barstool, trying to ignore the woman whispering in his ear. She's wearing five-inch heels and a black leather mini skirt. Her platinum hair is pulled back, showcasing the massive diamond earrings dangling from her ears. When we get closer, she leans back, arching her breasts in his face, and talks at a volume loud enough for me to hear. "Why don't we go someplace quieter, and we can talk about it more."

What the hell does she wanna talk about with my man?

"That's it!" Cullen's scream makes me jump. "That's the face," he says, pointing at me.

Pointing at *my face.*

Crutch bends down, looking.

I see Ray peek around from two barstools over. "What face?"

"Her jealous face," Ridge says, laughing. He's spun around on his own barstool, leaving the women staring at each other in question.

Marcum chuckles. "Like Ella rolling her eyes."

"But this is better," Cullen says, smiling.

I force myself to relax my face muscles, but I must do it wrong because everyone starts laughing even harder.

At this point, Holt still hasn't turned around.

But his lady friend definitely seems interested in all the fuss surrounding me. She looks at my pink sweater and simple khaki shorts and frowns.

"Well," Holt finally decides to join the conversation, "Avery, as enticing as that offer may be to most men, it's not something I'm up for exploring."

She cocks an eyebrow. "Really?"

"Really."

"And just why not?" she asks, obviously not used to being turned down.

Holt picks up his beer bottle and takes the last swallow. Cullen replaces it with a fresh one, and Holt nods his appreciation. "First of all, that man right there," he points at Ray, "is my father. And I don't think he wants a future daughter-in-law of his to do what you just offered to do. Second of all, there may still be some counties in Alabama where that's not even legal. And third—and arguably the most important—that woman right there," he points behind his back, right at me, "says I belong to her. She might not look like much of a fighter, but trust me, she's pretty damn scrappy." He leans closer like he's going to tell her a secret. "And she's fucking dynamite in bed."

Holy. Shit.

I can't even see straight I'm so embarrassed. My vision tunnels and my heartbeat thunders in my eardrums. I'm vaguely aware of

Holt spinning around and yanking me between his legs. I'm also vaguely aware of all the men in the extended Holt Hill family hollering and laughing like Holt just won another Super Bowl.

I blink, trying to clear the dizziness from my brain. After a second, I realize my mouth is open—like I'm waiting for a bug to fly in—so I snap it closed.

The stranger named Avery folds her arms across her chest and holds her head high, trying to save what little dignity she has left. "You don't know what you're missing if you think *she's* dynamite in bed." She smacks her lips together and eyes Holt like she can see right underneath his clothes. "Want my phone number? You know, for when you come to your senses and throw her out of your life?"

Oh, hell no. That fucking daughter of a shit-eater did not just say that.

And what a stupid question, by the way.

Holt looks at me, studying the anger and shock in my eyes, before turning back to her. "What a stupid question. And by the way, if you were a guy, I'd tell you to wash the lies out of your mouth with a dog turd."

We watch as Avery stomps off in a huff. Right then, Will comes around the bar, carrying a fresh case of beer. He looks at our faces and furrows his brow. "What'd I miss?"

Ridge pulls my barstool closer to his. "That was so damn funny."

He doesn't have to expand; it's pretty clear what he's talking about. "Yeah, funny for you. But what about the dads—Ray, even your dad?" Luckily, all the married men left about an hour ago, saving me from dwelling on it too much.

He smiles. "Oh, they thought it was funny too. It's not like they think Holt's a virgin."

I purse my lips together. "But what about me?"

He chokes on his beer. "You do realize you were married, right? I think Ray knows you're not a virgin."

Hmm. Good point.

Fortunately, I'm saved from discussing my sex life by my ringing phone. I quickly answer, asking the person on the other end to hold on. "It's the alarm company; I have to take this," I tell Ridge. I look over my shoulder and see Holt still playing pool with a couple of fans who struck up a conversation. "I'm gonna step outside."

Ridge takes a swig of his beer. "I'll go with you."

"Don't be silly. I'll stay by the door." I pat the barstool. "Save my seat." Despite the late hour, the bar is still busy, and I don't want to lose my spot.

The crowd outside has thinned down. There's only room for a couple of tables, and they're filled with people drinking beer in plastic cups from plastic pitchers. There's a surprising chill in the air, and I'm glad I wore a sweater instead of a sleeveless shirt. When I'm on hold with the alarm company, a couple of guys wave, trying to get my attention. I politely smile and turn away. After a couple of minutes, the alarm company resets everything. It looks like someone pulled on the front door to see if was open, but that's it. There was no other activity.

When I hang up the phone, one of the men catches me off guard, gently tapping on my shoulder. "Hey, everything okay? That looked like a serious phone call." He's got floppy brown hair and sunglasses hanging around his neck.

Apparently, he missed a memo too—that it's almost midnight and the sun's not out.

"It's fine. Everything's okay," I offer, trying not to engage him too much. It's pretty obvious by the little wobble in his step that he's drunk, and talking to drunk people can be cumbersome. And irritating.

"Hey, why don't you come join us for a drink?"

"Oh, no, thank you." I nod at the door. "I should head back in."

He sidesteps, somewhat blocking my way. "Oh, come on, we don't bite," he says, looking back at his friends.

I give a little snort. "Maybe next time."

"Don't be like that, sweetie. We're just wanting to have a good time." He reaches out, touching my arm.

I quickly pull away.

A calm, cool voice catches our attention. "I think the lady said no. I would listen if I were you."

I follow the sound over to the far side of the sidewalk. I squint, trying to make out the face in the dim light. The guy's wearing a white button down and navy slacks. "Colin?"

He walks up, placing himself between me and the stranger.

The stranger chuckles and holds his hands up. "No need to ruffle your feathers there, J Crew." Laughing he walks back over to his friends, mumbling under his breath, "You can have her. Looks too uptight for my taste."

Well, that's almost comical. Edward had to spend a lot of valuable time and money to try and make me more uptight because he thought I was too uncouth.

Colin turns around and smiles. "Problems?"

His mega-watt smile and spray tan are a little overwhelming. He's the CEO of his dad's real estate company. They have major money and, of course, are friends with Edward and his family. We were never especially close, but I guess I should be thankful for his chivalry. I'm not sure if I should hug him or shake his hand, so I just stand there. He wraps an arm loosely around my back and gives me a kiss on the cheek.

"It's good to see you, Colin."

"Indeed. It's definitely been a while. Since..." he pretends to be thinking about the timeframe, "before the divorce, if I remember correctly."

I smack my lips together. "Probably so."

"And you're doing well?" His tone is dripping with superiority, like he knows there's no way my life could be as good as his.

I fold my hands together and look down at the sidewalk. There's a crack, and I trace it with my sandal. "I'm doing very well. Thank you for asking."

His brow creases. "Let's see...you work at a little store, don't you?"

There's no point in correcting him. He knows I own the store; he just refuses to acknowledge it. "Yes, business is going well." I look at him, he's obviously waiting on me to return the question. "For you, too, I presume?"

He fake laughs and fiddles with his cufflinks. "You know the real estate market. It's on fire. Nothing stays on the market longer than a day."

"Well, I should get back—"

He interrupts me. "We've all missed you on the social scene. Things just aren't the same without you."

Oh, I highly doubt that.

He takes a step closer. "You look really good, Merit." His eyes trail down my body, making me feel dirty. He always did that. Right in front of Edward, too, and Edward would do nothing. Then, his voice lowers to a whisper. "Sexy. As always." He rubs his chin. His five-thousand-dollar watch glistens in my face. "Some of the other guys and I always talked about how jealous we were that Edward was the lucky bastard who got to bed you every night."

I take a couple of steps back, but I end up bumping into a table, basically trapping myself between it and him. He leans closer. His breath skirts across my face. "You know Edward was a fool for leaving you. I told him he should appreciate you more. Please you more. I told him you should hear from a man every single day just how beautiful you are."

"She does." I don't have to turn around to know whose voice that is. Chills instantly run down my spine. "She hears it from me."

Colin slides back on his heels, looking over my shoulder. "Well, if it isn't the great Holt Hill."

"That's right, asshole. And I'd prefer it if you stepped away from my girlfriend. Now."

Colin's lip twitches. "We haven't had the pleasure of meeting. I can only assume you wouldn't be speaking to me like that if you knew who I was."

"I don't give two shits who you are. It doesn't give you the right to talk to a woman like that. Can't you see she's uncomfortable? She doesn't want you near her."

He shrugs. "Merit and I have a longstanding friendship. Isn't that right, Merit?"

I look up and clench my fists at my side. Finally finding my voice, I speak up. "No, that's not right. You were Edward's friend, not mine. I always thought you were weird. Especially that eye-fucking thing you try to do. It makes you go cross-eyed. And I don't work at a store. I own it. But you already know that; you just refuse to acknowledge it."

Holt's chuckle is low and seductive. "There you have it." Sighing, he growls a warning, a threat that makes ice water run in my veins. "Now step the fuck away from my woman."

To the naked eye, Colin wouldn't look scared. But I see the tremble of his hands and the nervous tic of his eye. "You two deserve each other. Damn heathens."

Pushing the table out of the way, Holt floods my space. Taking my face in his hands, he looks me over. "He didn't touch you, did he? Hurt you?" His worry is evident.

"No, I'm fine."

Confident I'm telling the truth, a slow look of amusement settles across his face. "Cross-eyed, huh?"

I snort. "Yeah. He did it again tonight. It makes him look like he's about to pass out."

Tugging me behind him, I stop in front of the table of drunk guys. Floppy Hair is staring at me, jaw wide open. Another guy keeps fumbling for his cell phone, no doubt upset that he missed getting the altercation on video. "Gentlemen, I'm assuming you know Holt Hill," I say with a sweeping hand, flourishing it over Holt's body.

They mumble around, red-faced and embarrassed. "Uh...yeah. Hi, Coach."

Holt lifts an eyebrow. "Something I should know about?" he asks me.

"Nope. Just making friends," I say, waving at Floppy as we go back inside.

It's interesting to see the unspoken language that the boys all share—Holt with Ridge, Cullen, and Will. The three of them immediately stand at attention when we come inside, like they sense a change in the air based on Holt's mood. All Holt has to do is nod and make some sort of hand gesture, and it's like they all know what's going on. Breaking through the crowd, Ridge elbows his way to the front door, swinging it open and checking for danger. Satisfied the threat has gone away, he makes his way over to us. "Are you okay?"

I smile. "Of course, I'm fine."

Growling, he chastises himself. "I knew I should've gone outside with you."

I squeeze his arm. "Ridge, it's fine. I had to take a call from the alarm company. It's no big deal, nothing happened. It was just one of Edward's friends being a douchebag."

Holt slaps his best friend on the shoulder. "We're all good, brother. I promise." When Ridge doesn't move, Holt laughs, lightheartedly pushing him away. "Now, leave us alone. I'm gonna dance with my girl."

Pulling me into his arms, he sways back and forth to the music of a slow song blaring through the overhead speakers. Several other couples are dancing. Considering the late hour and the flowing booze, some of these couples may only be couples for tonight, if you catch my drift. Reaching up, he turns his ballcap around, giving him the freedom to bend closer to me. His lips graze the shell of my ear. "Hi."

"Hi. Did you win your game of pool?"

"Won one. Lost one."

I lift an eyebrow. "You mean you lost one on purpose, right? I've seen you play pool, and you kick butt. As with everything."

His laugh is low and breathy. "Everybody likes to win. Why not let someone win against the professional athlete." He shrugs. "It makes for a good story."

His hands press against the small of my back, begging me to be closer to him. I close my eyes, relishing the movement of his body.

Holt's larger than life. Not only physically but... dimensionally. He exists in a space all his own. It's like no one can touch him.

He's invincible.

The invincible Holt Hill.

As such, it feels like we're the only two people in the world. It doesn't matter what crowd is around us, mankind doesn't invade Holt Hill's universe.

When I open my eyes, he's staring at me. Watching me, absorbing me.

"Tell me again," I whisper.

He doesn't have to ask what I'm talking about. He knows. Whether he's reading my face or reading my mind, it doesn't matter. All that matters is *he knows*.

"I love you, Merit."

My hands snake around to the blond waves curling from underneath his hat. Forcing his face to mine, I kiss him. Sliding my tongue against his, I focus on the instantaneous reaction of my body. I savor the way he makes me feel, the way my body willingly responds to his touch, to his taste, to his power. It's like Holt's my generator—my lifeline—pumping heat and electricity through the still and quiet night. Never failing. Never stopping. Never leaving me cold or dark or hungry.

We kiss until we're both breathless and shaking.

"I really hope you're ready to get out of here," he says with a dramatic growl.

I snort halfway through my giggle. "Why?"

His devilish smile makes me weak in the knees. His fingers grip my hips—almost painfully—and he grinds his erection against me. "Because you're about to get fucked in the middle of this dance floor."

Taking a play from his book, I wink.

That's the only answer he needs.

Grabbing my ass, he hauls me into his arms, carrying me. My ankles instantly lock around his waist. Waving to the boys, he carries me out of the bar and home.

To our home.

Chapter 29

Merit

"Craig, are you all right?" I lean against a shelf, studying my delivery guy as he brings the last load of boxes through the back door. He's definitely been acting odd today.

"Yeah, absolutely." He stacks everything in the corner and leans on the hand truck. "So, I was just wondering... well, what I mean is..." he stumbles over his words.

"Craig, what is it?" I politely urge.

"Is it true you're dating Holt Hill?"

Why's he asking? "Yeah. Actually, I am."

The awkwardness in the air is dissolved by his smile. "Oh, wow. That's amazing." He shoves his hands in his pockets and rocks back on his feet. "I saw him play in the National Championship during his senior year of college. It was in Miami, so me and some buddies went. Best game I ever saw."

"Would you like to meet him?"

For a split second, I think Craig's about to faint.

"Are you serious? Really?"

I can't help but laugh. "Of course, I'm serious." I nod my head in the direction of the storefront. "He's out front."

His eyes nearly bug out of his head. "Right now?! He's out there right now?"

I don't want him to think I'm making fun of him, so I just nod.

"Oh, Merit, that would be freakin' awesome. Let me lock the truck, and I'll walk around front. Is that okay?"

"Sure." Locking the back door behind him, I make my way upfront. Leaning against the doorframe, I look around, taking in the beauty of the setting before me. It was a very busy morning, but this afternoon has been fairly slow. We haven't even had a customer in close to an hour. Kyra's sitting at the front counter, doing homework on her personal laptop. Holt and Heidi are sitting next to each other in the chairs, completely engrossed in the movie playing. Every time she giggles, Heidi playfully slaps his arm.

And who can blame them? *The Ghost and Mr. Chicken* is a classic.

I take the packing slips over to Kyra so she can scan them in the system when I'm immediately distracted by what's on her computer.

And it's definitely not homework.

"If you watch that video one more time, I'm gonna throw you out of my store."

She props her elbows on the counter. "I can't help it. It's like soft-core porn. Which is sometimes better than the hard stuff because you get to use your imagination."

Needless to say, when we were at the bar, Holt and I were completely oblivious to the fact that someone had their phone out and had videoed our entire dance, make-out session, and subsequent hasty retreat. And it goes without saying that our intimate moment was viral internet fodder by the next morning.

I scoot closer to her so Heidi won't overhear us. "You know Emily made a pass at Holt the other day."

Kyra's jaw drops. "You're kidding me? I hope you fired her ass." She shuts her laptop, mumbling underneath her breath, "What a moron."

"Holt said she apologized and immediately backed off when he turned her down."

"So, you didn't fire her?"

I shake my head. Right then, the front door buzzes, and Craig timidly walks in. I could be wrong, but it looks like he combed his hair and put on a clean shirt.

Holt and Heidi stand up, thinking a customer has come in and it's time for Heidi to work. Craig immediately starts to fangirl, bouncing from one foot to the other.

Walking around the corner, I grab his elbow and force him to walk within arm's distance of Holt. "Craig, this is my boyfriend, Holt. Holt, this is Craig, the best delivery man in the county and my friend."

It's one of the funniest interactions I've ever seen. I have to take four-thousand pictures with Craig's phone. He even asks Holt for a penny.

They're talking about football when my cell phone rings. I show Holt my home screen with my mom's picture flashing and point to the back room. He nods, understanding I'm leaving him alone with the needy fan. He should be used to it, though.

"Hey, Mom."

"Hey, sweetie. How are you?"

We chat for a few minutes, talking about each other's days.

"Well, what are your plans for this weekend?" she asks.

"Nothing really. We had Holt's football game last night. His team won again, of course. I think the kids are coming over tomor-row afternoon to swim. This will be the last weekend for it because the nights are starting to get pretty chilly. It's been a long and hot summer. In fact, I don't really remember any other summer in which we've still been able to swim in October. Do you? I was gonna come in and do some work, but I wanna see them, so I'll just save it for Monday. Why?"

"So, no bar visits?" I can hear the laugher in her voice.

Red hot flames of embarrassment fire in my body, like an engine combusting. "I knew it! I knew you knew! We've talked every dag-gum day, Mom, and you haven't said anything."

She laughs so hard she can hardly breathe. "I was just letting it soak in."

I flop down at the small table in the back. "Oh my gosh, everybody saw? Daddy? Granny?"

She snorts. "Of course, everybody saw. We live in the sticks... not in a cave."

A small river of shame runs through me, making me feel weak. Making me feel like I used to feel. "I'm sorry, Mom."

"You take that tone right out of your voice, Merit Eliza. Why are you sorry? You have nothing to be sorry for." She pauses for a second. "Besides, he looks like a great kisser."

I slap my hand against my forehead, but I'm unable to hide my laugh. It may be gross to know that my mom is thinking about Holt's kisses, but her comment does pull me out of my funk, instantly making me feel better. "And what about Daddy?"

"Well, it took him a few more days to come around. I mean, he did see his daughter dry-humping someone on the evening news."

"It was not on the evening news," I scoff.

"Might as well have been." I hear her take a drink of water. "Just so you know, he called your father to apologize."

"Who called?"

"Holt."

"Holt called Daddy?"

"Yep."

It takes me a minute to formulate a response. "What for?"

"To apologize for the video. He wanted your father to know that he respects you and would never objectify you to the world as just some plaything. He told your father that his intentions are pure."

"What intentions?" I whisper.

"Don't be stupid, girl. This is going *somewhere,* isn't it? Somewhere real?"

"Yes."

"You love him?"

I think before I answer. But it doesn't matter how hard I think, it doesn't change my mind. It doesn't make me regret what I'm about to say. "Yes."

"Have you told him?"

"No."

"And just why not?" Mom asks.

I fiddle with an ink pen, clicking it open and close. "Because I'm scared."

"What about him? Does he love you?"

"Yes. He's told me on more than one occasion." I get choked up just thinking about him saying the words. They're beautiful and overwhelming and sacred.

Mom sighs. "Merit, the past is the past. There's nothing you can do to change it. All you can do is move forward. Live a life full of happiness. Don't waste another single second being unhappy. That's power you are giving to Edward that he no longer deserves. It's your turn to be happy, sweet girl."

I jump a mile in my skin when Holt's arm snakes around my shoulder. "Hey, Marie," he calls in the phone.

I drop the phone, and it skitters across the table. I fumble around, getting it back in my hand. "Aghh. Sorry, Mom, I dropped you."

"Tell Holt I say hi back."

I roll my eyes and give Holt the message.

"Well, I better let you go. I love you."

"Love you, too, Mom."

Holt sits down in the chair next to mine. "Scared of what?"

My brow furrows. "Huh?"

"When I came in, I heard you saying you were scared of something."

I jump from my seat. Walking over to a shelf, I straighten a shoe box. "Oh nothing." I quickly switch the subject, "How did it go with Craig?"

Holt grabs the hem of my T-shirt and pulls me. Guiding me backward, he forces me to sit on the tabletop. Sliding his chair between my legs, he lays his head down on my stomach. "I'm mentally exhausted. He was a super-nice guy, but it felt like I was in the middle of a press junket. He just wouldn't stop talking." He lifts up, looking at me with his deep blue eyes. "And he's very happy to be the new owner of one of my shiny pennies."

"Thank you. I'll have the happiest delivery driver in the Southeast." I lick my lips, studying his beauty. His blond waves are a little longer than normal. He said he's going for a haircut next week. He knows I like the sexy scruff along the line of his firm jaw, so he hasn't shaved in two weeks. His bronzed skin is highlighted by the slight sunburn on the apples of his cheeks. My finger traces the freckles painted across the bridge of his nose. I drag my hand down his neck and circle his small scar.

"Did it hurt?"

"What? My injury?"

I nod. "I just realized that we've never talked about it. I've never told you how sorry I am, sorry that you had to stop playing the game that meant so much to you."

He sighs, and one side of his mouth tilts up. "So, ask me."

"Did it hurt?"

"Hurt like hell. But that's not the question you need to ask."

"What question do I need to ask?"

"*What happened,*" he says.

The Internet has thousands of pieces of information about Holt, and no matter how you search, articles about his career-ending injury pull up first. It's always at the top of the list. As always, the bad outweighs the good, at least where human curiosity is concerned.

July was the second anniversary of his injury. Apparently, he was at home in North Carolina and was attempting to change a light bulb when he fell off the interior, second-story balcony of his condo. He landed on the wooden coffee table in his living room. He broke a vertebra in his neck and tore nearly everything in his knee.

My brow furrows. "But I know what happened."

He pulls his chair closer and squeezes my waist. "Do you?" His voice is filled with an unusual urging, laced with surprise and anticipation.

My heart beats a little faster, and for some strange reason, worry shadows over me. "What happened?"

"I didn't fall off a balcony while changing a light bulb." He pauses, gauging my reaction. "I jumped off a cliff."

Huh? "You jumped off a cliff?"

"Yep."

What the hell? "Willingly?"

He laughs, gliding his hands across my thighs, making me shiver. "Yes, willingly. Very willingly, as a matter of fact."

A deep-seated fear covers my heart in concrete, weighing it down. My whisper is broken and strained. "Did you try to kill yourself?"

He jumps in shock. After a split second, he bursts out laughing. Wrapping his hand around my neck, he softly kisses me. "No. I wasn't trying to kill myself." Leaning back, he stares at me, adoringly. "You probably don't know this, but Ridge's family has a cabin in the Smoky Mountains. His grandparents retired there, and his family inherited it when they passed. We've all been there for vacation. It's beautiful. It's in a private, gated community that has its own hiking trails cut in the mountains. There's even a branch of the Little Pigeon River that runs through there.

"Well, that's where Anna wanted to go for her fifth birthday. Raylee was pregnant with Ty, so we wanted to make it special for her since it would be her last birthday as an only child. One day, we all went hiking. It's a trail we've all been on a thousand times. It's on a bluff, leading to the river, and the top has the most amazing views. What none of us knew was that heavy rains had been happening nearly every single day for the two weeks before our trip. The ground was soft."

I watch as his eyes cloud with painful memories of the past. A frown plagues his face. "She ran ahead of me. I should've stopped her, but I didn't." He shakes his head and his voice breaks. "I could see her, you know? I could see her so I thought she was safe."

My throat clenches, and my breath catches in my lungs, refusing to come out.

"She saw a flower that she wanted to pick. She was close to the edge of the ravine, but not so close I was worried about her falling. And then... the whole side just gave way and she fell."

I gasp, covering my mouth with my hand.

"She was there one second and gone the next." He swallows. "Like I said, we've been there a lot. I knew that trail. I knew what was below that trail's edge. About twenty feet down, there's a rock ledge that sticks out—part of a massive boulder, part of the mountain itself. It's about three feet wide. I raced up there, and there she was. Curled in a little ball and about to roll off the side."

He pulls his bottom lip against his teeth. "I jumped. There wasn't time to wait so I just jumped. Pulled her into my arms right as she was about to roll off the ledge. I mean, we were on a mountain. The next drop would've killed her."

Sighing, he drags his hands through his hair. When he doesn't say anything, I press him. "Was Anna okay?"

He smiles and makes a sweet little noise. "Kids are resilient. Ridge has seen a lot as a firefighter and paramedic, and he always says kids are like rubber bands. They bend and flop, and it takes a lot to break them. Well, he's right. Besides a few scratches and bruises, she was fine."

I shake my head at the truths he's just shared. "But you weren't," I state the obvious.

"Not exactly."

My finger reaches back out and traces his scar again.

He turns his neck, giving me a better look. "Blew the disc between C6 and C7." He lifts his leg and hitches his foot against the table. He rubs the tangle of scars on his left knee. "Shredded my ACL, PCL, and MCL." He sets his leg back down and stares at me.

He's literally just blown my mind. It takes me a minute to gather my thoughts. "How did you get out?"

"Ridge was there, of course, so he took charge of everything. He had rappelling gear at the cabin. We got Anna out of there, and then he got me."

"I don't understand. I mean, I watched a press conference about your injury. You did interviews after your medical retirement and talked about falling off the balcony."

He tugs on my ass, pulling me closer to him. "I lied."

"You lied?" My voice hitches, rising an octave.

"I promised not to lie to you. Reporters?" He chuckles, "Well, I made them no such promise."

"But how? How could something like this stay secret?"

"Will and Raylee immediately took Anna to the local hospital. But I went all the way back home to North Carolina."

"You drove home with a broken neck and a jacked-up knee? Weren't you in pain?"

His eyes widen. "Unbearable. But Ridge drove me. I just sat in the passenger seat writhing in agony." He snorts, "I didn't have any painkillers so I drank nearly a fifth of whiskey on the ride."

"Good lord, you're lucky alcohol poisoning wasn't added to the list. Why would you do that? Why not go to the hospital?"

"I spent my whole career trying to shield my family from the craziness of the paparazzi. If they knew what really happened, they would bombard them. They would be pounding on Raylee's door wanting interviews with Anna." His lips thin in anger. "There's no way I was allowing that to happen."

He brushes a hair from my face and twists it between his fingers. "So, we went to my condo. I took a shower, washed the mountain dirt off, and sobered up. We cooked up the story of falling off the balcony." He chuckles. "I think breaking my coffee table with a sledgehammer was Ridge's favorite part. And then...we called an ambulance.

"I lied to the doctors, but I told the truth to my coaches and the team owner. I didn't want anything to come back on me and affect my medical payout. It was determined that *how* I got my injury didn't matter, the outcome was the same. I couldn't play. So, knowing that my medical retirement was intact, they agreed to use the balcony fall as the official story. They knew I didn't want my family involved."

I sit, absorbing everything he said.

"I was in a neck and knee brace for two months. Then, I kicked ass in physical therapy. Lived in the gym. Got in the best shape of my life. I moved back here the following January and got my teaching job that summer. I was terrified I would hate coaching. Terrified it wouldn't be as fun as playing. But it is. I love it."

He licks his lips. "And I wouldn't have met you if I hadn't come back home. If I hadn't gotten injured, I'd still be in North Carolina. Playing, winning, trying to find peace with a life in the spotlight."

"Dating models?" I quip.

"Nah, I think this season was supposed to be a Grammy award-winning singer," he jokes.

I look down, watching his hands as they skim up and down my legs. The calloused graze of his fingertips is mesmerizing. Sliding off the table, I straddle him on the chair. I lean forward, kissing his scar. "I can't believe you did that. You risked your life for your niece. You could've died trying to save her." Holt's fierce love of his family makes me love him even more. I want him. Forever and ever. "I'm sorry you got hurt. But I'm not sorry that it made you mine."

As soon as I finish my sentence, his mouth is on my own. Exploring and tasting and branding me.

"Hey, Merit, do you have any more of the pink and yellow tie-dye socks back here?" Kyra's voice interrupts us. She says oops, but she doesn't really sound sorry.

There's a growling rumble deep in Holt's chest. His words fog against my neck, leaving moisture in their wake. "And what's the status on those new friends we're supposed to be getting?"

I laugh and snort. Pushing myself off him—despite my desire to do nothing but kiss him for the rest of the day—I dig in one of the new delivery boxes for socks. "I'll be there in a minute, Kyra."

When she turns the corner, walking back into the front, Holt hollers after her. "Make that a couple of minutes, Kyra."

I open my mouth to object, but the playful gleam in his eyes has me locking my jaw and biting back a smile. In one swift movement, he's by my side, hauling my body against his. Tingles fire from the top of my scalp to the bottom of my toes. His tongue darts out, licking the column of my neck. The moan falling from my lips is completely involuntary. My response to Holt is a reflex; it's a part of who I am now. It's imprinted into my soul and will last for the rest of my life and into eternity.

"The thought of having to wait until tonight before I can have your naked body beneath me is pure torture. I wanna spend all day wrapped in your love, baby." He suckles on the soft skin below my ear. "But I guess I'll have to settle for the next two or three minutes."

I grind myself against his erection. "And tell me, *sir*, what does the famous Holt Hill think he can do in the next ninety seconds?" Gifting him with a mischievous grin, I wink at him, giving him a dose of his own medicine.

"Oh, let me fucking show you." And with that, his mouth crashes back into mine.

Chapter 30

Holt

I jump up from the patio chair the second her picture flashes across my screen. Excusing myself, I quickly head inside and answer the phone in the middle of my assistant coach's living room. "Hey, are you on your way?"

"No." Her voice is filled with frustration and disappointment.

"What's wrong? What happened?"

"I went in the back to use the bathroom before leaving, and when I came back out front, the computer system had completely crashed. Everything—I mean *everything*—was gone. I nearly collapsed on the floor and had a panic attack. I've been on the phone with IT for over an hour. They think they can retrieve everything, but I have to stay here and test it as they work on it."

"Shit," I mumble under my breath. "And you have no idea what happened?"

"No, Heidi and I got the store all closed up. I went to the bathroom when she left; and when I came back, I was gonna sign off, but the computer screen was black. No screen saver. Nothing."

"Well, at least they think they can get the data back." I peek out the sliding glass door at the people on the back deck, drinking and talking. "I'm gonna head that way. I'll help you."

"Holt, you can't, that would be so rude. Your staff is celebrating a winning season. And you can't tell me that y'all aren't talking about the playoffs and what changes you wanna make before that starts."

She's right. Last night was the last game of the regular season, and we're undefeated. I can almost taste the State Championship. Last season, we lost in the second round of the playoffs. I was so proud of my team. It's hard enough to have a brand-new coach, but to make it to the playoffs during that coach's first year? It was freakin' awesome.

My assistant coach, Troy Skinner, has been planning this barbeque for weeks. All the football staff and their respective spouses are here. Several teachers too. Even the principal.

But does that really matter? Merit needs me.

"But you need me," I say.

She giggles and snorts. "I need you to do what? Turn the computer on and off and hit the enter button? I think I can handle that all by myself."

"It's getting late. I don't like you being there late at night all by yourself," I protest.

"Holt," her voice is firm and tender all at the same time. It's the voice I imagine she'll use with our children. "I appreciate the sentiment, but you forget that I was working late nights *way* before you sauntered into my store." She clears her throat. "With Bunny, I might add."

If I close my eyes, I can see her scrunching her nose. Reluctantly, I let her win the battle. "Point taken."

"Have fun, and I'll see you at home. Okay?"

I love it when she calls our house *home*.

Pocketing my phone, I spin around and nearly crash into Heidi. "Whoa." It takes a minute for her presence to register in my brain. "Heidi, what are you doing here?"

"I'm babysitting." She nods down the hall to the kids' room. She's got a bag of snack crackers in her hand. "Mrs. Skinner asked me to watch the kids so she could enjoy some adult time at the barbeque."

"I didn't know you babysat for Troy and Brittany. I haven't heard them mention it before."

She plays with her ponytail. "It's kind of a new development. I saw her in the grocery store a couple of days ago with the kids. I told her I would be happy to babysit anytime I wasn't working at the store." She peers behind my shoulder. "Speaking of, is Merit here yet?"

I shake my head. "No."

Her brow furrows. "Is everything okay? When I left the store, she said she was running home to change clothes and then heading this way." She looks at her watch. "I've already been here watching the kids for an hour."

I drag my hand across my chin. "The computer system crashed."

Her eyes widen. "At the store?"

"Yep."

"Oh man. Can it be fixed?"

"She thinks so. She's working with IT now."

She bites the side of her lip. "I'd go back and help her, but…" Her voice trails off as she looks back down the hallway.

I pat her shoulder. "It's fine. She knows she can call me if she has any problems."

Nodding, she smiles widely and shakes the bag of crackers. "I came out to get a snack for the kids. We're playing a card game. Why don't you come play a round? The kids would really get a kick out of it."

Before I can say no, she grabs my hand and drags me down the hallway.

I'm a little bit frustrated.

I get home later than expected, and Merit's nowhere to be found on my side of the house. I was really hoping she'd be sitting in the living room, waiting on me. Or better yet, lying in my bed.

Walking down the hall to the Children's Wing, I quietly open the door and immediately hear the tell-tale music from one of her old movies. Leaning against the doorframe of her own small living room, I fold my arms across my chest and silently watch her. Curled in a ball on the couch, she's wearing one of her near-see through cotton nightgowns and a cream color button-up sweater—one that she described as 'it's like wearing clouds'. Some song and dance number plays on the TV screen, and she taps her foot back and forth in beat. Her redwood hair waterfalls across the pillow. I bet it smells like pumpkin spice. That's her latest shampoo choice. Apparently, she had to change her scent when we decorated the front porch with pumpkins and a hay bale.

My birthday is next Saturday—technically the day before Halloween—but neighborhood trick or treating will happen that night, and she wants the house to look festive for when the kids come over.

"Are we really gonna keep doing this?" I ask.

She yelps in surprise. Balancing on her elbows, she pouts at me. "You scared the crap out of me."

"You didn't answer my question."

She cocks her head. "What question?"

"Are we really gonna keep doing this?"

Her face falls, and she immediately sits upright. Her hand rubs her sternum, drawing my attention to her breasts. "What?" she gasps.

She's so freakin' funny.

She thinks I'm talking about *us*.

I bite back a smile. "This back and forth. Me coming over to the Children's Wing. You coming over to the Big House. We haven't slept apart in weeks. Why can't we just move your stuff into my bedroom. *Our bedroom*."

A visible relief washes over her like a summer rain. She mimics me, folding her arms across her chest. "Because that's what dating people do. They have sleepovers. They don't *move in* together." She clicks her tongue together like my suggestion is pure ignorance.

Rolling my eyes, I push from the wall. Turning off her TV, I hold out my hand. "Fine. Will you sleepover with me tonight?"

She nibbles on her pink lips, flirting with me. "What's in it for me?"

"How about multiple orgasms? Would that work?"

Her face turns beet red. "Holt!"

Laughing, I tug her from the couch and pull her behind me, eager to get her to the bedroom and deliver on my promise.

"How was the barbeque? Was the food good?" she asks.

"It was all right. But you know me, I'm spoiled by Jeff's cooking."

"Did you talk about the playoffs? I know everyone is excited."

"We talked about it a little bit. I didn't wanna get into the specifics since so many people were there." I squeeze her hand. "Hey, you didn't tell me Heidi was gonna be there."

"Huh? Heidi was there?"

"Yeah, I thought you knew. She was babysitting the Skinner kids."

I watch from the corner of my eye as she shrugs. "Maybe she wanted to surprise me. I told her I was worried that I wouldn't really have anyone to talk to. I mean, I've gotten used to having Raylee and Ella and your mom to talk to at the football stuff, you know?"

I stop walking. Bending, I give her a quick, simple kiss. "Hey, you always have me."

I don't have to say more. She knows what I'm saying.

I'm saying I'm not like Edward. She's not just a pretty chess piece that I want to stand in the corner like a statue. I want her with me. All the time. I want her to talk and engage, voice her own opinion. Hell, anyone who actually knows her can see that Merit is the life of any party.

We silently walk down the hall, and I can't help but think that I love the sound of her bare feet on the marble floor. For some strange reason, that sound fills my heart with even more love for the beautiful woman by my side.

Once upstairs, I reach in the pocket of my jeans, pull out my cell phone, and plug it into the charger on the table outside the bedroom door.

"Why do you do that?"

I glance down at the table. "Leave my cell phone out here, you mean?"

"Yeah. You never put it on your nightstand, you always leave it out here. You do the same thing with me. You leave it on the table outside the Children's Wing."

"It's habit. Mom never let me and Raylee keep our cell phones in our bedrooms at bedtime. She thought we'd stay up all night playing on them. Once I made it to the pros, it became a sanity-saving decision. Since they had me on all that social media crap, I was getting notifications all night long. Don't get me wrong, it didn't wake me up because I sleep like the dead, but I'd get angry if I woke up to piss in the middle of the night and saw ten-thousand little lights flashing across my screen."

She pulls her own cell phone out of her sweater pocket and waggles it at me. "I have to sleep with mine next to me. What if the alarm company calls?"

I tuck her hair behind her ear. "I know. I don't mind. Like I said, it's just a habit for me."

"But what if something happens? An emergency? How will your family get ahold of you?"

Crossing the bedroom threshold, I shut the door behind us and nod at my nightstand. "That's what the house phone is for."

She blinks. "I can't believe I've never noticed the phone there before. Who has the number?"

"Just family."

I'm not surprised when she asks the next question. We all know Merit is curious. She leans over, wrapping her hand around my arm. "Has anyone ever called you on it? I mean, have you gotten an emergency call?"

My heart tightens just thinking about it. "Yeah. Back in February, actually."

Her breath catches in her chest. "What happened?"

"Dad thought Mom was having a stroke. Fortunately, it was just an adverse reaction to some new medication." I drag my hand through my hair. "Scared the shit out of me, though."

She reaches up and twists her fingers in my curls. "I'm sorry you were scared."

Damn, she's amazing.

Heading into the bathroom, we brush our teeth. She's still using the same green toothbrush I gave her on the first night we stayed together. She finishes and heads back into the bedroom while I change out of my jeans and T-shirt. I hear her turn the knob on the lamp, and the stream of light flowing into the bathroom darkens. When I come out, I find her standing in front of the window. She's opened the blinds and is looking out over the moonlit backyard.

I can't even describe how good it feels just to look at her.

Pulling her hair to the side, I kiss the nape of her neck, inhaling her scent. Sure enough...pumpkin spice.

I whisper against the shell of her ear. "I love you."

She suddenly spins around. Her hands glide down the side of my face and settle on my chest. Her lips open. A small noise escapes. But before she can say an actual word, she clamps her mouth shut.

Holy hell. This is it.

She's ready.

"What were you gonna say?" I ask.

She shakes her head, mumbling. "Nothing."

"Don't lie, Merit."

"Mmmm."

"You were gonna tell me that you love me. It's written all over your face."

She doesn't say anything. She just sways back and forth, scratching her fingernails in a loose pattern across my pectorals.

"Tell me the truth."

Her mouth opens and closes. Then, opens and closes again. Taking a shaky breath, she says the words I've longed to hear. "I'm in love with you, Holt."

Emotion strangles me. Now I'm the one afraid to talk. I'm afraid because words can't even begin to tell her what she means to me.

When I don't say anything, she must think my silence means I want more.

"Did I hurt your feelings? All the times you told me you loved me, and I didn't say anything back? All the times I demanded you say it to me again, again…and I just…stood there?"

My left arm folds across her lower back. With my free hand, I trace the curve of her cheekbone. "No, baby, you didn't hurt my feelings."

Her bottom lip sticks out just a little bit, and I can't wait to suckle it in my mouth. "I think it would've hurt my feelings," she admits. She blinks, her eyes widening with emotion. "If I had said it first, and you didn't say anything back."

"Merit, it didn't hurt me because I could see the love inscribed all over you, from head to toe, like it's tattooed on your skin. I could hear it in your heart, pulsing a rhythm just for me, every single time you kissed me. I could feel it in your body, aching for us to be joined as one, every single time we made love." I tip my forehead down, resting it against hers for a moment. "I know what you went through with Edward wasn't easy; and in many ways it was torturous. I know you don't like to dwell on it, but what he did to you was abusive, baby. You might not wear scars on the outside of your body, like some women; but that doesn't mean you don't carry them on the inside. Your spirit was shredded to pieces by that man."

I run my fingers down the elegant length of her neck and skim them across her collarbone. "I knew it might take some time for you to tell me you loved me, but that doesn't mean I didn't experience it. The words were already written on your heart…with invisible ink… made only for my eyes. And I've been reading them. Every. Fucking. Day."

She stands on her tiptoes and nuzzles against my jaw, scratching her face back and forth across the stubble that I've grown out, just for her. "I've loved you since before you loved me. I don't understand how people can say that love at first sight doesn't exist. I loved you. And I wanted you to fight for me." She licks her lips, licking my jaw in the process. "You did. Every minute of every day since we met. You didn't let me give up."

Pulling back just a smidge to look in my eyes, she smiles sweetly. "You brought me back. The *real me*." She leans up and kisses my lips. "And I'll never stop fighting for you too. You don't have to be afraid of me. You don't have to be skeptical." Her voice lowers, filling the space between us with truth. "Because we're real. Me and you. We are the real fucking deal, Holt Hill. I love you. I will fight for you until the last star dies and our bones are nothing more than dust. Because you are mine. And I'm never letting you go."

I can't believe this is happening. Part of me never thought she'd admit the truth—to herself or to me.

This is it.

This is the start of *our* forever.

I kiss her. And I mean, I fucking *kiss* her.

My tongue plunges into her mouth, fighting for space, and my teeth nip at her sweet bottom lip. My fingers graze against her breast when I pull the sweater down her shoulders, forcing her to take it off. I kiss up and down her neck, sucking hard, branding her with my mark. Reaching under her nightgown, I grab her panties and push them to the floor. When my fingers find her, she's soaking wet. "There's My Merit. You're so ready for me, baby. Always ready for me to pour my love into you."

I barely touch her clit, and her back bows, collapsing her body against mine. Dipping down, I slide two fingers inside of her, instantly finding the spot that makes her scream. I slowly make love to her with my hand, letting my body do the talking instead of my words. There's something about this slow and languid pace. It's laced with a longing and intensity that feels new and unexplored. Her arms cradle around my head, locking my mouth onto hers. And we're not even kissing.

Fuck me... we're... panting and licking and consuming. That's the only way to describe it. We are fucking consuming each other. She's exhaling the pain of her past, and I'm inhaling it, taking it as my own, refusing to ever give it back to her.

She's my world, my life, my eternity. And I'll be damned if I don't swallow her hurt and bury it down deep, locking it away so her life can be nothing but happiness.

Because that's what Merit deserves...happiness. And I'm gonna be the one to give it to her.

I twist my fingers and thumb her clit, and when her gasps and moans echo into the stillness of the room, I nearly lose my shit and come in my briefs.

"More. More, Holt," she whispers. Threading her fingers into my hair, she pulls and tugs, delighting in my hiss of my pain.

Firming my grip around her back, I lift her off the ground. Standing to my full height, her body settles into the new position. Her feet dangle in the air, her body too tense and impatient to even take the time to lock her legs around my waist. Her pussy swallows my fingers, eager and happy with our new position. I curl my fingers against her G-spot. When her body starts to shake with her impending orgasm, I crash my lips to hers, sucking her tongue into my mouth.

And when she comes all over me, I can barely keep my sanity. Her desire is everywhere—my stomach, my hands, her thighs. "My baby soaked me. Let me lick you clean."

"No!" Fogged by her passion, Merit's unaware of her volume and basically screams the word in my ear. She scrambles from my hold, and I gently set her on the ground, steadying her arms when she wobbles back and forth and nearly falls. She grabs the waistband of my boxer briefs, whining when they don't pass over my erection easily. With breathless anticipation, I help her, tossing my underwear on the ground next to hers. She looks down between our bodies. Her eyes grow heavy with desire, blinking slow and lazy. Grabbing my dick, she circles a drop of pre-cum around my thickened head.

Holy shit.

Just her touch makes my entire body tremble. My cock is so hard, it's actually borderline painful.

"Fuck this foreplay, *sir*. I need you. Now."

Oh, hell yes. I agree.

Scooping her into my arms, I lovingly place her on the bed. I barely lie down before she's making a move to straddle me. "Wait." My voice is so thick with hunger, it doesn't even sound like me. "Let me get a condom." When I roll it over the length of my erection, her eyes widen in yearning.

She finally pulls off her nightgown, giving me a full view of her amazing body. Her large breasts. The swell of her peaked nipples. The soft curve of her hips. Even the mole she has above her belly button.

It's all perfect.

She's perfect. Nudging my shoulder, she urges me to lie down. Climbing on top of me, she slowly feeds my cock into her body, one delicious inch at a time. Her back arches, and she loudly moans. Unable to stop myself, I do the same, howling into the room like a wild animal. We still for a moment, just absorbing the magnitude of the night, the feeling of being joined together.

When she starts to rock back and forth, my vision blurs. "Fuck me, Holt," she whispers. "Make love to me and fuck me—all at the same time."

The words tumble from my lips, soaked in gravel and honey. "Yes, baby." I grab her hips—hard—forcing her body even closer to mine. The friction is gloriously unbearable. It's nearly too much for me to process. The quicker she moves, the harder I pump into her. I can feel my need pulsing throughout my entire body—like I'm drowning in cum up to my eyeballs. When she explodes, I finally allow my own release to detonate.

My orgasm lasts forever, draining me, leaving me blissfully weak.

Sweaty and sticky and satisfied, her body collapses down on me, and I cover her in kisses. I'm out of breath, like I just ran sprints. I repeat the same command to her that she asked of me that night. "Tell me again."

She tenderly kisses my chest and grazes her fingernail across my nipple. "I love you, Holt."

I'm about to say it back when the house phone rings. We both look over at the nightstand like an alien is sitting on it smoking an after-sex cigarette. Panic grips my heart, and it feels like thunder is rumbling in my brain. I'm frozen, completely paralyzed with fear.

After several rings, Merit lifts her body off mine, severing our connection. I'm too stunned and terrified to even mourn the end of our intimacy. She reaches over and answers, her hand shaking. "Hello?"

I stare at her, unable to form a sentence.

"Yes, ma'am. It's Merit."

Who the heck is she calling ma'am?

Her eyebrow lifts. "Seriously?"

Shit. That sounds bad.

"Okay. We'll be right there." She hangs up the phone and lies down on the pillow next to me.

Please let the kids be okay.

All of a sudden, a smile tugs at the corner of her mouth. "We need to go to the hospital. Ella's having the baby."

All the dread wooshes out of me like a balloon popping. "Seriously?"

She giggles and snorts. "That's what I said."

Chapter 31

Holt

I lean back on the couch, watching Dad and Deke banter back and forth about the football game we're watching. I knew they'd get along, but to actually see it? It makes me pretty damn happy. Especially considering I'm about to ask for his daughter's hand in marriage.

It's been a perfect Thanksgiving holiday.

Well, except for the fact that Merit and I have to sleep in different beds.

We finally convinced Deke to take a few days off and come up for the holiday. With Merit preparing for today's Black Friday sale, there was just no way she could take off in the days leading up to Thanksgiving, let alone travel down to the farm.

We all went to Crutch and Ella's house for Thanksgiving yesterday. With Baby Harlan just being five weeks old, we wanted to make everything easy for Ella. That way, she could keep him in a routine—have him nap in his own bassinet and feed on his regular schedule. Of course, Jeff did all the cooking so Ella didn't have to worry about that. Today, we've been watching football while the women—except for Merit, who's busting her ass at the store—have been shopping.

Her parents and grandmother have been sleeping in the Children's Wing since Wednesday night, so that means Merit's been displaced to one of the downstairs guest rooms. When I first said Merit would be sleeping in one of the upstairs guest rooms, next to me, Deke made a face. We quickly amended that plan.

But they leave tomorrow.

Let's just say I don't plan on getting much sleep tomorrow night.

Ridge elbows me. "You still planning on talking to Deke?"

I haven't told many people my plan—just my parents and Ridge. I'm definitely not telling Raylee yet. She'll flip out. Plus, she's never been able to keep a secret. "Yeah, I wanna do it before all the girls come back from shopping."

"You sure about this?"

After everything I've been through, Ridge is a protective best friend. It's nice to have someone watching your back. "Yeah." I nod, taking a swig of my beer. "When I think about my future, she's all over it, brother."

"I'm glad. We all love her. She fits in perfectly."

A loud burst of laughter erupts from me. "She definitely fits in better than the date you brought to the family cookout two weeks ago." She made Bunny look like a Rhodes Scholar...with a virgin heart of gold. Laura completely ripped her a new one.

Cullen flops down on the couch next to us. "What are we talking about?"

Ridge sighs. "My last date."

Cullen rolls his eyes. "Oh, shit. That was painful. How could someone so cute be so dense?"

Ridge lifts an eyebrow. "Like your one-night stands from the bar are any better."

Cullen shrugs. "Point taken."

When the game pauses for halftime, everyone takes a break, meandering through the house for food or bathrooms. Except for Ridge, who goes into the gym to lift some weights. Catching up with Deke, I ask if he minds stepping outside so I can talk with him.

Marcum and Nate are in the backyard tossing the football. Marcum's always been an intuitive guy. It's one of the reasons he's a great cop. It only takes him a split second to see what's going on. "C'mon, Nate, take your Grandpa inside for some of that leftover pecan pie."

Deke walks to the edge of the pool. He splashes his hand through the water pouring off the rock waterfall. I watch him, wishing the flaming nerves in my stomach would settle down. I thought I was okay; I thought I could handle this... but I feel like I'm about to throw up. I didn't get this nervous before any of the Super Bowls I've played in.

Planting his hands on his hips, he looks up at my house. I'm halfway through stringing the outside Christmas lights, and I wonder if that's what he's looking at. His soft whistle makes my heart race like a damn thoroughbred. "Impressive house. Merit told us about it. She texted pictures to Marie, but even those didn't do it justice." He shakes his head. "And your cousin's place? From yesterday? That's a great piece of land."

"She grew up in this house, you know? Ella, I mean. I bought this house from her after her parents passed away."

"It's nice when something can stay in the family."

"Mmm-hmm."

He smirks, unimpressed with my answer.

Shit. Even my hands are sweating. I smear them across the front of my jeans. Deke walks over to one of the seating areas and leans back in a wicker chair, relaxing. Giving myself a few seconds to gain my composure, I grab a fresh beer from the outside fridge. "Need a drink?"

He chuckles. "If it'll calm your ass down, sure."

We'll this definitely isn't going as planned. Sitting across from him, I chug half my bottle in one swig. My leg bounces up and down. My lip twitches. I sit back. Then I sit forward. Then I sit back again.

"All right. What's the matter, son? You've been nervous all day, but this? This is just plain painful. Just say what you wanna say."

Leaning forward, I balance my forearms on my knees. Taking a deep breath, the words spew from my mouth like a geyser. "I'd like to ask for your daughter's hand."

"Her hand in what?"

I'm pretty sure my mouth falls open. I thought it was kind of self-explanatory. "Uhhh. Her hand in marriage, sir."

Deke bursts out laughing. "Relax, Holt. I'm just busting your balls. I know what you meant."

I don't embarrass easily. In fact, I can't even really remember the last time. But now? My cheeks burn hot like I just went swimming in a volcano.

Eventually his smile fades, and he studies me. "Why? And why so soon?"

Why? How do you explain something when there's no words to describe it?

I lean back and drag my hands through my hair. Just thinking about Merit makes me feel like a better man. A man who will do anything to make sure she's happy and cared for and loved. Forever.

"She's stubborn, you know?"

He nods, unable to hide the pride on his face.

"I'm sure she tried to hide it with Edward, but there's no way to hide something so fundamental. She wasn't even going to come to the door on our first date." I smile, thinking back to that night. "She scrunches her nose when she thinks another woman is hitting on me, and she refuses to admit she does it. And she nearly jacked up the toilet at the store because she wanted to fix it herself after she watched a video that told her what to do."

He chuckles, taking a sip of his beer.

"She's so damn beautiful. Her hair looks like the redwood trees I saw in California. Her eyes change color, depending on her mood. Her nose gets pink after an hour in the sun, and she secretly loves having tan lines because it gives her some weird sense of accomplishment. She loves dressing up, but would curl in a ball and die if she had to wear full makeup and high heels every day."

The smile slowly fades from his face as he tries to absorb all the details I'm throwing out.

Now that I've started, I just can't stop.

"She falls. All the time. She drops food on herself. She gets caught saying things she shouldn't be saying. It's like Murphy's Law was specifically written for Merit.

"She works so hard, for every single penny she's ever earned." I snort, thinking about her refusal to buy more than one smoothie a week. "And watches her spending like a stingy ninety-year-old who wants to be buried with every last dime. She doesn't care how many zeros are behind my net worth. Her love for me isn't contingent upon what I can buy her. She doesn't care that I used to throw a football and won the Super Bowl. She just cares about *me*. She loves *me*."

I take a breath, gathering my scattered thoughts.

"I love her, sir. I'm *in love* with her. When I close my eyes and think about my future, Merit's in it. There is no future for me without her. She's my family. I wanna marry her and have children and grow old. I wanna have family dinners. And teach our kids how to ride a bike. And have summer movie nights at the sod farm. I want it all. With her. With your daughter."

When he doesn't say anything, my apprehension skyrockets. Unable to handle the silence, I toss something else in the mix. "And she snorts when she laughs."

Eventually, Deke's eyes meet mine, and I'm blown away by the emotion in them. Wiping his face, refusing to shed a tear in my presence, he clears his throat and coughs. "So, you already have a ring?"

"The jeweler is working on it. I gave him a picture of her diamond and ruby bracelet from her great-grandma. I thought it would mean a lot if she had something that matched that. Something we could pass down."

He works his hand across his chin. "It doesn't bother you that she's a divorcee? That she's been married before?"

"Of course, it bothers me," I admit. "Because it should've been me. Edward is a waste of space, and I nearly lose my mind every time I think about the two of them together." I sigh. "But I'm focusing on the good, the fact that I get to spend the rest of my life with her."

"When are you wanting to pop the question?"

"Christmas. Really, I wanna ask her as soon as possible, but she's in her busy season. She'll be working like crazy between now and Christmas, so I'll just be patient and do it once things settle down."

Nodding, he stands up, stretching his back.

I rub my hands together. "So..."

"Yes, you have my blessing."

Holy hell. Did he just give me permission to marry his daughter?

Deke knocks my shoulder, jarring me out of my stupor. "You okay?"

I fall back and fold my hands behind my head. I can't stop smiling. I laugh in disbelief. "I never thought I'd get married. I can't believe it."

Deke finishes his beer. "What? A love and marriage skeptic?"

"In a past life, sir, absolutely. In our new life, with your daughter, it's game on."

Chapter 32

Merit

A noise wakes me up.

Holding my breath, I listen. But it's hard to hear anything above the pounding of my own heart.

"Holt." My whisper falls on deaf ears. His heavy breathing doesn't even falter. There's no easy way to wake him. There's basically only two options—bloodcurdling scream or elbow drop to the ribs.

Seeing as how I'm neither a horror film actress nor a professional wrestler, I guess I'm on my own.

I squint my eyes at his alarm clock. I guess I could make the alarm go off; he's trained his body to wake up to that obnoxious noise. But how could he not…he's got it set to rock-concert level. It's so loud I shit my pants every morning at the butt-crack of dawn.

Shaking my head, I decide to face this battle head-on. Sliding from the covers, I tiptoe across the bedroom, pausing every so often, trying to decipher the nighttime noises. A normal-size house has plenty of noises. The hum of electricity, the click of air conditioning, the settling of wood.

But this?

A mansion-size house has mansion-size noises. In fact, most nights, I wake up because I hear something. I usually take a bathroom break and force myself to settle and go back to sleep. But to-night is different. This noise sounded like something breaking.

Or something falling. Or something clattering across the floor.

I don't know why I'm nervous. Holt sets the house alarm every single night. He has to. Can you imagine what would happen if a thief got ahold of his Super Bowl ring?

Or his other Super Bowl ring.

Slowly, I turn the bedroom doorknob and peek outside. There's a lamp on the side table in the upstairs foyer casting everything in a soft glow. I sigh in relief.

Light always makes everything better.

Opening the door all the way, I step outside and take a quick survey of the hallway. All the bedrooms are dark. There's a small nightlight glowing in the laundry room. Leaning over the balcony railing, I look down the stairs.

Satisfied a mass murderer isn't mere feet away, I trudge back to the master bedroom. I'm about to shut the door when something catches my eye. Something lying on the floor of the kids' bedroom, right on the other side of the threshold.

Padding across the marbled tile, I'm shocked when I find Holt's cell phone.

What the hell?

I look behind me at the side table. The same table where he always sets his cell phone. Every single night.

How on earth did it get from there to here?

Did he drop it and not even realize it?

Did he sleepwalk and move it?

Surely, he didn't get a phone call; I would've heard it.

Wouldn't I?

Picking it up, I turn it over in my hands, checking it for damage. Everything looks intact. In fact, when I click for the home screen, our picture flashes back at me. It's a picture that Raylee took of us. Our heads are bent together. We're softly talking to one another, with huge smiles spread across our faces.

He had just won a football game.

Holt's always in a great mood after winning a football game.

I'm about to type the passcode to open his phone and look at the call log when his sleepy voice catches me by surprise. "Hey. You okay?"

The fright has my heart pounding again. It feels like a mariachi band is walking around inside of my body.

He shuffles across the foyer in his green boxer briefs. His blond curls point in every direction, and his blue eyes are hooded with sleep. Just the sight of him wets my body with desire. He leans against the doorway, with furrowed brow, and nods at the phone in my hand. "What's wrong?"

I wiggle it back and forth. "This was laying on the floor."

He cocks his head to the side. "On the floor?"

"Yeah, right there," I say, pointing. "Did you get a phone call or something?"

He snorts. "You think a phone call on my cell phone would wake me up?" He lifts an eyebrow, slowly enunciating every word, "Through the closed bedroom door? While I'm sleeping?" He gives me a lazy smile. "You *have* met me, right?"

I roll my eyes. "Hardy har."

He holds out his hand, motioning for his phone. He clicks through the screens. "It doesn't show any phone call." Lifting one shoulder, he shrugs. "I must have knocked it off the table before bed and not even realized it."

Grabbing me by the hand, he leads me back to bed, depositing his cell phone in its normal spot along the way. Pulling me against his body, his hands wrap around me, possessively holding me against him. I crane my neck. My lips graze against his jaw, and his facial scruff scratches me. "What caused you to wake up?" I ask.

"What?"

"What woke you up?"

His words choke around a yawn. "I had to take a piss. And I saw you weren't in bed." Leaning over me, he looks down, studying my face in the moonlight. "What about you? What woke you up?"

All of a sudden, my sleepy mind goes blank. *Why did I wake up?* "Oh..." I fumble through my words, "I...I heard a noise."

"A noise?"

"Yeah." I lovingly pat his cheek. "I looked around. It was nothing." Sighing, I snuggle into my pillow and close my eyes. "I probably dreamed it."

Chapter 33

Merit

"There's no way we can have that amount of food delivered in just two hours. I would have to completely shut down the kitchen for every other order."

I just ordered fifteen-hundred dollars in pizza, pastas, and sandwiches. And that was even after using a coupon. In two hours, the house is going to be overrun with football players, their families, coaches, cheerleaders, and...well, everyone. When Holt kissed me goodbye, he tasked me with getting food. I don't plan on failing.

"This food is for Holt Hill and his football team. They just won the State Championship today. They're on the bus, driving back from the game, and they're starving. Is there anything that can be done?"

I've resorted to name dropping.

Of course, it might backfire. What if this guy doesn't watch football? He could be a fan of synchronized swimming, for all I know.

"Give me two-and-a-half hours," he says.

I bounce up and down on the balls of my feet. "Thank you so much!"

I confirm the delivery address and slide Holt's black American Express card in the back pocket of my jeans. I'll put it back in the top drawer of his desk in just a minute. I need to change my shirt first because I spilled blue slushie on myself at the game.

I soak my shirt in stain remover and search the closet for something perfect. I settle on a bright green, off-the-shoulder sweater and a black tank top—because I refuse to wear strapless bras ever again. They were a staple with the outfits Edward made me wear. They're not comfortable, and at least one boob always falls out. Staring at myself in the mirror, I drag the ponytail holder from my hair and pile it into a messy bun instead. I could stand to put on some more eye makeup or fresh lipstick. I reach for the eyeliner and then toss it back in the drawer.

I'm in too good of a mood to fiddle with more makeup.

I'm about to head back to the Big House to join the rest of Holt's family when the reminder alarm on my phone buzzes.

Oh crap. I nearly forgot.

The other day I ran across this amazing woman on a craft website who has phenomenal handcrafted ornaments. They're designed around kids' sports and activities, and they have a nameplate where you can add a name personalization if you want. It's something I could do with a glitter pen. I have no doubt they would sell like hot cakes at the store. It's December 3rd, so the Christmas frenzy is in full force. I know if Kyra puts them on the store's social media pages, we'll be sold out in no time. I reached out to her, inquiring about buying her whole stock, and she said today was the only day she was free to talk.

Sitting on the couch, I pull up her contact information and call. After five minutes, we reach a price of three-thousand dollars for everything. When I give her my business credit card number, I nearly fall off my seat when she says it's declined.

"But that's impossible. Can you try it again?"

Confusion and horror rip through me when she confirms it was declined again. Apologizing, I drag my personal credit card from my purse and nearly collapse in a puddle of tears when she says that card is being declined too.

What the hell is happening? Am I a victim of identity theft? My brain fogs with one terrifying theory after the other. This has to be one of the most embarrassing moments of my life. "I'm so sorry. I have no idea what's happening. Let me call the card company and get this sorted out. Can I call you back Monday?"

She sucks in a breath, holding it. "Listen, you seem really nice, but I've had another offer from someone in Texas to buy my whole stock. I was just trying to be fair because you reached out first, but I can't wait until Monday. I need the money. We're buying my daughter a car for Christmas."

Shit.

I can't let this inventory slip through my fingers. It'll be a money-maker. And considering I'm stuffing all my extra cash in a manila envelope in the bottom of my panty drawer, I don't want to lose out. I plan on making a big installment payment to Holt after the first of the new year. He's never once asked me to pay him back, but I plan to.

I have to.

"Wait. Can you try one more card?" Reaching in my back pocket, I pull out Holt's credit card and slowly read her the numbers. A sick feeling swirls in my stomach when she tells me it's approved and she'll ship everything out on Monday. Burying the guilt deep inside, I promise to tell him what happened as soon as I see him. I can just write him a personal check, I reason. It's no big deal.

Everything will be fine.

Holt will completely understand.

I call the twenty-four-hour customer service line on the back of my business credit card. Come to find out, a website that I made a purchase on one year ago was compromised with a data breach, and customer card information was stolen. The credit card company shut down my credit card for security reasons. And since my personal card is linked to my business card under the same main account, they shut it down too. They have overnighted new cards to me and instruct me to destroy the old ones. I guess they emailed all this to me today, but I was a little busy watching my boyfriend become a state-winning coach.

By the time I make it back into the Big House, Holt's family has taken care of almost everything. The men have coolers lined up outside, filled with waters and sodas, and the women have set out paper plates and napkins and store-bought cookies and candy.

"There you are, sweetie. We thought you got lost. Did you get the food ordered?" Teresa asks, wrapping an arm around me.

Trying to shake off the drama of the past few minutes, I nod. "It should be here right after everyone else, assuming the busses are still getting back to the school on time."

"They are." She looks down, searching my hands. "Do you want me to put his credit card back in the office? I'll probably lock that door since so many people will be here."

"Oh sure." I give her the card and busy myself in the kitchen, trying to forget the regret of using Holt's money.

Borrowing.

I mean, borrowing Holt's money.

Holt traces the line of my spine. "Tell me again."

Kissing his bare chest, I lift my head, giving myself a chance to stare at his handsome face in the moonlight of the bedroom. "You are a state-winning coach."

He licks his lips. "Not that. The other thing."

I don't think Holt will ever know just how sexy he is. Every movement his body makes is like an aphrodisiac. He moves with ease and grace, power and strength. Like a predator. He's so comfortable in his body. And the rest of us mere mortals aren't even worthy to look upon him.

I pout, pretending to think. "Hmmm. What other thing?"

Grabbing my hair, he yanks my head back, exposing my neck. Burying his teeth against my soft skin, he tickles the sensitive area with his tongue, making me squirm. "Fine. Fine." Wriggling away, I lean over him. My hair falls forward, framing us like a weeping willow. "I love you."

Reaching up, he grabs my face. Lovingly pulling me to him, he kisses me.

And I love it when Holt kisses me.

Eventually, I settle back down, nuzzling against his chest and wrapping my leg over his. "Everyone seemed to have a good time tonight."

"I think we could've sat around and stared at each other all night long, and it still would've been fun. It's called a winner's high."

"I'm just glad the food lasted as long as it did," I say.

Holt laughs. "Yeah, those teenage boys act like wolves when they're hungry." He kisses the top of my head. "Thanks for ordering the food, by the way. I gotta say, I was surprised they could deliver so much food on such short notice."

I giggle. And snort, of course.

He jiggles me. "What?"

"Well, at first, it wasn't gonna be here in time."

"What changed?" he asks.

"I sort of name-dropped your name. Fortunately, the guy's a football fan."

He chuckles. "So, my fame got us pizzas?"

"Don't forget the pasta. That alfredo was on point." It really was. I stole some when no one was watching and hid it in the fridge for tomorrow.

"I was too busy talking to everyone. I never really got a chance to eat."

"Ohhh. It's so hard being the number one high school football coach in the state of Alabama," I tease.

"Haha," he enunciates with sarcasm. Grabbing a strand of my hair, he twirls it around his finger. "At least we didn't have too many crashers."

There were a couple of people who showed up uninvited—some of the fans who think they're actually part of the coaching staff. But they left immediately when Holt told the guys about them. Granted, most people would leave when you see four men who look like Crutch, Ridge, Cullen, and Will coming at you, with scowls on their faces.

"Speaking of," he adds, "it was nice that you invited Heidi to come over."

"Yeah, I mean, she was a cheerleader up until this year. I thought it would be nice for her to celebrate such a big accomplishment with the team."

I could tell she was super excited and grateful to be included. She gave Holt the biggest hug ever and monopolized his conversation until I asked her to help me clean up where someone accidentally spilled a bowl of spaghetti on the big Christmas tree in the living room. Holt and I decorated it last Sunday, so I nearly had a heart attack when a meatball rolled between the branches and got lost in the artificial foliage.

"It was funny to see how excited the kids were. Did you see Anna asking the boys for their autographs in case they become famous?" Holt asks.

I laugh. "How could I? I was preoccupied watching Laura. She did *not* like the attention that Nate was getting from some of the freshman cheerleaders."

He laughs. "No, she did not." I feel him shake his head. "I can't believe he'll be in high school next year. I wish he was zoned for my high school. He's gonna be a phenomenal ball player."

We spend the next few minutes in silence. My fingertips draw circles across the sharp lines of his stomach, including the deep V-shaped muscle of his hip. I smirk to myself when his cock jumps underneath the sheets.

He rubs my shoulder, getting closer and closer to my naked breast. Interrupting his obvious plans, I ask him a serious question. "Why teaching and coaching? Why did you wanna do that after your injury?"

"Well, my degree is in physical education and kinesiology. After graduation, Mom made me apply for my state teaching certificate, here in Alabama. I had never really thought about being a teacher, but Mom visited once when I was helping out with a football camp. She said I had a gift."

"You just got drafted with one of the biggest packages ever offered by the NFL, and Teresa still made you get a teaching certificate?"

"Yep...and I renewed it every five years to keep it active."

"And now, look at you." I smell his skin, soaking up the scent of his soap. "I'm so proud of you, Holt."

"What about you?"

"What about me?"

"What do you want for your future? Your professional future, I mean."

My brow furrows. "Uhhh, *sir*, I have this little thing called *Run and Jump and Twirl*."

He scoffs, "I know that. I wanna know if you want more than that. Are you happy? With the store?"

"I love the store." My words come out a little more slowly than anticipated.

He holds me closer. "Mer, I don't have to see your face to be able to read it."

When I don't say anything, he pushes. "Tell me the truth."

I'm about to tell him something I've never told anyone. Well, except for Kyra one night when we were drinking. "You know how Kyra is getting her master's degree in graphic design?" I wait for him to answer. "Well, she has all these great ideas. She shows me all this amazing stuff that's she's designed, and it just blows my mind. I'd love to expand and have a stationery store. You know—letterhead, notepads, invitations, greeting cards. Even fridge magnets and chip clips and cups. Kyra is so talented; she can do anything. If I could have it next door, that would be awesome. We could just cut out the middle wall and have one huge store." I sigh, thinking about the possibilities. "We could do it together, you know? Be partners. Then, I wouldn't have to worry about her moving home and leaving me after she graduates this coming spring."

"So do it." His comment makes everything seem so simple.

It's anything but simple.

I turn my head, resting my chin in the crook of his shoulder. "You're damn crazy."

He chuckles. "Why?"

"Uhhh... it cost money for something like that. Like a lot of money. I'd have to sell both kidneys just to afford *half* of a printing machine." I shrug, "Not to mention, it's irresponsible for me to even think about stuff like that. I mean, I might not even have my store forever. I have the farm to think about."

"You wanna work the farm?" His confusion is obvious.

He's so cute. I kiss the freckles on his nose.

"It's called a family farm, Holt. That means family has to run it. Daddy still has a lot of good years left, but there will come a time when he wants to retire. He's worked hard and he deserves that."

"I know you love the farm, but I thought the store was your dream."

"The store *is* my dream, but my family has worked too hard for the farm. I'll never let it die. I couldn't live with myself if I let that happen."

"So, that's always been the plan? For you to take over for Deke?"

I shake my head. "Not always, no. It's supposed to pass from father to son. When Daire was born, we all knew the legacy would survive for another generation." Even after all these years, emotion strangles me when I talk about my infant baby brother. "Then, he was gone." Holt kisses the top of my head again, giving me time to compose myself. "When I got married, we just assumed that I would have a son, and Daddy would be able to teach him everything about the farm. It could pass from grandfather to grandson. But of course, that didn't happen. It's just the reality of the situation. I'm divorced, and there's no little boy spending his summers at the sod farm learning how to shovel fertilizer and run tractors. So, it's on my shoulders. I have to think about that legacy and put it above my own wants and dreams."

It's so long before he says something, for a second, I think he's fallen asleep.

"So, you need a son?" The teasing taunt in his voice can't hide the desire now bubbling underneath. "I think I know how we can make that happen. I might've read about it in a book once." He reaches around and cups my breast, fondling my nipple.

Giggling, I push his arm away. "I don't think so. My parents— my granny—would kill me if I got pregnant out of wedlock."

All of a sudden, he rolls out from under me. Turning the tables, he pins me against the bed. He slides my arms above my head and stretches me. The bedsheet falls down, exposing me to the waist. Even in the darkness, I can see the blue in his eyes. The moonlight reflects in them, and they mimic the rise and fall of the ocean's waves. "Really? Something to keep in mind, then."

He shouldn't say things like that.

Make unspoken promises in the night.

I search his face for the truth, wondering if he's lying to me. He says he doesn't lie to me. Is this when it starts? The lies? The broken vows? The shattered gospel?

But I don't see anything but honesty. Honesty and love and adoration.

Is this really my life?

Is this wordless commitment true?

Is it real?

Is Holt Hill real?

Shifting over me, he slides down my body, grazing his tongue between my breasts and down my stomach.

My heart pounds, and my thighs rub against him searching for friction. "What are you doing?" My whisper is husky and breathless.

He looks up at me, underneath heavy, sex-lusted eyes. And once again, he reads my mind. "I'm making sure you're real, of course."

Leaving me with his signature wink, he disappears under the covers and buries his head between my legs.

Chapter 34

Holt

Well, she finally told me her favorite movie.

White Christmas

And she watches it all year long, multiple times a year. And she's finally sharing it with me. It's a Sunday afternoon, and I convinced her to stay home from work. She's been working so many hours I feel like I've barely seen her. Now that school's out for the holidays, I want a little one-on-one time. Christmas and New Year's will be spent with family and friends, and I want a day to monopolize her all to myself.

"You sure you don't wanna watch it in the theater room? The quality will be better."

She cocks her hand on her hip and glares at me, like I just told her blueberry pancakes have been outlawed by Congress. "Holt Hill, there's no Christmas tree in the theater room. I know you're not suggesting we watch *White Christmas* with no Christmas tree next to us."

She's so freakin' funny.

"Mer, you watch this movie in July. There's no Christmas tree up in July. What's the difference?"

She shakes her head like I'm a moron and walks into the kitchen, mumbling to herself. "There's a difference. You know there's a difference."

Turning on the TV, I slide in her DVD. The movie is on one of my streaming devices, but she also refuses to watch it on anything but her DVD. I'm about to sit on the couch when my cell phone buzzes, showing the front doorbell camera has picked up movement. It can't be family. They always use the door by the garage. I don't even have time to pull up the camera and look before someone's pounding on the door. In fact, they're pounding so damn hard, I'm worried they might break the damn thing.

"Holt! Open up!"

Hearing Crutch's voice, I trot over to the door and throw it open. "Hey!" Glancing behind him, I see his truck in the circular driveway that only one-time guests or strangers use. He didn't even shut his door. I point to it. "You left your door open. You're gonna drain your battery."

I walk back into the living room, and I'm surprised when he follows me instead of heading back out to shut his truck door.

"You're about to be arrested."

What did he say? His voice sounds weird. I pick up the remote and turn down the volume of the soundtrack song playing on the DVD title screen. "Huh?"

"You're about to be arrested."

My heart drops. "Shit. Are you kidding me?" I flop my hand to the TV. "We're about to watch a movie."

This is just freakin' great. I can't even erase the sarcasm from the voice in my head.

Don't get me wrong, I'm all for a good charity arrest. But it's eight days before Christmas, and I just did an arrest in the spring. Last time, I was locked up until I raised thirty-thousand dollars, and I couldn't donate it myself. Luckily, I still have a few generous friends in the NFL. It was for a good cause, but it still took me close to twenty-four hours before getting enough money to get released.

"Hey, Crutch!" Merit walks out of the kitchen holding a big bowl of popcorn. She pops a kernel in her mouth and holds the bowl out to him. "Want some? I used real butter."

Crutch just stares at her. It's actually kind of unsettling. His face is pale and worried.

"Crutch, can't you just postpone for me? Tell them I'll raise double at the next one and I—"

He yells, cutting me off. "Holt! I'm not talking about a fucking charity arrest. You are about to be arrested. For real."

Okay. This isn't funny.

My mind feels heavy, and my throat closes up. "What? For what?"

There's a one-second beat. One second when my life is still normal.

And then my whole world turns upside down.

The doorbell camera buzzes on my cell phone again. This time the person doesn't even knock on my front door. He does, in fact, break it down.

Merit immediately drops the bowl of popcorn all over the floor.

Suddenly, it feels like hell is raining down in my living room. Everything moves in slow motion, and my vision blurs with adrenaline. Police are everywhere. Police *from* everywhere—city police, sheriff's department, state troopers. Men are screaming. They scatter through my house in all directions. A framed picture gets knocked off the wall and shatters.

A city officer is pointing a gun at me. Directly in my face. In my living room. In front of my Christmas tree.

From the corner of my eye, I see Crutch scoop Merit into his arms and pull her out of harm's way.

"Put your hands in the air! Put your hands in the air!"

"Turn around!"

"Don't move!"

A thousand different instructions are being hurled at me. I can't process it. My brain can't understand a single command. Someone violently grabs my shoulders and shoves me across the room, bouncing me against the wall. The air whooshes from my lungs. Yanking my arms behind my back, I feel the handcuffs close around my wrists.

What's weird is I can actually hear it.

Despite all the noise echoing in the room, I can hear the rattle of the metal cuffs. It reverberates in my brain. The noise is in my soul. It shatters my existence.

"Holt Hill, you are being arrested under suspicion of having an inappropriate teacher-student relationship. As defined by Alabama law, a felony count is present when a school employee has sexual contact with a student under the age of nineteen."

"What?" My voice is hoarse and weak.

One of the officers looming over me shouts in my ear. "You heard what he fucking said, you pervert!"

They pull me back from the wall. Merit's staring at me, wide-eyed, with tears streaming down her face. Crutch is whispering to her, his mouth constantly moving. The pain on her face breaks me even more.

This can't be happening. Can't they see they have it wrong? They have the wrong guy.

"You made a mistake. You have the wrong guy." My feeble protest doesn't get very far.

A rally of cries come from nearly every person in the room.

"Shut the fuck up!"

"Give it a fucking rest, man."

"Asshole millionaires. Laws don't apply to y'all, right?"

"Having sex with a minor is more than a mistake!"

All of a sudden, a distant and familiar voice can be heard, screaming and screeching. "Don't say anything! Don't say anything!" Ella races down the hall from the Children's Wing, waving her arms in the air. "Don't say any—" She's cut off by two state troopers. They flank around her, blocking her movement.

Crutch erupts like a wild animal. Pushing through the crowd, he knocks grown men to the side like they're nothing more than paper dolls. "Get your fucking hands off my wife!"

Fortunately, the state troopers listen and take a step back. Ella slides between them and rushes into his arms. Their hug is cut short, though, because she catches my eye and immediately runs over to me. Crutch has to grab her waist and physically restrain her from getting in the way of the men holding me captive. "Don't say anything! Nothing until an attorney is present. Promise me!"

Two men shove me, trying to get me out of her line of sight.

Another person growls at Crutch. "Sergeant Crutchfield, get your family under control before we toss you out. You should be arrested for trying to warn this offender."

But I'm not an offender.

Someone recites my Miranda Rights, but it just sounds like white noise. Another holds a piece of paper in my face, assuming I have enough brain power to actually digest what's in front of me. I can barely recall my own name, let alone read a fucking legal document. "As you can see, we have a search warrant. We'll be going through this place with a fine-tooth comb. Whatever you tried to hide, we will find it." He yanks his head toward what used to be my front door. "Get him out of here."

"Holt!" Merit reaches for me, but Ella holds her tight.

"We can't go with him, Merit. We have to stay here. I need your help. We need to video the search and make note of everything they take. I need your help, okay?" Ella talks to Merit like she's a child, giving her a job, hoping it calms her down.

It doesn't.

I shake my head, pleading with Merit, praying she can see the truth written all over my face. "I didn't do this."

And then... I'm hauled out of my house and loaded into the back of a police cruiser.

Chapter 35

Holt

A nightmare.

Actually, a nightmare doesn't even come close to describing it.

My face feels flushed and raw, like I've spent a week fighting a fever. My head is pounding. My body is sore. My muscles cramp. My lips are cracked. And my soul? It feels like it's been run through a garbage disposal.

At least I'm not handcuffed anymore.

"So, you understand this doesn't look good for you. Evidence is evidence, right?" The woman on the other side of the metal table stares at me. She pushes her glasses up on her nose, and for a moment, I'm reminded of Laura.

Lieutenant Liz Archer with the Alabama Bureau of Investigation—the ABI.

Apparently, she's planning on getting me to confess.

But how can I confess to something I didn't do?

I swallow. "I understand what you're saying, how it looks. But it's wrong. I didn't do anything."

She rummages around in the file in front of her. Picking up a paper, she reads. "'I had such a good time with you tonight. It's getting harder to hide my feelings. There's no other place I'd rather be than with you. Inside of you.'" She lifts an eyebrow. "Sound familiar?"

We've been through this. "No."

"But this text was sent from your phone." She pats the stack in front of her. "It's just one of hundreds. Sent from *your phone.* Sent by *you.*"

"It was not sent by me. I told you, I have never had any inappropriate relationship with Heidi Trevors. She's a student at my school, and she works part time for my girlfriend. That's it."

She leans back and folds her arms across her chest. "How do you explain everything then? The texts. The pictures." She pushes a picture in front of me. A picture that suspiciously looks like me and Heidi making out in my truck.

But it's not. It's from the night I drove Heidi home and she hugged me. The angle just makes it look bad.

I hit the picture with my finger. "That's not what it looks like. I told you. That was a hug, and I pulled away as soon as she hugged me."

Who even took that picture anyway? It's from outside the truck.

"Look, she's a cute girl. You're a good-looking guy. You're used to getting lots of attention from women. Maybe it started innocently enough, a little flirting. But you had to know you were playing with fire. She's seventeen."

"I know she's seventeen! That's why I didn't hit on her!" I shake my head, realizing I'm not wording anything correctly. "I didn't flirt with her, nor did I even *want* to flirt with her. She's a student, a child. I would never do that. Not to mention, I'm in a relationship. I love my girlfriend."

She purses her lips and makes an uninterested sound. "The girlfriend who owns the store?"

"That's right."

"The store where you got Heidi a job so she could be closer to you? Make it easier for y'all to steal some alone time with one another?"

"What? Of course not. Merit hired Heidi of her own accord. I just made an introduction. Heidi was saving money, and Merit wanted to help her."

Scowling, she digs back through her papers. When she starts reading another text, I nearly poke my own eardrums out. "'I can't do this anymore. I've decided I'm not leaving Merit. We're done. Whatever this was, it's over. We're nothing but friends. And remember what I told you. Tell no one, or I will make your life a living hell. I have enough money and power to do anything I want.'" She clears her throat. "You sent this to Heidi at three a.m. the night you won the State Championship. I understand you had a party that night? It was your last romantic interaction with her? The last time you and Heidi were physically intimate?"

What the fuck. "There was no *last* romantic interaction because there was never a *first* romantic interaction."

She completely ignores me. "Fortunately, she's a very strong girl. She refused to cower to your threat. She went to the police that very morning. My office was immediately brought in to spearhead the investigation. Do you know that I had dozens of people from all agencies working on this twenty-four-seven for the past two weeks?" She chuckles cynically. "What can I say? You made it all very easy for us. Sure, you deleted the texts from your phone, but the cloud holds onto everything." She leans forward, resting her elbows on the table. "You may be smart on the field, but you're dumb as hell with electronics."

The anger in my voice is palpable. "I don't know how many times I have to tell you. I did not send those messages. Someone must be spoofing my phone number. And I did not have a relationship with Heidi. No touching, no kissing, no sex. Nothing!"

She glowers at me. It's clear she's weighing her options on how she wants to proceed. Finally, she breaks the silence. "She can describe your genitalia."

"Excuse me?"

"You have a scar," she says with a smirk. "On the inside of your left thigh, in the groin area, right next to your..." Her voice trails off.

She's right. I do.

We went on a field trip in first grade to a working farm. Ridge and I snuck away from the group, and I tried to climb over a fence. I didn't realize there was barbed wire at the top. I bled like a stuffed pig. Got seven stitches.

How in the world could Heidi know such a thing? There's no way.

I can feel my life slipping away from me with every word I say. I can't believe I actually thought this was some kind of misunderstanding that I could clear up with a few questions. "I'm done talking. I need to contact my lawyer."

There's a ferocious pounding on the door and a scuffle of noise, making me jump. I think this room is supposed to be soundproof, but there's no mistaking Crutch's voice. I can't hear what he's saying—or screaming—but I know it's him.

Lieutenant Archer's chair scrapes across the floor. Sliding outside, she pulls the door behind her, but it doesn't latch. "What's going on out here?!" She interrupts whatever fight is happening.

Crutch's voice is filled with exasperation. "I'll say it again... there's no way Holt Hill did this. If you'd just let me—"

She warns, "I've already told you to stay out of this investigation, Sergeant. If you even say the name Holt Hill again, I'm gonna make sure the Sheriff takes your badge. Understand?"

Crutch has a pretty low voice. But when he's pissed? It sounds deadly. "I'll do whatever the fu—"

"Crutch!" Marcum interrupts him. I hear footsteps. He must be walking down the hallway toward us. I can hear the worry and concern the moment Marcum opens his mouth. "I told you to leave." He sighs, saying it again. "You need to leave, son."

"But—" Crutch immediately protests.

"Stop. You have a family to think about now. A wife and a son. You need to leave before you get kicked out of here...as a civilian." I hear him clap Crutch on the shoulder.

Archer clears her throat. "Thank you for your assistance, Lieutenant Marcum."

"Well..." If I close my eyes, I can literally picture Marcum, hands in his pockets, rocking back and forth on his heels. "I've heard you don't mess around. Threatening to take a man's badge is serious business." He clicks his tongue. "You know, my wife has been after me to turn my own badge in. Retire."

No one says anything. Not Archer or the others who I know are standing around.

"I guess now is as good of a time as any," Marcum says.

"Pardon?" Archer asks.

"I just turned in my papers. I've got over a year of sick days built up. Consider my retirement effective immediately." He snaps his fingers. "Oh, and the family just hired me as a private consultant. Not another word to my client until he has an attorney present." He flings the door open and leans his head in the room. "Shut the hell up, Holt. Listen to what Ella said."

He barely has time to finish his sentence before they're pushing him out of the room.

A minute later, Archer comes back in. "I'm sorry for the disturbance. Where were we?"

"We weren't anywhere." I lean forward, splaying my hands across the table. My word is simple but decisive. "Attorney."

When she leaves the room, I try to hold it together.

I try to hold it together because the camera in the corner of the ceiling is still flashing red, still recording.

But I can't help it.

Burying my face in my hands, I cry.

Chapter 36

Holt

I've been fingerprinted.

I've been strip searched.

I've had a mug shot taken.

I've given a DNA sample.

I've had a health screening.

I've even had my dick photographed.

Dressed in my new khaki-colored jail scrubs and rubber sandals, my hand shakes as I hold the phone. I'm scared to even put the damn thing to my ear.

It has bite marks on it.

Who the hell bites a telephone?

He answers on the first ring. I don't say hello. "I didn't do it."

Dad chokes with emotion. "Of course, you didn't do it, son. We all know that."

Turning away from the officers watching me, I wipe away a tear. *Guards.* Are they called guards when you are in jail? Taking a deep breath, I steel myself. "Where are you?"

"At your house. We're all at your house. What do you need us to do?"

"Look in my desk drawer. I don't know if it's in the top left drawer or top right drawer, but there's a card for my NFL union lawyer.

Call him. His cell number is on there. Don't stop calling until he answers."

"Okay. We can do that. What else?"

"I have to stay here. In jail." I nearly die. That's a sentence I never imagined myself having to say. "They said my arraignment won't be until Tuesday afternoon. They're taking the full forty-eight hours."

"What! Why?"

"They said it's going slower because of the holidays. We've got to get the lawyer here. He's a new guy. Since I moved back home, they assigned me someone licensed to practice in Alabama. I think he's out of Atlanta."

"We're on it, son. I'll drive there and kidnap him if I have to."

I rub my eyes. "Dad, these calls are recorded."

"Oh." He stumbles over his words. "It was just a figure of speech."

"I know."

"What else do you need?"

"You have to put money in my temporary account for me to be able to call you. You can call the jail tomorrow and do that. Is that okay?"

"Yeah, of course. Crutch is here now. He can help me with that."

"Merit?" I ask, trying to hide the quiver in my voice.

The look on her face when I was being arrested will haunt me for all eternity.

"She's fine."

Dad's many things in life, but a good liar is not one of them. "Dad."

He smacks his lips. "She's inconsolable. She's too upset to even talk. Your mom called Marie. She's on her way up here now."

Great. Nothing like having your future mother-in-law thinking you're a child predator.

The officer—*guard*—motions for me to hurry up. Ending my call, I'm escorted back to my cell. The metals bars are slammed shut, locking me in.

If you punch someone while you're in jail, is it bad?

Like, will I get re-arrested?

Because this attorney is in serious danger of getting his ass kicked.

I knew I was in for trouble when he showed up with his gelled hair and five-thousand-dollar cufflinks.

"So, we can just take a plea deal. I should be able to talk them down to community service and probation."

I toss my hands in the air. "Sure, registering as a sex offender is no big deal, right?"

He's not even paying attention to me; he's just writing notes with his quill pen. Finally, he looks up. "Pardon?"

"You want me to take a plea deal. I'll have to register as a sex offender."

He scoffs, "It's fine. Don't worry about it. It's not like you have future employment to worry about; you're a multi-millionaire. And I can make sure you keep your medical retirement income."

"I'll tell you again. I'm not pleading guilty to something I didn't do."

He looks at me like I'm a simpleton with no intelligence in my head. "Listen, I've only seen a handful of the text messages. There's no denying they came from your phone. Why fight this?" He sits back and crosses his legs. "I'm licensed to practice law in Georgia, Florida, and Alabama. Do you know how many of you profession-al athletes I've represented just this year alone in sex-crime related cases? Fourteen. You're lucky number fifteen. And you know what all of you say in the beginning? 'I didn't do it. I'm not guilty.' But then we see the evidence, and you all quickly change course. Why not save everyone some time and money, especially yourself. We'll come to an arrangement with prosecutors, and you can celebrate Christmas at home."

I try to rein in my anger. My emotions have been all over the place, completely draining me. Not to mention, I'm exhausted. The thought of laying my head on the stained plastic mattress makes me want to bash my brains in, so I've been sleeping sitting up against the cinder block wall with my head on my knees. "There's one difference between those fourteen and me," I enunciate slowly so he can understand me through the fog of his overpriced education. "I. Am. Not. Guilty." I lick my lips and look at the clock on the wall. "And I expect you to say that in one hour at my arraignment."

I guess they could've put me in the city jail. Technically, my house is in the city limits. But, instead, I've been at the county jail, in the basement of the courthouse, next door to the sheriff's department. At least, they can take me to the courtroom via a back elevator, and I'm not being dragged through who-knows-what-hell-hole of paparazzi that may be here. My douchebag lawyer said the arraignment is closed to the general public, save for some hand-selected reporters.

I asked if I could change clothes, but my request was denied before it was even considered. Apparently, they aren't concerned with my inmate scrubs swaying the judge's opinion of me. They smell like bleach, and they're scratchier than hay. I can't wait to get out of them.

When I walk into the courtroom, my senses are jarred with the sound of a thousand camera flicks. There's no flash photography but that doesn't stop the sound. My stomach is wound in tight nerves. My body feels weak, like it's on the verge of collapse. I want to jump on the table and scream to everyone that I'm innocent. Can't they open their eyes and fucking see the truth.

My family crowds the first couple of rows, worry and concern etched across their faces. It's hard to even imagine them happy. One could easily assume they've always looked like this—hard and frozen, anxious and defeated.

And then there's Merit.

She's wearing black. One of Edward's fucking black dresses.

At least this one is demure with cap sleeves and a high collar. I can't see her legs, but I can only assume it's at a more respectable length than what Edward always preferred.

But what really gets me is her red-rimmed eyes, her swollen cheeks, and her chapped lips. She's wearing pink lipstick, trying to disguise the cracks and flaky skin, but I can still tell. I've made it one of my purposes in life to memorize everything about her, and I can see the difference.

And the difference is because of me.

I've caused her this pain, this anguish.

I can't believe I'm putting her through this.

I'm not sure why Heidi is lying, but I must've done something to deserve this. Karma from my past? Whatever it is, I'm now the cause of Merit's pain. I'm not quite sure how to live with that.

The hearing is a blur—blessedly fast and painfully slow at the same time. My bail is set at five million. I have to surrender my passport, and I'm going to be fitted with an ankle monitor. Before I leave the courtroom, my attorney tells me he'll be in touch after New Year's and that he hopes I'll spend the holidays re-examining my position on taking a plea deal.

I lean close, growling in his ear. His over-powering cologne makes me gag. "I *have* reconsidered." His face lights up, excited with the idea of quick, easy money. "You're fucking fired."

Chapter 37

The World

"I *could tell something was wrong with him the second I met him. Just a feeling, you know? It's like some big secret was lurking just beneath the surface. He made a pass at me once. I turned him down, of course. I mean, hello? I work for your girl- friend. When Heidi came to work with us, things got even worse. I caught them in the back room once. I mean, they weren't kissing or having sex or anything, but you could tell something like that had just happened right before I walked back there. I tried to talk to Heidi about it. She's just a kid. I told her it was wrong for him to take advantage of her, but she was in love. I hate that he stole her innocence. Poor Merit was just clueless. As for me, I'm gonna be living with the trauma of this for a long time. When I found out he was arrested, I immediately quit. It's just time for me to focus on self-healing. I pray justice is served."*

Emily Edmondson
Former Employee at Run and Jump and Twirl

"This is an epidemic. These professional athletes, they're treated like gods. They're paid millions and millions of dollars to run a ball

up and down a field of green AstroTurf. Why? Why do we place such value on this kind of entertainment? What's happened to the arts? Watching plays and concerts? We assign such a high worth to these men—and that's all they are, men. That's why they think they can do whatever they want. They take everything to excess— drinking, drugs, money-spending, and sex. And if the sex isn't given freely, they take it. They just take it. And who better to take it from than a young, impressionable girl? A girl you're supposed to be mentoring, teaching. Throw the book at him. That's the only way these guys will ever learn."

Betty Taylor-White
Cable News Commentator

"There's definitely a level of mental illness here. Of course, I haven't had the opportunity to interview Holt Hill, but in my professional opinion, he seems to fit the characteristics of narcissistic personality disorder. He has extreme self-importance. In his mind, he has the right to engage in a romantic relationship with anyone he wants. Age or consent doesn't matter to him. There needs to be better mental health services and screenings in place for these professional athletes—really, for anyone in a position of power. There is still a stigma with these groups surrounding psychiatric services. Proper counseling and medication might have prevented this situation altogether."

Dr. Alexander Crawford
Psychiatrist and Department Head

"Thank you all for coming to this press briefing today. I know it's been an unimaginable few days for our school, our teachers, and most importantly, our students. Needless to say, I never thought I

would be up here saying these words about a man I once considered a dear friend, a trusted colleague, and a valued member of this community. Effective immediately, Holt Hill is no longer on staff at our school. He is no longer serving in either a teaching or coaching capacity. Our administration has been fully cooperating with all law enforcement agencies, and we will continue to do so. Our students are our number one focus, and we will be providing free counseling services when school starts back after the holiday break. We encourage our families to take advantage of this opportunity together. We need to make sure our children understand sexual consent. The administration, Board members, and classroom teachers will work together to strengthen our school environment so every child feels safe. We are in talks with a local charity to establish a hotline where students or their families can report any activity or interaction that makes them feel threatened, uncomfortable, or defenseless. I pray you enjoy the rest of the holiday season and please don't hesitate to reach out to my office if you have any concerns."

Principal Ted Adams
Rockdale High School

"He was my high school sweetheart, and we reconnected during his first year in the NFL. Holt has always been very intense, especially with his emotions. Before I even knew what was happening, we were living together. He's a very different person behind closed doors. He knows how to work the cameras. He knows how to manipulate the fans. He gives out pennies, and people just swoon. That wasn't even his idea; it was mine. A lot of things happened in our relationship that I wish I could change. Maybe if I were strong enough to stay with him, I could've saved this poor girl. I'm just glad that his true colors are finally showing. I'm glad that no oth-

er woman will have to endure what we have. It's time all women stand up and fight for themselves. We are worthy!"

Delaney Fitts
Former Girlfriend

∝

"Fuck him. What a pervert."

"He should be castrated, and his balls fed to pigs."

"My little brother goes to that school. There's a sex tape, y'all!!!!! Just wait...it's gonna be released on Christmas Day. Once I get the link, I'll post it here."

"That's what money gets you. Stupid decisions and jail."

"Our schools should do a better job of protecting our kids."

"I guess that girlfriend of his sucks in bed. Otherwise, why would he step out with a seventeen-year-old?"

"Why does he give out pennies anyway? He's a multi-million-aire. He can spare a fucking dollar."

"My sister's best friend has an uncle who's a janitor at the school. The entire school knew what was happening—teachers, students, counselors, everybody. And they did nothing to stop it. They didn't wanna lose the state championship. Football was the only thing they were concerned about."

"Someone said he took a dick pic and sent it to the girl. Anyone know how I can find it? Any leaks of their texts?"

"I am a survivor of a non-consensual, long-term sexual assault. And some of the comments in this blog are not only insensitive, but extremely vicious and sickening. Yes, the facts will eventually play out in a court of law, but we need to remember that all survivors of sexual assault, sexual trauma, grooming, and domestic violence, deserve to be treated with the utmost respect. Forget about him being a professional athlete and millionaire; the focus should be on his status as a teacher and coach. This is a prime example of how power dynamics can warp a young person's mindset. This is exact-

ly why every state in our country has laws to protect our students. Schools should be a safe environment."

"He's a sicko and should spend the rest of his life getting raped in prison. That'll teach him."

"He's hot. I wish he would've been my teacher when I was in high school. I totally would've hit that."

"He has money. Why didn't he just buy her off? I'm more than willing to be his fuck-buddy if the price is right. Hell, I'd do it for minimum wage. Have you seen him without a shirt?"

"I hope someone cuts off his dick and sticks it down his throat."

"I can't believe Holt Hill is a child molester. I heard she wasn't his first victim. He used to be my hero. I wanted to be just like him. Not anymore. I guess the world would be a better place without him."

Fan Blog

Chapter 38

Merit

I throw up a little in my mouth.

"Merit, get away from the window." Ridge's voice is firm yet sympathetic.

I take one last look at the paparazzi and media vans lining our street, just beyond the huge pecan trees. They're busy taking video and photographs of the yard signs scattered across the yard. Apparently, some brazen people decided to break the public right of way and trespass onto our property last night. Every sign has a vile message.

Rapist.

Predator.

Liar.

Future Prison Bitch.

Money Can't Buy Everything.

Justice for Heidi.

Her name wasn't even supposed to be released to the press, but somehow it was. Some of the text messages too. I mean, *we* haven't even seen all the messages. How can the tabloids have them? And not only have them, but print them?

Before I close the blinds, I see a familiar face. I can't make out her features, but I know it's her...Chloe. She texted me last Sunday night after the arrest was made public. I don't even know how she got my number. I remember her words.

Keep your head low and always say no comment. Even when I ask you. Scream it in my face if you have to. Don't fall for the bait.

Ridge wraps an arm around me and leads me back into the living room. "C'mon. I've got the security worked out."

Holt's where he's been for days—sitting on the couch, blankly staring out the glass doors, watching the waterfall splash into the serene swimming pool. He made it home that Tuesday night after making bail. His homecoming was bittersweet. He wanted to be happy, but a stoic depression bubbled under the surface, begging to drown his strong and happy personality. Despite Mom being in town, I had been sleeping in Holt's bed while he slept in the jail cell. She didn't say anything about it, nor did she say anything when I trudged up the stairs that night, telling him I would see him upstairs.

But I didn't see him upstairs.

He never came to bed.

He's taken to sleeping on the couch.

On Thursday, he sent me home with Mom for Christmas. I was miserable without him. We barely even talked. His cell phone is being held as evidence, and with the Christmas holiday, the local store was sold out of a replacement. He ordered two new phones, but they hadn't come in yet; so, the times we did talk, it was via the cell phone of whomever was with him at the time. As soon as the sun came up the day after Christmas, I headed back.

I was shocked to see him. It looked like he had aged ten years in those few days.

He's lost. He's a shadow. He's punishing himself for something he didn't do. On top of that, he's scared that we don't believe him. I can see it. His eyes flicker around to each of us when he thinks we aren't paying attention. He's just waiting for one of us to call him a liar.

Despite his melancholy, the house has been a bustle of somber activity. No one wants to leave him alone. Ridge and Cullen have been taking turns staying in one of the guest rooms, depending on

Ridge's schedule at the firehouse. Ray and Teresa are also staying here most nights. After I came back from my parents' house, I started sleeping back in my bed in the Children's Wing, giving him space in his own bed, hoping he could get some rest. But that didn't happen. He still slept on the couch. If that's what you can even call it—tossing and turning and shouting out in nightmares.

Ridge sits in front of him on the coffee table. "Holt." When he doesn't look over, Ridge waves some papers in front of his face, trying to get his attention. "Holt."

Blinking, he looks at us. "Yeah?"

"I've got it all lined up."

Holt nods.

"So right now, some city officers are coming by every two hours. As we can see, that's not enough protection. Crutch has lined up some deputies and city officers whom he trusts to patrol twenty-four hours a day during their off time until the security firm can start. I talked to the owner, and he hopes a team can be in place Tuesday, after New Year's. In the meantime, their installation people will be here tomorrow to start on the fence, the security gates, and the cameras."

Holt looks down at the ankle monitor on his leg. "So, I'm making my house my prison."

Ridge shakes his head. "They're some crazy people out there. It's not safe. If they can get into the yard, they can get into the house. Is that what you want?"

Holt looks over at me. His vibrant blue eyes are void of the spark I love, the dancing waves are gone. He swallows, finally answering Ridge. "You know it's not. I'll do whatever I have to do to protect her."

His declaration makes my lip quiver. I'm trying to be strong for him, but it's not easy. I feel like I'm teetering on the edge of a huge cliff about to fall into a lake of quicksand. The store's been closed. When Kyra went to put up a sign last Monday, she said paparazzi were already there. She also had to shut down the social media pages because people were posting horrible comments.

I believe Holt. Really, I do. There's nothing in my soul that says he did this. Nothing in my heart.

I don't know why Heidi is doing this. I don't know why she is lying. She seemed like a good kid. I thought she was my friend.

And I have no idea how the texts were done. They say they came from Holt's phone. I don't know how... there has to be an answer, an explanation.

"Do you have the other stuff?" he asks.

Shuffling through the papers, Ridge holds up a couple of pages. He nods, telling Ridge to give them to me. Ridge slides them in front of me and points with an ink pen. "Sign here and here."

My brow furrows. "What am I signing?"

Holt leans back and drags his hands through his hair. Normally, Holt's every action is done with confidence, sending tingles through my body. Now, he just looks exhausted. "I'm adding you to my main checking account."

"Wh...What?" I fumble over my words. "Why?"

He looks out the window again. "I can barely string a sentence together, let alone take care of the house. I figured you could help me pay the bills when they come in."

I study his face. Every line, every curve. The hard set of his jaw. He's lying. I slam the ink pen down. "Bullshit."

He sighs. "Just sign it, Mer."

"No. Why on earth would you add me to your bank account? I don't want your money. I just want you."

He shoots up from the couch, anger pulsing in his temples. "You want me?! You don't think I want that too?! I may be going to fucking prison, Merit. I need to know you're taken care of. This is your home now. I need to know that you're safe. I don't wanna sit behind bars worrying about you counting every damn penny."

His outburst has drawn some attention. Marcum and Teresa lean out the office door, watching us. I lift my eyebrows, hoping to get some support from his mom, but she just smiles softly.

"Please," Holt pleads. His voice is strained and cracked.

What can I do? Biting the side of my lip, I nod, and sign my name on the dotted line.

For a second, I think he's going to laugh. I'm not sure if I've ever let him win a battle this easy. Instead of laughing, he walks away. "The bank will send over your checks and debit card this afternoon. I'm going to take a shower."

When I walk into the kitchen, I catch Jeff and Cullen huddled in conversation. Joining them at the large island, I grab a plate to make a sandwich with the assortment of meats and cheeses Jeff has laid out.

"They just canceled? I mean, the wedding is Sunday. On New Year's Eve. They'll never find another caterer," Cullen says.

Jeff grabs a marbled piece of roast beef and layers it on my bread. Apparently, I am picking out the wrong pieces. Turning back to Cullen, he shrugs. "I know. It was a huge order. A great way to close out the year. Fortunately, the vendors weren't delivering the food until tomorrow. Most of them have agreed to credit us."

"Did they say why? Any explanation?"

Jeff shifts in his seat, looking uncomfortable.

"Dad, what is it?"

Jeff rubs his jaw, debating before finally giving in. "They know that we're friends with Holt. They're a prominent family and don't want to give the illusion," he says with air quotes, "of supporting an accused sexual predator."

Cullen curses underneath his breath.

All of a sudden, it feels like the air is sucked out of the room. It's filled with an unspoken tension, almost tangible around us. Looking up, we see Holt standing in the corner of the huge kitchen.

Cullen slides back from the barstool. "Holt. It's no—"

Holt immediately cuts him off. "Stop. Can't you see, Cullen? It's just the beginning. This isn't just going to ruin my life; it's going to ruin everyone's. Y'all need to distance yourself from me. Run as far away as you can."

Cullen shakes his head, growling. "We're fighting this with you. We're not going anywhere."

"I'm fucking toxic!" Holt barks back.

"Enough." Ella steps in the room, commanding attention. Defiantly lifting her head in the air, she passes an order. "We're ready. Come to the dining table. Nate's finished."

Grabbing a baseball cap from the corner bar, Holt places it on his head, covering his damp waves. Drops of water dot the shoulders of his green T-shirt. Grumbling, he follows behind her. "He shouldn't even be here."

That's just another way Holt's been punishing himself. He refuses to see any of the kids. Raylee said he wouldn't even accept Anna's phone call on Christmas Day. The only exceptions are Nate, because Marcum showed up with him today, and Baby Harlan—affectionately called Hardy—because Ella is still breastfeeding.

Ella checks the baby monitor hooked to her waistband. Hardy is sleeping in a new crib in the kids' room upstairs. "You know he's a tech wizard," she says, talking about Nate. "He's already been a valuable resource. Be appreciative."

We all gather around the huge dining table, tucked in the corner of the living room. Despite his mood, Holt holds out a chair, nodding for me to sit next to him. When his hand brushes against my side, he quickly whispers an apology. "Oh, sorry."

I hate it. And it makes my fragile heart break a little more.

Marcum nods, giving Nate the floor. He slides one of the new cell phones in front of Holt. "So, this is the duplicate phone. It's set up just like your old one. Same phone number, same email address, same apps. I downloaded everything from the cloud. If someone calls or texts your old number, it will show on this. But keep in mind, the police will see it too. They have your old phone and your cloud information. In addition, since it's a ghost clone, you won't actually be able to answer any phone calls that come in. You'll just see them in the call log history." He slides the other new phone over. "This is the new phone. It has your new phone number and your new email address. I established a new cloud backup with a new password. I also changed the usernames and passwords on all your apps—bank accounts, credit cards, even your music app. I have everything written down here." He hands Holt a piece of paper.

Ray leans forward, resting his forearms on the table. "The texts?"

Marcum pats Nate on the shoulder. "When Nate downloaded the old cloud information, all of the alleged correspondence downloaded." He nods at one of the cell phones. "It's on there. We also sent a secure file to the new lawyer with all of the messages."

"And they'll be here when?" Ray asks.

Ella answers, "January 10th. That'll give them time to get moved and set up."

After firing his lawyer through the union, Holt asked Ella for a referral. In her consulting business, she works with lawyers all over Alabama and the surrounding states. Her recommendation was a bulldog criminal attorney out of Mobile. He's actually the attorney who first asked for her assistance as a consultant. He's persistent. And expensive. He's bringing one junior attorney and three paralegals with him. Holt's having to rent two houses for them—indefinitely. They plan on living here during the week and going back home on the weekends.

Ridge hits his knuckles against a massive stack of papers. "And this?"

Ella takes a deep breath. "It's the text messages and phone logs."

Holt sits up straight. "There are that many messages?"

Marcum clears his throat. "We have several copies; but yes, there are a lot of messages." He gives Ella a knowing look.

She picks up where he left off. "We have multiple copies because in our opinion, we should all read them."

Holt's face immediately pales. "What? Even I don't wanna read them."

"You don't really have a choice, Holt. The more eyes we have on these, the better. No one knows you better than us. We can help spot inconsistencies, even in the language and style. I think it's the best idea."

Moaning, Holt knocks his hat up and drags his hands down his face. After several seconds, when he doesn't say anything, Ray urges him to make a decision. "Son?"

Tugging his hat back down, he sighs, taking the weight of the world on his shoulders. "Yeah. Sure."

Quietly, Nate passes out the clipped packages to each of us. Holt doesn't like that. "You saw these? You read them, Nate?"

Nate clicks his tongue. "Does it matter? They're not real."

Just like the rest of us, Nate has unwavering faith in Holt.

When the packet is placed in front of me, I stare at it. What I really want to do is tear it into shreds and line a bird cage with it. It's vile and disgusting and filled with lies. *I'm not sure how.* But it is.

Holt leans in, getting closer to me than he's gotten in the past several days. "You don't have to do this, you know?"

What a stupid question.

"Of course, I do. I'll do anything to help you. You know that." I purse my lips, biting back tears. "I love you, Holt."

Chapter 39

Merit

Holy shit.

Why did I think I could do this?

I press my nose against the window of Ridge's truck. The parking lot is filled with media. There's even a tent set up. A couple of reporters and paparazzi are milling around on the sidewalk in front of the store. Taking a deep breath, I reach for the handle, cracking open the door.

"Merit," Ridge nudges my shoulder, "wait for Crutch."

A split second later, Crutch parks caddy-corner in front of us. Jumping out, he immediately starts yelling and pointing at the crowd. His hand protectively hovers over the weapon on his belt. "Y'all need to back up. This parking lot is private property, and the development owner has a tow truck on standby. You need to back up to the small strip of grass in the right of way next to the road." They all moan and grumble. Crutch shrugs. "I don't know why y'all are complaining. I've said the same thing to you multiple times a day for the past two weeks."

"Yeah, but it actually looks like she's coming to work today." A small lady with perfectly coifed hair points in our direction with her microphone.

A guy, videoing with his cell phone, breaks through the crowd and starts to yell. "This is a free country. We can go wherever the hell we want."

Crutch doesn't back down. Instead, he walks right up to him. He towers over the guy by a good seven inches. His voice lowers, and I can hear his intimidating growl from here. "Wanna bet."

Eventually, the majority of the crowd is back where they're supposed to be, after a couple of other deputies and officers join Crutch. With trembling hand, I climb out of the truck. Shoving my bags higher on my shoulder, I look at the short distance between us and my storefront, and it looks completely insurmountable. Like I'm climbing Mount Everest. Like I'm about to crawl across shattered lightbulbs on hands and knees.

Ridge comes around, meeting me. "You sure you're ready for this?"

I don't have any other choice. The store has been closed for more than two weeks. Which means no income for more than two weeks. Sure, I lost three employees—Emily, Kim, and the fucking lying bitch—but I still have Kyra's salary and rent and utilities and everything. Plus, I still have Holt to pay back. I have to do everything I can to get him some money; his legal fees are going to be astronomical.

So, there's not a choice. Not really.

With wide eyes, I nod. "I'm ready."

The moment we step out from the shelter of the truck, all hell breaks loose. The masses start yelling and screaming, vying for my attention. Ridge wraps his arms around me and holds his hand over my face, trying to shield me from their cameras.

"Merit! Did you know? Did you know he was cheating on you?"

"Merit! How does it feel to be sleeping with a pedophile?"

"Merit! Did you hire the victim so your boyfriend could be close to her? Are you an accomplice?"

"Merit! Are you staying with him? Why haven't you left?"

"Merit! Is it true that you're sleeping with his best friend?"

My heart thunders in my chest so rapidly I think I'm having a heart attack. I focus on the ground, focus on putting one foot in front of the other. When I stumble, Ridge keeps me upright.

Out of the corner of my eye, I see Kyra's car in the distance. "Ridge, it's Kyra."

Following my sightline, he spots her. Hollering at Crutch, he motions for him to get her. I'm relieved when Crutch jogs over and gives Kyra the same treatment. It feels like it takes an hour for us to reach the door. I'm shaking so badly I can't even get the keys in the lock. I fumble, dropping them to the ground. Wordlessly, Ridge grabs them and opens the door. Kyra and I stumble through the threshold like drunks looking for a beer. I haven't seen her in person since before Holt was arrested. Flinging my bags to the floor, we collapse into each other's arms. When she whispers that she's missed me, a few silent tears fall from my eyes.

When we finally separate, I look around, taking stock of my store. I'm assaulted by the Christmas inventory that never had a chance to be sold, including what's left of the beautiful handcrafted ornaments. Which did, in fact, sell like hot cakes and were lined up to completely sell out in the week before Christmas.

In the week my life fell apart.

There's no point in beating around the bush. "Fifty percent off," I tell Kyra. "We have no choice."

"All the Christmas stuff, right?"

I blow a raspberry, thinking. "Fifty percent off everything."

"Everything!"

"Yep. We need customers and good rapport. The sale will get them in, and then we'll rebuild the rapport." I smile holding out my hand for her. "Me and you."

"I'm gonna do a perimeter check before I leave. I'd stay, but I'm in the middle of a robbery investigation." Crutch points to my cell phone on the counter. "Call my cell if you need anything at all. Understand?"

I give him a quick hug. "Thank you so much. I'm sure things will settle down in a few days."

He and Ridge share a knowing look, making me uneasy.

After he leaves, Kyra and I get busy working. Thirty minutes later, Ridge is still pacing around the store. He's clearly babysitting us. I slap my hands on my hips. "What do you think you're doing?"

He lifts an eyebrow. "You know, I remember a time when Holt said you were meek and wouldn't talk."

I snort. "A lot of things have changed, huh?"

He drags a hand down his face and then taps his chin. "You can say that again."

"Ridge, you're exhausted. You just got off from your shift at seven this morning. You need to go get some sleep."

"And leave you here alone?"

I look around. "This is my happy place. We'll be completely fine here." I smile weakly. "But what we really need are customers. And they're not gonna come in with some big dude stalking around the store."

"She's right," Kyra chimes in.

There's a low hum in the back of his throat. "Fine." He points at the crowd. "But promise neither one of you will set foot outside without calling us first."

I have to make twenty promises, but eventually he leaves.

Kyra sighs. "If I didn't have a boyfriend, I would totally be into Ridge."

The look on her face is so damn funny, I can't help but laugh.

And laughing feels really good.

Five hours.

We've been open for five hours, and no one has come in.

Not one single customer.

Kyra's behind the front counter, working designs on her computer, and I'm sprawled on the floor, watching an Elvis movie on the big-screen TV. Scrambling to my feet, I stretch my back. I can't just sit here anymore, waiting for something to happen that we both know won't. What customer in their right mind would want to fight a pile of photographers just to get a pair of kids' tennis shoes at fifty percent off?

Plus, my nerves are wearing thin. I feel torn. I want to be here, but I also want to be home with Holt. Watching over him. Protecting him.

This is a never-ending nightmare. It's like I'm dying a slow death. Every second of every day another piece of me crumbles. I don't know how much more I can take.

The man I love is walking around with an ankle monitor.

"I'm going to the back."

Kyra nods, not even glancing up from her screen.

I stop in the doorway, unable to take another step. It feels like I have a two-ton anvil sitting on my heart, weighing me down. My feet are frozen in place. "Do you believe him?" My question shocks even me.

Sighing, Kyra carefully considers her answer. "I never saw anything inappropriate between them. Nothing. Ever. I'm mean, sure, she might've had a little crush on him, but I never saw him encourage her."

"You didn't answer my question."

"I don't know what to believe," she says honestly. "The messages. The phone calls. You even said yourself that you have no idea how they got on his phone." She taps her fingers against the countertop. "But I know that I believe in you. And if you believe him, that's the only thing I need to hear." She shrugs. "For what it's worth, I know he loves you. Without a doubt, he is totally and completely in love with you."

Unfortunately, that does little to comfort me.

Sitting at the table in the back, I stare at my bag, listening to the whispers of the paperwork lurking inside. It calls to me, like a siren calling to a sailor. Pulling the packet in front of me, I flip to the first page and start reading.

Holt: So... last night was interesting.

Heidi: Definitely.

Holt: Did you get your car?

Heidi: Yeah. My uncle finally got it started.

Holt: Good.

Holt: I just wanted to apologize again for kissing you last night.

Heidi: Why? I'm not sorry.

Heidi: In fact, it's all I can think about.

There's a five-minute break before the next message is sent.

Holt: When can I see you again?

Heidi: Well, that's up to you, isn't it? You're the one with all the power.

I read until my eyes are blurry. I read until I'm sick and twisted in knots. The messages range from common chatter to highly sexual content. Some would even be considered too vulgar for your average pornographic flick.

I know Holt's in touch with his body, aware of his sexual prowess. But this? This is a whole new level.

What the hell am I talking about?

Holt didn't write these messages.

Did he?

Unable to control myself, I collapse in grief. Burying my head in my hands, I cry. I cry like I did the day he got arrested. When he came home, I vowed not to lose it in front of him. I vowed to be strong. But how strong can one woman be? How faithful? How loyal?

I cry until I'm empty. Until there's nothing left of me. Nothing but a shell. My eyes are swollen, my throat is raw, and my chest is sore. I close my eyes, praying for clarity. I want someone to give me the answer. I want someone to tell me what to do.

Because I don't have a fucking clue.

So, I do what any rational adult woman would do; I call my mom.

"Hey, sweetie. How is your first day back?"

I have to clear the snot from my throat before I can even talk. "It's terrible. No one's come in. And by no one, I mean not one single person. Not even our mail lady. She opened the door—literally an inch—and put the mail on the floor. I mean, it's like I have a contagious disease."

Mom takes a deep breath. "Well, we're talking about some serious charges. We're not talking about running a red light, Merit."

I mumble, telling her I know.

"You have some people who are scared. Scared for their children to go to school. Scared for what our young women have to experience as they grow up. It's like our society—our world—has just resigned itself to the fact that sexual assault and inappropriate sexual behavior is the norm. When it's a horrific and hideous crime that should be fully and appropriately punished. Others are upset, thinking they've been fooled all these years by a celebrity who they thought was a good guy. And then there's always those who love to hear bad news, whether it's true or not. Wicked chaos is their lifeline. They cling to the evil because it gives them a target to cast their stones."

I pinch the bridge of my nose. I have a pounding headache. "I read the messages."

There's nothing but silence on the other side of the phone.

"There's so many of them," I continue. "And there's a log of phone calls. Some are an hour long."

"So, the leaked messages on the news? On the Internet?" Mom asks.

"Yep. Verbatim. I have them in writing."

Mom exhales. "Oh, Merit, that's not good. Those messages are..." she pauses, trying to be diplomatic, "very suggestive."

I snort. "It's not much of a suggestion, Mom, when nothing is left to the imagination. 'Your tight, young, virgin pussy makes my cock throb' isn't exactly a secret code."

"How'd you get them?"

"Holt. He had everything downloaded from his cloud account. We all have copies—me, his parents, all of us."

"And he didn't write them? But they're on his phone?"

"That's what he says." My voice wavers, putting me on the edge of tears again.

"And do you believe him?"

Well, that's the million-dollar question, isn't it.

I'm surprised Mom can even hear my whispered answer. "Should I? Should I believe him? Tell me what to do, Mom."

"Honey, I can't tell you what to do." She waits a few seconds, thinking about what she wants to say. "Follow your heart, Merit. Follow your heart, and we will support you no matter your decision or the outcome."

Follow my heart.

How can I follow something that's breaking?

Just as promised, Ridge is there to escort us out. Crutch is working so Cullen is Kyra's assigned protector for the walk back to her car. I set the alarm, and as soon as we're on the sidewalk, we're assaulted by a brash reporter and a guy with a camera.

A reporter I happen to know.

"Merit! Has Holt confessed to you? Are you moving out of his house? Leaving him?"

Chloe's voice rings in my ears. Ridge shields me with his hand, blocking the camera's view as I lock the door to the store. "What the hell, Chloe?" Exasperation pours from him. "Get the hell out of here. The other reporters are gonna think it's okay to block the store."

Sure enough, from the corner of my eye, underneath the glowing parking lot lights, I see several of them jump up. They meander back and forth, trying to decide if they should race over.

Ridge buries me against his side, navigating me across the sidewalk.

"How much has he told you, Merit? Is the guilt eating him alive?" Chloe halfheartedly tries to shove a microphone in my face.

I'm looking down, watching my tennis shoes take step after step. When suddenly, an unexpected wave of calm washes over me. It actually takes me by surprise, and my legs falter, jostling me against Ridge's shoulder.

The feeling is new. And completely welcome.

The past few weeks I've been walking on a glass bridge. A glass bridge filled with cracks. Slowly wobbling from side to side. Just waiting on it to shatter and send me plummeting to the ground.

And now?

For some reason, I feel steady. Strong. Powerful.

In control.

Ducking away from Ridge, I spin around, facing Chloe head-on. My movements catch everyone off guard. Cullen and Kyra stop walking. Even Chloe takes a little jump back.

Lifting my head, I take a deep breath. "The guilt isn't eating him alive because he did nothing wrong. He's not guilty."

Chloe's eyes widen. With an almost imperceptible movement, she shakes her head, secretly telling me to stop talking. Just like her text said, she wants me to ignore her. She wants me to say 'no comment' and keep moving.

But I'm done with that.

Ridge grabs my elbow. I ignore him.

She swallows and begrudgingly asks another question. "What do you mean, he's not guilty?"

"I mean, he's not guilty. Completely innocent of all charges."

Her face almost looks pained. "What about all of the evidence?"

"Evidence isn't evidence until it's fully investigated and vetted by all parties."

"Meaning what? You're saying Holt Hill was framed?" The cameraman takes a step closer, getting a better angle.

"What I'm saying is... Holt Hill is innocent. Anyone who actually knows him knows the truth. Holt could never—would never—do what he is being accused of. And we will fight until the whole world knows that."

"So, you're staying with him? Supporting him?"

I nod firmly, the epitome of confidence. "I'm never leaving."

"So, you're staying with him? Supporting him?"

I nod firmly, the epitome of confidence. "I'm never leaving."

Chapter 40

Merit

I grab another ornament from the tree and gently place it in the storage container. The tree is the last Christmas decoration I need to put away. Side glancing at Holt, frustration builds in my chest. It's bubbling beneath the surface, building pressure so tight it makes my sternum hurt.

Sitting on the damn couch.

That damn fucking couch.

I hate it.

It's become his tomb.

"Wanna help me?" I ask, trying to keep my voice neutrally happy.

He stares out the glass doors, once again watching the water from the stone waterfall drop into the swimming pool. A cold front has come through, and the backyard grass is coated with frost. When he doesn't answer, I ask him again. But instead of answering me, he peppers me with his own question.

"Did you hear the latest one?" he asks.

"Huh? The latest one of what?"

"A former White House aide is accusing me of groping her. Said it happened when the team visited the White House after the National Championship win my junior year." He scoffs, shaking his head with a cynical laugh. "I wasn't even there. I was in the hospital having my appendix out."

Sighing, I put down another ornament and fold my arms across my chest. "So, we'll fight it. Just like all the others."

He doesn't answer. He just shrugs.

A sliver of bitterness slices through my heart. "Do you plan on doing anything today?"

He bounces his leg, watching the small movement of his ankle monitor. "Sure. I was thinking of going to work today. You know at the high school around teenagers. Then, I thought I would go out to eat. Maybe catch a flick at the theater." He lifts an eyebrow. Dropping the sarcasm, his voice lowers. "C'mon, Mer, really? What do you think I'm doing today?"

"Not a damn thing from what I can see." I walk closer to him. My bare feet slap against the marble floor. "Do you even remember that the lawyer's coming tomorrow." I can't hide my indignation.

He licks his lips and his jaw tics. "Of course, I remember the lawyer's coming tomorrow. You think I don't know? I'm paying an ass-load of money to rent him and his team two houses. Fucking houses, Merit. Giant ones. And that's on top of all the legal fees."

I dramatically flop my arms in the air. "They're trying to prove your innocence, Holt. I don't care if you have to rent them the fucking Taj Mahal and buy them ponies. Do it."

"I am doing it! I'm doing everything everybody wants!" He points at the window. "Right now, there's five strangers—in houses I've paid for—looking at every aspect of my life. I'm under a microscope. Things that I thought were private will never be private again." He drags his hand across his face, tugging his facial hair. "And it's not just them! It's the police. They're reading *our* messages, Merit. Mine and yours. And if you remember, sometimes, we didn't exactly keep our text messages in the PG realm. Doesn't that bother you?"

Yes, it does. "Not if it helps get you out of this. If it helps you, I'd rent a sky banner and fly our dirtiest text all over the southern U.S."

Lacing his fingers on top of his head, he closes his eyes and sighs.

I bite my lip. "You're not fighting hard enough. Every single day and night, you sit on that couch, drowning in your thoughts. You're in prison already."

His eyes dart open. Slowly lowering his hands, he stares at me.

"You don't talk to me. You don't share your feelings with me." I nudge the edge of the rug with my toe. "And you won't even touch me."

His whisper is barely audible. "Excuse me?"

"You heard me."

Anger flashes in his eyes, turning his beautiful blue eyes black. "You want me to touch you?" He holds up his hands. The hands I love. Rough-hewn and calloused from constantly throwing footballs and lifting weights. "With these hands?" He can't hide the disgust in his voice. "These hands are accused of touching a child. And you want them on you?"

I can't take it anymore. He's drowning in guilt over something that he's not even guilty of.

I need to scream.

I need to fight.

I need to break something.

Seeing as how I'm not a particularly violent person, I grab a throw pillow and heave it across the room. I'm mortified when it bounces off a bookshelf and sends a blue vase crashing to the ground. Glass shards scatter across the floor, making me jump.

My mouth drops open. "Uhhh... was that expensive?"

His eyebrow cocks, and a small little smirk tugs at the corner of his mouth. "It was a gift from my coach's wife after my first touchdown run in the NFL. It was tradition. She gave a gift to every player after their first major play."

Nodding, I consider apologizing.

Normally, I would apologize.

But these aren't exactly normal circumstances.

"Well, good." I plant my hands on my hips. "I mean, this is the liveliest I've seen you in days. Maybe I should head to that trophy room and see what I can bust next." I turn and start to walk away, carefully checking my path for pieces of broken glass. "I wonder what happens when you flush a Super Bowl ring down the toilet."

A pounding noise stops me in my tracks. Holt's stomping across the top of the coffee table. He didn't even take time to walk *around* it. He just decided to walk *over* it. Jumping down, he stalks across the room. With powerful and purposeful intent. Like a lion stalking a zebra. He grabs my arms, clutching them tightly.

His shining and vibrant blue eyes are back. They study my face, searching for my wants, searching for my needs. His hair is longer than normal, and the blond waves curl around his neck, drawing attention to the tensed muscles of his shoulders. They've been knotted since the second the police stormed in the house. I wish I could take some of his pain, some of his stress, and carry it for him. Give him some relief.

I take a deep breath, inhaling his scent.

My mouth dries. My heart thunders. My stomach clenches. I find it hard to breathe. My brain drowns in a fog. When he licks his lips, I nearly faint because my desire is so intense.

"You want my hands on you?" he growls.

"Yes. I want your hands on me. I want your mouth on mine." My throat makes a weird tingly noise when I swallow. "I want you inside of me."

Before I can even finish my sentence, his mouth crashes down on mine. Pushing his tongue into my mouth, he tastes me and steals the breath from my lungs. Pulling from his grasp, my fingers claw at him, desperate to trace the firm lines of his back and tangle in his hair.

His kiss is fierce and feverish. Eventually, he tugs my sweatshirt off and curses under his breath when he sees he still has a tank top and sports bra to contend with. I help him, quickly stripping my torso naked. When his own T-shirt hits the ground, I dip my body, tracing my tongue across his perfectly sculpted chest. He moans, and my body immediately responds. I'm in the crosshairs of that fine line between pleasure and pain. My hardened nipples turn to stone and my clit throbs.

Holt grabs the waistband of my leggings. Stepping away, I push my pants to the floor, nodding for him to do the same to his sweat pants. Unwilling to be disconnected for even a second, Holt pulls me back into his arms before I'm finished. I stumble around with my toes trapped in my leggings. Flopping my left foot back and forth, my pants eventually fly through the air.

Holt grabs my ass and lifts me. My legs wrap around his waist. The heat from his groin feels like a fire against my damp panties. He walks over to a tall side table and sets me down. The wood is cold against my sensitive skin. Leaning me back, he removes my panties. Slowly. Painfully slowly. It's a complete contradiction to our actions so far.

He drags a finger through my folds, spreading my wetness, down my ass and up to my clit. He doesn't linger—it's one swift, fluid movement. And it makes my body contort and buck, leaving me longing for more. I watch in awe as he slides his underwear lower, freeing his massive erection. Long and hard. Swollen purple and red with pumping blood. Begging for release.

Anticipation consumes me, making my vision blur.

With one hand, he strokes his cock, readying himself. With the other, he grabs me, pulling me closer. When my legs balance on his shoulders, he kisses my right ankle.

And then...

He slams into me.

Not softly.

Not slowly.

Not gently.

His hands grip my hips, and he thrusts into my depths, immediately hitting my wall, finding the sweet spot that makes my back arch and my eyes close.

We moan. We scream.

He hammers into me with wild abandon, freeing his anger and frustration and bitterness. Tension builds in my body. I can feel every part of him. He fucks me like the world is ending. Like it may be the last time we ever feel anything this good.

More. More. More.

His hands drift up to my shoulders, and he uses the new traction to drive me to the brink of insanity. I yell—a screeching mumble of incoherent words— relishing in my orgasm, and I'm vaguely aware of him doing the same, finding relief in his own release.

It's takes several minutes for my euphoria to settle. Several minutes for me to even have the strength to open my eyes.

And then?

Then, it all ends.

It ends in a way it's never ended before.

I watch the joy leak from his eyes, like air from a balloon. He backs away from me, leaving me empty and cold. Immediately pulling his boxer briefs over his still-erect dick, he turns and walks away. Balancing against the glass door to the outside, he leans his forehead against it, trying to absorb the cold winter air. Sighing, he closes his eyes.

I watch his reflection.

Watching him feels wrong.

Like I'm a stranger invading his space.

Like I don't belong here.

Like he regrets what we just did.

Like... he regrets me.

"I..." He trips over what he wants to say. "I shouldn't have done that."

I study his back. The seductive curve of his spine. The alluring roundness of his ass. The strong contours of his shoulders. The powerful lines of his legs. "Wh-what?" My voice is groggy.

"I shouldn't have done that. Not with these allegations looming over us."

I blink back tears. What the hell am I supposed to say to that?

A deep sadness sucks every piece of happiness from my soul. And then, a slithering snake of rage curls around my heart.

Jumping down from the table, I rush around gathering my clothes. I don't even bother to put them on. I just hug them in my arms, listening to my bare feet as they slap against the floor.

I refuse to look at him.

I refuse to give him the satisfaction of seeing my emotions.

And just when I think he can't be a bigger asshole, he proves me wrong. "I forgot to wear a condom," he says.

Snorting, I fling my leggings over my shoulder. "Don't worry about it, shithead. I'll stop by the drug store on my way to work and get the morning-after pill."

I'm already walking down the hallway when I hear his parting words. "I love you, Mer."

I don't respond.

Because what's left to say?

Chapter 41

Holt

They've only been here a half hour, and I'm already on my second bathroom break. I don't even have to piss. I just have a nervous, dread-filled energy and can't stay seated.

Right now, there's a five-person legal team sitting at the dining room table in my living room. And Ella.

I check my watch, wondering where Marcum is. Right then, the new security system intercom buzzes. For the time being, there's a security guy out front working the gates. "Mr. Hill, Patrick Marcum has arrived. He's coming through the security gate now."

I walk down the hall, wanting to have a quick word with Marcum by myself before he joins the group. I'm surprised to see Marcum's not alone when he comes in from the garage. "Nate?" My brow furrows. Today's a school day; he should be in school. "Everything okay?"

Nate shuffles past me. Looking down, he shifts the backpack on his back.

"Sorry, I'm late," Marcum says. "Nate's gonna do his homework in your office, if that's okay?"

"Yeah, of course." I shrug in question, "Is he sick?"

Marcum shakes his head. "Not sick. Suspended."

"Suspended!" I grab Nate's shoulder before he gets farther away from me. "What happened?"

Slowly, he looks up, and I'm shocked to see the nasty purple and blue shiner on his face. "You have a black eye," I say, pointing out the obvious.

The look on his face tells me all I need to know.

But... I still ask him anyway. "What the hell happened?"

He swallows. "Don't worry about it, Holt."

My eyes harden and my voice drops, giving him a warning. "Nate."

He sighs. "They were saying things about you that aren't true. I couldn't let them do that."

"Who was?"

"Some guys at school. Don't worry about them. They're bullies. They deserved what they got. Stupid asswipes."

"Hey!" Marcum raises his voice and points at the office. "In there. Shut the door and do your homework. Not a peep. You hear me?"

"Yes, sir." Taking his marching orders, Nate disappears, shutting the door.

Depression consumes me, making it hard to breathe. My heart thunders, and a tight vise circles around my heart.

It's happening. The kids are starting to get hurt.

I'm ruining everyone's lives.

I can't fucking stand this. I feel like I'm losing my mind.

I want my life back. I want my family back. I want my reputation back.

Fuck Heidi. And fuck her lies.

"Hey," Marcum wraps a hand around my shoulder. "He's fine." He chuckles. "In fact, he's more than fine. He took down four of those little shits."

I drag my hand across my face. "Brent and Stephanie must hate me. Their son just got suspended because of me."

"Nah, they trust his judgment. They know he's a smart kid." He swings his large briefcase on his shoulder. "Now, introduce me to this top-tier legal team of yours."

The same questions. Over and over. For six hours.

And it's going to be this way for months. Who knows, maybe years.

"So, nothing inappropriate, ever?" Mr. Harrison, the high-priced lawyer asks again. "Accidental touching?"

"I told you the only time was when I gave her a ride home from the school parking lot. She hugged me. I backed away, gave distance." I shrug, trying to think back over the past few months. "She may have hugged me after we won the State Championship, but I can't remember. I hugged a thousand people that day and night."

"And electronic contact? Phone calls, texts, emails?" Jacob, the junior associate, asks. He furiously scribbles notes and keeps glancing at his laptop. My table is covered in laptops and notepads and scattered with the transcripts of my supposed love history with Heidi.

I count to five in my head before I answer, trying to stave off some of my pissed-off tone. "Nothing. I have never texted or called Heidi. Ever. Merit did, but not me."

"And just to confirm, you are saying," he taps some of the papers, "these messages aren't yours."

Ella explained this is part of the process. They ask the same questions multiple times and compile all the different answers to get to the truth. Even a slight variation in an answer can give them something new. Something to follow, something to search.

"The messages aren't mine. My fingers didn't type those messages. My fingers did not call her phone number. I never, ever texted or called Heidi, despite what my phone records show. Despite what her phone records show."

"So, your assertion is you're being framed?" Mr. Harrison pushes his glasses on the bridge of his nose. It reminds me of Laura. And then it reminds me of Lieutenant Liz Archer with the ABI and how the world thinks I'm a sexual predator.

"That is one hundred percent what I'm saying."

Jacob clicks around on his screen. "Well, as you know, you told us money was no object." He lifts an eyebrow, waiting for me to nod. "We've already hired two different IT and metadata experts. They specialize in cell phone and cloud data. In fact, Ella has vetted them on a couple of our cases. At this point, their findings are preliminary, but they're both coming to the same conclusion."

When he doesn't say anything, I swing my hands through the air. "And that is..."

"Nothing was hacked. Nothing was spoofed. The outgoing text messages physically came *from* your cellular device, and the incoming text messages physically came *to* your cellular device. Same thing with the phone calls. Your phone actually made those phone calls. Unless they find something new, there is no disputing that."

"I can dispute it. Because I didn't do it." I sit back in the chair and drag my hands through my hair. Marcum pushes a fresh bottle of water in front of me.

Mr. Harrison clears his throat. "Let's assume the data isn't wrong. If the data is correct, and you're saying you didn't send the messages then there is only one reasonable explanation." All heads swivel in his direction. "Someone gained access to your cell phone and used it, explicitly for the purpose of framing you for this charge."

Yep. And that thought makes me sick to my stomach.

"You've got top-notch security," he continues. "Cameras line the outside of your property. Do you have cameras inside your home as well?"

A couple of the paralegals look around, searching for mounted cameras on the ceiling.

I shake my head. "This is all new. And no, there aren't any cameras on the inside."

"What do you mean new?"

"The keypad gates, the fence around the entire property, the cameras, and of course, the security guards. All of that came after my..." I still hate saying the word arrest, so I just skip over it. "The only camera I had before was just a normal doorbell camera that I ordered off the Internet and hooked up to my smart devices. But it was only for the front door so I could see when deliveries were being made. The wrought iron fence was around a portion of the backyard, to keep the swimming pool closed off, you know, for insurance purposes. And each door had an alarm keypad for setting the system and for keyless entry, on both the exterior and interior of the door."

"And the alarm keypads were connected to an actual alarm company?" Jacob asks.

I'm taking a drink of water so Ella answers for me. "Yes, we've used the same alarm company since I lived in the house. If the alarm goes off, they call requesting the private password. If they don't get an answer, they send the police out."

"But until recently, you didn't have cameras at any of the other doors or windows, besides the front door?"

"That's right."

"And did you set the house alarm each night? When going to sleep?"

I nod yes.

"And who has the alarm code? The code for the door keypads, the keyless entry?"

"It's the same code for both. And just my family has it," I answer.

Jacob points at the notepad in front of me. "Can you make a list for us?"

"I'll type up a list and email it out," Ella says. "Holt can let me know if I'm missing anyone."

I offer a small smile to my cousin. I'm pretty damn miserable with all of this questioning, but the fact remains, I don't know what I would do without her. She's really amazing at all this stuff.

"Well, in looking at the transcripts, every single text message and phone call occurs in the late-night hours and early morning hours. Basically, overnight, while the rest of the world is sleeping." Mr. Harrison taps his ink pen on the table, thinking. "So, you're proposing that someone bypassed the alarm, snuck into your house, creeped up to your bedroom, took your cell phone, sent text messages and made phone calls—some of which were an hour long—replaced the cell phone, left the house, and reset the alarm." He leans forward in his chair. "And you're suggesting that occurred nearly every single night for over three months?"

Jacob slaps his hands on the table, scoffing. "I think you would notice if someone kept coming into your bedroom during the dead of night and snatched your phone from the nightstand."

"I don't sleep with my phone in the bedroom."

"Huh?" Jacob furrows his brow, and Mr. Harrison cocks his head.

"I never sleep with my phone in the bedroom. I always leave it on a table in the hallway. And I keep my bedroom door shut. I've done the same thing since I was a teenager."

Mr. Harrison wiggles his head back and forth. "Okay. I guess that makes the scenario a little more plausible, but still... I just don't see someone taking that amount of risk. I mean, we're talking about dozens and dozens of breaking and entering, with an intruder being in your home for sometimes hours at a time. The likelihood of getting caught is just too great. Plus, I just don't see how you could sleep through something like that."

"I sleep like the dead. There's not much that wakes me up."

Jacob smacks his lips together, making a popping noise. "But what about your girlfriend?"

"What about her?"

"You said that she *officially* lives in the connected apartment, but that you both have shared a bedroom for the past couple of months, isn't that correct?"

I glance around the table. "Yeah, so?" I don't bother to elaborate that we've not shared a bed since I came home from jail. They know everything else about me, I'd like to keep the problems with my current sex life to myself. I've pretty much been a dick to Merit lately, and I don't really feel like calling myself out.

Mr. Harrison picks up where Jacob left off. "Well, Holt, you sleep like the dead, but what about her?"

"She…" I pause, collecting my thoughts, "sleeps like a normal person."

"And yet she never woke up and caught an intruder."

He doesn't ask it like a question, so I don't answer him.

"Do the two of you always sleep in your bedroom in the master residence?"

"Most recently, yeah. In the beginning of our relationship, we went back and forth, between her bedroom and mine." I have to clear my throat to get the words out. My mouth is starting to go dry, and an uncomfortable feeling settles low in my stomach.

"So, it's reasonable to say that some of the communication with Heidi came on nights when you were sleeping in the connected apartment. Is that right?"

My throat clenches. I nod.

"And where did you keep your cell phone on those nights, Holt?"

My voice shakes. "A table outside of the Children's Wing…I mean, apartment. In the hallway."

"So, we're making the astronomical assumption that the intruder would know which nights you slept in the apartment, and where to go looking for your cell phone, correct?"

Anger curls in my chest, and I feel like pummeling his face for even insinuating what I think he's insinuating.

Marcum jumps in. "I think we may be delving into territory that we don't need to be in. Implying that Merit may have something to do with this is outside the realm of possibility."

Mr. Harrison scoffs. "And I thought my wife depleting one of our bank accounts to buy her boyfriend and his mom a luxury SUV and a Hawaiian vacation was outside the realm of possibility too. But it still happened."

Jacob jumps in. "Is there an alarm keypad—some sort of lock—between the apartment and the rest of the house?"

He reads my face.

"So, she's had free rein of your house since the day she moved in?"

"What you're offering doesn't make any sense," Ella says. "Merit and Heidi met through Holt. Allegedly, Holt's first phone call to Heidi was on the night her car broke down, after he dropped her at her house. Merit didn't even know Heidi on that date."

Jacob cocks an eyebrow. "Says who? Merit? Heidi? Heidi could've gone shopping in Merit's store two years ago and none of us would know. I mean, she did hire Heidi as soon as Holt suggested it, right? If we are saying the text messages and phone calls are a frame job, then Heidi's car breaking down is a hoax too. I mean, it's a pretty elaborate plan. Whatever happened and whoever it happened with, I don't see a seventeen-year-old-kid coming up with it by herself. If we take a step back and look at it objectively, it definitely looks like a long-con."

My ears start to ring. It's so damn loud I can't even hear myself think.

Acid churns in my stomach, making me sick.

My heart pounds against my chest, making it hard to breathe.

I break out in a cold sweat.

My vision blurs, turning my periphery black.

My fingers go numb.

It feels like I'm fucking dying.

And still... they bombard me with question after question.

Exactly how long have you known Merit Browning?

Has she ever been in any financial trouble?

Wasn't she previously married? To someone very wealthy?

You gave her full access to your house?

She sleeps beside you?

Does she have the code to your phone?

Have you been giving her any money?

Do you think she could've made the phone calls and text messages without you knowing? Without waking you?

Have you ever caught her wandering through the house at night?

She's the only one with clear access to your phone every single night, all night long.

She's the only one with access.

She's the only one with access.

She did it.

She did it.

She did it.

For money. She wants your money. She wants it all.

I've never been someone whose life flashes before his eyes in moments of great danger or peril. Even when I jumped off that cliff after Anna... nothing. No major memories. No major epiphanies. I was simply living in the moment.

But now?

Now, every minute I've ever spent with Merit plays through my shattered and paralyzed mind. A broken video loop playing in a broken mind.

What stands out, like a bright shining spotlight, is seeing her with my cell phone in her hand. In the middle of the night. With no reasonable explanation. Even her lie didn't sound convincing that night. *"I heard a noise."*

Yeah, right.

Every word she's ever spoken tumbles through my mind, like jumbled clothes in a washing machine.

"I mean, you're like obscenely rich."

"I've been thinking that maybe, just maybe, I could start looking for a part-time associate."

"I wanna take everything from you. Every fucking thing."

I jerk away from the table. My chair overturns, clattering loudly against the floor. I can't even walk straight. Stumbling, I drag my limp body across the living room and lean against a tall side table.

The same table I fucked her on just yesterday.

I can't believe she would do this to me. She was supposed to be different from all the others. I love her. She was supposed to love me. My soul is obliterated. I'll never be the same again.

And then… I hear her sweet voice.

Or what used to be her sweet voice—up until five minutes ago.

"Hi."

She's standing on the opposite end of the room with a cardboard carrying-box of coffee in one hand and a huge bag filled with pastries in the other. Apparently, she went to the expensive coffee shop by her store. Why on earth would she do that? For some reason, just staring at the name of the coffee shop on that bag pisses me off.

Slowly my confusion and hesitation morph into bitterness and resentment.

When no one says anything, she takes a few tentative steps in our direction. "I thought, maybe, everyone could use a little break." She lifts the bag. "I brought coffee and snacks." Setting everything on the small section of the table we're not using, she digs through the bag and pulls out a box. Opening it, she tries to show off the chocolate croissants inside. One falls out and splats against the floor. "Oops." Afraid to put it back in the box with the others, she sits it on top of a coaster.

Normally, I'd find her hijinks cute.

But now? Now, it just seems like a lie.

"What are you doing here?" There's no disguising the harshness in my voice.

Her eyes flicker around the room. "I…I thought you could use a break."

"You're supposed to be at work."

She folds her hands in front of her and glances down. "I wanted to check on you."

"You mean you wanted to spy on me," I snap.

"Holt!" Ella warns, pinning me with her stare.

"Excuse me?" Merit's whisper is shaky.

It fillets my cracked heart, wide open. I rub my sternum, wondering if I'm actually having a heart attack. "I can't believe you would do this to me."

She bites her bottom lip. "Do what?"

"Frame me."

She jumps back, like I shot her. "What? What are you talking about?"

"You were the only one with access to my cell phone all those nights. And you know my passcode. You did it, didn't you? You sent the text messages to Heidi. You made the phone calls."

Her face pales to white and her vibrant hazel eyes die, the color fading to black. Her body trembles. She looks like she's about to be sick.

She doesn't even have the decency to answer.

I scoff, fighting the urge to destroy everything in my path. "Was it always about the money?"

"It... it was never about the money."

Jacob takes out his cell phone and starts filming. I don't even think Merit notices.

I drag my hand down my face, my fingers traveling the well-worn path of worry I've carved since my arrest. "I know about the three-thousand dollars."

She holds her breath. "What?"

"You charged three-thousand on my credit card."

She studies the ground and awkwardly shifts from one foot to the other. "I was gonna pay you back."

"I trusted you. I let you in my life." I take a step in her direction, but she backs away. And that makes me even angrier. "I paid off your loan. I gave you a place to live. Hell, I just added you to my bank account!"

"I didn't ask for any of that," she whimpers.

"No, you just put me in jail so you could enjoy it all."

When she finally looks up, tears are streaming down her face.

A couple of months ago, I swore I would do anything to never see her cry. I guess a lot of shit can happen in just a couple of months.

"Why are you doing this?" she asks.

"Me?! You're the one who did it."

I nearly collapse when she answers. "You're right. I did."

A couple of people in the room gasp.

My words come out in a growl, pained and animalistic. "What? What are you saying?"

She takes a step in my direction, gaining the distance she lost. Lifting her chin in the air, she stares straight at me. Even through the cascade of silent tears flooding her eyes, I can see the hollow depths of her soul. The soul—just yesterday—I thought was beautiful and perfect and made by God's hand just for me. "Whatever you think I did, I did it. The texts, the phone calls. Heidi and I did this together. You were never supposed to figure it out. I didn't pin you as that smart of a man." She sniffles, trying to gain control of her breaking voice. "What did you expect me to do, Holt? Edward left me high and dry, eating peanut butter and jelly sandwiches. I had a store to support, a farm to worry about. I did what I had to do. No, no, I take that back. I did what I *wanted* to do. Just like every other woman you've ever dated."

I can't even see straight. Purple and white spots dance behind my eyes, and I feel dizzy. I reach back, searching for something to hold to steady myself. "The money?"

Wiping her eyes, she shrugs. "Like I said, you're obscenely rich."

There are those words again.

Unable to control my rage, I grab the nearest thing—a remote control—and throw it across the unoccupied side of the room. It bounces off the wall, sending pieces everywhere. The batteries roll across the floor. From the corner of my eye, I see Nate watching us from the doorway. Shame and embarrassment immediately mix with my sadness.

Merit wipes her nose with her hand. "Funny thing is, I thought you could read my face? See the truth on it?"

I swallow. "So did I."

Folding her hands back in front of her, she studies the floor. For a few minutes neither of us say anything. Eventually, she nods. Her whisper is barely audible. "Goodbye, sir."

Turning on her heels, she walks away.

To be continued in...
The Believer's Game: The Skeptic's Duet Book Two
Available Now.

Gratitude

It happened again.

I wrote words.

I dreamed about them, obsessed over them, and then put them on paper.

I pray from the depths of my soul that everyone loves every page, every paragraph, every sentence, every freakin' syllable.

This world that I've built feels tangible—first with Crutch and Ella, and now, with Holt and Merit. I want the Hill Family Universe to grow and thrive and prosper. And… I'm terrified that it won't. I think it's my life's biggest fear (to date).

So, I need to extend my utmost appreciation to every single person who bought, downloaded, read, loved, rated, and reviewed The Reality Duet. I'm a super small fish in a really big pond, and the words and affirmations of encouragement from those who reached out to me after reading The Reality Duet made all the difference… in my heart and in my psyche.

Thank you. I love you.

I hope I never let you down.

A super big thank you, peppered with hugs and kisses to those who offered to be a part of the Halcie Dawn Permanent ARC Team. I'm blessed beyond measure that you want to support me during this crazy dream-quest of me becoming a writer. The fact that y'all are willing to take time out of your lives and schedules to read my books and help me shape them into the very best versions they can be is nothing short of spectacular. Thank you for your friendship, hard work, eagerness to promote my novels on social media, and all-around awesomeness! Thank you... Heather S.S., Jenney M, Ashley R, Erica A, Ali S, Amber W, Jennifer S, Jessica V, Jessica A, Kandi S., and Sambora C.

Thank you to everyone on social media who has posted about The Reality Duet and/or The Skeptic's Duet. So far, everyone has been so very nice. Let's hope that continues. Haha! Seriously, for indie authors, word of mouth is everything; and I'm so honored and thankful for every post, repost, tag, and mention.

Thank you so very much to Erica Anderson with Get Lit Author Services. You have been so kind and supportive. I'm so glad Instagram brought us together! Your content creation is perfection, and a huge weight (aka burden) was lifted from my heart when we started collaborating. Your work on my graphics, reels, and ARC Team set-up has given me the gift of time and allowed me to better focus on writing and editing. Thank you!

Thank you to my friend, mentor, and super-amazing author, Kelly Elliott. You always take time out of your busy day to answer any question I may have. I'm so grateful that Elaine put me in contact with you. I pray every day for your continued growth, success, and happiness.

Thank you to Stacey Blake with Champagne Book Design for designing the most gorgeous covers ever for The Skeptic's Duet. You are an absolute dream to work with—so responsive and attentive. Even when you knew something probably wouldn't look good, you still changed it just so I could look at it and say... "Umm, yeah, no." I'm so grateful that Elaine put me in contact with you. (Elaine for the "win" again!) Lord willing, I'll be able to keep writing and publishing, and we'll be able to work together five hundred more times!

Thank you to Elaine York with Allusion Publishing for being YOU—my editor and my friend. I'm so blessed that you agreed to accept me as a client. Can you believe we've been through four books together now?! Thank you for your continued work and support on The Reality Duet (aka my obsessive need and compulsion to make post-publication edits). And thank you so much for working, reviewing, editing, and formatting The Skeptic's Duet. The entire Hill Family is floating around in my brain, just begging for their stories to be told, and I can't wait for you to read them. I value your opinion—oh, so much—and I want nothing more than to make you proud of me. I hope I do...

To Dandy and Big, the most amazing parents ever...I love you. Thank you for supporting me, always giving me hope, and pumping me with confidence when I start to doubt my abilities. I am so lucky to have you in my life, and my love for you both knows no bounds. And to Dandy, thank you for being the Ultimate Permanent ARC Team Member! You read, read, read until your eyes are blurry just to help me.

To my Boo Boo Bear... I can't believe you are eighteen, and I refuse to acknowledge any other birthdays that you will have in the future. Don't grow up on me! Just kidding, of course. I am so honored to be your mother, and I am excited to watch you grow in the next steps of your life—graduating high school and attending college. You are so intelligent, kind, loving, funny, and empathetic. You make every day better. You make every day worth living.

To Kuntry, my husband and my best friend, thank you for your unwavering love and support. This past year was unprecedented for us. I never thought I would lose a job and be unemployed at the age of forty-three, completely starting over in my career. Not once during these past fourteen months (as I'm typing this), did you ever make me feel like a burden or anything less than your equal. Every morning, you kissed me goodbye and headed out to your beyond-stressful job, working hard for every single cent you brought home to our family. No matter the day, the hour, or the minute, you love me like the world is ending. You're mine. And I'm never letting you go.

To the Lord my God, my Almighty Savior Jesus Christ... Thank you. Your blessings pour over me. I am loved and worthy by Your Grace.

About the Author

HALCIE DAWN is a happy and blessed wife and mother. She attended the University of Alabama where she graduated with a bachelor's degree in Business Management. A lifelong avid reader, her love affair with books started with the original *The Babysitter's Club* series when she was in the third grade and morphed into a love of all things romantic. After years of thought, she finally placed finger to keyboard and penned her first contemporary romance. *The Reality Duet—Escaping Our Reality* (Book One) and *Finding Our Reality* (Book Two) released in November 2024. When not writing or reading by the swimming pool, she can be found watching true crime documentaries or *Psych* (for the millionth time). Halcie lives in Alabama with her amazingly wonderful, funny, kind, and handsome husband and son. And she lives next door to her parents, whose antics often have her laughing so hard she pees her pants. But without a doubt, the star of the home is the family morkiepoo, Princess Doodle Fluffybutt.

Connect with me:
Website: www.halciedawn.com
Instagram: halciedawnromance
Facebook: www.facebook.com/halciedawn
Facebook Reader Group: www.facebook.com/groups/
halciedawndaydreamers
TikTok: www.tiktok.com/@halciedawnromance